A
Free
Man
of
Color

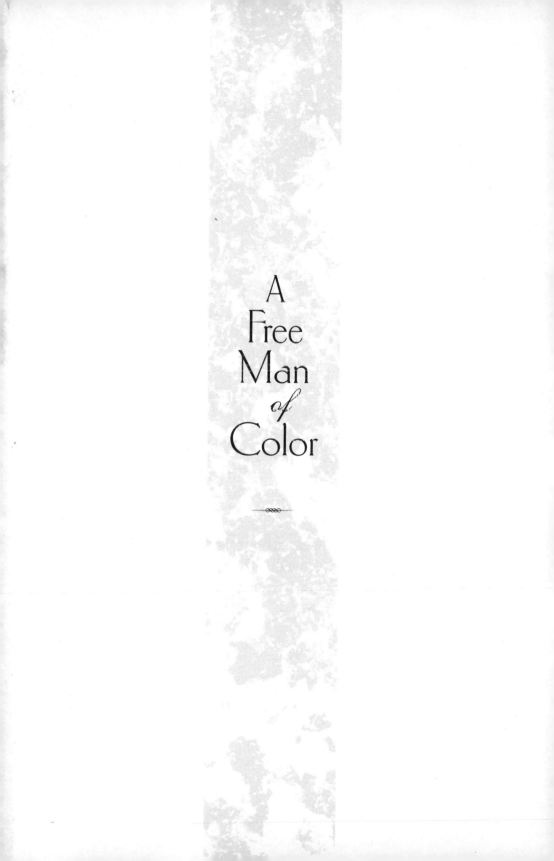

BANTAM BOOKS

New York

Toronto

London

Sydney

Auckland

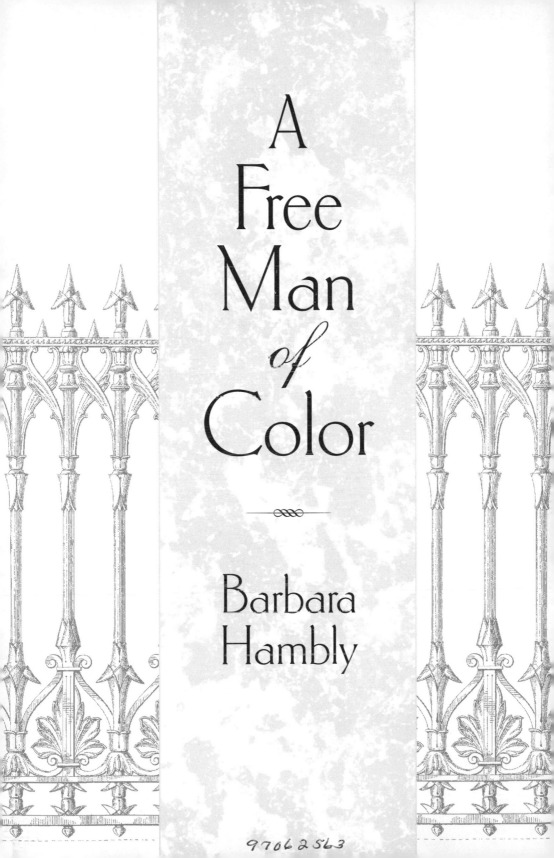

A
Free
Man
of
Color

Barbara
Hambly

All my thanks and humble gratitude go to Octavia
Butler for her time and consideration in reading the
original of this manuscript and for her invaluable
comments; to George Alec Effinger for his support
and advice about local New Orleans customs;
and to Leslie Johnston and the rest of the research
staff at the Historic New Orleans Collection
for all their help.

A FREE MAN OF COLOR
A Bantam Book / July 1997

Book design by Donna Sinisgalli.

**Library of Congress Cataloging-in-Publication
Data**

Hambly, Barbara.
A free man of color / by Barbara Hambly.
p.   cm.
ISBN 0-553-10258-3
1. Afro-American men—Louisiana—New Orleans—
History—19th century—Fiction.   I. Title.
PS3558.A4215F74   1997
813'.54—dc20   96-44942
                                    CIP

*Published simultaneously in the United States and
Canada*

Bantam Books are published by Bantam Books, a
division of Bantam Doubleday Dell Publishing
Group, Inc. Its trademark, consisting of the words
"Bantam Books" and the portrayal of a rooster, is
Registered in U.S. Patent and Trademark Office and
in other countries. Marca Registrada. Bantam Books,
1540 Broadway, New York, New York 10036.

PRINTED IN THE UNITED STATES OF
AMERICA

BVG   10 9 8 7 6 5 4 3 2 1

For
Brother Ed

AUTHOR'S NOTE

In any work of fiction dealing with the American South, a writer runs into the problem of language and attitudes—specifically not only words and phrases but outlook, upbringing, and unspoken assumptions, which, though widely held and considered normal at the time, are appalling today.

The early 1830s were a time of great change in America. President Andrew Jackson's view of democracy was very different from the eighteenth-century vision of the country's founders. Civil War and Reconstruction lay a generation in the future, and the perception of blacks—by the whites and by the blacks themselves—was changing, too.

In New Orleans for most of the nineteenth century, it would have been as offensive to call a colored—that is, mixed-race—man or woman "black," as it would be today to call a black person "colored." Both words had connotations then that they do not have now; both words are freighted now with history, implications, and inferences unimaginable then.

I have tried to portray attitudes held by the free people of color toward the blacks—those of full or almost-full African descent, either slave or free—and toward the Creoles—at that time the word meant fully white descendants of French and Spanish colonists—as I have encountered them in my research. Even a generation ago in New Orleans, the mothers of mixed-race teenagers would caution their children not to "date anybody darker than a paper bag." Light skin was valued and dark skin discredited, and a tremendous amount of energy went into making distinctions that seem absurdly petty today. An intricate hierarchy of terminology existed to categorize those of mixed race: *mulatto* for one white, one black parent; *griffe* or *sambo* for the child of a mulatto and full black; *quadroon* for the child of a mulatto and a full white; *octoroon* for a quadroon's child by a full white; *musterfino* or *mameloque* for an octoroon's child by a full white. (I've seen alternate meanings for *griffe*, *sambo*, and *musterfino*, so there's evidently some question about either what the records were talking about, or whether the people at that time used the same words for the same things.)

White Creoles, by the way, had an intricate hierarchy of words to categorize *each other* as to social standing and how long their families had been prominent in New Orleans society, so they evidently just liked to label things. Americans, of course, simply did not count.

I have not attempted to draw parallels to any modern situation or events. I have tried to construct a story from a historical setting, using the attitudes and outlooks—and, of necessity, terminology—of that time and place. I have attempted, to the best of my ability, neither to glamorize nor to conceal. The territory is touchy for those who have suffered, or whose families have suffered, from the prejudices and discrimination that once was—and still is to some extent—commonplace. To them I apologize if I have inadvertently offended. My goal is, as always, simply to entertain.

O N E

Had Cardinal Richelieu not assaulted the Mohican Princess, thrusting her up against the brick wall of the carriageway and forcing her mouth with his kisses, Benjamin January probably wouldn't have noticed anything amiss later on.

Now, THERE's a story for the papers. January considered the tangle of satin and buckskin, the crimson of the prelate's robe nearly black in the darkness of the passageway save where the oil lamp that burned above the gate splashed it with gory color, the grip of the man's hand on the woman's buttocks and the way her dark braids surged over his tight-clenched arm. *Certainly the American papers: Cardinal Richelieu Surprised with Leatherstocking's Sister.* It was a common enough sight in the season of Mardi Gras, when the February dark fell early and the muddy streets of the old French town had been rioting since five o'clock with revelers—white, black, and colored, slave and free, French and American—bedizened in every variation of evening costume or fancy dress. God knew there were women enough yanking men off the high brick banquettes into doorways and carriage gates and public houses on Rue Royale and Rue Bourbon and all over the old quarter tonight. He wondered what Titian or Rembrandt would have made of the composition; he was turning politely to go when the woman screamed.

The fear in her voice made him swing around, just within the arch of the gate. The oil lamp's light must have fallen on his face, for when she screamed a second time, she cried his name.

"Monsieur Janvier!"

A stride took him to the grappling forms. He seized His Eminence by the shoulder and tossed him clear out of the carriageway, across the brick banquette, over the dark-glittering stream of the open gutter and into the oozy slops of Rue Ste.-Ann with a single throw—for January was a very big man—making sure to cry as he did so in his most jovial tones, "Why, Rufus, you old scamp, ain't nobody told you . . . ?"

Timing was everything. He'd learned that as a child.

Even as his victim went staggering into the jostle of carriages, he was bounding after him, catching the man's arm in a firm grip and gasping, "Oh, my God, sir, I'm terribly sorry!" He managed to yank the enraged churchman out of the way before both could be run down by a stanhope full of extremely Cooperesque Indians. "I thought you were a friend of mine! My fault entirely!" Richelieu was pomegranate with rage and thrashing like a fish on a hook, but he was also a good half foot shorter than January's six-foot three-inch height and hadn't spent nine years carrying cadavers—and occasionally pianofortes—on a daily basis. "I do beg your pardon!"

January knew the man would hit him the moment he let go and knew also that he'd better not hit back.

He was correct. It wasn't much of a blow, and at least Richelieu wasn't carrying a cane, but as the scarlet-masked villain flounced back across the gutter and disappeared into the dark maw of the gate once more, January was surprised by his own anger. Rage rose through him like a fever heat as he tasted his own blood on his lip, burning worse than the sting of the blow, and for a time he could only stand in the gluey street, jostled on both sides by gaudy passersby, not trusting himself to follow.

I've been in Paris too long, he thought.

Or not long enough.

He picked up his high-crowned beaver hat, flicked the mud from it—it had fallen on the banquette, not in the gutter—and put it back on.

The last time he'd let a white man strike him, he'd been twenty-four. An American sailor on the docks had cuffed him with casual violence as he was boarding the boat to take him to Paris. He'd thought then, *Never again.*

He drew a long breath, steadying himself, willing the anger away as he had learned to will it as a child.

Welcome home.

Music drifted from the pale, pillared bulk of the Théâtre d'Orléans immediately to his right, and a mingled chatter of talk through the carriageway to the courtyard of the Salle d'Orléans that had been his goal. The long windows of both buildings were open, despite the evening's wintry cool—not that New Orleans winters ever got much colder than a Normandy spring. That was something he'd missed, all these past sixteen years.

In the Théâtre, the Children's Ball would just be finishing, the main subscription ball getting ready to begin. The restless, fairy radiance of the newfangled gaslights falling through the windows and the warmer amber of the oil lamps on their chains above the intersection of the Rue Ste.-Ann and Rue Royale, showed him proud, careful mamas clothed as classical goddesses or Circassian maids, and watchful papas in the incongruous garb of pirates, lions, and clowns, escorting gorgeously costumed little boys and girls to the carriages that awaited them, drawn up just the other side of the gurgling gutters and tying up traffic for streets. With the Théâtre's long windows open he could hear the orchestra playing a final country dance—"Catch Fleeting Pleasures"—and he could identify whom they'd got to play: That had to be Alcée Boisseau on the violin and only Philippe Decoudreau could be that hapless on the cornet.

January winced as he picked up his music satchel from beside the wall where he'd dropped it in his excess of knight-errantry, wiped a trace of blood from his lip and thought, *Let's not do that again.* The Mohican Princess was long gone, and January hoped, as he made his way toward the lights and voices of the courtyard that lay behind the Salle d'Orléans' gambling rooms, that Richelieu had gone into the gambling rooms or upstairs to the Salle as well. The colored glimmer of light from the courtyard, slanting into the dark of the passageway, showed him a couple of green-black cock feathers from the woman's headdress lying on the bricks at his feet.

The woman had called his name. She had been scared.

Why scared?

To any woman who would come unaccompanied to the Blue Ribbon Ball at the Salle d'Orléans , being thrown up against the wall and kissed by a white man was presumably the point of the evening.

So why had she cried out to him in fear?

Colored lanterns jeweled the trees in the court, and the gallery that stretched the length of the Salle's rear wall. In the variegated light, Henry VIII and at least four of his wives leaned over the gallery's wooden railings, laughing amongst themselves and calling down in English to friends in the court below. January didn't have to hear the language to know the Tudor monarch was being impersonated by an American. No Creole would have had the poor taste to appear with more than one woman on his arm. A curious piece of hypocrisy, January reflected wryly, considering how many of the men at the Blue Ribbon Ball tonight had left wives at home; considering how many more had escorted those wives, along with sisters, mothers, and the usual Creole regiments of cousins, to the subscription ball in the Théâtre, directly next door.

Both the Salle d'Orléans and the Théâtre were owned by one man—Monsieur Davis, who also owned a couple of gambling establishments farther along Rue Royale—and were joined by a discreet passageway. Most of those gentlemen at the subscription ball tonight would slip along that corridor at the earliest possible moment to meet their mulatto or quadroon or octoroon mistresses. That was what the Blue Ribbon Balls were all about.

Ayasha, he recalled, had hardly been able to credit it when he'd recounted that aspect of New Orleans life. None of the ladies in Paris had. "You mean they attend balls on the *same night,* with their wives in one building and another with their mistresses *a hundred feet away?*"

And January, too, had laughed, seeing the absurdity of it from the vantage point of knowing he'd never go back again. There was laughter in most of his memories of Paris. "It's the custom of the country," he'd explained, which of course explained nothing, but he felt an obscure obligation to defend the city of his birth. "It is how it is."

Allowing a white man to strike him without raising a hand in his own defense was the custom of the country as well, but of that, he had never spoken.

Why would she struggle? And who was she, that she'd known his name?

He paused beneath the gallery, his hand on the latch of the inconspicuous service door that led to offices, kitchen, and service stair, scanning the court behind him for sight of that deerskin dress, that silly feathered headdress that more resembled a crow in a fit than anything he'd actually seen on the Choctaws or Natchays who came downriver to peddle filé or pots in the market.

Most of the women who came to the quadroon balls came with friends, the young girls chaperoned by their mothers. Women did come alone, and a great deal of outrageous flirting went on, but those who came alone knew the rules.

Above him, one of Henry VIII's wives trilled with laughter and threw a rose down to a tobacco-chewing Pierrot in the court below. The gaudy masks of the wives set off their clouds of velvety curls, chins and throats and bosoms ranging from palest ivory through smooth café-au-lait. In London, January had seen portraits of all the Tudor queens and, complexion aside, none of the originals had been without a headdress. But this was one of the few occasions upon which, licensed by the anonymity of masks, a free woman of color could appear in public with her hair uncovered, and every woman present was taking full and extravagant advantage of the fact.

The French doors beneath the gallery stood open. Gaslights were a new thing—when January had left in 1817 everything had been candlelit—and in the uneasy brilliance couples moved through the lower lobby and up the curving double flight of the main stair to the ball-room on the floor above. As a child January had been fascinated by this festival of masks, and years had not eroded its eerie charm; he felt as if he had stepped through into a dream of Shelley or Coleridge where everything was more vivid, more beautiful, soaked in a crystal-line radiance, as if the walls of space and time, fact and fiction, had been softened, to admit those who had never existed, or who were no more.

Marie Antoinette strolled by, a good copy of the Le Brun portrait January had seen in the Musée du Louvre, albeit the French queen had darkened considerably from the red-haired Austrian original. January recognized her fairylike thinness and the way she laughed: Phlosine Seurat, his sister Dominique's bosom friend. He couldn't remember the name of her protector, though Dominique had told him, mixed up with her usual silvery spate of gossip—only that the man was a sugar planter who had given Phlosine not only a small house on Rue des Ramparts but also two slaves and an allowance generous enough to dress their tiny son like a little lace prince. At a guess the Indian maid was another of his sister's friends.

He looked around the courtyard again.

There were other "Indians" present, of course, among the vast route of Greek gods and cavaliers, Ivanhoes and Rebeccas, Caesars and corsairs. *The Last of the Mohicans* was as popular here as it was in Paris. January recognized Augustus Mayerling, one of the town's most fash-ionable fencing masters, surrounded by a worshipful gaggle of his pupils, and made a mental note to place bets with his sister when he saw her on how many duels would be arranged tonight. In all his years of playing the piano at New Orleans balls, January had noticed that the average of violence was lower for the quadroon balls, the Blue Ribbon Balls, than for the subscription balls of white society.

And even on this night of masks, he noted that those who spoke French did not mingle with those who spoke English. Some things Carnival did not change.

He'd laughed about that, too, in Paris, back when there'd been reason to laugh.

Don't think about that, he told himself, and opened the service door. *Just get through this evening. I wonder if that poor girl . . . ?*

She was standing in the service hall that led to the manager's tiny office, to the kitchen and the servants' stair.

At the sound of the opening door she whirled, her face a pale blur under the mask and the streaks of war paint. She'd been watching through the little door that led into the corner of the lobby, and for a moment, as she lifted her weight up onto her toes, January thought she'd flee out into the big room, into which he could not follow. He noted, in that instant, how absurdly the cheap buckskin costume was made, with a modern corset and petticoat beneath it, and a little beaded reticule at her belt. Her dark plaits were a nod to Monsieur Cooper, but she wore perfectly ordinary black gloves, much mended, and black slippers and stockings, splashed with mud from the street.

She seemed to lose her nerve about the lobby and turned to flee up the narrow stair that led to the upstairs supper room and the little retiring chamber beside it, where girls went to pin up torn flounces. January said, "It's all right, Mademoiselle. I just wanted to be sure you were all right."

"Oh. Of course." She straightened her shoulders with a gesture he knew—he'd seen it a hundred times, or a thousand, but not from an adult woman . . . . "Thank you, Monsieur Janvier. The man was . . . importunate." She was trying to sound calm and a little arrogant, but he saw from the way the gold buckskin of her skirt shivered that her knees were still shaking. She nodded to him, touched her absurd headdress, loosing another two cock feathers, and started to walk past him toward the courtyard again. It was well done and, he realized later, took nerve. But when she came close January got a better look at what he could see of her face and knew then where he had seen that squaring of the shoulders, those full lips; knew where he had heard that voice.

"Mademoiselle Madeleine?"

She froze, and in the same moment realization took hold of him, and horror.

"Mademoiselle Madeleine?"

Her eyes met his, her mouth trying for an expression of cool surprise and failing. She was a woman now, wasp-waisted with a soaring glory of bosom, but the angel-brown eyes were the eyes of the child he remembered.

She moved to dart past him but he put his body before the door, and she halted, wavering, tallying possible courses of action, even as he'd seen her tally them when her father would come in after the piano lessons and ask whether she would like a lemon ice before her dancing teacher arrived.

Mostly, January remembered, she would ask, "Might we play another piece, Papa? It's still short of the hour."

And old René Dubonnet would generally agree. "If it's no trouble for Monsieur Janvier, ma chère. Thank you for indulging her—would you care for some lemon ice as well, when you're done, Monsieur?"

Not an unheard-of offer from a white Frenchman to his daughter's colored music master, but it showed more than the usual politeness. Certainly more politeness than would be forthcoming even from a Frenchman these days.

He realized he didn't know what her name was now. She must be all of twenty-seven. If she hadn't spoken he might not have known her, but of course she had known him. He and the waiters in their white coats and the colored croupiers in the gaming rooms were the only men in the building not masked.

All this went through his mind in a moment, while she was still trying to make up her mind whether to deny that she knew him at all or to deny that she was the child who had played modern music with such eerie ferocity. Before she could come to a decision he gestured her to the empty office of the Salle's master of ceremonies and manager, one Leon Froissart, who would be safely upstairs in the ballroom for some time to come. Had he been in Paris January might have taken her arm, for she was trembling. But though she must be passing herself as an octoroon—and there were octoroons as light as she—as a black man he was not to touch her.

Only white men had the privilege of dancing, of flirting with, of kissing the ladies who came to the Blue Ribbon Balls. The balls were for their benefit. A man who was colored, or black, freeborn or freedman or slave, was simply a part of the building. Had he not lost the habit of keeping his eyes down in sixteen years' residence in Paris, he wouldn't even have looked at her face.

She left a little trail of black cock feathers in her wake as she preceded him into the office. The room was barely larger than a cupboard, illumined only by the rusty flare of streetlights and the glare of passing flambeaux that came in through the fanlight over the shutters; the cacophony of brass bands and shouting in the street came faintly but clearly through the wall.

She said, still trying to bluff it through, "Monsieur Janvier, while I thank you for your assistance, I . . ."

"Mademoiselle Dubonnet." He closed the door after a glance up and down the hall, to make sure they were unobserved. "Two things. First, if you're passing yourself as one of these ladies, some man's plaçée or a woman looking to become one, take off your wedding ring. It makes a mark through the glove and anyone who takes your hand for a dance is going to feel it."

Her right hand flashed to her left, covering the worn place in the glove. She had big hands for a woman—even as a little girl, he remembered, her gloves had always been mended on the outside edge, as these were. Maybe that was what had triggered the recollection in his mind. As she fumbled with the faded kid he went on.

"Second, this isn't anyplace for you. I know it isn't my place to say so, but why ever you're here—and I assume it's got something to do with a man—go home. Whatever you're doing, do it some other way."

"It isn't . . ." she began breathlessly, but there was guilty despair in her eyes, and he held up his hand for silence again.

"Some of these ladies may be as light as you," he continued gently, "but they were all raised to this world, to do things a certain way. They mostly know each other, and they all know the little tricks—who they can talk to and who not. Who each other's gentlemen are and who can be flirted with and who left alone. Even the young girls, with their mothers bringing them here for the first time for the men to meet, they know all this. *You don't.* Go home. Go home right now."

She turned her face away. She had always blushed easily, and he could almost feel the color spreading under the feathered rim of the mask. He wondered if she'd grown up as beautiful as she'd been when he taught her pianoforte scales, simple bits of Mozart, quadrilles and the rewritten arias on which he got his students used to the flow and the story of sound. She had a wonderful ear, he recalled; those hands that tore out the sides of her gloves could span an octave and two. He remembered how she'd attacked Beethoven, devouring the radical music like a starving woman eating meat, remembered the distant, almost detached passion in her eyes.

Horns blatted and drums pounded in the street, as a party of maskers rioted by. Someone yelled "Vive Bonaparte! À bas les américains!" What was it now? Ten years? Twelve years since the man's death? And he was still capable of starting riots in the street. "Salaud!" "Crapaud!" "Athéiste!" "Orléaniste . . . !"

He saw the quicksilver of tears swimming in her eyes.

"I'm telling you this for your own protection, Mademoiselle Dubonnet," he said. "If nothing else, I know these girls. They gossip like cannibals cutting up a corpse. You get recognized, your name'll be filth. You know that." He spoke quietly, as if she were still the passionate dark-haired child at the pianoforte, who had shared with him the complicity of true devotees of the art, and for a moment she looked away again.

"I know that." Her voice was tiny. From his pocket January drew one of the several clean handkerchiefs he always carried, and she took it, smudging her war paint a little in the process. She drew a deep breath, let it go, and raised her eyes to his again. "It's just that . . . there was no other way. My name is Trepagier now, by the way."

"*Arnaud* Trepagier?" His stomach felt as if he'd miscalculated the number of steps on a stairway in the dark.

He'd heard his sister's friends gossip about the wives and the white families of the men who bought them their houses, fathered their children, paid for their slippers and gowns. For any white woman to come, even masked, even protected by the license of Carnival, to a Blue Ribbon Ball was hideous enough. But for the widow of Arnaud

Trepagier to be here, dressed like Leatherstocking's worst nightmare less than two months after her husband's body had been laid in the Trepagier family crypt at the St. Louis cemetery . . .

She would never be received anywhere in the parish, anywhere in the state, again. Her husband's family and her own would cast her out. The Creole aristocracy was unforgiving. And once a woman was cast out, January knew, whether here or in Paris, there was almost nothing she could do to earn her bread.

"What is it?" he asked. She had never been stupid. Unless she had fallen in love with intense and crazy passion, it had to be something desperate. "What's wrong?"

"I have to speak with Angelique Crozat."

For a moment January could only stare at her, speechless and aghast. Then he said, "Are you *crazy?*"

He'd only been back in New Orleans for three months, but he knew all about Angelique Crozat. The free colored in their pastel cottages along Rue des Ramparts and Rue Claiborne, the French in their close-crowded town houses, and the Americans in their oak-shaded suburbs where the cane fields had been—the slaves in their cramped outbuildings and attics—knew about Angelique Crozat. Knew about the temper tantrums in the cathedral, and that she'd spit on a priest at Lenten confession last year. Knew about the five hundred dollars' worth of pink silk gown she'd ripped from bosom to hem in a quarrel with her dressmaker, and the bracelet of diamonds she'd flung out a carriage window into the gutter during a fight with a lover. Knew about the sparkle of her conversation, like bright acid that left burned holes and scars in the reputations of everyone whose name crossed her lips, and the way men watched her when she passed along the streets.

"I must see her," repeated Madame Trepagier levelly, and there was a thread of steel in her voice. "I *must.*"

The door opened behind them. Madeleine Trepagier's eyes widened in shock as she stepped around Froissart's desk, as far from January as the tiny chamber would permit. January's mind leaped to the soi-disant Cardinal Richelieu, and he turned, wondering what the hell he would do in the event of another assault—in the event that someone guessed that Madame Trepagier was white, alone here with him, to say nothing of the woman she was seeking.

But it was only Hannibal Sefton, slightly drunk as usual, a wreath of flowers and several strings of iridescent glass Carnival beads looped around his neck. "Ball starts at eight." His grin was crooked under a graying mustache, and with alcohol the lilt of the well-bred Anglo-Irish gentry was stronger than usual in his speech. "Like as not Froissart'll fire your ass."

"Like as not Froissart knows what he can do with my ass," retorted January, but he knew he'd have to go. He'd been a performer too long not to begin on time, not only for the sake of his own reputation but for those of the other men who'd play in the ensemble. Managers and masters of ceremonies rarely asked who was at fault if the orchestra was late.

He turned back to Madame Trepagier. "Leave now," he said, and met the same quiet steeliness in her eyes that he had seen there as a child.

"I can't," she said. "I beg you, don't betray me, but this is something I must do."

He glanced back at Hannibal, standing in the doorway, his treasured fiddle in hand, and then back at the woman before him. "I can leave," offered Hannibal helpfully, "but Froissart'll be down here in a minute."

"No," said January, "it's all right."

Madeleine Trepagier's face was still set, scared but calm, like a soldier facing battle. She'd never survive, he thought. Not if La Crozat guessed her identity . . . .

"Listen," he said. "I'll find Angelique and set up a meeting between you at my mother's house, all right? I'll send you a note tomorrow."

She closed her eyes, and some of the tension left her shoulders and neck; she put out a hand to the corner of the desk to steady herself. She too, realized January, had heard everything there was to hear about Angelique Crozat. A deep breath, then a nod. Another black cock feather floated free, like a slow flake of raven snow.

"All right. Thank you."

They left her in the office, Hannibal checking the corridor, right and left, before they ducked out and hastened up the narrow, mildew-smelling flight of the service stair. In the hall January retrieved another cock feather from the bare cypress planks of the floor, lest Richelieu happen by and be of an observant bent. With luck once the music started everyone would be drawn up to the ballroom, and Madame Trepagier could slip away unnoticed. It shouldn't be difficult to hire a hack in the Rue Royale.

Didn't I tell myself fifteen minutes ago, 'Let's not do this again'? An interview with Angelique Crozat—spiteful, haughty, and so vain of the lightness of her skin that she barely troubled herself to treat even free colored like anything but black slaves—a clout in the mouth from Cardinal Richelieu promised to be mild in comparison. At least being struck was over quickly.

"Who's the lady?" asked Hannibal, as they debouched into the little hall that lay between the closed up supper room and the retiring parlor.

"A friend of my sister's." The parlor door was ajar, showing the tiny chamber drenched in amber candlelight, its armoire bulging with costumes for the midnight *tableaux vivants* and two girls in what was probably supposed to be classical Greek garb stitching frantically on a knobby concoction of blue velvet and pearls.

"In case you've forgotten, that kind of tête-à-tête's going to get you shot by her protector, and it probably won't do her any good, either."

They passed through an archway into the lobby at the top of the main stair. The open stairwell echoed with voices from below as well as above, a many-tongued yammering through which occasional words and sentences in French, Spanish, German, and Americanized English floated disembodied, like leaves on a stream. Pomade, roses, women, and French perfumes thickened the air like luminous roux, and through three wide doorways that led into the long gas-lit ballroom, only the smallest breath of the night air stirred.

Hannibal paused just within the central ballroom door to collect a glass of champagne and a bottle from the bucket of crushed New

England ice at the buffet table. One of the colored waiters started to speak, then recognized him and grinned.

"You fixin' to take just the one glass, fiddler?"

Hannibal widened coal-black eyes at the man and passed the glass to January, ceremoniously poured it full, and proceeded to take a long drink from the neck of the bottle.

> *"Oh, for a beaker full of the warm South,*
> *Full of the true, the blushful Hippocrene.*
> *With beaded bubbles winking at the brim,*
> *And purple-stainéd mouth."*

He solemnly touched the bottle to January's glass in a toast, and resumed his progress toward the dais at the far end of the ballroom. January collared two more glasses for Jacques and Uncle Bichet, who awaited them behind the line of potted palmettos. The waiter shook his head and laughed, and went back to pouring out champagne for the men who crowded through the other doorways from the lobby, clamoring for a last drink before the dancing began.

As he settled at the piano—a seven-octave Erard, thick with gilt and imported at staggering cost from Paris—and removed his hat and gloves, January thought he caught a glimpse of the creamy buff of a buckskin gown in the far doorway. He swung around, distracted, but the shifting mosaic of revelers hid whoever it was he thought he'd seen.

Concern flared in him, and anger, too. *Damn it, girl, I'm trying to keep you from ruining yourself!* His hands passed across the keys, warming up; then he nodded to Hannibal and to Uncle Bichet, and like acrobats they bounded into the bright strains of the *Marlboro Cotillion. First thoughts were best—I'm getting too old to be a knight-errant.* His lip smarted and he cringed inwardly at the thought of seeking out and interviewing Angelique Crozat later in the evening.

And for what? So that she could come up here anyway . . .

But why would she come up? He'd seen her relax at the thought that she didn't have to find the woman herself, saw the dread leave her.

He'd probably been mistaken.

He hoped he'd been mistaken.

Men were leading their ladies in from the lobby, forming up squares. Others came filtering through the discreetly curtained arch that led to the passageway from the Théâtre next door, greeting their mistresses with kisses, their men friends with handshakes and grins of complicity, while their wives and fiancées and mothers no doubt fanned themselves and wondered loudly where their menfolk could have got to.

The custom of the country.

January shook his head.

All of Madeleine Trepagier's family, and her deceased husband's, were probably at that ball. He'd never met a Creole lady yet who didn't have brothers and male cousins. True, if they didn't know she'd be here they wouldn't be expecting to see her, but there was always the risk. With luck the first dances—cotillion, waltz, Pantalon—would absorb their attention, giving the woman time to make her escape.

If that was what she was going to do.

The skipping rhythms of the cotillion drew at his mind. He knew that for the next hour, music would be all he'd have time to think about. Whatever she decided to do, she'd be on her own.

It was her own business, of course, but he had been fond of her as a child, the genius and the need of her soul calling to the hunger in his. She had to be desperate in the first place to come here. Quiet and well-mannered and genuinely considerate as she had been as a child, she had had the courage that could turn reckless if driven to the wall. He wished heartily that he'd had time to escort her back to the Trepagier town house himself.

He was to wish it again, profoundly, after they discovered the body in the parlor at the end of the hall.

Benjamin January's first public performance on the piano had been at
a quadroon ball. He was sixteen and had played for the private parties
and dances given during Christmas and Carnival season by St.-Denis
Janvier for years; he was enormously tall even then, gawky, lanky,
odd-looking, and painfully shy. St.-Denis Janvier had hired for him
the best music master in New Orleans as soon as he'd purchased—and
freed—his mother.

The music master was an Austrian who referred to Beethoven as
"that self-indulgent lunatic" and regarded opera as being on intellec-
tual par with the work hollers Ben had learned in his first eight years
in the cane fields of Bellefleur Plantation where the growing American
suburb of Saint Mary now stood. The Austrian—Herr Kovald—
taught the children of other plaçées and seemed to think it only the
children's due that their illegitimate fathers pay for a musical as well as
a literary education for them. If he ever thought it odd that Ben did
not appear to have a drop of European blood in his veins it was not
something he considered worthy of mention.

Ben was, he said quite simply, the best, and therefore deserved to be beaten more, as diamonds require fiercer blows to cut. Common trash like pearls, he said, one only rubbed a little.

Herr Kovald had played the piano at the quadroon balls, which in those days had been held at another ballroom on Rue Royale. Then, as now, the wealthy planters, merchants, and bankers of the town would bring their mulatto or quadroon mistresses—their plaçées—to dance and socialize, away from the restrictions of wives or would-be wives; would also bring their sons to negotiate for the choice of mistresses of their own. Then, as now, free women of color, plaçées or former plaçées, would bring their daughters as soon as they were old enough to be taken in by protectors and become plaçées themselves, in accordance with the custom of the country. Society was smaller then and exclusively French and Spanish. In those days the few Americans who had established plantations near the city since the takeover by the United States simply made concubines of the best looking of their slaves and sold them off or sent them back to the fields when their allure faded.

At Carnival time in 1811, Herr Kovald was sick with the wasting illness that was later to claim his life. As if the matter had been discussed beforehand, he had simply sent a note to Livia Janvier's lodgings, instructing her son Benjamin to take his place as piano player at the ball. And in spite of his mother's deep disapproval ("It's one thing for you to play for me, p'tit, but for you to play like a hurdy-gurdy man for those cheap hussies that go to those balls . . ."), he had, as a matter of course, gone.

And, except for a break of six years, he had been a professional musician ever since.

The ballroom was full by the time the cotillion was done. January looked up from his music to scan the place from the vantage point of the dais, while Hannibal shared his champagne with the other two musicians and flirted with Phlosine Seurat, who had by this time discovered that powdered wigs and panniers were designed for the stately display of a minuet, not the breathtaking romp of a cotillion. Between snippets of Schubert, played to give everyone time to regain their breaths, January tried again to catch sight of Madeleine Trepagier—if that was she he had thought he'd glimpsed in the ballroom doorway—or of Angelique Crozat, or, failing either of them, his sister Dominique.

He knew Minou would be here, with her protector Henri Viellard. During the four years between Dominique's birth and January's departure for Paris, he had known that the beautiful little girl was destined for plaçage—destined to become some white man's mistress, as their mother had been, with a cottage on Rue des Ramparts or des Ursulines and the responsibility of seeing to nothing but her protector's comfort and pleasure whenever he chose to arrive.

The practical side of him had known this was a good living for a woman, promising material comfort for her children.

Still, he was glad he'd been in Paris when his mother started bringing Minou to the Blue Ribbon Balls.

He caught sight of her just as he began the waltz, a flurry of pink silk and brown velvet in the wide doorway that led to the upstairs lobby, unmistakable even in a rose-trimmed domino mask as she grasped the hands of acquaintances, exchanged kisses and giggles, always keeping her alertness focused on the fat, fair, bespectacled man who lumbered in at her side. Viellard appeared to have been defeated by the challenge of accommodating his spectacles to the wearing of a mask—he was clothed very stylishly in a damson-colored cutaway coat, jade-green waistcoat, and pale pantaloons, and resembled nothing so much as a colossal plum. When the waltz was over Dominique fluttered across the dance floor to the musicians' stand, holding out one lace-mitted hand, a beautiful amber-colored girl with velvety eyes and features like an Egyptian cat's.

"First I heard Queen Guenevere had her dresses made from *La Belle Assemblée.*" Benjamin gestured to the fashionable bell-shaped skirt, the flounced snowbank of white lace collar, and the sleeves puffed out—Dominique had recently assured him—on hidden frameworks of whalebone and swansdown. Like every woman of color in New Orleans she was required to wear a tignon—a head scarf—in public, and had used the license granted by a masked ball to justify a marvelous confection of white and rose plumes, of wired and po-

maded braids, of stiffened lace dangling with tasseled lappets of rose
point in every direction, the furthest thing from the grace of Camelot
that could be imagined.

Women these days, January had concluded, wore the damnedest
things.

"Queen Guenevere is for the *tableaux vivants,* silly. And I'm just
appallingly late as it is—you can't get any kind of speed out of waiters
during Carnival, even in a private dining room—and I've just found
out Iphègénie Picard doesn't have her costume for our tableau finished! Not," she added crisply, "that she's alone in that. Iphègénie was
telling me—"

"Is Angelique Crozat here?" In the three months he'd been back
in New Orleans, January had learned that the only way to carry on a
conversation with Dominique was to interrupt mercilessly the moment the current appeared to be carrying her in a direction other than
the one intended.

She said nothing for a moment, but the full lips beneath the rim
of the mask tightened slightly, and the chill was as if she'd imported a
chunk of New England ice to cool the air between them. "Why on
earth do you want to talk to Angelique, p'tit? Which I wouldn't
advise, by the way. Old man Peralta has been negotiating with Angelique's mama—for his son, you know, the one who doesn't have a
chin—and the boy's crazy with jealousy if any other man so much as
looks at her. Augustus Mayerling's had to pull him out of two duels
over her already, which he hasn't any right to be getting into—Galen,
I mean—because of course negotiations are hardly begun . . ."

"I need to give her a message from a friend," said January mildly.

"Better write it on the back of a bank draft if you want her to read
it," remarked Hannibal, coming around to lean on the corner of the
piano. "In simple words of one syllable. You ever had a conversation
with the woman? Very Shakespearean."

Reaching out, he extracted two of the plumes from Dominique's
hat and twisted his own long hair into a knot on the back of his head,
sticking the quill ends through like hairpins to hold it in place. "Full
of sound and fury but signifying nothing." Dominique slapped at his

hands but gave him the flirty glance she never would have given a man of her own color, and he hid a grin under his mustache and winked at her, thin and shabby and disreputable, like a consumptive Celtic elf.

"I haven't had the pleasure," said January wryly. "Not recently anyway, though she did call me a black African nigger when she was six. But I've heard conversations she's had with others."

"I've done that two streets away."

"She'll be here." Dominique's tone was still reminiscent of the ominous drop in temperature that precedes a hurricane. "And I don't think you'll find her manners have improved. Not toward anyone who can't do anything for her, anyway. Well, I understand a girl has to live, and I don't blame her for entertaining Monsieur Peralta's proposals, but . . ."

"What's wrong with Peralta?" January realized he'd run aground on another of those half-submerged sandbars of gossip that dotted New Orleans society—Creole, colored, and slave—like the snags and bars of the river. One day, he knew, he'd be able to negotiate them as he used to, unthinkingly—as his mother or Dominique did—identifying Byzantine gardens of implication from the single dropped rose petal of a name. But that would take time.

As other things would take time.

In any case he couldn't recall any scandal connected with that dignified old planter.

"Nothing," said Dominique, surprised. "It's just that Arnaud Trepagier has only been dead for two months. Arnaud Trepagier," she went on, as January stared at her in blank dismay, his mind leaping to the fear that she had somehow recognized Madeleine, "was Angelique's protector. And I think—"

"Filthy son of a whore!"

All heads turned at the words, ringingly declaimed. There was, January reflected, something extremely actorlike in the way the dapper little gentleman in trunk hose and doublet had paused in the archway that led through to the more respectable precincts next door, holding the curtains apart with arms widespread and raised above the level of his shoulders, as if unconsciously taking up as much of the opening as was possible for a man of his stature.

The next second all heads swiveled toward the object of this epithet, and there seemed to be no doubt in anyone's mind who that was. Even January spotted him immediately, by the way some people stepped back from, and others closed in behind, the tall and unmistakably American Pierrot who'd been spitting tobacco in the courtyard earlier in the evening.

For an American, he spoke very good French. "Better a whore's son than a pimp, sir."

Waiters and friends were closing in from all directions as the enraged Trunk Hose strode into the ballroom, raising on high what appeared to be the folded-up sheets of a newspaper as if to smite his victim with them. A pirate in purple satin and a gaudily clothed pseudo-Turk in pistachio-green pantaloons and a turban like a pumpkin seized Trunk Hose by the arms. Trunk Hose struggled like a demon, neither ceasing to shout epithets nor repeating himself as they and the sword master Mayerling hustled him back through the curtain to the Théâtre d'Orléans again. The American Pierrot only watched, dispassionately stroking his thin brown mustache beneath the rim of his mask. A Roman soldier, rather like a bonbon in gilt papier-mâché armor, emerged from the passageway, flattening to the side of the arch to permit the ambulatory Laocoön to pass, then crossed to Pierrot in a swirl of crimson cloak. Pierrot made a gesture that said, *It's what I expected.*

Hannibal tightened a peg and touched an experimental whisper from the fiddle strings. "I'll put a dollar on a challenge by midnight."

"You think that Granger's gonna hang around wait for it?" demanded Uncle Bichet promptly. Whose uncle Uncle had originally been no one knew—everyone called him that now. He was nearly as tall as January and thin as a cane stalk, claimed to be ninety, and had old tribal scarring all over forehead, cheekbones, and lips. "I say by the time Bouille shakes free of his family over in the other hall Granger's out of here. And where you gonna get a dollar anyway, buckra?"

"And let people say he ran away?" contradicted Jacques unbelievingly. "I say eleven."

"That's William Granger?" Like everyone else who'd been following the escalating war of letters in the New Orleans *Bee,* January had pictured the railway speculator as, if not exactly a tobacco-spitting Kaintuck savage, at least the sort of hustling American businessman who came to New Orleans on the steamboats with shady credit and a pocket full of schemes to get rich quick. That might, he supposed, be the result of the man's spelling, as demonstrated in his letters to the *Bee*'s editor, or the speed with which his accusations against the head of the city planning council had degenerated from allegations of taking bribes and passing information to speculators in rival railway schemes to imputations of private misconduct, dubious ancestry, and personal habits unsuited to a gentleman, to say the least.

Not that Councilman Bouille's rebuttals had been any more dignified in tone, particularly after Granger had accused him of not even speaking good French.

January shook his head, and slid into the bright measures of *Le Pantalon*. The crowd swirled, coalesced, divided into double sets of couples in a rather elongated ring around the walls of the long ballroom. Creole with Creole, American with American, foreign French with foreign French . . . . Bonapartist with Bonapartist, for all he knew.

He saw the young Prussian fencing master emerge from the passageway to the other ballroom, the offending newspaper tucked under one arm, and scan the crowd, like a scar-faced, beak-nosed heron in Renaissance velvet and pearls. The purple pirate stepped through the curtain behind him and conferred with him rapidly—a silk scarf covered the corsair's hair but nothing in the world could prevent his copper-colored Vandyke from looking anything but awful in contrast. Then Mayerling moved off through the crowd to speak with Granger, who had clearly brushed aside the encounter and was asking Agnes Pellicot if one of her daughters would favor him with a dance.

Agnes looked him up and down with an eye that would have killed a snap bean crop overnight and made excuses. January had heard his mother remark that her friend would have her work cut out for her to successfully dispose of Marie-Anne, Marie-Rose, Marie-Thérèse, and Marie-Niege, but Kaintucks were Kaintucks.

Her own protector having crossed over to join his fiancée in the Théâtre, Phlosine Seurat waved, and Mayerling joined her in a set with a very young, fair, chinless boy in a twenty-dollar gray velvet coat.

The tide of the music drew January in—the "tour des mains," the "demi promenade," the "chaine anglaise"—and for a time it, and the joy of the dancers, was all that existed for him. Hidden within the heart of the great rose of music, he could forget time and place, forget the sting of his cut lip and the white man who'd given it to him, who had the right by law to give it to him; forget the whole of this past half year. For as long as he could remember, music had been his refuge, when grief and pity and rage and incomprehension of the whole of the bleeding world overwhelmed him: It had been a retreat, like the gentle hypnotism of the Rosary. With the gaslight flickering softly on the keys and the subliminal rustle of petticoats in his ears, he could almost believe himself in Paris again, and happy.

As a medical student he had played in the dance halls and the orchestras of theaters, to pay his rent and buy food, and after he had given up the practice of medicine at the Hôtel Dieu, music had been his living and his life. It was one of his joys to watch the people at balls: the chaperones waving their fans on the rows of olive-green velvet chairs, the young girls with their heads together giggling, the men talking business by the buffet or in the lobby, their eyes always straying to the girls as the girls' eyes strayed toward them. January saw the American Granger stroll over to the lobby doors to talk to the gilt Roman, controlled annoyance in the set of his back. Something about the way they spoke, though January could hear no words, told him that the Roman was American as well—when the Roman spat tobacco at the sandbox in the corner he was sure of it. Uneasiness prickled him at the sight of them. He neither liked nor trusted Americans.

The young man in the gray coat likewise made his way to the lobby doors, looked out uneasily, then gravitated back to the small group of sword masters and their pupils. Mayerling and Maître Andreas Verret were conversing in amity unusual for professional fencers, who generally quarreled at sight; their students glared and fluffed like tomcats. Gray Coat orbited between the group and the doors half a dozen times, fidgeting with his cravat or adjusting his white silk domino mask. Waiting for someone, thought January. Watching.

"*Drat* that Angelique!" Dominique rustled up to the dais with a cup of negus in hand. "I swear she's late deliberately! Agnes tells me two of her girls need final adjustments in their costumes for the tableau vivant—they're Moth and Mustardseed to Angelique's Titania—and of course Angelique's the only one who can do it. It would be just like her."

"Would it?" January looked up from his music, surprised. "I'd think she'd want her group to be perfect, to show her off better."

Minou narrowed her cat-goddess eyes. "She wants *herself* to be perfect," she said. "But she'd always rather the girls around her were just a little flawed. Look at her friendship with Clemence Drouet— who might stand some chance of marrying a nice man if she'd quit trying to catch a wealthy protector. She designs Clemence's dresses . . . . Well, look at her."

She nodded toward the narrow-shouldered girl who stood in deep conversation with the fair young man in gray, and January had to admit that her dress, though beautiful and elaborately frilled with lace, accentuated rather than concealed the width of her hips and the flatness of her bosom.

"She designed the gowns for all the girls in her tableau," went on Dominique in an undertone. "I haven't seen them finished, but I'll bet you my second-best lace they make Marie-Anne and Marie-Rose look as terrible as Clemence's does her."

"She's that spiteful?" It was a trick January had heard of before.

Dominique shrugged. "She has to be the best in the group, p'tit. And the two Maries are younger than she is." She nodded toward Agnes Pellicot, a regal woman in egg yolk silk and an elaborately wrapped tignon threaded with ropes of pearls, now engaged in what looked like negotiations with a stout man clothed in yet another bad version of Ivanhoe. Marie-Anne and Marie-Rose stood behind and beside her, slim girls with abashed doe eyes.

They must be sixteen and fifteen, thought January—he recalled Agnes had just borne and lost her first child when he had departed for

France—the same age, probably, at which Madeleine Dubonnet had been married to Arnaud Trepagier.

And in fact, he reflected, there wasn't that much difference between that match and the one Agnes was clearly trying to line up with Ivanhoe. They were technically free, as Madeleine Dubonnet had been technically free, marrying—or entering into a contract of plaçage—of their own free choice. But that choice was based on the knowledge that there was precious little a woman could do to keep a roof over her head and food on her table except sell herself to a man on the best terms she could get. Why starve and scrimp and sell produce on the levee, why sew until your fingertips bled and your eyes wept with fatigue, when you could dress in silk and spend the larger part of your days telling servants what to do and having your hair fixed?

A girl has to live.

Then Angelique Crozat stepped into the ballroom, and January understood the iciness in his sister's voice.

True, a girl must live. And even the most beautiful and fair-skinned octoroon could not go long without the wealth of a protector. That was the custom of the country.

And true, the social conventions that bound a white woman so stringently—to coyness and ignorance before marriage, prudishness during, and hem-length sable veils for a year if she had the good fortune not to die in childbed before her spouse—did not apply to the more sensual, and more rational, demimonde.

But it was another matter entirely to appear at a ball in the dazzling height of Paris fashion two months after her lover was in his tomb.

Her gown was white-on-white figured silk, simply and exquisitely cut. Like Dominique's it swooped low over the ripe splendor of her bosom and like Dominique's possessed a spreading wealth of sleeve that offset the close fit of the bodice in layer after fairylike layer of starched lace.

But her face was covered to the lips in the tabbied mask of a smiling cat, and the great cloud of her black hair, mixed with lappets of lace, random strands of jewels, swatches of red wigs, blond curls, and the witchlike ashy-white of horsetails—poured down like a storm of chaos over her shoulders and to her tiny waist. Fairy wings of whalebone and stiffened net, glittering with gems of glass and paste, framed body and face, accentuating her every movement in a shining aureole. She seemed set apart, illuminated, not of this world.

A triple strand of pearls circled her neck, huge baroques in settings of very old gold mingled with what looked like raw emeralds, worked high against the creamy flesh. More strands of the barbaric necklace lay on the upthrust breasts, and bracelets of the same design circled her wrists, and others yet starred the primal ocean of her hair.

Fey, brazen, and utterly outrageous, it was not the costume of a woman who mourns the death of her man.

The young man in gray left Clemence Drouet standing, without a word of excuse, and hastened toward that glimmering flame of ice. He was scarcely alone, for men flocked around her, roaring with laughter at her witticisms—"What, you on your way to a duel?" of an armored Ivanhoe, and to a Hercules, "You get that lion skin off that fellow down in the lobby? Why, your majesty! You brought all six of your wives and no headsman? How careless can you be? You may need that headsman!"

In spite of himself, January wanted her.

The young man in gray worked himself through the press toward her, holding out his hands. She saw him, caught and held his gaze, and under the rim of the cat's whiskers the red lips curved in a welcoming smile.

Timing is everything. And quite deliberately, and with what January could see was rehearsal-perfect timing, just as the boy was drawing in breath to speak, Angelique turned away. "Why, it's the man who'd trade his kingdom for a horse." She smiled into the eyes of the dazzled Roman and, taking his hand, allowed him to lead her onto the dance floor.

As they departed, she smiled once more at the boy in gray.

It was as neat and as cruel a piece of flirtation as January had seen in a lifetime of playing at balls, and it left the boy openmouthed, helpless, clenching and unclenching his fists in rage. Leon Froissart, a fussy little Parisian in a blue coat and immaculate stock, bustled over with a young lady and her mother in tow—Agnes must be ready to spit, thought January, seeing that neither Marie-Anne nor Marie-Rose was present in the ballroom at that moment—and performed an introduction, offering the girl's gloved hand. The boy shoved it from him and raised his fist, Froissart starting back in alarm. For an instant January thought the boy really would strike the master of ceremonies.

Then at the last minute he flung himself away, and vanished into the crowd in the lobby.

Shaking his head, January swung into the Lancers Quadrille.

By the dance's end, when he was able once more to pay attention to the various little dramas being enacted in the ballroom, Agnes Pellicot had been rejoined by her two daughters, and it was blisteringly clear that Minou's predictions concerning Angelique's use of her design skills had been correct. Marie-Anne and Marie-Rose were both clothed now in gowns quite clearly designed to complement Queen Titania's moondust skirts and shimmering wings, and just as clearly designed to point up the older girl's awkward height, and the sallow complexion and rather full upper arms of the younger. Both girls were confused and on the verge of tears, knowing they looked terrible and not quite knowing why, and Agnes herself—no fool and considerably more experienced in dressmaking—seemed about to succumb to apoplexy.

Languishing, giggling, smiling with those dark eyes behind the cat mask, Angelique dispatched Marc Anthony to fetch her champagne and vanished into the lobby, the tall tips of her wings flickering above the heads of the crowd.

"I'll be back," said January softly and rose. Hannibal nodded absently and perched himself on the lid of the pianoforte as Uncle and Jacques disappeared in quest of negus. As January wove and edged his way reluctantly through the crowd toward the doors, a thread of music followed him, an antique air like faded ribbon, barely to be heard.

Best do it now, he thought. The picture of the doll-like six-year-old in his mother's front parlor returned to his mind, lace flounced like a little pink valentine, clutching the weeping Minou's half-strangled kitten to her and shaking away January's hand: "I don't have to do nothing you say, you dirty black nigger."

And Angelique's mother—that plump lady in the pink satin and aigrettes of diamonds now chatting with Henry VIII, rather like a kitten herself in those days—had laughed.

The Creoles had a saying, *Mount a mulatto on a horse, and he'll deny his mother was a Negress.*

Angelique was at the top of the stairs, exchanging a word with Clemence, who came up to her with anxiety in her spaniel eyes; she turned away immediately, however, as a rather overelaborate pirate in gold and a blue-and-yellow Ivanhoe claimed her attention with offers of negus and cake. January hesitated, knowing that an interruption would not be welcome, and in that moment the boy in gray came storming up and grabbed hard and furiously at the fragile lace of Angelique's wing.

She whirled in a storm of glittering hair, ripping the wing still further. "What, pulling wings off flies isn't good enough for you these days?" she demanded in a voice like a silver razor, and the boy drew back.

"You b-bitch!" He was almost in tears of rage. "You . . . stuh-stuh-strumpet!".

"Oooh." She flirted her bare shoulders. "That's the b-b-best you can do, Galenette?" Her imitation of his stutter was deadly. "You can't even call names like a man."

Crimson with rage, the boy Galen raised his fist, and Angelique swayed forward, just slightly, raising her face and turning it a little as if inviting the blow as she would have a kiss. Her eyes were on his, and they smiled.

But her mother swooped down on them in a flashing welter of jewels, overwhelming the furious youth: "Monsieur Galen, Monsieur Galen, only think! I beg of you . . . !"

Angelique smiled a little in triumph and vanished into the dark archway of the hall with a taunting flip of her quicksilver skirts.

"A girl of such spirit!" the mother was saying—Dreuze, January recalled her name was, Euphrasie Dreuze. "A girl of fire, my precious girl is. Surely such a young man as yourself knows no girl takes such trouble to make a man jealous unless she's in love?"

The boy tore his eyes from the archway into which Angelique had vanished, gazed at the woman grasping him with her little jeweled hands as if he had never seen her in his life, then turned, staring around at the masked faces that ringed him, faces expressionless save for those avid eyes.

"Monsieur Galen," began Clemence, extending a tentative hand.

Galen struck her aside, and with an inchoate sound went storming down the stairs.

Clemence turned, trembling hands fussing at her mouth, and started for the archway to follow Angelique, but January was before her. "If you'll excuse me," he said, when their paths crossed in the mouth of the hallway, "I have a message for Mademoiselle Crozat."

"Oh," whispered Clemence, fluttering, hesitant. "Oh . . . I suppose . . ."

He left her behind him, and opened the door.

"How *dare* you lay hands on me?"

She was standing by the window, where the light of the candles ringed her in a halo of poisoned honey. Her words were angry, but her voice was the alluring voice of a woman who seeks a scene that will end in kisses.

She stopped, blank, when she saw that it wasn't Galen after all who had followed her into the room.

"Oh," she said. "Get out of here. What do you want?"

"I was asked to speak to you by Madame Trepagier," said January. "She'd like to meet with you."

"You're new." There was curiosity in her voice, as if he hadn't spoken. "At least Arnaud never mentioned you. She can't be as poor as she whined in her note if she's got bucks like you on the place." Behind the cat mask her eyes sized him up, and for a moment he saw the disappointment in the pout of her mouth, disappointment and annoyance that her lover had had at least one $1,500 possession of which she had not been aware.

"I'm not one of Madame Trepagier's servants, Mademoiselle," said January, keeping his voice level with an effort. He remembered the flash of desire he had felt for her and fought back the disgust that fueled further anger. "She asked me to find you and arrange a meeting with you."

"Doesn't that sow ever give up?" She shrugged impatiently, her lace-mitted hand twisting the gold-caged emeralds, the baroque pearls against the white silk of her gown. "I have nothing to say to her. You tell her that. You tell her, too, that if she tries any of those spiteful little Creole tricks, like denouncing me to the police for being impudent, I have tricks of my own. My father's bank holds paper on half the city council, including the captain of the police, *and* the mayor. Now you . . ."

Her eyes went past him. Like an actress dropping into character, her whole demeanor changed. Her body grew fluid and catlike in the sensual blaze of the candles, her eyes smoky with languorous desire. As if January had suddenly become invisible, and in precisely the same tone and inflection in which she had first spoken when he came in, she said, "How *dare* you lay hands on me?"

January knew without turning that Galen Peralta stood behind him in the doorway.

It was his cue to depart. He was sorely tempted to remain and spoil her lines but knew it wouldn't do him or Madeleine Trepagier any good. And Peralta would only order him out in any case.

The boy was trembling, torn between rage and humiliation and desire. Angelique moved toward him, her chin raised a little and her body curving, luscious. "Aren't we a brave little man, to be sure?" she purred, and shook back her outrageous hair, her every move a calculated invitation to attack, to rage, to the desperate emotion of a seventeen-year-old.

Stepping past the ashen-faced boy in the doorway, January felt a qualm of pity for him.

"You . . . you . . ." He shoved January out of his way, through the door and into the hall, and slammed the door with a cannon shot violence that echoed all over the upstairs lobby.

It was the last time January saw Angelique Crozat alive.

THREE

Bitch, thought January, his whole body filled with a cold, dispassionate anger. *Bitch, bitch, bitch.*

Anger consumed him, for the way she had looked at him, like a piece of property, and at the knowledge that this woman had flitted and cut and stolen her way through the life of the woman who had once been Madeleine Dubonnet. That for one moment he had wanted her—as probably any man did who saw her—disgusted him more than he could say. His confessor, Père Eugenius, would probably call it repentance for the Original Sin, and he was probably right.

Back in the ballroom, major war appeared to have broken out.

January heard the shouting as he crossed the upstairs lobby, which was completely deserted, men and women crowding the three ballroom doors. Monsieur Bouille's shrill accusations rode up over the jangling background racket of a brass band playing marches in the street outside. "A swine and a liar, a scum not fit to associate with decent society. . . ."

Granger, thought January wryly. Bouille had used precisely the same wording in his latest letter to the *Bee*.

"You call me a liar, sir? Deny if you will that you helped yourself to bribes from every cheapjack railway scheme—"

"Bribery may be how you Americans do business, sir, but it is not the way of gentlemen!"

"Now who's the liar?"

There was a roar and a surge of the crowd, and Monsieur Froissart's helpless voice wailing, "Messieurs! Messieurs!"

January slipped unnoticed along the back of the crowd, to where Hannibal, Uncle Bichet, and Jacques were sharing a bottle of champagne behind the piano. He had never played a white subscription ball that hadn't included beatings with canes, pistol whippings or kicking matches in the courtyard or the gaming rooms—*So much,* he thought wryly, *for the vaunted Creole concept of "duels of honor."* If it wasn't a Bonapartist taking out his spite on an Orléaniste, it was a lawyer assaulting another lawyer over personal remarks exchanged in the courtroom or a physician challenging another physician following a lively fusilade of letters in the newspapers.

"Wagers now being taken." Hannibal poured out a glass of champagne for him. "Jacques here insists it'll be swords. . . ."

" 'Course it'll be swords," argued the cornetist. "Bouille spends half what he earns at Mayerling's salle des armes and he's crazy to try it out! He's been challenging everyone he meets to duels!"

January shook his head, and sipped the fizzy liquid. "Pistols," he said.

"*Pistols?* Where's your *élan?*"

"Americans always use pistols."

"Told you," said Uncle Bichet to Jacques.

On the whole, the quadroon balls were far better run. January wondered whether that had something to do with the fact that these men didn't legally control their mistresses the way they did their wives and so had to make a better impression on them, or if the simple social pressure of Creole families caused the men to drink more.

"Live pigs at thirty paces," decreed Hannibal solemnly, and gestured with a crawfish patty. "*Arma virumque cano* . . . Did you encounter La Crozat?"

"Monsieur Bouille, you forget yourself and where you are." Over the heads of the crowd—and January could look over the heads of most crowds—he saw a snowy-bearded, elderly gentleman in the dark blue satins of fifty years ago interpose himself between William Granger and Jean Bouille, who were squared off with canes gripped clubwise in their hands.

"I do not forget myself!" screamed Bouille. "Nor who I am. I am a gentleman! This canaille has insulted me in public, and I will have my satisfaction!"

Granger inclined his head. His accent was a flatboat man's twangy drawl but his French was otherwise good. "When and where you please, sir. Jenkins . . ."

The Roman soldier stepped forward, putting up a nervous hand to steady his laurel wreath as he inclined his head.

"Would you be so good as to act for me?"

"Only think!" wailed Monsieur Froissart. "I beg of you, listen to Monsieur Peralta's so sensible words! Surely this is a matter that can be regulated, that can be talked of in other circumstances."

The city councilman sneered contemptuously and lifted his cane as if fearing his opponent would turn tail; Granger returned the look with a stony stare and spat in the direction of the sandbox. Froissart looked frantically around him for support, and at the same moment January felt a touch on his shoulder. It was Romulus Valle, the ballroom's majordomo.

"Maybe you best get another set started, Ben?" The elderly freed man gestured at the eager faces crowding to see more of the drama. "Give these good people something else to think about?"

January nodded. If there was one thing that could distract Creoles from the prospect of a duel, it was a dance. Jacques and Uncle Bichet took their places; though Hannibal's hands shook a little as he picked up fiddle and bow, there was nothing unsteady about the way he sliced into the most popular jig and reel in their repertoire. Sets were forming even as Froissart and the senior Monsieur Peralta shepherded the combatants out into the lobby and presumably down to the office.

And let's hope, thought January dourly, *that our bonny Galen and*

*la belle dame sans merci didn't decide the office was a more private venue
for their tête-à-tête than the parlor. That would be all it needs, for Galen's
father to find the pair of them coupling like weasels on the desk.*

Cross passes. Footing steps. Casting off and casting back, and
swooping into the grand promenade.

"I'm going to *strangle* that woman!" Dominique had changed into
her costume for the tableaux, and, as Guenevere, had dispensed with
the corsets and petticoats of modern dress, unlike at least four of the
assorted Rebeccas and Juliets circulating in the crowd. Without them
she looked startlingly sensual, thin and fragile and very reminiscent of
the girls of January's young manhood in their high-waisted, clinging
gowns. He had never adjusted to the sight of women in the enormous
petticoats and mountainous sleeves of modern dress.

"Not only does she disappear without helping Marie-Anne and
Marie-Rose—and after making them wear those *frightful* dresses in the
first place, and Agnes is ready to spit blood!—but because I'm hunting
high and low for her I miss the only real excitement of the evening!"

"She'll be in the parlor," pointed out January mildly. "She still
has to fix her wings."

"Ben, I *looked* in the parlor. It was the first place I looked. *And* in
the supper room. And it would have served that . . . that uppity tart
right if he'd torn those wings right off her back." Minou adjusted the
fall of one floor-length sleeve of buttercup yellow and straightened the
dark curls of her chignon. "Did you *hear* what she told her mama
about price and terms to take back to Peralta Père? If I ever saw
such a . . ."

"I've looked everywhere." Marie-Anne Pellicot, her long oval face
visibly beautiful despite a domino mask of exactly the wrong shade of
gray-green for her pale crème-café complexion, hurried up, vexation
replacing her earlier tears. "It's nearly eleven! She promised to dress
our hair. . . ."

Her sister was right behind her. January heard Ayasha's voice in
his mind: *A designer who knows what she's doing can guide beauty to a
woman's form or make that selfsame woman ugly, just in the way she cuts
a sleeve.* He knew what his wife would have guessed—and said—about

Angelique, just from looking at those two dresses, on those two particular girls.

For all her tartness, Ayasha had been a kind woman. She'd never have let Angelique anywhere near those poor children's hair.

"If the parlor is the first place you looked, look again," advised January. The music had soothed away his anger, and he was able to look dispassionately at Angelique and at the situation, only wondering what he was going to say to Mme. Trepagier to keep her from undertaking some other mad attempt to see the woman. He hadn't liked the hard desperation in her eyes as she had said, *I must see her. I MUST.* "She and Galen may have gone somewhere else for their quarrel, but if she's going to repair those wings she'll have to go back where there's light."

"Galen?" Marie-Anne looked surprised. "Galen left after what she said to him in the lobby. Which was horrible, I thought—he can't help it if he stammers."

"Galen." January sighed. "He came back."

"*Tiens!*" Dominique flung up her hands. "Just what we need! That . . . that . . ."

"Wasn't that you who slammed the door?" asked Marie-Rose, trying vainly to tug the lower edge of her bodice into a more flattering position on her hip.

"Have you checked the attics?" Hannibal swiped rosin onto his bow with an expert lightness of touch. "Those back stairs go up as well as down."

"I swear I'm going to . . . Ah! There's Henri." The annoyance melted from Minou's face, replaced by a mischievous brightness at the sight of her elephantine beau emerging awkwardly through the curtain of the passageway to the Théâtre. She stroked a tendril of her hair into the slightest hint of seductive dishabille. "I must go, p'tit. It's one thing to let your protector see you in all your glory in a tableau, but it does mean he's wandering about the ballroom unattended while you're getting yourself ready." She flitted away like a primrose-and-black Gothic butterfly, leaving Marie-Anne and Marie-Rose to their own devices.

"Clemence might know," said Marie-Anne, not in the least disconcerted by the abrupt departure. As January had said to Mme. Trepagier, they all knew the rules.

"Is she still here? I thought she went after Galen."

Hannibal poked January in the back with the bow, and mimed fingering a keyboard. "She'll have to comb her hair when she's done, anyway," the violinist pointed out practically. "They can catch up with her then." And he led the way into the opening bars of a waltz.

In the blaze of gaslight and candle glow, January's eyes followed his sister and her protector around the double circle of the waltzers, annoyed in a tired way—as Angelique annoyed him now—at the thought of how she literally dropped everything to dance attendance on this man whose mother, sisters, female cousins, and quite possibly fiancée were standing stiff-backed in a corner of the Théâtre d'Orléans, chatting with other deserted ladies and pretending they had no idea where their errant menfolk had got to just now.

Marie-Anne and Marie-Rose deserved better.

Minou deserved better.

Didn't they all?

The ballroom was full, this waltz among the most popular of the repertoire. There were more men than women present now, watching the dancers, talking, flirting a little with the unmarried girls under their mamas' wary eyes. The costumes made a fiery rainbow, bright and strange, in the brilliant light, like the enchanted armies of a dream. He could identify groups from the *tableaux vivants,* theme and design repeated over and over, nymphs and coquettes of the ancien régime. Dreams for the men who owned these women, or sought to own them; a chance to see their mistresses in fantasy glory. *You don't love a sang mêlé whose mother bargained with you for her services. You love Guenevere in her bower, you love the Fairy Queen on Midsummer's Eve.* For the young girls, the girls who were here to show off their beauty to prospective protectors, the occasion was more important still.

No wonder Agnes Pellicot's face was stone when she hurried through the ballroom and then out again. No wonder there was poison in her eyes as she watched Euphrasie Dreuze trip by, an overdressed, overjeweled pink dove. Where January sat at the pianoforte he could look out through the triple doors of the ballroom to the lobby and see men and women—clothed in dreams and harried by the weight of their nondream lives—as they came and went.

Angelique's mother caught Peralta Père as the elderly planter re-entered the ballroom, asked him something anxiously. The old man's white brows pulled together and his face grew grim. *Telling him about the quarrel,* guessed January, *and asking if he's seen either Galen or Angelique.* The old planter turned and left abruptly, pausing in the wide doorway to bow to a group of chattering young girls who entered, clothed for a tableau as the Ladies of the Harîm.

January returned his attention to the keys. That was one dream he preferred not to regard too near.

There were about six of them, mostly young girls—he didn't know their names. Minou had told him, of course, but even after three months back he was still unfamiliar with the teeming cast of the colored demimonde. Though he had never in his life seen Ayasha in anything but sensible calicos or the simple, ivory-colored tarlatan that had been her one good dress—the dress in which they had buried her last August—still the sight of the Arabian ladies tore at the unhealed flesh of his heart.

From the waltz they slid into another Lancers, almost without break. Dimly, the sounds of quarreling could be heard when the curtain to the passageway was raised. The night was late enough for just about everybody to be drunk, both on that side of the passageway and this. Still he didn't look up, seeking such nepenthe as the music had to offer.

Maybe it was because Ayasha had laughed at the latest fad for things Arabic. "They think it's so glamorous, the life of the harîm," she had said, that lean, hook-nosed face profiled in the splendor of the cool Paris sun that poured through the windows of their parlor in the Rue de l'Aube. Beadwork glittered in her brown hands. "To do nothing except make yourself beautiful for a man . . . like your little plaçées. As if each of them assumes that she's the *favorite* of the harîm, and not some lowly odalisque who spends most of her day polishing other women's toenails or washing other women's sheets. And the harîm is of course always that of a wealthy man, who can afford sorbets and oils and silken trousers instead of cheap hand-me-downs that have to last you three years."

She shook her head, a Moroccan desert witch incompletely disguised as a French bonne femme. The huge black eyes laughed in a face that shouldn't have been beautiful but was. "Like dreaming about living in one of these castles up here, without having seen a castle, which look horribly uncomfortable to me. And of course, the dreamer is always the queen."

Ayasha had left Algiers at the age of fourteen with a French soldier rather than go into the harîm her father had chosen for her. When January met her, even at eighteen she had risen from seamstress to designer with a very small—but spotlessly clean—shop of her own, and had little time for the romantic legends of the East.

But the sight of a woman with henna in her hair, the smell of sesame oil and honey, could still shake him to his bones.

He could not believe that he would never see her again.

When he looked up at the conclusion of the Lancers, the sword master Augustus Mayerling stood beside the piano.

"Monsieur Janvier?" He inclined his head, neat pale features overweighted by a hawk-beak nose and marred from hairline to jawbone with saber scars. His eyes were a curious light hazel, like a wolf's. "I am given to understand that you've practiced as a physician."

"I'm a surgeon, actually," said January. "I trained at the Hôtel Dieu in Paris. After that I practiced there for three years."

"Even better." The Prussian's fair hair was cropped like a soldier's; it made his head seem small and birdlike above the flare of his Elizabethan ruff. Like Hannibal, he spoke with barely an accent, though January guessed it came from good teaching rather than length of time spent in the United States.

"Bone and blood is a constant. I would prefer a man who understands them, rather than one who spent six years at university learning to argue about whether purges raise or lower the humors of the human constitution and how much mercury and red pepper will clarify a man's hypothetical bile. That imbecile Bouille's challenged Granger to a duel," he added, evidently not considering a Paris-trained surgeon's current position at the piano of a New Orleans ballroom a subject of either surprise or comment. "Children, both of them."

The lines at the corners of his eyes marked Mayerling as older than he looked, but he was still probably younger than either his student or the man that student had challenged. January didn't say anything, but the lines deepened just slightly, ironically amused. "Well-paying children," admitted Mayerling, to January's unspoken remark. "Nevertheless. Bouille's wife is the sister to two of the physicians in town—physicians who actually studied medicine somewhere other than in their uncles' back offices, you understand—and the third has money invested in Monsieur Granger's prospective LaFayette and Pontchartrain railway company. The others who have been recommended to me seem overfond of bleeding. . . . I trust that your remedy for a bullet in the lung does not involve a cupping glass? It is to my professional interest, you understand, to know things like this."

Considering how nearly every young Creole gentleman bristled and circled and named his friends at the most trivial of slights, it wasn't surprising that Mayerling, Verret, Crocquère, and the other fencing teachers would be on intimate terms with every medical man for fifty miles.

January shuddered. He knew several who would resort to just that, accompanied by massive purges and a heavy dose of calomel— salts of mercury—for good measure.

"You think they'll accept a physician of color?"

The sword master appeared genuinely surprised. "It is of no concern to me what they accept. Jean Bouille is my student. The American shall accept your ministrations or die of his wounds. Which, it is of little interest to me. May I count upon you, sir?"

January inclined his head, hiding his amusement at the extent of the Prussian's imperial arrogance. "You may, sir."

Mayerling produced his card, which January pocketed, and accepted one of January's in return. Mayerling's said simply, *Augustus Mayerling. Sword Master.* January's was inscribed, *Benjamin Janvier. Lessons in Piano, Clavichord, Harp, and Guitar.* Underneath the lines were repeated in French.

"I can't find her anywhere," wailed Marie-Rose at twenty minutes until midnight, coming up while Minou was flirting with Hannibal across the palmettos that screened the dais on both sides. Henri had returned to the respectable purlieus of the establishment with promises to be back in time for the tableaux; even the senior M. Peralta, pillar of rectitude that he was and assiduous in his attentions to Euphrasie Dreuze, had been back and forth several times.

By the way the old man was watching the lobby outside the ballroom, January guessed he had no idea where his son was. The boy was only seventeen. If he'd sent him home or banished him to the Théâtre he wouldn't be watching like that.

And Euphrasie Dreuze, quite clearly aghast at the possibility that her daughter might have whistled at least some percentage of the Peralta fortune down the wind, was like a pheasant in a cage, flitting in and out from ballroom to lobby in a fluffy scurry of satin and jewels. January dimly recalled his mother telling him that Etienne Crozat, owner of the Banque Independent and stockholder in half a dozen others, had paid Euphrasie Dreuze off handsomely upon his marriage. Her concern might, of course, stem entirely from care for her daughter's welfare, but the woman's reputed fondness for the faro tables and deep basset were probably the actual cause of the increasingly frenzied look in her eye.

When the Roman, Jenkins, returned from negotiations downstairs, he, too, loitered around the lobby with an air of searching for someone, but at the moment January couldn't see him.

"It's just like her," sighed Minou, as Marie-Anne, Marie-Rose, and one of the Ladies of the Harîm—shedding an occasional peacock eye in her wake—scampered off after the next waltz to make another canvass of the courtyard. "I asked Romulus to check the gambling rooms, but even Angelique wouldn't have gone down there. Maybe vanishing like this is part of her plan."

"No woman wears a getup like that and disappears before the *tableaux vivants*," Hannibal pointed out. He turned away to cough, pressing a hand briefly to his side to still it, and the candlelight glistened on the film of sweat that rimmed the long fjords of his retreating hairline.

"No," retorted Minou. "But if she's not back in another few

minutes Agnes is going to have to fix her daughters' hair, and every-body knows Agnes is just dreadful at that sort of thing. And now we can't find Clemence either. If Henri comes back and so much as speaks to another woman, have a waiter slip some mysterious potion to him to render him unconscious, would you, p'tit?"

"You'll need a sledge to get him home."

"I'm sure Monsieur Froissart will oblige. Why does everything have to go wrong at these affairs?" She fluttered away again, sleeves billowing like white and gold sails.

"I don't know why she'd take an hour and a half at it," said Hannibal, plucking at the strings again, and turning a key. "Any of the girls down in the Swamp—the Glutton or Railspike or Fat Mary—can have you begging for mercy inside five minutes. Seven, if you're dead to start with." He coughed again.

"Maybe that's the reason they're working the Swamp instead of having some banker buy them a house on Rue des Ursulines?"

"Surely you jest, sir." The fiddler grinned, and drained the last of his second bottle of champagne. "Though I'd trade a week's worth of opium to see what the Glutton would wear to one of these balls."

"What I'd trade for," remarked January, beginning to sort through his music and his notes for which tableau would be first, "is to know where they *could* have gone for an hour and a half. The building's filled. If Peralta Père and Phrasie Dreuze are that puzzled, it's got to mean they've asked in the courtyard and the gambling rooms whether anyone saw the two of them leave." He reached up and took the empty bottle from Hannibal's unsteady grasp.

"Easy," said Hannibal. "They could have gone through the pas-sageway to the Théâtre. Those boxes above the stage are curtained. Angelique's white enough to pass. It's not easy to tup a woman in a gown like that—twelve petticoats at the least, not to speak of the wings—in a box, but it can be done, if you don't mind leg cramps."

"Peralta would know that," pointed out January.

"And there's lot o' competition for them boxes," added Uncle Bichet, who had been following the entire intrigue with interest.

Minou strode over to them from the direction of the lobby doors, Agnes Pellicot at her heels, like a pair of infuriated daffodils. January

saw both of them look automatically in the direction of Euphrasie
Dreuze, seated in the triple bank of spindly gilt chaperones' chairs
with two of her cronies, fanning herself with what looked like an acre
of ostrich plumes and watching the archways into the lobby with a
wild and distracted eye.

"I have done what I can," announced Agnes, her protuberant
brown eyes flashing grimly. "Whore and bitch she might be, but she
can fix hair. How such a woman could have been so . . ." She gave
up with a gesture. "This is the big chance for Marie-Anne and Marie-
Rose to be seen, to be admired at their best. If that conceited light-
skirt doesn't turn up . . ."

"I'll move her tableau to last." January shifted the Rossini aria
he'd arranged as Angelique's music in behind the Mozart dances that
would usher in the Harîm.

"Don't you dare!" cried a masked woman in a red-and-gold hash-
ish dream of a Sultana costume. Her fantasia of dyed ostrich plumes
tossed like storm clouds as she shook her head and shed a faint snow-
fall of shreds. "We're on last. It serves her right if she misses her
place."

"Rachelle, of course if she shows up after you go on, we'll put her
on last," said Minou coaxingly. "Think how unfair it would be to
punish Emilie and Clemence and the two Maries. And where *is* Clemence?"

"I think she left when Galen did," put in Marie-Rose.
"Iphègénie's aunt saw someone wearing that gray-green dress in the
courtyard."

"Tell you what," said January, as the Sultana Rachelle's bronze
mouth puckered dangerously. "We'll do that mazurka as an extra, to
give everybody a little more time. Minou, you checked back on the
parlor lately? She's got to go back there one time or another if she's
going to fix those wings of hers. It's the only place where she'd have
room to work."

"Hussy," whispered Agnes Pellicot, her face like a hurricane sky.
"*Bandeuse!* Coming to the ball like this, two months or less after
Arnaud Trepagier is in his tomb, to see what else she can catch! If
she'd had any decency she would have left the tableau, turned her

position in it over to someone else! She can't be needing money. After all he gave her, the jewels he lavished on her, slaves, a house fit for royalty, horses and a carriage, even! You saw those pearls and emeralds she had about her neck! He'd ride in from his plantation every night to be with her, even took her to the opera . . . fie!"

She stormed out into the lobby again in wrath.

"Dare one infer," murmured Hannibal, turning over a page of the mazurka, "that Mama had some plans for Peralta Fils and the fair Marie-Rose?"

"Sounds like it," agreed January philosophically. "Shall we?"

The brisk dance was entering its third variation when Minou reappeared in the hall, her face ashy in the dark frame of her hair. January, glancing up from the piano, saw the flutter of her sleeves with the shaky wave of her hands, the way the jeweled pomander chain at her waist vibrated with the trembling of her knees. With a quick gesture he signaled Hannibal to carry the figure as a solo—hoping his colleague wasn't going to engage in any adventures with the tempo, as he sometimes did at this stage of an evening—and leaned from the piano's seat.

"What is it?"

"I . . ." Minou swallowed hard. "You'd better come."

"What happened?" He hadn't known his sister long, but he knew that under the empty-headed frivolity lay considerable strength of mind. It was the first time he'd ever seen her unnerved.

"In the parlor," she said. "Ben, I think she's dead."

From the time he was fourteen years old, January had wanted to study medicine.

St.-Denis Janvier had sent him to one of the very fine schools available to the children of the colored bourgeoisie—where he had been looked upon askance, as he had in his music lessons, for his gangly size and African blackness far more than for his mother's plaçage—which boasted a science master who had trained in Montpellier before returning to his native New Orleans to teach.

Monsieur Gomez had been a believer in empiricism rather than in theory and had trained him as a surgeon rather than a physician. For this direction January was infinitely and forever grateful, despite his mother's sneer and frown: "A *surgeon,* p'tit? A puller of teeth, when you could have an office and a practice of wealthy men?"

But his reading of the medical journals, the endless quibblings about bodily humors and the merits of heroic medicine—his experience with the men who prescribed bleeding for every ill and didn't consider a patient sufficiently treated until he'd been dosed with salts of mercury until his gums bled—convinced him early on that he could never have adopted a livelihood based so firmly on ignorance, half truths, and arrogant lies.

Instead he had dissected rabbits and possums netted in the bayous and cattle from the slaughterhouses; had roved at will through Monsieur Gomez's meager library and had followed the man on his rounds at the Charity Hospital, learning to set bones, birth babies, and repair fistulas regardless of which bodily humor was in ascendance at the time. He had been more than a student to Gomez, as Madeleine Dubonnet had been more than a student to him; rather, he had been, as she had been, a secret partner in a mystery, a junior co-devotee of the same intricate gnosis.

He had fought alongside Gomez in Jackson's army when the British invaded and afterward had tended the wounded with him. When yellow fever had swept the city for the first time in the summer before his departure for France, he'd worked at his mentor's side in the plague hospitals.

But from the start, Gomez had told him to be a musician.

"That Austrian drill sergeant is the best friend you have, p'tit." Gomez's Spanish-dark eyes were sad. "You have talent. If you were a white man, or even as bright-skinned as I, you could be a truly fine doctor. But even in Europe, where they don't look at a black man and say, 'He's a slave,' they'll still look at you and say, 'He's an African.' "

January had sat for a long time, looking down at the backs of his huge ebony hands. Very quietly, he said, "I'm not."

"No," agreed Gomez. "Were you an African—living in Africa, I mean, in the tribes—I daresay you'd have found your way to the healing trade. They're not all savages there, whatever the Americans may say. You have the healer's hands and the memory for herbs and substances; you have the lightness of touch that makes a good surgeon, and the speed and courage that are the only salvation of a man under the knife. And you have a surgeon's caring. You'd have been exceptional, either in the one world or the other. But you're not an African either."

January was silent. He'd already encountered too many of his mother's friends—too many of his classmates' parents—who gave him *that* look. Who said—or didn't say—"He is . . . very *dark* to be Monsieur Janvier's son, is he not?"

With one white grandparent—whoever that had been—he was only *sang mêlé* by courtesy in those days. He knew how, in colored society, one white grandparent was looked down upon by those who had two or more. Even in those days it had been so. Now it was worse, now that the colored artists and craftsmen of the city, the colored businessmen who owned their own shops, were being met by the newly arrived Americans flooding into the city and taking up plantations along the river and the bayous. They were being called "nigger" by illiterate Kentuckians and Hoosier riverboat men who wouldn't have been permitted through those artists' and craftsmen's and businessmen's front doors.

These days, the colored had stronger reasons than ever to proclaim themselves different—entirely different—from the black.

Maybe he could have practiced medicine in New Orleans, he thought, if he were as light as Monsieur Gomez, as light as the one or two other colored physicians in practice there—even as light as his own mother.

She was a mulatto. He, with three African grandparents, was black.

"I'll make them change their minds," he said.

That was before the war.

Despite Napoleon's betrayal, St.-Denis Janvier, like most Creoles, regarded himself as French. When January spoke to him about going to study in Europe, it was assumed by both that he would study in France. But by the time he was old enough to undertake the journey, fighting had broken out afresh between England and France, and between England and the United States. There was little enough fighting on land in Louisiana, except toward the end during Pakenham's disastrous attempt at invasion, but it wasn't a safe time to be on the sea. Thus January was twenty-four, and a veteran of battle, battlefield surgery, and a major epidemic, before he set sail for Paris, to study both medicine and music, subjects that in some fashion he could not explain seemed at times to be almost the same in his heart.

He had found Monsieur Gomez to be mostly right. He studied and passed his examinations and was taken on as an assistant surgeon in one of the city's big charity hospitals, but no one even considered the possibility of his entering private practice. In any case it was out of the question, for St.-Denis Janvier died of yellow fever in 1822, shortly after his adopted son was admitted to the Paris College of Surgeons. He left him a little, but not enough to purchase a practice or to start one on his own.

He had still been working at the Hôtel Dieu two years later, when a black-haired, hook-nosed, eighteen-year-old Moroccan seamstress had brought in a fifteen-year-old prostitute who sometimes did piece-work for her, the girl hemorrhaging from self-induced abortion.

The girl had died. Ayasha had left, but later, coming away from the hospital, January had found her crying in a doorway and had walked her home.

He was not making enough as a doctor to marry, and by then he knew that he never would.

But Paris was a city of music, and music was not something that whites appeared to believe required a white father's blood.

Angelique Crozat had been bundled together in the bottom of the armoire in the retiring parlor, beneath a loose tangle of cloaks and opera capes.

"I looked to see if she might have stowed her wings in here." Minou was still a little pale, her voice struggling against breathlessness as she glanced from her tall brother back to the silvery form stretched on its scattered bed of velvet and satin, the face a deformed and discolored pearl in the particolored delta of hair. One extravagant sleeve was torn away from the shoulder, and a drift of white swans-down leaked out onto the dark satin of the domino beneath her. Beside her, the wings lay like the brittle, shorn-off wings of the flying ants that showed up on every windowsill and back step after swarming season. January knelt to touch the needle dangling loose from the torn netting at the end of its trailing clew of silk.

"She was under the cloaks. I saw just a corner of her dress sticking out and remembered there was no one else in the ballroom wearing white."

"Did you pull off her mask?"

Minou nodded. "She had it on when I—when I found her. I thought she might have been still alive. . . . I swear I don't know what I thought."

This room, like Froissart's office, had not been included when the building was converted to gaslight. Instead, branches of expensive wax candles burned against glass reflectors all around the walls. It was a haunted light, after the brilliance of the gas, as if the whole chamber had been preserved in amber long ago, and the woman who lay on the cloaks were no more than some beautiful, exotic relic of an antediluvian world. But under the eerie, tabby-cat face shoved up onto her forehead, there was no mistaking the bluish cast of the skin, the swollen tongue, and bulging, bruised-looking eyes. There was certainly no mistaking the marks around her neck.

Behind them, Leon Froissart whispered, "My God, my God, what am I to do? All the gentlemen in the ballroom . . ."

"Send someone for the police," said January. "God have mercy on her." He crossed himself and offered an inward prayer, then turned the lace-mitted hand over in his. There was blood under all her nails; two of them had been pulled almost clear of their beds in the struggle, and dabs of red stood on her skirt and sleeves like the fallen petals of a wilting rose.

He was thinking fast: about the passageway from the ballroom to the Théâtre, about the courtyard with its teeming, masked fantasies. About the Coleridge dreams ascending and descending the double stair to the lobby, and the double doors opening from lobby to gaming rooms, and from gaming rooms to the street.

"Now, immediately, as soon as possible. Keep anyone from entering or leaving the building and send someone over to the Théâtre and tell them to do the same. If anyone tries to leave tell them we've found a large sum of money and we have to identify the owner. But mostly just tell Hannibal and the others to play that Beethoven contradanse.

It should keep everybody happy," he added, turning to see the look of horror that swept Froissart's face.

Belatedly, he remembered he was no longer in Paris, shifted his eyes quickly from the white man's eyes and modified the tone of command from his voice. "You know the police are going to want to talk to everyone."

"Police?" Froissart stared at him in horror. "We can't send for the police!"

January looked up, startled into meeting his eyes. Froissart was a Frenchman of France, without the American's automatic contempt for persons of color, but he'd been in the country for years. Still, an American wouldn't have flushed or have turned his glance away in shame.

"Some . . . some of the most prominent men in the city are here tonight!" There was pleading in his voice.

The most prominent men in the city and their colored mistresses, thought January. Any one of whom can be headed out the side door this minute, masked and disguised as who-knows-what.

And French or not, Froissart was white. January looked down again and made his tone still more conciliating, like the wise old uncle common to so many of the plantations. "Believe me, Monsieur Froissart, if I had a choice between what your guests'll say about your calling the police, and what the police'll say if you don't call—if it was me, I'd call."

Froissart said nothing, staring in fascinated horror down at the dead woman's face. The beautiful light skin of which she had been so vain was suffused with dark blood, the delicate features—indistinguishable from a white woman's—contorted almost beyond recognition.

"I could be dismissed," he whispered in a wan little voice. "M'sieu Davis wants no trouble in this house, not in the gaming rooms, not in the Théâtre. . . ." He swallowed hard. "And bien sûr, she is only a plaçée . . ."

January could see where that was going. *The custom of the country . . .* So could Dominique; she gestured toward the door with her eyes, and January bent down closer to the body, his motion deliberately drawing Froissart's attention. "You see how her neck's marked?" The man would have had to be an idiot not to note the massive bar of bruise circling the white throat like a noose, but Froissart knelt at his side, leaned attentively, fascinated by the gruesome melding of beauty and death. Dominique slipped from the room with barely a rustle of silk petticoat.

"She was strangled with a cloth or a scarf, like a Spanish garrote. A woman could have done it as easily as a man. She was wearing a necklace of pearls and emeralds earlier—see where the pressure drove the fixings into her skin?" His light fingers brushed the ring of tiny cuts. "They took it off her afterward. So it's a thief. . . . Which means they might strike here again."

"Again!" gasped Froissart in horror.

January nodded, remaining on his knees in spite of an overwhelming desire to thrust the nattering fool aside and fetch Romulus Valle. Romulus could organize an unobtrusive cordon around both the ballroom and the Théâtre while he himself could have enough time alone to examine the body and see if Angelique had been raped as well as robbed.

But such a cordon—such an examination—would never be permitted.

"Of course none of the gentlemen in the ballroom would have done this—why would they have needed to steal? But one of them may have seen something. And there's nothing says they have to take off their masks or give their right names when the police ask them questions."

And if you believe that, he thought, watching the groping quest for guidance in the manager's eyes, *I have the crown jewels of France right here in my pocket, and I'll let you have them cheap at two thousand dollars American. . . .*

"But . . . But how will it look?" stammered Froissart. "I depend on the goodwill of the ladies and gentlemen. . . . Of course, there must be a discreet investigation of some sort, conducted quietly, but can it not wait until morning?" He dug in his waistcoat pocket, took January's hand, and slapped four gold ten-dollar pieces into his palm.

"Here, my boy. I'll send for Romulus, and the two of you can get her to one of the attics. Romulus can have the room tidied up in no time, and there'll be another four of these if you hold your tongue."

He started to rise, looking around him—possibly for Dominique—and January touched his arm, drawing his attention again. "You know, sir," he said gravely, "I think you may be right about a private investigation. Myself, I wouldn't trust the police now that they have so many . . . Well, maybe I shouldn't say it about white men, sir, but I think you know, and I know, that some of these Kentuckians and riffraff they have coming down the river nowadays . . . And putting them on the police force, too!"

"Exactly!" cried Froissart, with a jab of his stubby, bejeweled finger. January saw all recollection of Dominique's presence in the room evaporate from Froissart's face and felt a mild astonishment that he'd remembered, out of all his mother's crazy quilt of gossip, that Froissart had been furious with chagrin over the construction by Americans of the new St. Louis Hotel Ballroom on Baronne Street.

But as if January had rubbed a magic talisman he'd found in the street, Froissart launched into an extended recital of the insults and indignities he had suffered, not only at the hands of the Americans on the police force but of the Kentucky riverboat men, American traders, upstart planters and every newcomer who had flooded into New Orleans since Napoleon's perfidious betrayal of the city into United States hands.

During the recital January continued to kneel beside Angelique's body, touching it as little as possible—she was, after all, a white man's woman—but observing what he could.

Lace crushed and broken at the back of her collar, knotted with the gaudy tangle of real and artificial *chevelure*. In the dim light of the candles it was hard to tell, but he didn't think there were threads caught in it, though there might be some in her dark hair. Fluffs of swansdown from her torn sleeve were scattered across the gorgeous Turkey carpet, thickest just to the left of the low chair. A cluster of work candles stood on the small table immediately to the chair's right, draped with huge, uneven winding-sheets of drippings. They'd been there when he'd come in. She'd been fixing her wings, he remembered, by their light. In France it would have been an oil lamp, but mostly in New Orleans they used candles. The drippings were distorted from repeated draughts—people had been in and out of the parlor all evening, fixing their ruffles or looking for her. Froissart was lucky the table hadn't been kicked over in the struggle. The whole building could have gone up.

Swansdown wasn't the only thing on the carpet. A peacock eye near the chair told him that Sultana girl in the blue lustring had been here. A dozen calibers of imitation pearls were trodden into the carpet: Marie-Anne had had large ones on her mask and bodice, and the drop-shaped ones he'd seen on the sleeves of the American Henry VIII's Anne Boleyn. Mardi Gras costumes were never made as well as street clothes, and ribbons, glass gems, and silk roses dotted the floor among thread ends of every color of the rainbow. In the padded arm of the velvet chair a needle caught the light like a splinter of glass.

Drunken laughter floated in from the Rue Ste.-Ann through the single tall window that nearly filled one side of the room. The brass band still played in the street. Shouts of mirth, a woman's shrill squeak of not entirely displeased protest. Men cursed in French, German, slangy riverboat English, and there was a heavy splash as someone fell into the gutter, followed by whoops of drunken laughter.

January glanced at the window, not daring to break Froissart's self-centered oblivion by walking over to check whether there were marks on the sill. The killer could have stepped out one of the ballroom windows and walked along the gallery, he supposed. But with the heat of the ballroom, other revelers had taken refuge on the gallery, and such an escape would not have gone unseen.

Carnival rioted below, thick in these narrow streets of the old French town, drowning the sounds of the ballroom itself. In the growing upriver suburbs, in their tall brick American houses on the new streets along the tracks of the horse-drawn streetcars, Protestants would be shaking their heads about the goings-on. Though perhaps, reflected January, a number of those Protestant wives wondered—or tried not to wonder—where their husbands were tonight.

Last summer everyone in the ballroom—everyone in the streets— everyone in the city—had been through the horrors of a double epidemic: yellow fever and Asiatic cholera, worse than any that had gone before. They had survived it, mostly by clearing out of town if they could afford to, taking refuge in the lakeside hotels of Mandeville and Milneburgh or on plantations. Typical of the Creoles, they celebrated the victory rather than mourned the loss. But there was no guarantee that in five months it wouldn't return.

He remembered Ayasha and crossed himself again. There was no guarantee about anything.

"They simply do not understand." Froissart's voice brought him back to the present. The man was now well worked into his theme. January kept an expression of fascinated interest in his face, but barely heard him. It was only a few hundred feet to the Cabildo, and ordinarily a woman—even a beautiful one—was quite safe walking about the streets alone, provided she kept out of certain well-defined districts: the waterfront or the bars along Rue du Levée; the Swamp or the Irish Channel.

But Carnival was different.

"Americans have no finesse, no sense of how things are done!" Froissart's gesture to heaven was worthy of Macbeth perishing in the final act.

"They sure don't, sir." *If he's buying, I'll sell it to him.*

"The Americans, they don't know how to behave! They don't know how to take mistresses. They think it's all a matter of money. For them, money is everything! Look at the houses they build, out along the Carrolton Road, in the LaFayette suburb and Saint Mary! I recall a time—not ten years ago it was!—that the whole of the city of Jefferson was the Avart and Delaplace plantations, and a half-dozen others, the best sugar land on the river. And what do they do now? They build a streetcar line, they tear up the fields, and the next thing you know, you have these dreadful American houses with their picket fences! Exactly that which that canaille Granger proposes to do along Bayou Saint John! Him, fight a duel? Pffui!"

He flung out his hands in indignation—evidently challenges to duels, like trouncings with canes or fistfights in the court downstairs, did not come under the same category as murder.

"Why, in my office this evening, the way he and those sordid friends of his behaved! A disgrace! They are not gentlemen! They have no concept! They cannot tell Rossini from 'Turkey in the Straw'!"

"You're right about that, sir," agreed January gravely. As he spoke he felt a deep annoyance at himself, to be playing along as he had played along during his childhood and adolescence, falling back into the old double role of manipulating a white man's illusions about what a man of color was and thought. Still, the role was there, script and inflections and bits of business, a weapon or tool with whose use he was familiar, though he felt dirtied by its touch. "In Paris, the Americans were the same way. Every ball I'd play at, you could tell right where the Americans were sitting."

"And that is why we cannot summon the police tonight," concluded Froissart, turning regretfully back to the beautiful, ruined woman lying between them. "They do not understand how to do these things quietly, discreetly. Of course, of course they must be summoned in the morning—after I have spoken to Monsieur Davis. . . . Of course he will want to summon them. . . ." He chewed his lip in an agony of uncertainty, and January remembered the mother of one of his friends in Paris, who would put aside bills "for a few days until I know I have the money" and then eventually burn them unread.

Angelique's body was a bill that would be burned unread. Not because she was an evil woman or because she had harmed every life she touched, but only because she was colored and a plaçée.

"Well, what would you?" sighed Froissart—January could almost see Mme. du Gagny sliding yet another dressmaker's dun into that nacre-and-rosewood secrétaire. "It is how it is. . . . Good heavens, how long have we been here? People will begin to ask. . . . You must return to your piano and say nothing, nothing. Be assured that the matter will be taken care of in the morning."

January inclined his head and arose. "I'm sorry," he said humbly. "I was so shaken up by seeing her here like this, I . . . It took me a while to get my thoughts back. Thank you for your patience with me."

Froissart beamed patronizingly. "One understands," he said, as if he himself hadn't gone fishbelly green at the sight of the body—

January guessed he was one of those who headed for Mandeville at the first of the summer heat and had never been through an epidemic at firsthand in his life. "Of course, the shock of it all. I hope you are better."

"Much," said January, wondering if he should fake a spell of dizziness with the shock and rejecting the idea—and his own consideration of it—with loathing. He made a show of looking around as if he'd forgotten something, playing for as much time as he could scrape. "Much better."

Froissart turned and left the jewelbox room with its grisly occupant, and January perforce followed. He glanced back at the crumpled body, the grasping and greedy woman who had assumed he was a slave because his skin was darker than hers. Still, she did not deserve to be forgotten like an unpaid bill. *I did my best,* he apologized. More, certainly, than he would ever have accorded her in life.

As he left he laid the four coins Froissart had given him gently on the table by the door.

"Romulus!" called Froissart. "Romulus, I . . ."

They emerged from the hallway into the lobby in time to see a small party of blue-clothed city guardsmen arrive at the top of the stairs.

Froissart stopped, goggling, as if he hoped these were another group of revelers, like Robin Hood's Merry Men or the Ladies of the Harîm.

But none of them were masked. And no Creole he knew, thought January, would have the wit to dress that much like an out-at-elbows upriver Kaintuck, with a shabby, flapping corduroy coat many years out of fashion and too short in the sleeves for his loose-jointed height.

Minou slipped past them, startlingly invisible for someone so beautiful and brightly clad, and melted into the crowd in the ballroom like snow on the desert's dusty face. The tall officer stepped forward and laid a black-nailed hand on Froissart's arm.

"Mr. Froissart?" Interestingly, he got the pronunciation right. " 'Fore you and your boy head on back to the ballroom, we'd like to talk to you." His tone was polite but his backcountry dialect so thick that his English was barely comprehensible.

Two of the guards were heading into the ballroom. The music ceased. Silence, then a rising clamor. January could already hear that the tenor of the noise from the gaming rooms and the downstairs lobby had changed as well.

"What . . ." stammered Froissart. "What? . . ."

The tall man touched the brim of his low-crowned hat, and spit a stream of tobacco in the general direction of the sandbox. He was unshaven, noisome, and the sugar-brown hair hanging to his shoulders was stringy with grease. "Abishag Shaw, lieutenant of the New Orleans police, at your service, sir."

FIVE

"This is an outrage!" The plump Ivanhoe who'd been negotiating with Agnes Pellicot stationed himself foursquare in the central of the three ballroom doorways, ornamental sword drawn as if to reenact Roncevaux upon the threshold. Looking past him, January was interested to note that the invisible barriers that had separated the Americans—the Roman, Henry VIII, Richelieu—from the Creoles seemed momentarily to have dissolved. "None of us had the least thing to do with that cocotte's death, and I consider it an insult for you to say that we have!"

"Why, hell, sir, I know you got nuthin' to do with it." Police Lieutenant Abishag Shaw, though he replied in English, did not appear to have any trouble understanding the man's French. He folded his long arms, stepped closer to the doorway and lowered his voice as if to exclude the three constables grouped uncertainly behind him, their eyes on the curtained passage to the Théâtre next door. "But I also know men like yourselves don't miss much of what goes on around them, neither. Anything happen out of the ordinary—an' maybe you wouldn'ta knowed it was out of the ordinary at the time—

you'd a seen it. That's what I'm countin' on to help me find this killer."

The Creoles muttered and whispered among themselves in French. January heard a man start to say in English, "She's only a . . ." The concluding words, *nigger whore,* remained unsaid, probably more because the speaker realized that saying them would damage his chances with the dead woman's fellow demimondaines than out of any consideration of good taste. Old Xavier Peralta turned his head. "She was a free woman of this city, sir," he said quietly. "She is entitled to this city's justice."

"I agree," said Ivanhoe. "But there is no need for us to unmask to tell you what we have seen tonight."

Shaw scratched his unshaven jaw. "Well," he said in his mild tenor voice, "in fact there is." And he aimed another long stream of tobacco juice into the nearest spittoon, missing by only inches—not bad at the distance, January thought.

"Malarkey!" barked Henry VIII. Only men were visible in the doorway, but January could see the silken bevies of women grouped in the other two entries, watching with eyes that held not love, but worried calculation, like the occupants of a sinking vessel computing the square footage of the rafts.

From the parlor a wailing shriek sliced the air: "Angelique, my baby! My angel! Oh dear God, my baby!" Other voices murmured, soothing, weeping, calming.

January's eyes returned to the faces of the men. It was absurd to suppose the murderer was still in the ballroom, or anywhere in the Salle d'Orléans. Henri Viellard certainly wasn't, having beaten a hasty retreat through the passageway to the concealing skirts of his mother, sisters, and aunts, who would be willing like any group of Creoles to perjure themselves for the good of the family. William Granger likewise seemed, as the Kaintucks put it, to have absquatulated. In fact only a small group of men remained in a room that had been crammed with a preponderance of them moments before. The ladies in the Théâtre d'Orléans must have wondered why their menfolk had developed so sudden a craving for their company.

January hoped this man Shaw had the wits to set a guard in the

Théâtre's lobby as well as in the court and at the doors from the gaming rooms to the Rue Orléans outside.

Augustus Mayerling was one of those who remained, arms folded, at the rear of the group. His students, perforce, stood their ground as well, unwilling to have it said of them that they fled while their master remained, although a number of them didn't look happy about it.

"This is ridiculous," declared Ivanhoe. "You overstep your authority, young man."

"Well, maybe I do," agreed Shaw and absentmindedly scratched his chest under his coat. "But if'n you was to be murdered, Mr. Destrehan, I'm sure you'd like to know that the police was keepin' all suspects and witnesses in the same buildin' until they could be asked about it."

"Not if it meant all but accusing my friends of the deed!" The Knight of the Oak scowled darkly under his helmet's slatted visor at this offhandedly correct deduction of his identity. "Not if it meant needlessly impugning their reputations, running the risk of exposing their names to the newspapers—"

"Now, who said a thing about newspapers?"

"Don't be a fool, man," snapped Bouille, who from his well-publicized quarrel with Granger over the past few months had reason to know all about newspapers. He seemed to have either drunk himself to the point where he didn't care about the risk to his reputation, or more probably simply had no concept that his reputation could be at risk. "Of course the newspapers will get any list you make. And publish it."

"Froissart," ordered a truly awful Leatherstocking, "send one of your people to the police station and get Captain Tremouille and let us end this comedy."

" 'Fraid the captain's off this evenin'," said Shaw.

"He'll be at the LaFrennière ball," said Peralta quietly. He turned back to Shaw, the gaslight glittering on the lace at his throat and wrists. "I understand your position, Lieutenant, but surely you must understand ours. There are men here who cannot afford to have their names dragged through the American newspapers, which, you must admit, display very little discretion in their choice of either subject matter or terms of expression. If you cannot take our information without demanding our names, I fear we must stand on our rights as the leading citizens of this town and refuse you our assistance."

Under a narrow brow and a hanging forelock of grimy hair, Shaw's pale eyes glinted. He spat again and said nothing.

Quietly, January said, "Lieutenant?" He wasn't sure how the man would take a suggestion from a colored, but every second the impasse lasted increased the chance of someone finding a good reason to forget the whole matter. The man at least seemed to be willing to investigate a plaçée's death, which was something.

Shaw considered him for a moment, lashless gray eyes enigmatic under a brow like an outlaw horse's, then walked to where he stood.

Very softly January said, "The women will know who's who. Have a man in the room take down color and kind of costume when these men give their testimonies masked and match up the descriptions with the women later."

Shaw studied him for a moment, then said, "You're the fella found the body."

January nodded, then remembered to lower his eyes and say, "Yes, sir."

"Froissart tells me you kept him talkin' and kept the place from bein' blockaded."

January felt his face heat with anger at the master of ceremonies' casual shifting of criminal blame. He forced calm into his voice. "That wasn't the way it happened, but I can't prove that. He was going to have the body taken up to an attic, clean up the room, and not call the police until morning. Maybe not call the police at all." He wondered for a moment whether this man would have preferred it that way . . . but in that case he'd have found some reason not to come quickly. "I kept him talking to give my sister time to bring you here."

"Ah." The policeman nodded. His face, ugly as an Ohio River gargoyle, was as inexpressive as a plank. " 'Xplains why a private citizen all dressed up like Maid Marian brung the news, 'stead of an employee of the house." His English would have earned January the beating of his life from his schoolmasters or his mother, but he guessed the man's French was worse. "Now I think on it, 'xplains why anyone brought the news at all. So Miss Janvier's your sister?"

"Half-sister. Sir."

"Beautiful gal." The words might have been spoken of a Ming vase or a Brittany sunset, an admiring compliment without a touch of the lascivious. He turned back to the assembled planters, bankers, and merchants crowded in the ballroom door. "Gentlemen," he said, "as a representative of equal justice in this city, I can't say I approve of divagatin' from the law, but I understand yore reasons, and I'm bound to say I accepts 'em." He shoved back the too-long forelock with fingers like cotton-loom spindles. "With your permission, then, I'll note down what any of you saw anonymously, and I thank you for doin' your duty as citizens in figurin' out the circumstances of this poor girl's death and findin' the man what killed her. I will ask that you be patient, since this'll take some little time."

There was an angry murmur from the ballroom. January saw several of the men—mostly Americans—glance toward the curtained passageway and guessed they'd have a number of desertions the moment Shaw was out of sight. "Mr. Froissart," said Shaw softly, "could you be so kind as to lend us your office for the interviews? It'll likely take most of the night, there bein' so many. Would it trouble you too much to make coffee for the folks here? Boechter," he added, motioning one of his constables near, "see to it nobody wanders in off'n the street, would you?"

Or wanders out, thought January, though he guessed Constable Boechter wasn't going to be much of a deterrent if Peralta or Destrehan grew impatient and decided to quit the premises. Shaw motioned him over and said, "Maestro? I'd purely take it as a favor if while you're waitin' you'd play some music, give 'em somethin' to listen to. Sounds silly, but music doth have charms an' all that."

January nodded. He wondered whether it was chance, or whether this upriver barbarian truly knew the Creole mind well enough to understand that by turning the nuisance into a social occasion with food, coffee, and music, he would keep his witnesses in the room. "If it's as well for you, Dominique and I can wait to be interviewed last.

Sir. You may want to get through as many of these as you can before they get bored and start walking out."

The lieutenant smiled for the first time, and it changed his whole slab-sided face. "You may have a point, Maestro. I think I'll need to talk to your sister first off, to get the shape of what it is I'm askin'." He spoke softly enough to exclude not only the men grouped in the ballroom doorway, but Froissart and his own constables. "I take it your sister's here with her man?"

"He'll have gone by this time," said January. "Half the men here tonight just slipped back through to the Théâtre; their wives and mothers are going to swear they were with them all night on that side. I doubt there's anything you can do about that."

Shaw spat again—he had yet to make his target—but other than that kept his opinion to himself. "Well, we can only do what we can. You may be waitin' a piece. . . . What is your name?"

"January. Benjamin January." He handed him his card.

Shaw slipped it into the sagging pocket of his green corduroy coat. "Like they say, it's the custom of the country."

From his post on the dais, January could watch the entire long ballroom and hear the surge and babble of talk as now one masked gentleman, now another, exited for questioning. Those who really didn't want to be questioned slipped off the moment Shaw was out of sight, but the Kaintuck's instinct had been a wise one: Romulus Valle replenished the collation on the tables with fresh oysters, beignets, and tarts newly baked from the market, and the somber glory of coffee, and this, combined with the light, calming airs of Mozart and Haydn, Schubert, and Rossini, created a partylike atmosphere. No Creole, January knew, was going to leave a party, certainly not if doing so would rob him of the chance to talk about it later. Secure in the knowledge that they were masked, wouldn't be identified, and that none of this really had anything to do with them, most stayed, and in fact more than a few returned from the Théâtre rather than lose out on the novelty.

Augustus Mayerling set up a faro bank in a corner and systematically fleeced everyone in sight. A slightly spindle-shanked Apollo got into a furious argument with one of the several Uncases present and had to be separated by three of Mayerling's students before another duel ensued. Jean Bouille quoted to everyone who would listen the exact content of the letters William Granger had written to the *Courier* about him, and verbatim accounts of what he had written in return in the *Bee*.

The older women like Agnes Pellicot, and the daughters they had brought to show, had the best time: The men took the opportunity of a new experience to flirt with the young girls, and the mothers gossiped to their hearts' content. January reflected that his own mother would burst a blood vessel to think that she hadn't deigned to show up tonight and so had missed something her cronies would be discussing for weeks.

Only now and then could Euphrasie Dreuze's weeping be heard. Once Hannibal turned his head a little and remarked, "That was a good one." And when January frowned, puzzled, he explained, "You have to have lungs like an opera singer to make your grief carry through two closed doors and the corridor."

"She did lose her daughter," said January.

"She lost a son in the cholera last summer and went to a ball the same night she heard the news. Got up in black like an undertaker's mute, true, leaving streaks of it on every chair in the Pontchartrain Ballroom and telling everyone present how prostrate she was with grief, but she stayed till the last waltz and went out for oysters afterward. I was there."

Old Xavier Peralta evidently hadn't been apprised of this piece of gossip, however, for he gathered up a cup of coffee and slipped quietly from the ballroom; January saw him turn in the direction of the corridor from the lobby. Whatever he felt about the woman during negotiations for her daughter's contract, grief was grief.

His was the only sign of bereavement. Men sipped whisky from silver hip flasks or from the tiny bottles concealed in the heads of their canes and flirted with the girls. Probably fearing that he'd be asked to pay for all four if they stayed, Monsieur Froissart released Jacques and Uncle Bichet, but after he was questioned by the guards, Hannibal returned with another bottle of champagne and continued to accompany January's arias and sonatinas with the air of a man amusing himself. January suspected that the other two had only gone as far as the kitchens anyway, where they would sit trading speculations with Romulus Valle until almost morning.

As people moved in and out of the ballroom or through the lobby past the doorways, January kept watching the crowd, searching for the golden buckskin gown and the silly crown of black cock feathers. It would have been insanity for her to remain, but he could not put from his mind the fleeting impression he had had of her presence in the ballroom after he'd begun to play; could not forget the hard desperation in her eyes as she'd said, *I must see her . . . I MUST.* He wondered what she so urgently needed to discuss with the dead woman, and whether Angelique's death would make matters better for her, or worse.

Taking his advice—or perhaps simply following the dictates of logic—Shaw questioned all the men first and turned them out of the building, then the women, who were quite content to remain; though after the departure of the men most of the buffet vanished as well. Monsieur Froissart was under no illusions about which group constituted his more important clientele. A few gentlemen waited for their plaçées in the lobby downstairs or in the gambling rooms. Others, conscious of wives, mothers, and fiancées in the other side of the building, simply left instructions with coachmen—or in some cases employees of the ballroom—to see the ladies home. Few of the plaçées complained or expressed either indignation or annoyance. They were used to looking after themselves.

It was nearly five in the morning when January was conducted by a guardsman down the rear stairway—out of consideration to those still in the gambling rooms—and into Froissart's office.

The place smelled overwhelmingly of burnt tallow and expectorated tobacco. "I'd have started with the mothers, myself," sighed Lt. Shaw, pinching off the long brownish winding sheet from one of the branch of kitchen candles guttering on the desk. In his shirtsleeves the resemblance to a poorly made scarecrow was increased, his leather galluses cutting across the cheap calico of his shirt like wheel ruts, his long arms hanging knobby and cat scratched out of the rolled-up sleeves. Windrows of yellow paper heaped the desk's surface, and a smaller pile on the side table next to a graceful Empire chair marked where the clerk had sat. January wondered how accurate the notes on the costumes were.

He was a little surprised when Shaw motioned him to a chair. Most Americans—in fact most whites—would have let a man of color stand.

"You're right about that, sir," he said. "They're the ones who would have seen anything worth seeing."

Coffee cups stood in a neat cluster in one corner of the desk— presumably brought in by the men when they were questioned. Even at this hour, voices clamored drunkenly in the street, though the general tenor had lowered to a masculine bass. The brass band, wherever it was, was still going strong, on its fifth or sixth iteration of the same ten tunes. On the way from the back stairs to the office January had heard the noise from the gambling rooms, as strong now as it had been at seven-thirty the previous evening.

"Now, there's a fact." Shaw stretched his long arms, uncricking his back in a series of audible pops. "I sure wouldn't want to go bargainin' with one of them old bissoms, and I don't care what her daughter looked like. I seen warmer Christian charity at Maspero's Slave Exchange than I seen in the eyes of that harpy in yellow. . . . Leastwise this way the daughter gets the good of it, and not some rich man who's got a plantation already. You know Miss Crozat?"

"By reputation," said January. "I met her once or twice when she was little, but her mama kept her pretty close. She was only seven when I left for Paris in 1817, and she wasn't a student of mine. I taught piano back then, too," he explained. "I expect I'd have met her sooner or later, now I'm back. Her mother and mine are friends."

"But your sister says you say you talked to her tonight."

January nodded. "I'd been charged by a friend to arrange a meeting with her at my mother's house, tomorrow afternoon . . . this afternoon. I haven't had time to talk to my mother about it yet. I've lived with my mother since I came back from Paris in November. It's on Rue Burgundy."

Shaw made a note. "Any idea what the meetin' was about? And could I get the name of your friend?"

"I have no idea about the meeting. If it's all the same to you . . . sir," he remembered to add, ". . . I'd rather keep my friend's name out of this. The message was given in confidence."

It was his experience that white men frequently expected blacks or colored to do things as a matter of course that would have been a dueling matter for a white, but Shaw only nodded. The rain-colored eyes, lazy and set very deep, rested thoughtfully on him for a time, shadowed in the rusty glare that fell through the fanlight, as Madame Trepagier's had been shadowed. "Fair enough for now. I might have to ask you again later, if'n it looks like it has some bearin' on who took the girl's life. Tell me about your talk with her."

"It wasn't much of a talk," said January slowly, sifting, picking through his recollections, trying to excise everything that would indicate that the one who sent the message was white, Creole, a woman, a widow . . . connected to Angelique . . . present in the building . . .

With his dirty, dead-leaf hair and lantern-jawed face, Abishag Shaw gave the impression of an upriver hayseed recently escaped from a plow tail, but in those sleepy gray eyes January could glimpse a woodsman's cold intelligence. This man was an American and held power, for all his ungrammatical filthiness. As Froissart had said, there was a world of matters the Americans did not understand, and chief among them the worlds of difference that separated colored society from the African blacks.

"She refused to meet with my friend. She said she'd received notes before from . . . my friend, that she had nothing to say to . . . them." He changed the last word quickly from *her,* but had the strong suspicion that Shaw guessed anyway. "She said her father was an important man, and that my friend had best not try any . . . little tricks."

"What kind o' little tricks?" asked Shaw mildly. "You mean like brick dust on the back step? Or accusin' her of being uppity an' gettin' her thrashed at the jailhouse?"

"One or the other," said January, wondering if he'd let the answer go at that.

Shaw nodded again. "She say anythin' to you? About you?"

Genuinely startled, January said, "No. Not that I remember."

"Insult you? Make you mad? Phlosine . . ." He checked a note. "Gal named Phlosine Seurat says she heard the door slam."

"It was Galen Peralta who slammed the door," said January. "He came in—"

"Galen Peralta? Xavier Peralta's boy? One she had the tiff with earlier?" Shaw sat up and took his boots off the desk, and spat in the general direction of the office sandbox.

January regarded him with reciprocal surprise. "Didn't anyone else tell you?"

The policeman shook his head. "When was this? Last anybody saw of the boy was when he tore that fairy wing o' hers in the lobby, an' she went flouncin' off into that little parlor in a snit. Last anybody saw o' her, for that matter. This Seurat gal—an' the two or three others who was up in the upstairs lobby—say the boy stormed off down the stairs, and somebody says they seen him in the court, but they don't remember if that was before or after or when."

"There's a way in from the court to the passage outside this office," said January. "He could have changed his mind, had what they call l'esprit d'escalier . . ."

"Bad case of the I-shoulda-said," agreed Shaw mildly, sitting back again. Outside, men's voices rose in furious altercation; there was the monumental thud of a body hitting the wall that made the building shake. "I dunno how many sweethearts come to grief from one or the other of 'em comin' up with just the right coup de grâce halfway down the front walk. Go on."

"If he came up the back stairs nobody in the lobby downstairs, or upstairs, would have seen him. Because he did come in, as I think she knew he would. She thought I was him, when I first came into the room, before she turned around, and she had her lines all ready for him. The boy had a temper. And there isn't a seventeen-year-old in the world with the sense to just walk away."

"God knows I didn't," said Shaw, getting up and stretching his back. "Near got me killed half a dozen times, when I came up with just the right thing to say to my pa when he was likkered. And you left then?"

January nodded. "Yes, sir. There was no reason for me to stay, and the boy would have ordered me out in any case. My sister and Marie-Anne Pellicot were hunting for Mademoiselle Crozat for the rest of the night. Galen's father, too. I thought at the time the two of them went off somewhere to have their fight in more privacy, but it may be that he left fairly soon—during the jig and reel we started up to distract everyone from Bouille and Granger—and that she was still in the room fixing her wing when the murderer came on her."

The colorless eyebrows quirked. "Now, where you get that from?"

"Here." January got to his feet, Shaw following in his wake. They climbed the dark of the back stairs, turned right at the top, to where a sleepy constable still guarded the parlor door. A cup and a half-eaten pastry lay on the floor beside his chair. He got to his feet and saluted.

"We got everything up off that rug, Mr. Shaw. The mother took the girl away, like you said she could."

"And no sign of them geegaws that's missin'?"

"No, sir." The man unlocked the door.

The candles were guttering in here, too. The windows had been shut, and the room had a crumpled look and smelled of smoke and death. The brass band outside had silenced itself, and the voices of the few passersby rang loud.

January crossed at once to the stiffened gauze wings, still leaning where Dominique had propped them, against the armoire that had concealed Angelique's body. He reached down, very carefully, and touched the needle, hanging by the end of the thread. "Mostly if a woman stops sewing she'll stick the needle into the fabric to keep the thread from pulling free," he said. "Few things drive a woman crazier than having to rethread a needle when she hasn't planned on it. I don't know why this is."

Shaw's ugly face cracked into a smile again. "Now, there's a man been married." He looked around for someplace to spit, found no spittoon, and opened the window and shutter a crack to spit out across the balcony. January hoped Cardinal Richelieu was on the street beneath.

While Shaw was so engaged, January glanced down at the table, where the candles had been pushed aside around the top of a cardboard dress box. January lifted the box gently and angled it to the light, studying the dozen different colors of ribbon laid out in it, the innumerable tag ends of thread; two needles and fourteen pins; the peacock eye and the pearls and a large number of shreds of dyed and undyed ostrich plume. A ball of swansdown shreds the size of a sheep's stomach. Lace snagged from someone's petticoat.

Half a dozen hooks and eyes. Somebody's corset lace. The servants of both ballroom and theater would be picking up pounds of this kind of trash all morning.

From the midst of it he picked a leaf of swamp laurel. "The Roman in the golden armor," he said. "Jenkins, I think Granger said his name was. He was wreathed for victory."

"You got quite an eye for furbelows." Shaw strolled back, hands in pockets, as if only such bracing kept his gawky body upright. "That was smart, 'bout the costumes."

"My wife was a dressmaker." January turned the bits of thread, pearl, ribbon in his kid-gloved fingers. There were two ways a man could have said what Shaw did, even as there were two ways he could have earlier remarked on Minou, *Beautiful gal.* "There never was a time when I wasn't surrounded by ribbons and lace and watching her match them up into some of the prettiest gowns you ever saw."

He smiled, remembering. "There was a lady—some baron's wife —who drove her crazy, asking for more of this and more of that and not offering to pay a sou for it. Ayasha put up with this till this old cat started coming on to her about how a Christian woman would have thrown it in as lagniappe. Then she just changed the color of the ribbons on the corsage—and mind you, that color was all the crack that year, and this old harpy was delighted with the change—and I've never seen one woman get so ugly so fast."

He shook his head, and saw Shaw's gray eyes on him again, as if hearing the pain that lurked under the joy of any memory of her.

"Your wife was an Arab?"

"Moroccan—Berber," said January. "But a Christian, though I don't know how much of any of it she believed. She died last summer."

"The cholera?"

He nodded and picked up a pink velvet rose that had to have come from Dominique's mask, tiny in his huge hands. "She would have been able to tell you every person who'd been in this room from these bits. My sister can probably tell you most of them."

"Don't mean whoever done it leaked beads and ribbons here to be obligin'," remarked Shaw. "If that Peralta boy was in plain evenin' dress, less'n she tore off a button there'd be nuthin' to show. Now that Jenkins . . ."

"He was looking for her," said January. "Prowling in and out of the ballroom and the lobby. He could have come in here."

"You hear this tiff of theirs? In the lobby?"

"Everybody did. She flirted with Jenkins. From what I hear, she flirted with everybody, or at least everybody who had money."

"Even though Peralta's daddy's been . . . What? Buyin' her for his son?"

"Not buying *her*," said January, though he could tell from Shaw's voice that the policeman knew the plaçées were technically free. "Bargaining to buy her contract. That way the boy doesn't get skinned out of his eyeteeth, and the girl doesn't have to look like a harpy in front of her protector—and her mother can come right out and say, 'I want to make sure you don't marry some Creole girl and leave my child penniless with your baby,' where the girl can't. It's all arranged beforehand. Signed and sealed, no questions."

Shaw considered the matter, turning the leaf of swamp laurel in his hand. "Smart dealin'," he said. "What kid's gonna pick himself even a half decent girl on his first try? When I think about the first girl I ever fell in love with—Lordy!" He shook his head. "You think Miss Crozat was flirtin' with the Noblest Roman of 'em All to run up her price?"

"If she was, it was working. The boy was wild when he came into the room. But whether an American would have arrived at the same arrangement as a Frenchman is anybody's guess."

Shaw regarded him for a moment from narrowed eyes, as if weighing this criticism of the habit American planters had of simply buying a good-looking slave woman and taking her whether she would or no. But he only stepped to the window and spat again.

January followed him to the lobby, where Hannibal Sefton slept curled on a sofa under the flicker of the gaslights while two servants picked up stray champagne cups and swept beads and silk flowers, cigar butts and ribbons, from the brightly colored rugs. The ballroom gaped dim and silent to their right. When they descended the main stair, Shaw sliding snakelike into his weary old green coat, even the gambling rooms behind their shut doors were growing quiet.

A constable met them in the downstairs lobby, where a broad hall led to the silent dark of the court. The air smelled of rain and mud. Dawn light was bleeding through the half-open doors.

"We've searched the building and the attics, sir," said the man, saluting. "Nothing."

"Thank you kindly, Calvert." He pronounced it as the French did. Someone—probably Romulus Valle—had placed January's hat and music satchel on a console in the lobby. January and Shaw walked out into the courtyard together, Shaw turning back to crane his neck and look up at the Salle d'Orléans, rising above them in a wall of pale yellow and olive green.

There was always something indescribably shabby about this time of the morning in Carnival season, with streets nearly empty under weeping skies and littered with vivid trash. Crossing the courtyard, Shaw looked around him at the gallery, the plane trees, the colored lanterns doused and dark, then walked down the carriageway that let onto Rue Ste.-Ann, watching the occasional fiacre pass filled with homebound revelers and hearing the deep-voiced hoots of the steamboats on the river.

A woman strolled by, singing "Oystahs! Git yo' fresh oystahs!" in English, and on the opposite banquette two gentlemen in evening dress, still masked, reeled unsteadily from post to post of the overhanging gallery. A woman improbably clad as a Greek goddess accosted them, her masked face beaming with smiles.

"Now I wonder what she does for a livin'?" Shaw mused, and spat copiously in the gutter.

"Not the same as these ladies here tonight," January said quietly, hearing again the man in the ballroom and Froissart's dismissive, *she is only a plaçée, after all.* . . . He stooped to pick up the single curl of black cock feather that lay wet and forgotten against the alley wall.

Shaw looked back at him, surprised. "Now I may be a upriver flatboat boy with no classical education, but I know the difference between a courtesan an' a streetwalker, mask or no mask."

"Does it make a difference?" asked January. "Sir?"

"To me?" asked Shaw. "Or to Mr. Tremouille, when I go back to the Cabildo an' tell him what we got here?"

January started to say, *You tell me,* and shut his mouth on the words. The man was police, the man was white, the man was American. He might have said it to a Creole under the same circumstances, but the uneasiness returned to him, consciousness of the man's power to harm.

Shaw rubbed his face again, grubby with brown stubble like a layer of dirt.

"A woman was kilt," he said. "She bein' a free woman, an' a householder in this city, that meant the tax she paid was payin' my salary, so it sorta obligates me to avenge her death, don't it? I be violatin' any code of conduct if I was to call on your sister this afternoon?" He patted the sheaf of yellow notepapers that stuck out of the pocket of his sagging coat, and donned his disreputable hat.

"Send her a note this morning giving her the time," advised January. "That way she can get one of her girlfriends, or probably our mother, to play duenna. Four o'clock's a good time. She'll be awake and made up by then, and whatever's going on at the Crozats' won't be until eight or so. You have her address?"

Shaw nodded. "Thank you kindly," he said. "I was a constable here last Carnival time—and Lordy, I thought I'd stepped into one of my granny's picture books!—and it stands to reason there's gonna be more pockets picked now than any other time. And if a stranger kills a stranger, you don't hardly never catch him, less'n he does something truly foolish with his loot. But somethin' tells me it's a rare thief who'd kill for jewels at a ball in a place like this. And there was plenty of women comin' an' goin' through this tunnel, gussied up just as costive or more so. If somebody killed Miss Crozat for them necklaces she was wearin', it was a damn fool way to go about it."

He stepped out onto the brick banquette, spat into the gutter, and walked away into the weeping dawn, his coat flapping around his slouching form. January watched him out of sight, stroking the black cock feather with his fingertips.

The ochre stucco cottage on Rue Burgundy was silent when January reached it. It was one of a row of four. He listened for a moment at the closed shutters of each of its two front rooms, then edged his way down the muddy slot between the closely set walls of the houses to the yard, where he had to turn sideways and duck to enter the gate. The shutters there were closed as well. The yard boasted a privy, a brick kitchen, and a garçonnière above it.

When first he had lived there, his sister had occupied the rear bedroom, his mother the front, the two parlors—one behind the other—being used for the entertainment of St.-Denis Janvier. Although he was only nine years old, Benjamin had slept from the first in the garçonnière, waiting until the house lights were put out and then climbing down the rickety twist of the outside stair to run with Olympe and Will Pavegeau and Nic Gignac on their midnight adventures. He smiled, recalling the white glint of Olympe's eyes as she dared them to follow her to the cemetery, or to the slave dances out on Bayou St. John.

His younger sister—his full sister—been a skinny girl then, like a black spider in a raggedy blue-and-red skirt and a calico blouse a slave woman would have scorned to wear. Having a back room with access to the yard had made it easy for her to slip out, though he suspected that if she'd been locked in a dungeon, Olympe would still have managed to get free.

Olympe had been fifteen the year of Dominique's birth. The two girls had shared that rear chamber for only a year. Then Dominique had occupied it alone, a luxury for a little girl growing up. But then, Dominique had always been her mother's princess, her father's pride.

Presumably Dominique had occupied the room until Henri Viellard had come into her life when she was sixteen. By that time St.-Denis Janvier was dead, leaving his mistress comfortably off, and Livia Janvier had married a cabinetmaker, Christophe Levesque, who had died a few years ago. The rear room that had been Olympe's, then Dominique's, had been for a short spell Levesque's workshop. Now it was shut up, though Minou was of the opinion that her mother should take a lover.

January stepped to the long opening and drew back one leaf of the green shutters, listening at the slats of the jalousie for his mother's soft, even breath.

He heard nothing. Quietly, he lifted the latch, pushed the jalousie inward. The room was empty, ghostly with dust. He crossed to the door of his mother's bedroom, which stood half-slid back into its socket. Slatted light leaked through the louvers of the doors to the street. The gaily patterned coverlet was thrown back in a snowstorm of clean white sheets. Two butter-colored cats—Les Mesdames—dozed, paws tucked, on the end of the bed, opening their golden eyes only long enough to give him the sort of gaze high-bred Creole ladies generally reserved for drunken keelboat men sleeping in their own vomit in the gutters of the Rue Bourbon. There was water in the washbowl and a robe of heavy green chintz lay draped over the cane-bottomed chair. The smell of coffee hung in the air, a few hours old.

Euphrasie Dreuze, or one of her friends, he thought. They had come to her for comfort, and Livia Janvier Levesque had gone.

January crossed the yard again, his black leather music satchel under one arm. There was still fire in the kitchen stove, banked but emitting warmth. The big enamel coffeepot at the back contained several cups' worth. He poured himself some and carried it up the twisting steps and drank it as he changed his clothes and ate the beignets and pastry he'd cadged from the ballroom tables in the course of the night. Half his gleanings he'd left at Hannibal's narrow attic, stowed under a tin pot to keep the rats out of it, though he suspected the minute he was gone one or another of the girls who worked cribs in the building would steal it, as they stole Hannibal's medicine, his laudanum, and every cent he ever had in his pockets.

Before eating he knelt on the floor beside his bed and took from his pocket the rosary he'd had from his childhood—cheap blue glass beads, a crucifix of cut steel—and told over the swift decades of prayers for the soul of Angelique Crozat. She had been, by his own experience and that of everyone he'd talked to, a thoroughly detestable woman, but only God could know and judge. Wherever she was, she had died unconfessed and would need the prayers. They were little enough to give.

It was nearly nine in the morning when he dismounted his rented horse at the plantation called Les Saules where, up until two months ago, Arnaud Trepagier had lived.

A coal-dark butler clothed in the black of mourning came down the rear steps to greet him. "Madame Madeleine in the office with the broker," the man said, gesturing with one black-gloved hand while a barefoot child took the horse's bridle and led it to an iron hitching post under the willows scattered all around the house.

The house itself was old and, like all Creole plantation houses, built high with storerooms on the ground floor. The gallery that girdled it on three sides made it look larger than it was. "She say wait on the gallery, if it please you, sir, and she be out presently. Can I fetch you some lemonade while you're waiting?"

"Thank you." January was ironically amused to see that the servant's shirt cuffs were less frayed and his clothing newer than the free guest's. The long-tailed black coat and cream-colored pantaloons he'd worn last night had to be in good condition, for the appearance of a musician dictated in large part where he was asked to play. But though he'd made far more money as a musician than he'd ever made as a surgeon at the Hôtel Dieu—or probably would ever make practicing medicine in New Orleans—there'd never been a great deal to spare, taxes in France being what they were. Now, until he made enough of a reputation to get pupils again, he would have to resign himself to being more down-at-heels than some people's slaves.

The butler conducted him up the steps to the back gallery and saw him seated in a cane chair before redescending to cross the crushed-shell path through the garden in the direction of the kitchen. From his vantage point some ten feet above ground level, January could see through the green-misted branches of the intervening willows the mottled greens and rusts of home-dyed muslins as the kitchen slaves moved around the long brick building, starting the preparations for dinner or tending to the laundry room. It seemed that only those who went by the euphemism "servants"—in effect, the house slaves—warranted full mourning for a master they might have loved or feared or simply accepted, as they would have accepted a day's toil in summer heat. The rest simply wore what they had, home-dyed brown or weathered blue and red cotton calicoes, and the murmur of their voices drifted very faintly to him as they went about their duties.

Les Saules was a medium-size plantation of about four hundred arpents, not quite close enough to town to walk but an easy half-hour's ride. The house was built of soft local brick, stuccoed and painted white: three big rooms in a line with two smaller "cabinets" on the back, closing in two sides of what would be the sleeping porch in summer. Panes were missing from the tall doors that let onto the gallery, the openings patched with cardboard, and through the bare trees January could see that the stucco of the kitchen buildings was broken in places, showing the soft brick underneath. In the other direction, past the dilapidated garçonnière and the dovecotes, the work gang weeding the nearby field of second-crop cane looked too few for the job.

He recalled the heavy strands of antique pearls and emeralds on Angelique Crozat's bosom and in her hair. Old René Dubonnet, he remembered, had owned fifteen arpents along Lake Pontchartrain,

living each year off the advances on next year's crop. Like most planters and a lot of biblical kings, he had been wealthy in land and slaves
but possessed little in the way of cash and was mortgaged to his back
teeth. There was no reason to think Arnaud Trepagier was any different.

But there was always money, in those old families, to keep a town
house and a quadroon mistress, just as there was always money to send
the sons to Paris to be educated and the daughters to piano lessons
and convent schools. There was always money for good wines, expensive weddings, the best horseflesh. There was always money to main-
tain the old ways, the old traditions, in the face of squalid Yankee
upstarts.

Many years ago, before he'd departed for Paris, January had
played at a coming-out party at a big town house on Rue Royale. It
had not been too many months after the final defeat of the British at
Chalmette, and one of the guests, the junior partner in a brokerage
house, had brought a friend, an American, very wealthy, polite, and
clearly well-bred, and, as far as January could judge such things, handsome.

Only one French girl had even gone near him, the daughter of an
impoverished planter who'd been trying for years to marry her off.
Her brothers had threatened to horsewhip the man if he spoke to her
again.

"Monsieur Janvier?"

He turned, startled from his reverie.

Madeleine Trepagier stood in the half-open doors of the central
parlor, a dark shape in her mourning dress. Her dark hair was
smoothed into a neat coil on the back of her head, eschewing the
bunches of curls fashionable in society, and covered with a black lace
cap. Without the buckskin mask of a Mohican maid and the silly
streaks of red and blue paint, January could see that the promise of her
childhood beauty had been fulfilled.

He rose and bowed. "Madame Trepagier."

She took a seat in the other cane chair, looking out over the
turned earth and winter peas of the kitchen garden. Her mourning
gown, fitting a figure as opulent as a Roman Venus's, had originally

been some kind of figured calico, and the figures showed through the home-dyed blackness like the ghostly tabby of a black cat's fur, lending curious richness to the prosaic cloth. Her fingers were ink-stained, and there were lines of strain printed around her mouth and eyes.

And yet what struck January about her was her serenity. In spite of her harried weariness, in spite of that secret echo of grimness to her lips, she had the deep calm that arose from some unshakable knowledge rooted in her soul. No matter how many things went wrong, the one essential thing was taken care of.

But she looked pale, and he wondered at what time she had returned to Les Saules last night.

"Thank you for your concern last night," she said in her low voice. "And thank you for sending me away from there as you did."

"I take it you reached home safely, Madame?"

She nodded, with a rueful smile. "More safely than I deserved. I walked for a few streets and found a hack and was home before eight-thirty. I . . . I realize it was foolish of me to think . . . to think I could speak to her there. I'd sent her messages before, you see. She never answered."

"So she said."

Her mouth tightened, remembered anger transforming the smooth full shape of the lips into something bitterly ugly and unforgiving.

January remembered what Angelique had said about "little Creole tricks" and his mother's stories about wives who'd used the city's Black Code to harass their husbands' mistresses. For a moment Mme. Trepagier looked perfectly capable of having another woman arrested and whipped on a trumped-up charge of being "uppity" to her—though God knew Angelique *was* uppity, to everyone she met, black or colored or white—or jailed for owning a carriage or not covering her hair.

But if Angelique had told him to take her a warning about it last night, it was clear she hadn't exercised this spiteful power.

The woman before him shook her head a little and let the anger pass. "It wasn't necessary for you to come all the way out here, you know."

Something about the way that she sat, about that strained calm, made him say, "You heard she's dead."

The big hands flinched in her lap, but her eyes were wary rather than surprised. She had, he thought, the look of a woman debating how much she can say and be believed; then she crossed herself. "Yes, I heard that."

From the woman who brought in her washing water that morning, thought January. Or the cook, when she went out to distribute stores for the day. Whites didn't understand how news traveled so quickly, being too well-bred to be seen prying. Having set themselves up as gods and loudly established their own importance, they never ceased to be surprised that those whose lives might be affected by their doings kept up on them with the interest they themselves accorded only to characters in Balzac's novels.

"You heard what happened?"

Her hands, resting in her lap again, shivered. "Only that she was . . . was strangled. At the ballroom." She glanced quickly across at him. "The police . . . Did they make any arrest? Or say if they knew who it might be? Or what time it happened?"

Her voice had the flat, tinny note of assumed casualness, a serious quest for information masquerading as gossip. *Time?* thought January. But as he studied her face she got quickly to her feet and walked to the gallery railing, watching an old man planting something in the garden among the willows as if the sight of him dipping into his sack of seed, then carefully dibbling with a little water from his gourd, were a matter of deepest importance.

"Did they say what will happen to her things?" she asked, without turning her head.

January stood too. "I expect her mother will keep them."

She looked around at that, startled, and he saw the brown eyes widen with surprise. Then she shook her head, half laughing at herself, though without much mirth. When she spoke, her voice was a little more normal. "I'm sorry," she said. "It's just that . . . All these years I've thought of her as some kind of . . . of a witch, or harpy. I never even thought she might have a mother, though of course she must. It's just . . ." She pushed at her hair, as if putting aside tendrils of it that fell onto her forehead, a gesture of habit. He saw there were tears in her eyes.

He had been her teacher when she was a child, and something of that bond still existed. It was that which let him say, "He gave her things belonging to you, didn't he?"

She averted her face again, and nodded. He could almost feel the heat of her shame. "Jewelry, mostly," she said in a stifled voice. "Things he'd bought for me when we were first married. Household things, crystal and linens. A horse and chaise, even though it wasn't legal for her to drive one. Dresses. That white dress she was wearing was mine. I don't know if men feel this way, but if I make a dress for myself it's . . . it's a part of me. That sounds so foolish to say out loud, and my old Mother Superior at school would tell me it's tying myself to things of this world, but . . . When I pick out a silk for myself and a trim, and linen to line it with—when I shape it to my body, *wear* it, make it mine . . . And then to have him give it to her . . ."

She drew a shaky breath. "That sounds so grasping. And so petty." They had the ring of words she'd taught herself with great effort to say. "I don't know if you can understand." She faced him, folded her big hands before those leopard-black skirts.

He had seen the way women dealt with Ayasha when they ordered frocks and gowns, when they came for fittings, and watched what they had asked for as it was called into being. "I understand."

"I think that dress made me angriest. Even angrier than the jewelry. But some of the things—my things—he gave her were quite valuable. The baroque pearls and emeralds she was wearing were very old, and he had no right to take them. . . ."

She paused, fighting with another surge of anger, then shook her head. "Except of course that a husband has the right to all his wife's things."

"Not legally," said January. "According to law, in territory that used to be Spanish—"

"Monsieur Janvier," said Madeleine Trepagier softly, "when it's only a man and a woman alone in a house miles from town, he has the right to whatever of hers he wishes to take." The soft eyes burned suddenly strange and old. "Those emeralds were my grandmother's. They were practically the only thing she brought with her from Haiti. I wore them at our wedding. I never liked them—there was supposed to be a curse on them—but I wanted them back. I needed them back. That's why I had to speak to her."

"Your husband died in debt." Recollections of his mother's scattergun gossip slipped into place.

She nodded. It was not something she would have spoken of to someone who had not been a teacher and a friend of her childhood.

"It must have been bad," he said softly, "for you to go to that risk to get your jewels back. Do you have children?"

"None living." She sighed a little and looked down at her hands where they rested on the cypress railing of the gallery. He saw she hadn't resumed the wedding band she'd put off last night. "If I lose this place," she said, "I'm not sure what I'm going to do."

In a way, January knew, children would have made it easier. No Creole would turn grandchildren out to starve. His mother had written him of the murderous epidemic last summer, and he wondered if that had taken some or all. Louisiana was not a healthy country for whites.

"You have family yourself?" He recalled dimly that the Dubonnets had come up en masse from Santo Domingo a generation ago, but could not remember whether René Dubonnet had had more than the single daughter.

She hesitated infinitesimally, then nodded again.

A governess to nieces and nephews, he thought. Or a companion to an aunt. Or just a widowed cousin, taken into the household and relegated to sharing some daughter's room and bed in the back of the house, when she had run a plantation and been mistress of a household of a dozen servants.

"There any chance of help from your husband's family?"

"No."

By the way she spoke the word, between her teeth, January knew that was the end of the topic.

She drew breath and straightened her back, looking into his face. "You said there are . . . rules . . . about that world, customs I don't know. I know that's true. We're all taught not to look, not to think about things. And you're right. I should have known better than to try to find her at the ball." Against the pallor of her face her eyebrows were two dark slashes, spots of color burning in her cheeks. What had it cost her, he wondered, to go seeking a woman she hated that much? To take that kind of risk?

Why was she so concerned about what time Angelique had died?

"Is there some sort of rule against me going to speak to her mother? Surely there wouldn't be gossip if I went to pay my respects?"

"No," said January, curious and troubled at once. "It isn't usual, but as long as you go quietly, veiled, there shouldn't be talk."

"Oh, of course." Her brows drew down with quick sympathy. "I'm sure the last thing the poor woman needs is . . . is some kind of lady of the manor descending on her. And the less talk there is, the better." She moved toward the parlor doors in a rustle of starched muslin petticoats, then paused within them. For a woman of her opulent figure she moved lightly, like a fleeing girl.

"Is she—Madame . . . Crozat?"

"Dreuze," said January. "Euphrasie Dreuze. She went by both. Plaçées sometimes do." Dominique was still called *Janvier,* but his mother had been called that, too, for the man who had bought her and freed her.

"I see. I . . . didn't know how that was . . . dealt with. Would she see me? Would it be better for me to wait a few days? I'm sorry to ask, but you know the family and the custom. I don't."

He remembered the despairing screams from the parlor where Euphrasie Dreuze's friends had taken her, and Hannibal's tale about the son who had died. Remembered Xavier Peralta crossing the crowded ballroom full of angrily murmuring men, a cup of coffee carefully balanced in his hand, and how the gaslight had spangled the jewel-covered tignon as the woman had caught the boy Galen's sleeve, babbling to him in panic of her daughter's love.

"I don't know," he said. "I knew Madame Dreuze when Angelique was a little girl. She worshiped her then, treated her like a porcelain doll. But women sometimes change when their daughters grow."

His own mother had. Nothing had been too good for Dominique: Every bump and scratch attended by a doctor, every garment embroidered and tucked and smocked with the most delicate of stitches, every toy and novelty that came into port purchased for the little girl's delight. Three months ago, just after his return from Paris, he'd come down to breakfast in the kitchen to the news that Minou had contracted bronchitis—"She's always down with it, since she had it back in '30" had been his mother's only comment as she casually turned the pages of the *Bee.* It had been January, not their mother, who'd gone over to make sure his sister had everything she needed.

Certainly his mother had never wasted tears over him. The news of Ayasha's death she greeted with perfunctory sympathy but nothing more. There were days when he barely saw her, save in passing when he had a student in the parlor. But then, he'd never had the impression his mother was terribly interested in him and his doings.

Because he had three black grandparents instead of three white ones?

It was with Dominique—who had been only a tiny child when he'd left—that he had wept for the loss of his wife.

"A moment." Madame Trepagier vanished into the shadows of the house. January returned to his chair. From the tall doorway of one of the side rooms a girl emerged, rail slim and ferret faced, African dark, wearing the black of home-dyed mourning but walking with a lazy jauntiness that indicated no great sense of loss. She sized up his clothing, his mended kid gloves, the horse tethered beneath the willows in the yard, and the fact that he was sitting there in a chair meant for guests, with a kind of insolent wisdom, then tossed her head a little and passed on down the steps, silent as slaves must be in the presence of their betters.

And indeed, he could scarcely imagine Angelique Crozat or her mother or his own mother, who had been a slave herself, speaking to the woman.

The woman was a slave, and black.

He was free, and colored, though his skin was as dark as hers.

He watched the slim figure cross through the garden toward the kitchen, like a crow against the green of the grass, saw her ignore the old man tending to the planting, and noted the haughty tilt of shoulder and hip as she passed some words with the cook. Then she went on toward the laundry, and January saw the cook and another old woman speak quietly. Knowing the opinions his mother's cook Bella traded with the cook of the woman next door, he could guess exactly what they said.

Not something he'd want said about him.

"I've written a note for Madame Dreuze."

He rose quickly. Madame Trepagier stood in the doorway, a sealed envelope in her hand. "Would you be so good as to give it to her? I'm sorry." She smiled, her nervousness, her defenses, falling away. For a moment it was the warm smile of the child he had taught, sitting in her white dress at the piano—the sunny, half-apologetic smile of a child whose playing had contained such dreadful passion, such adult ferocity. He still wondered at the source of that glory and rage.

"I always seem to be making you a messenger. I do apologize."

"Madame Trepagier." He took the message and tucked it into a pocket, then bowed over her hand. "I'm a little old to be cast as winged Mercury, but I'm honored to serve you nevertheless."

"After two years of being Apollo," she said smiling, "it makes a change."

He recognized the allusion, and smiled. In addition to being the god of music, Apollo was the lord of healing. "Did you keep up with it?" he asked, as he moved toward the steps. "The music?"

She nodded, her smile gentle again, secret and warm. "It was like knowing how to swim," she said. "I thought of you many times, when the water was deep. You did save my life."

And turning, she went back into the house, leaving him stunned upon the steps.

SEVEN

A square-featured woman in the faded calico of a servant answered January's knock at the bright pink cottage on Rue des Ursulines. The jalousies were closed over the tall French windows and a muted babble came from the dimness beyond her shoulder. There was a smell of patchouli and a stronger one of coffee.

"You lookin' for your ma, Michie Janvier?" she asked. "She in the back with Madame Phrasie." She curtsied as January regarded her in surprise.

"I'm looking for Madame Euphrasie, mostly," he said, as the woman stood aside to admit him. She had the smoother skin and unknotted hands of a longtime house servant. At first glance, in the shadows under the abat-vent, he would have put her near his own forty years, but as his eyes adjusted to the dim room he realized she couldn't be more than twenty-five. "How is she?"

The woman hesitated, then said, "She bearin' up." There was a world of weighted words and unspoken thought in that short phrase.

"Bearin' up, huh," said Agnes Pellicot shortly, from the green brocaded settee she shared with two other beautifully dressed, still-handsome women with fans of painted silk in their hands. The older,

Catherine Clisson, had been three years ahead of January in Herr Kovald's music classes, a slim girl with high cheekbones for whom, at the time, he had nursed a sentimental and hopeless love. The younger, rounded and pretty in an exquisite rose-and-white striped dress, was Odile Gignac, his mother's dressmaker.

"Bearin' up enough to collect every earbob and pin, and cut the silver buttons off every one of her daughter's dresses, is how she's bearin' up."

"A woman can grieve her daughter and still fear for her own future, Agnes," said Clisson gently. "You know she had nothing beyond what Angelique sent her every month."

"God knows it was Angelique who paid her bills, more times than not," added Gignac, crossing herself. The daughter of respectable free colored parents, she was one of the small minority of sang melés who accepted the plaçées on their own terms as friends as well as customers, though it was understood they did not speak on the public streets. "*And* her gambling debts, from what I hear. It's that poor child Clemence that fainted dead away when she came here this morning and heard."

Agnes only sniffed. January deduced the matter of young Peralta still rankled.

"Judith," Clisson went on in her soft voice, "please be so good as to fetch Monsieur Janvier some coffee. Or should I say Ben?" she added, her dark eyes sparkling with a friendship she'd never shown him when they were young. "I've missed you twice by your mama's. It's good to catch up with you at last."

January smiled, too. He'd been fourteen when she, far too proud of her own position to take the slightest notice of a gawky coal-black lout such as he had been, had become the mistress of a middle-aged Creole with a plantation on Lake Pontchartrain. January's adoration had lasted for years. On the nights when Monsieur Motet came into town he had been drawn to loiter on the opposite banquette of her cottage on Rue des Ramparts in an agony of jealous speculation, though they had not spoken since she had left Herr Kovald's class.

Funny, what time did.

The memory brought back all those other memories. He'd played with Odile and her brother as children, though her parents had looked askance at a plaçée's son, and had sent her to a Select Academy for Colored Females at an early age. A queer sense of pain touched him, which he recognized as a kind of pins-and-needles of the heart: feeling coming back into memories long buried and numb.

This city had been his home. These people had been his home.

In turning his back on Froissart and Richelieu, and on the thick heat of the fever summers, he had turned his back on them as well.

"I'd forgotten how beautifully you played." Clisson laid down her fan, French lace on sandalwood sticks, costly and new. "I didn't even think about it during the dancing, but afterward, when you were playing to keep everyone amused . . . The Rossini almost made me cry. I was sorry to hear about your wife."

He smiled down at her from his height. "I didn't think you even noticed how I played when we had class together," he said, with the rancorless amusement of shared old times. "You're still with Monsieur Motet?"

Her smile was no more than the tucking back of the corners of her lips, the velvet warming of her eyes. It told him everything even before she nodded, and he felt for her a rush of gladness. "Are you taking students, now you're back?" she asked. She spoke almost as if it had been a given, a foregone conclusion for all those years, that he would eventually return. He wanted to tell her he hadn't intended to return at all.

"I think your mama said you were. My daughter Isabel's eight. I've taught her a little, but it's time she had a good teacher."

January was opening his mouth to reply when a woman's voice cried out in the rear of the house, a sharp gasp, rising to a shriek. "There it is! There! I told you! Oh God—"

A break, a murmur, January and Clisson and Gignac all on their feet in the sliding doorway that separated the darkened parlor from the still-darker bedchamber. "Oh, my child! Oh, my poor little one! Murder! Oh God, murder—"

"What the—" began January.

"Of course it was murder," said Clisson, puzzled. "Nobody ever said it wasn't."

The door to the bedroom sliced open and Euphrasie Dreuze stumbled through, clutching something in her fat jeweled hand. "My God, my God, look!" she sobbed at the top of her lungs. "My poor little girl was hexed to death! Someone hid this in her mattress; she was sleeping next to this all along! It drew death down on her! It drew death!"

"Phrasie, don't be a goose." Livia Levesque emerged from the bedroom on her friend's heels and made an unsuccessful grab at the filthy little wad of parchment and bone.

Euphrasie Dreuze wrenched herself free. Only five years older than January, she was plumper than she'd been when first he had seen her but retained the impression of kitten-soft cuddliness that had attracted a well-off young broker thirty years before. Her chin was pouchy and deep lines graven on either side of her painted mouth, but she was still a lovely woman, fair-skinned even among quadroons, with small, grasping hands. Even for day wear her tignon was orange silk, glittering with an aigrette of jewels.

With a shattering sob she brandished what she held. January took it, turned it over in his hands. A dried bat, little bigger than a magnolia leaf.

A gris-gris. A talisman of death.

"Madame Dreuze, Madame Dreuze," bleated Clemence Drouet, fluttering at her heels the way she had fluttered at Angelique's, her round face still gray with shock and tears. "Please don't. . . ."

"Throw that piece of trash out," commanded Livia sharply and snatched it from her son's hands.

Even as she did so, Euphrasie turned with a hysterical cry upon the servant girl Judith, frozen in the act of pouring coffee from a pot at the sideboard.

"You did this!" Euphrasie shrieked, smashing cup and saucer from the girl's hands. "You black slut! You planted it there, you wanted my child to die!" Her hand lashed out, quick as a cottonmouth striking, and clapped the girl on the ear. Judith gasped and tried to run, but the room was choked with furniture, new and English and thick with carving. Odile and Pellicot clogged the door to the other half of the parlor, Clemence and Euphrasie herself that to the bedroom.

"You did it, you did it, you did it!" Euphrasie struck her again, knocking her white head scarf flying, her gesture almost an identical echo of Angelique's last night, when she had struck young Peralta. "You cheap, lazy whore! You dirty black tramp!" She caught Judith by the hair, dragging her forward and shaking her by the thick pecan-colored mass until the girl screamed. "You wanted her dead! You wanted to go back to that mealymouthed white bitch! You hated her! You got some voodoo and got her to make gris-gris!"

"Phrasie!" Clisson caught the hysterical woman's wrist. "How can you, with Angelique dead in her bed there?"

"Phrasie, don't be a fool." Livia thrust herself into the fray, slapped Euphrasie loudly on her plump cheek.

Euphrasie fell back, opening her mouth to scream, and Livia picked up the water pitcher from the sideboard. "You scream and I dump this over you."

Clisson, Odile, and Agnes Pellicot promptly retreated to the doorway, hands pressing their mountains of petticoats back for safety. January reflected that they'd all known his mother for thirty years.

Euphrasie, too, wisely forbore to scream. For a moment the only sound was the girl Judith sobbing in the corner, her hair a tobacco-colored explosion around her swollen face. The smell of coffee soaking into wool carpet hung thick in the air. Outside a woman sang "Callas! *Hot* callas *hot*!"

Then Euphrasie burst into fresh tears and flung herself onto the bosom of the only male present. "They murdered my little girl!" she howled. "My God, they witched her, put evil on her, so someone was drawn to kill her!"

Livia rolled her eyes. January's mother was small and delicate, like her younger daughter but not so tall, almost frail looking, with fine bronze skin and Dominique's catlike beauty. At fifty-seven she moved with a decisive quickness that January didn't recall from her languid heyday, as if her widowhood, first from Janvier and then from Christophe Levesque, had freed her of the obligation to be alluring to men.

"She hated her!" Euphrasie moaned into January's shirt. "She ran away, again and again, going back to that uppity péteuse. She hated my angel, she wanted her dead so she could go back. . . ."

Livia meanwhile set the pitcher down, picked up Judith's head scarf and the unbroken saucer and cup, and said to the sobbing servant, "Get a rag and vinegar and get this coffee sopped up before the stain sets." She thrust the scarf into the girl's hands. "Put this back on before you come back. And wash your face. You look a sight. And you"—she pointed at Clemence, sagging gray faced against the side of the door, both lace-mitted fists stuffed into her mouth—"don't you go faint on me again. I haven't time for that." She looked around for the gris-gris but January had retrieved it from the floor and slipped it into his coat pocket.

"It was that woman," Euphrasie wailed, clutching January's lapels. "That stuck-up white vache! That nigger bitch, she'd run off, trying to go home, and that Trepagier, she'd tell that girl how if my Angelique were to die, she'd take her back. I know it. That Trepagier set her up to murder my child, my only little girl! Oh, what am I going to do? They drew down death on her and left me to starve!"

"Phrasie, you know as well as I do Etienne Crozat left you with five hundred a year," said Livia tartly. "Benjamin, pull her loose or she'll hang on to you weeping till doomsday. You'd think it was *her* funeral tomorrow and not her daughter's."

Odile Gignac meanwhile had helped Clemence Drouet to one of the overstuffed brocade chairs, where the girl burst into shuddering tears, handkerchief stuffed in her mouth, as if all her life she had been forbidden to make a sound of discontent or grief. "There, there, chérie," murmured the dressmaker comfortingly. "You mustn't cry like that. You'll make yourself ill."

January had to reflect that his sister was right about the Drouet girl's dresses: Like her costume last night, this one—also designed by Angelique, if Dominique spoke true—though costly and beautiful, made her look like nothing so much as a green-gold pear.

"That Trepagier put her up to it! She put her up!" It was astonishing how Madame Dreuze could keep her face buried in his sleeve without either muffling her voice or disarraying her tignon. "She hated her like poison! They poisoned my child, the two of them together!"

"Angelique was strangled," Livia reminded her dryly. She went to the sideboard and handed January a clean napkin from a drawer as he fished vainly in his pockets for a handkerchief. "And you can't very well say Madeleine Trepagier turned up at the Orleans ballroom and did it. Get that child out of here, Odile. She's been nothing but underfoot since . . ."

"Why not? She could have come in through the Théâtre . . ."

"With all the Trepagier family in the Théâtre to recognize her? And that hag of an aunt of hers?"

"That black slut Judith did, then! Why not? She hated my child. . . ."

At Livia's impatient signal, Catherine Clisson came forward and eased the weeping woman from her leaning post. Clisson relieved Ben of his napkin and proceeded to dry Euphrasie's eyes as she guided her toward the settee. Livia Levesque took her tall son's arm and steered him briskly toward the door, and January went willingly, unnerved by the accuracy of Madame Dreuze's chance shot.

"I swear," declared Livia, as they descended the two high brick steps to the banquette, "it's like a summer rainstorm in there, between those two watering pots." She pulled her delicate knit-lace gloves on and flexed her hands. "Give me my parasol, Ben."

"Why does she say the girl Judith hated Angelique?" January handed his mother the fragile, lacy sunshade she had thrust into his hands on the way through the door. "I take it Judith belonged to Madeleine Trepagier?"

Like the jewels and the dresses, he thought. *When there's only a man and a woman alone in a house miles from town . . .*

The thought conjured up was an ugly one.

Livia opened the sunshade with a brisk crackle of bamboo and starch, despite the fact that the day was milkily overcast. Even so far back from the river, the air smelled of steamboat soot.

"She's carrying on as if *she* were wronged, not her daughter murdered," the elderly lady sniffed. "*And* not her only child, as she's been saying. She has two sons still living, one of them a journeyman joiner with Roig and the other a clerk at the Presbytère, but they're not the ones who've been giving her gambling money and buying her silk dresses. Etienne Crozat left her a house and five hundred a year when he married André Milaudon's daughter in '28, so she hasn't any room to talk." She moved with small, quick steps along the brick banquette, the river breeze stirring the pale green chintz of her bell-shaped skirts. Like Catherine Clisson, she was dressed very plainly and very expensively, her tignon striped pale green and white and fitting her fine-boned face like the petals of a half-closed rose. A gold crucifix sparkled at her throat, and Christophe Levesque's wedding ring gleamed through the fragile net of the mitt.

"And Madame Trepagier?"

She cocked her head up at him. "Arnaud Trepagier was free to do with his own Negroes as he pleased," she said, in that deep voice like smoky honey that both her daughters had inherited. "I think the girl used to be his wife's maid, but as far as I'm concerned that's of a piece with giving her his wife's dresses and his wife's jewelry. That cook of Angelique's was Trepagier's, too, and a good one, for a Congo."

He remembered the way Angelique had looked at him, the slight, impersonal regret in her eyes as she'd said, *You're new*. He knew his anger at her was wrong, for he was alive and she was dead, but he felt it all the same.

His mother spoke as if she'd never sweated in a cane field at sugaring time, had never been bought and sold like a riding mare. January remembered huddling in terror in the gluey, humming blackness of a dirt-floored cabin, holding his little sister and fighting not to cry, wondering if the Frenchman who was buying his mother would buy him, too, and whom he'd have to live with if he was left behind.

Olympe had told him once that buying them hadn't been their mother's idea. He had no clue where she'd gotten this information, or if it was true.

"The whole time she was hunting through that room for a gris-gris—and she turned the place upside down, with Angelique lying there in her bed in that white dress looking like the Devil's bride—she was picking up every brooch, earring, and bracelet she could find and putting them in her reticule." Livia paused at the corner of Rue Burgundy to let her son cross the plank that spanned the cypress-lined gutter and hold out his hand to help her over.

"And a fair pile of them there were, too. Some of them were

French and old—antique gold, not anything a wastrel like Arnaud Trepagier would have the taste to buy for a woman and surely too tasteful for any of Angelique's asking. If that silly heifer Clemence thinks she's going to get a keepsake out of her she's badly mistaken. Every stitch and stone of it's going to be in the shops tomorrow, you mark my words, before Madame Trepagier can claim them back."

"Can she?"

"I don't suppose Trepagier made a will. Or Angelique either. That girl Clemence kept blundering around underfoot, hinting that Angelique had promised her this and promised her that, but a fat lot of good that'll do her. I never saw anybody who looked so much like a sheep. Acts like one, too."

A carriage passed in front of them, curtains drawn back to show a pair of porcelain-fair girls and an older woman in a fashionable bonnet and lace cap. Livia remarked, "Hmph. Pauline Mazant has her nerve, setting up as chaperone to her daughters—the whole town knows she's carrying on an affair with Prosper Livaudais. And him young enough to be her son, or her nephew anyway."

She turned her attention back to January and the matter at hand. "At Trepagier's death, presumably the jewelry would revert to Angelique, and then to her mother—those brothers of hers wouldn't touch it, and small blame to them. But Madame Trepagier may sue her for the more expensive pieces, like that set of pearls and emeralds, if they ever find them, and the two slaves. The cook should fetch a thousand dollars at least, even if she can't make pastry, and the girl nearly that."

Only his mother, reflected January wryly, would keep track of the relative price of her friends' servants.

"Unless Phrasie decides to keep them for herself. She's only got the one woman now and she can't cook worth sour apples, but she may sell them and keep the cash, to prevent La Trepagier from getting them back. Weeping about the hardship of her lot all the while, of course. And God alone knows what she owes in faro games."

They walked in silence for a few minutes, threading their way among servants, householders, men and women abroad on the errands of the day. The air was warm without brightness, heavy with the strange sense of expectation that the dampness frequently seemed to bring. Even here, at the back of the old town, the well-dressed servants of the rich came and went from the small shops, the dressmakers and furniture builders, the milliners who copied the latest French styles, the dealers in books and linen, soaps and corsetry. Here and there the tall town houses of the wealthy lifted above the rows of brightly painted stucco cottages or the old Spanish dwellings, built half a story above the ground for coolness—the voices of children sounded like the cries of small birds from courtyards and alleyways. A pair of nuns walked slowly down the opposite banquette, black robes billowing a little in the wind off the river—they stopped to buy pralines from a woman in a gaudy head scarf, then moved on, smiling like girls. From far off a riverboat whistled, a deep alto song like some enormous water beast. Livia made a little detour to avoid the puddles where a man was washing out the stone-paved passageway into a court, and past its shadows January glimpsed banana plants, palmettos, and jasmine.

"You know anything about what kind of terms Madame Dreuze was negotiating with Monsieur Peralta?"

"Euphrasie Dreuze hasn't the wits to negotiate the price of a pineapple in the market," retorted Livia coolly. "She was trotting back and forth for weeks between her daughter and Monsieur Peralta, pretending she was 'checking' with that harpy and really taking her instructions, and a pretty bargain it was, too. She wanted that piece of downtown property on Bourbon and Barracks, six seventy-five a year *and* a clothing allowance, household money plus freehold on whatever young Peralta might give her."

January didn't even bother to ask how his mother had come by those figures.

"Grasping witch. Personally I can't see how Peralta Père would countenance it, because he'd be just laying his son open for a drain on the capital. And her playing bedroom eyes with Tom Jenkins since last May. Père et fils, they're well rid of her."

A cat blinked from an iron-grilled balcony. Two boys ran by, chasing a hoop.

"Tell me about Madeleine Trepagier," said January.

"You knew her." Livia angled her parasol though there was no sunlight strong enough to cast shadow. "She was one of your piano students. Madeleine Dubonnet."

"I know." January felt that much admission was better than trying to remember a lie. "The one who played Beethoven with such . . . rage." He was surprised his mother remembered the students he'd had before he left.

His mother's dark eyes cut sidelong to him, then away. "If she had rage in her she had a right to it," she said. "With a drunkard of a father who married her to one of his gambling friends to cancel a debt. Oh, the Trepagiers are a good family, and Arnaud had three plantations, if you want to call that piece of swamp in Metairie a plantation. Good for nothing but possum hunting is what I've heard, and wouldn't fetch more than fifteen dollars an acre even now, and less than that back when he sold it to that American." The inflection of her voice added that as far as she was concerned, the American was a tobacco-chewing flatboat man with fleas in his crotch.

"I've ridden past Les Saules," he remarked, to keep her on track.

"It's been going downhill for years." Livia dismissed it with a wave of her hand. "Cheap Creole cane. It won't produce more than eight hundred pounds an acre, if the cold doesn't kill it. *And* three mortgages, and lucky to get them. Arnaud Trepagier was a fine gentleman but not much of a planter, and they say the woman's a pinchpenny and works her slaves hard, not that slaves won't whine like sick puppies if you make them step out any faster than a tortoise on a cold day. God knows what the woman's going to do now, with all the debts he left. I'd be surprised if she could get ten dollars an acre for that land. That worthless brother of Trepagier's left town years ago, when he sold his own plantation, also to an American"—there was that inflection again—"and got cheated out of his eyeteeth on railroad stock. And I'd sooner peddle gumbo in the market than go live with Alicia Picard—that's Dubonnet's sister—and her mealy-mouthed son."

January almost asked his mother if she wanted to go back over the battlefield and slit the throats of anyone she'd only wounded in the first fusillade, but stopped himself. Behind them, a voice called out, "Madame Levesque! Madame Livia!" and January turned, hearing running footsteps. The woman Judith was hurrying down Rue Burgundy toward them, her hand pressed to her side to ease a stitch. She'd put on her head scarf again, and against the soft yellows and rusts and greens of the houses the dull red of her calico dress seemed like a smear of dark blood.

"Madame Livia, it isn't true!" panted Judith, when she had come up with January and his mother. "It isn't true! I never went to a voodoo woman or made any gris-gris against Mamzelle Angelique!"

Livia looked down her nose at the younger woman, in spite of the fact that Judith was some five inches taller than her. "And did you run away?"

The slave woman was, January guessed, exactly of his mother's extraction—half-and-half mulatto—but he could see in his mother's eyes, hear in the tone of her voice, the exact configuration of the white French when they spoke to their slaves. The look, the tone, that said, *I am colored. She is black.*

Maybe she *didn't* remember the cane fields.

And Judith said, "M'am, it was only for a night. It really was only for a night." As if Livia Levesque had been white, she didn't look her in the face. "She'd whipped me, with a stick of cane. . . . I really would have come back. Madame Madeleine, she told me I had to. . . . I never would have gone to a voodoo."

"Did Monsieur Trepagier take you away from Madame Madeleine and give you to Angelique?" asked January.

Judith nodded. "Her daddy bought me for her. Years ago, when first they got married. I'd waited on her, fixed her hair, sewed her clothes. . . . She was always good to me. And it made me mad, when Michie Arnaud give that Angelique her jewelry and her dresses and her horse, that little red mare she always rode. She tried not to show she cared, same as she tried not to show it when he'd taken a cane to her."

She shook her head, her eyes dark with anger and grief. "There'd be nights when she'd hold on to me and cry until nearly morning, with her back all bleeding or her face marked, then get up and go on about sewing his shirts and doing the accounts and writing to the brokers, until I'd have to go out back and cry myself, for pity. Later when he gave me to that Angelique, sometimes I'd run away and go back, just to see her. I did when Mamzelle Alexandrine died—her daughter—long of the fever. She was my friend, Madame Livia. But I'd never have hurt Angelique. I go to confession, and I know that's a sin. Please believe me. You have to believe. And as for her saying Madame Madeleine put me up to a thing like that . . . I never would have! *She* never would have!"

Livia sniffed.

Gently, January asked, "Would the cook? She was Madame Madeleine's servant too, wasn't she?"

"Kessie?" Judith hesitated a long time. "I—I don't think so, sir," she answered at last. "I know she left a man and three kids at Les Saules, but I know, too, she's got another man here in town. And she didn't . . . didn't hate Angelique. Not like I did. For one thing," she added with a wry twist to her lips, "if anything happened to Angelique, Kessie wouldn't be able to steal from the kitchen, like she was doing. She might have put graveyard dust someplace in the bedroom, but she wouldn't have done that kind of a ouanga, a death sign."

She looked from Livia's cool face to January's, anxious and frightened, her hazel eyes wide. "I go to church, and I pray to God. I don't go to the voodoo dances, Sundays. You have to believe me. Please believe me."

January was silent. He wondered if his mother was right, if Euphrasie Dreuze would sell off her daughter's two slaves quickly, for whatever she could get, to avoid Madeleine Trepagier's bringing suit to get them back. He wondered if Judith knew, or guessed, what would happen to her.

But Livia only cocked her sunshade a little further over her shoulder and asked, "And why are you so fired up all of a sudden that I have to believe you?"

"She'll tell that policeman that I had something to do with Angelique's death," whispered Judith. "She'll tell him Madame Madeleine and I did it."

"Policeman?"

"That tall American one, as tall as you, Michie Janvier. He's at the house now. He's askin' questions about you."

"About *me?*"

Madame Madeleine Trepagier
Les Saules
Orléans Parish
Friday afternoon
15 Fev. 1833
Madame Trepagier—

 *My attempt to deliver your note to Madame Dreuze met
with no success. She has conceived the opinion that at your
instigation, the slave woman Judith obtained a death talisman
from a voodoo and placed it in Angelique Crozat's house, and
that this was what drew Mlle. Crozat's murderer to her. She has
expressed this opinion not only to five of her friends—Catherine
Clisson, Odile Gignac, Agnes Pellicot, Clemence Drouet, and
Livia Levesque, all free women of color of this city—but I
believe to the police as well. Though I doubt that the police will
take any action based on what is quite clearly a hysterical accusation, that she made this accusation told me it would do no
good for me to plead your cause.*

 It appears that Madame Dreuze is in the process of gather-

ing together all jewelry in her late daughter's house preparatory to selling it as quickly as possible. Moreover, I have reason to suspect that she intends to sell both slave women—Judith and the cook Kessie—as soon as she can, to forestall any claim you may make upon them. I strongly suggest that you get in touch with Lt. Abishag Shaw of the New Orleans police and take whatever steps you can to prevent Madame Dreuze's liquidation of her daughter's valuables until it can be ascertained which of these items are, in fact, yours by right.

Please believe that I remain your humble servant,

Benj. January, f.m.c.

It was, January reflected, rubbing a hand over his eyes, the best he could do. Dappled shade passed over the sleeve of his brown second-best coat like a coquette's trailing scarf, and on the bench beside him, two young laundresses with heaped willow baskets on their laps compared notes about their respective lovers amid gales of giggles. By the sound of it, the Irish and German girls in the front of the omnibus—maids-of-all-work or shop assistants, grisettes they'd have been called in Paris—were doing the same. A carriage passed them, the fast trot of its two copper-colored hackneys easily outpacing the steady clop of the omnibus's hairy-footed nag.

It was perhaps intelligence that would have been more kindly conveyed by a friend in person rather than by note, but even had he gone back to Desdunes's Livery and rented another horse to ride out again to Les Saules the moment Judith had told him about Lt. Shaw's visit to the Crozat household, January doubted he could have returned to town before two. And two o'clock, murder and wrongdoing aside, was the hour at which, three times a week, the daughters of Franklin Culver had their music lesson, at fifty cents per daughter per hour, or a grand total of four dollars and fifty cents each Friday. If he thought Shaw would place the slightest weight on Euphrasie's accusations it would have been a different matter, but his warning was one that could as easily be conveyed by note, and he had not the smallest doubt that Madeleine Trepagier would act upon it with all speed.

He sighed, and rubbed his eyes again. On either side of Nyades

Street cleared lots showed where cane fields had once rattled, dark green, hot, and mysterious. A double line of massive oaks shaded the road, draped in trailing beards of gray-green moss, and far off to his left he could glimpse the green rise of the levee, and the gliding, silent smokestacks of the riverboats beyond. Past the oaks stood new American-style houses, built of wood or imported New England brick, brave with scrollwork and bright with new paint, gardens spread about them like the multicolored petticoats of market women sitting on the grass. After the enclosing walls and crowding balconies of the French town, the American town seemed both airy and a little raw, its unfinished streets petering out into rows of oaks and syca-mores or ending in the raw mounds of the cane fields, bare looking or just beginning to bristle with the first stubble of second or third crops. A black man was scything the grass in one yard behind a white-painted picket fence; a woman with a servant's plain dark dress and an Irishwoman's fair complexion walked a baby in a wicker perambulator down the footpath by the roadside, trailed by a small boy in a sailor suit and a smaller girl in frilly white with a doll.

The houses glittered with windows, the farthest dwellings imagin-able from the sordid cabins of the Irish Channel just upriver from the French town, or the filth of the Girod Street Swamp. Not that his mother—or any of the old French planters—would admit that there was any difference in the quality of the inhabitants. "They are Ameri-cans," Livia—or Xavier Peralta, for that matter—would say, with the tone Bouille had used of his opponent Granger, with the look in her eyes like the eyes behind those velvet masks regarding Shaw from the doorway of the Orleans ballroom last night.

He suspected that because they could afford such houses—be-cause they owned so many steamship companies and banks, so much of the money that kept the old French planters going from sugar crop to sugar crop—only made the situation worse.

"Ma! The nigger music teacher's here!"

The small boy's bell-clear voice carried even through the shut back door of the house, and January felt his jaw muscles clench even as he schooled his face to a pleasant smile when the housemaid, wiping flour-covered hands on her apron, opened the kitchen door. The knowledge that the girls' white drawing master also had to come to the back door was of little comfort.

Franklin Culver was vice-president of a small bank on the American side of Canal Street. He owned four slaves: the housemaid Ruth, the yardman Jim, and two other men whose services he rented out to a lumberyard. January suspected that if any of the three daughters of the household knew that his given name was Benjamin, they'd call him by it instead of Mr. January. He could see that the matter still profoundly puzzled Charis, the youngest. "But slaves don't have last names," she'd argued during the first lesson.

"Well, they do, Miss Charis," pointed out January. "But anyway, I'm not a slave."

Upon a later occasion she'd remarked that slaves didn't speak French—French evidently being something small girls learned with great labor and frustration from their governesses—so he could tell she was still unclear about the entire concept of a black man being free. He suspected that her father shared this deficiency. He didn't even try to explain that he wasn't black, but colored, a different matter entirely.

Still, the girls were very polite, unspoiled and charming, clearly kept up with their daily practicing, and four-fifty a week was four-fifty a week. Three dollars of that went to Livia, and two or three from what he earned teaching small classes in her parlor on Monday, Wednesday, and Friday afternoons. They didn't have the passion, or the gift for music, that Madeleine Dubonnet had had, nor the secret bond of shared devotion, but he'd instructed far worse.

He occasionally asked himself what he was saving for, squirreling away small sums of money in his account at the Banque de Louisiane. A house of his own?

In New Orleans? Paris had been bad enough, knowing that he was a fully qualified surgeon who would never have his own practice—or never a paying one—sheerly because of the color of his skin. Even as a musician his size and color had made him something of a curiosity, but at least people on the streets of Paris did not treat him like an idiot or a potentially dangerous savage. At least he didn't have to alter his manner and his speech in the interests of making a living, of not running afoul of the Black Code. At least he could look any man in the eyes.

In the few months he had been back he had found himself keeping almost exclusively to the French town, among the Creoles, who had not been brought up with the assumption that all those not of pure European descent were or should be slaves.

But the thought of returning to Paris turned his heart cold. During the weeks after Ayasha's death he had nearly gone crazy, expecting to see her around every corner, striding up the cobbled hill of Montmartre or arguing with market women, a straw basket of apples and bread on her hip—looking for her, listening everywhere for her voice. One night he'd gone walking for hours in the rain, searching the streets, half persuading himself that she wasn't really dead. He'd ended up sobbing at three in the morning on the steps of Notre Dame, the blue-beaded rosary wrapped around his hands, incoherently praying to the Virgin for he knew not what. He knew then that he had to leave that city or go mad.

And where else was there for him to go?

He listened to Charis's careful simplifications of Mozart airs, to Penelope's mechanical cotillions, and Esther's studied, overemphatic mutilation of *Childgrove;* gave them exercises and new pieces to learn; watched and listened for patterns of mistakes. He was conscious of pacing himself, giving the attention and care necessary but offering nothing beyond. Weariness had caught up with him, between his early ride to Les Saules and the exhausting scene at the house on Rue des Ursulines, with no sleep the night before. As a result he felt a curious disorientation in this overdecorated room, with its fashionable German furniture of heavily carved black walnut and slick upholstery, its beaded lampshades and fussy breakfronts and printed green wallpaper—a very American house, unlike the pared simplicity of Les Saules or his mother's simple cottage on Rue Burgundy. Sixteen years ago, when he'd left, most of this land had been cane fields, and English was a language one seldom heard in New Orleans.

His mind feeling thick and heavy, he dozed on the omnibus as it

clopped its way down Nyades Street. The walk back to his mother's
house revived him a little, and there was enough time, before his
pupils arrived at four, to go back to the kitchen and beg a dish of
beans and rice from Bella, the woman who had cooked and cleaned
and done the laundry almost as long as his mother had lived there.
After he ate he went into the parlor, where his mother was reading the
newspaper, and played some Bach to clear his mind and warm up his
hands. The children, ranging in ages from seven to fourteen and in
colors from the clear medium brown of polished walnut to palest
ivory, appeared a few minutes later, and he switched his mind over to
the disciplines of teaching again, studying the way those small hands
labored over the keys and guessing half instinctively how their minds
interpreted what they were doing with rhythm and sound.

One was the child of a plaçée and a white man; the others, offspring of well-off artisans, merchants, leaders of the colored community who wanted their children to have a little more than they
themselves might have had.

He wondered what Charis Culver—or her father—would have
made of that.

When the last of them had gone he crossed the yard, climbed the
narrow stair to his room above the kitchen, and slept, all the windows
open against the heat that rose from below. But his dreams were
uneasy, troubled by images of Madeleine Trepagier in her silly deerskin dress and cock feathers standing on an auction block, while
masked men in rich satins called out bids for her in the rotunda of the
St. Charles Hotel. He was aware of one figure moving at the rear of
the group, a figure he could barely see, shrouded, with the bound jaw
of a corpse. Every time that figure raised its hand the bidding halted
for a moment, uneasily, and when it continued it flagged, as if none
dared bid against that greenish, dreadful shape.

A crashing, thumping noise woke him, like giant's footfalls in the
room beside his bed. Bella, he realized. She was hitting the ceiling of
the kitchen with a broom handle to tell him it was seven o'clock. The
Grand Ball of the Faubourg Tremé Militia Company began in two
hours. His head thick with the dissatisfied, incompleted ache of day-
time sleep, he lay for a moment feeling the moist air from outside

walking over his face, rippling silently at the thin white curtains. The smell of lost bread and coffee drifted up with the kitchen's warmth, and the ache, the longing, the wanting to wake up completely and find Ayasha still lying in the bed beside him passed over him as a dark wave would have passed across a sleeper on the beach, salt wetness lingering for hours after the drag and force were gone.

Somewhere in his mind an image lingered—part of a dream?—of the slave block in the St. Charles Hotel, empty save for a couple of black cock feathers and a lingering sense of despair.

Angelique's funeral was to be at noon.

Sipping what he hoped would be a restorative cup of café noir at one of the tables scattered under the market's brick arcade and listening to the cathedral clock chime four-thirty, January wondered if he'd be able to sneak in some sleep before then.

"Maybe they're both terrible shots," said Hannibal, dusting powdered sugar from the beignets off his sleeves. New Orleans had one of the best systems of street lighting in the country, and even beyond the arcade the sooty predawn murk was streaked and blotted with amber where iron lanterns hung high above the banquettes. "Maybe they'll just miss each other and we can all go home."

"Maybe somebody'll discover I'm the long-lost heir to the throne of France, and I can give up teaching piano."

January glanced uneasily around him. Curfew was seldom enforced during Carnival, and for the most part the city guardsmen only bothered those who were obviously slaves or poor, but still he felt wary, unprotected, to be abroad this late.

"Creoles will end a swordfight after first blood—everybody in town is each other's cousins anyway. With bullets it's hard to tell." He shrugged. "With Americans it's hard to tell. Mostly they shoot to kill."

Across the street the shutters of the Café du Levée were still flung wide, the saffron light blurred by river mist but the forms within still visible: the elderly men who had fled the revolution in Santo Domingo and younger men who were their sons, playing cards, drinking absinthe or coffee, denouncing the filthy traitorous Bonapartists and lamenting the better life that had existed before atheism, rationalism, and les américains. Many wore fancy dress, coming in as one by one the balls and dances around the French town wound to conclusion, and all around January at the tables beneath the arcade, men—and a scattering of women—in evening clothes or masquerade garb rubbed elbows with market women and stevedores just starting their day as the revelers were ending theirs. Pralinières and sellers of beignets or callas moved among them, peddling their wares fresh from the oven out of rush baskets; a coffee-stand sent white steam billowing into the misty dark. If some few of the gentlemen at the other tables looked askance at Hannibal for eating with a colored man, the lateness of the hour and the laxness of Carnival season kept them quiet about it. In any case, Hannibal was well enough known that few people commented on his behavior anymore.

Beyond the arcade's brick pillars dyed gold by lamplight, past the dark lift of the levee, the black chimneys of steamboats clustered like a fire-blasted forest in the dark, spiked crowns glowing saffron with the fire reflected within and glints of that feral light catching the gilded trim of flagstaffs and pilothouses. The thin fog tasted of ash, and drifting smuts had already left streaks on the two men's shirtfronts and cuffs.

"Monsieur Janvier."

Augustus Mayerling appeared in the shadows of the arcade. He had removed his mask but wore the Elizabethan doublet of black-and-green leather he'd had on for Thursday night's ball. Despite his short-cropped hair and the four saber scars that marked the left side of his face and must, January reflected, make shaving a nightmare for him, the high-worked ruff and the odd glare of the café's lights gave his beaky features an equivocal cast, almost feminine in the iron gloom. "Hannibal, my friend. I had not looked to see you."

"What, and miss a duel?" As usual for this hour of the morning the fiddler looked as if he'd been pulled through a sieve, but his dark eyes sparkled with irony. "The single, solitary chance of an entire lifetime to see a Creole and an American actually taking potshots at each other? Heaven forfend." He raised the backs of his fingers to his forehead in the manner of a diva quailing before circumstances too awful to endure. "It's all a matter of timing," he explained and went back to the dregs of his coffee.

> *"When now Aurora, daughter of the dawn,*
> *With rosy luster purpled o'er the lawn . . .*

"The very hour, my friends, when the sporting establishments in the Swamp customarily close their doors and disgorge the flatboat crews into the—er—I suppose I have to call it a street. They'll still be drunk, but not drunk enough yet to pass out, and they don't go back to work until sunrise. If I come along to the duel I only have to worry about *one* bullet."

"I like to see a man who is provident as well as talented." Mayerling nodded gravely, then held out a gloved hand to January. "Thank you again for agreeing to accompany us. It's a nuisance, and cuts into your rest—and mine, I might add—but they seem to think their manhood will fall off in the dirt if they are deprived of the chance at least to put their lives in danger to prove the veracity of their claims. You're familiar with their quarrel?"

"Only that it's the biggest shouting match since that last mayoral election when the editors of the *Argus* and the *Courier* got into that fistfight in the Café Hewlett," said Hannibal cheerfully.

"I gather Granger started out by accusing Bouille of deliberately voting against the proposed streetcar route of his LaFayette company in favor of another one that he says would favor the French population."

January finished the last scrap of beignet, and he and Hannibal followed the Prussian through the clutter of tables and patrons toward the street. "Bouille came back saying Granger was only angry because he, Bouille, hadn't accepted the bribes offered by the LaFayette and Pontchartrain railway, and from there they went on to accuse each other of cowardice, bastardy, enticing young girls to run away from convents in order to lead them to ruin, infamous personal habits, and accepting a slap in the face from the mayor without demanding retribution."

January tucked his music satchel under his arm and sprang lightly across the gutter, the weight of his black leather medical bag a weirdly familiar ballast in his hand.

"I am armed with more than complete steel," quoted Hannibal expansively. *"The justice of my quarrel."*

"My mother says she can't believe Bouille didn't accept whatever bribes Granger was handing out because Bouille's palm is greasier than a candlemaker's apron, but that Granger makes his money stealing cows in St. Charles Parish and selling them back to their owners, so what does he care about his silly streetcar line anyway? I'd forgotten," he added reminiscently, "how much I loved New Orleans politics."

The sword master gave him a quick grin. "Better than Balzac, no? I am a peaceful soul . . . no, it's true," he added, seeing January's eyebrows shoot up. "Fighting is either for joy, or for death—to push and test yourself against your friend, or to end the encounter as quickly as possible so that your enemy does not get up again, ever. This silliness . . ." He waved a dismissive hand, as they dodged through the early traffic of carts and drays and handbarrows in the flickering oil-lit darkness of Rue du Levée.

Mayerling's students were waiting for them around the corner on Rue Condé, clustered beside a chaise and a barouche. It was a smaller group than had formed his court at the quadroon ball, but the faces were much the same. The red Elizabethan costume was familiar and the rather sissified Uncas; a blue-and-yellow Ivanhoe and a corsair who looked as if he'd be more familiar with the interior of a jewelry shop than the deck of a pirate vessel. City Councilman Jean Bouille had eschewed his Renaissance trunk hose in favor of evening dress and a crimson domino. January wondered if this had something to do with uneasiness about the possible dignity of his corpse.

"Come to watch the show?" January asked, as he, Mayerling, and Bouille got into the chaise. He stowed his medical bag under his feet—the usual collection of cupping glasses, calomel, opium, and red pepper. At least, he thought, this would be a straightforward matter of wounds, bleeding, possibly broken bones. The four revelers piled into the barouche and dragged Hannibal in after them, all plying him in turn with their flasks, to be rewarded with an impassioned recitation of Byron's "Destruction of Sennacherib," as the vehicles pulled forward.

"They have come to witness justice being done against a perjured and impotent Kaintuck swine," declared Bouille, with comparative mildness and restraint, for him. "For me, I am glad of their presence. I would not put it past that infamous yellow hound to appear with a gang of like-minded bravos and ambush us, for he knows well he cannot prevail honestly in a man's combat."

Mayerling only raised his colorless brows.

Crowded close against him—the single seat of the two-wheeled chaise barely accommodated three people at the best of times, and only the Prussian's slightness made it possible for a man of January's size to fit—January said softly, "Young Peralta's taking it hard, isn't he? Mademoiselle Crozat's death."

The strange eyes cut to him, then away.

"It takes a lot to make a Creole absent himself from backing a friend's honor."

"The boy is a fool to mourn," said Mayerling, his voice cold. "The woman was evil, a poisonous succubus with a cashbox for a heart. Whoever he marries will have cause to thank the person who wielded that scarf."

January glanced in surprise at the ivory profile. "I didn't know you knew her." He remembered the way the Roman had lurked and lingered in the ballroom, the way masculine conversation stopped when she appeared, like a glittering idol of diamonds, in the ballroom doorway, the way all men had clustered around her.

Except, now that he thought back on it, Mayerling.

"Everyone in this city knows everyone," replied the sword master. "Trepagier was one of my students. Did you not know?" He returned his attention to the road.

The duel itself went as such things customarily did. The two carriages followed the Esplanade to the leaden, cypress-hung waters of Bayou St. John, and as dawn slowly bleached, the mists reached a patch of open ground on the Allard plantation, near the bayou's banks, overshadowed with oaks the girth of a horse's body.

Granger, too, had decided against the possibility of being carried dead back to his family in the white baggy costume of Pierrot, and had worn evening dress instead. His second, however, still sported the gleaming pasteboard armor of the Roman legions, while the purple pirate with his unfortunate copper-colored beard held the heads of their phaeton's team. Both Granger and Bouille, January noticed, wore dark coats whose buttons were noticeably small and inconspicuous.

Mayerling produced the pistols, a pair of his own Mantons that Jenkins and the blue-and-yellow Ivanhoe examined minutely. While the fencing master loaded the pistols, the seconds made a last effort—albeit a fairly perfunctory one—to talk their principals out of battle: January heard Granger state loudly, "Were I not given the opportunity to sponge away this impudent crapaud's bilious spewings in blood I would be forced to reenact the final scenes of *Macbeth* upon his verminous person." A remark clearly intended for Bouille's ears since Granger, an American speaking to two other Americans, said it in French.

Bouille replied—to his own seconds, but in loud English—that he had no fear of "a canaille who can no more pass himself for a gentleman than our surgeon can pass himself for a white man. One cannot pretend to be what one is not."

And January, standing next to Mayerling, saw the sword master's ironic smile. Bouille, that champion of Creole culture, like Livia Levesque, had evidently forgotten that he'd fled a typesetter's job in France ahead of a couple of sordid lawsuits and a welter of bad debts. Mulattos were not the only ones to suffer amnesia on horseback.

January and Hannibal prudently retired to the shelter of the oak trees fifty feet away. Mayerling, with what January considered reckless confidence in both men's aim, remained where he was. "You going to bleed whoever gets hit?" inquired Hannibal irreverently, leaning his chin on a horizontal bough.

January nodded. "And purge them. Two or three times."

"Couldn't happen to more deserving men."

There were two loud reports. Egrets squawked in the misty bayou. January peered around the deep-curved limbs of the tree in time to see William Granger stalk back to his phaeton and climb in. Bouille was expostulating to the little cluster of fencing students.

"You see?" the city councilman crowed triumphantly. "The coward has outsmarted himself! In fear of my marksmanship he selected an impossible distance—fifty feet—at which he himself could not hit the door of a barn! Myself, I saw the shoulder of his coat rent asunder by my bullet."

While the exultant Bouille and his fellow pupils toasted one another and Hannibal with more hip flask brandy, Mayerling, with the air of a naturalist in quest of a new species of moth, paced off the spot where Granger stood and searched the surrounding trees until he found the bullet. Given even the most flattering estimate of its trajectory, it would have missed the American by yards. "More work in the gallery," he said to Bouille, returning like the ghost of another century through the knee-deep ground mist, white ruff and sleeves pale in the dawn gloom. "Or less at your writing desk."

They climbed into the vehicles once again.

The entire colored demimonde, past and present, turned out for Angelique's funeral, Euphrasie Dreuze weeping in too-tight weeds and covered with veils that hid her face and trailed to her knees. From his position at the organ of the mortuary chapel of St. Antoine, January counted and tallied them: The chapel itself was small, but the overwhelmingly female audience did not overcrowd its hard wooden pews. In New Orleans' climate of fevers and family ties there were few women who didn't possess mourning dresses, but January was aware that if Angelique had been better liked many of those tricked out in well-fitting plum- and tobacco-colored silks would have worn black even if it didn't show off their figures. Few women of color looked really good in black.

As the pallbearers—handsome if embarrassed-looking young men, Angelique's surviving brothers and two cousins—slid the coffin past the hanging curtain and into the oven tomb in the upstream wall of the cemetery, Madame Dreuze threw herself full-length on the ground before it, sobbing loudly.

"Oh, Madame," whispered Clemence Drouet, dropping to her knees beside her, "do not yield that way! You know that Angelique . . ." She was one of very few clothed in black, which did nothing for the ghastly pallor that underlay her warm, mahogany-red coloring. Her eyes were swollen, and tears had left gray streaks in the crepe of her bodice.

"Phrasie, get up," said Livia Levesque calmly. "You're going to trip the priest."

Euphrasie permitted herself to be raised to her feet by the younger of her two sons.

"There is no justice," she cried, in ringing tones. "*That Woman* used witchcraft to murder my girl, and no one will do anything to bring her to her just deserts." She turned toward the assembled group, the beautiful veiled ladies of the Rue des Ramparts, their servants, and a scattering of the merchants who served them. They stood crowded close, for the tombs rose up around them like a little marble village, tight-packed as the French town itself. January reflected that one didn't have far to seek for the source of Angelique's penchant for theatrics.

"I told that dirty policeman how it was! Told him about the injustices That Woman had perpetrated on my innocent, before she hounded her to death! And he as much as told me they weren't going to investigate, they weren't going to prosecute . . . they weren't going to lift a finger to avenge my child!"

She threw back her veils to display a puffy, tear-sodden face framed by large earrings of onyx and jet, an enormous gold crucifix on her black silk breast. Obviously reveling in the role of tragedy queen, she turned to January, her lace-mitted hands clasped before her. "Ben, for the love of your own sweet mother, help me bring That Woman to justice, who witched my girl and brought down death on her. I beg you."

"What?" said January, horrified. Lack of sleep slowed him down, and the delay was fatal; Euphrasie stepped forward and enveloped him in a heavily scented embrace and laid her head on his breast. He stared wildly around him, at Euphrasie's friends, his mother's friends, all gazing at him as if waiting for him to agree to the absurd demand.

Then Livia's voice cut the silence. "Phrasie, don't ask my son to do anything for love of me. Just because somebody put a piece of voodoo trash in your daughter's bed doesn't mean her death has the smallest thing to do with her man's wife, much less does it give you leave to drag poor Ben into what isn't his business, or yours either."

"It is my business!" Euphrasie whirled, drawing back from January but keeping a hold on his hands. "My only child's murder is my business! Bringing the murderess to justice is my business! That policeman—that *American*—would let That Woman get away with the crime as if she'd strangled her with her own two hands—which I'm not sure even now she didn't do!"

"Madame Dreuze—" bleated the priest.

"Tell him." Madame Dreuze's plump finger, glittering with a diamond the size of a pigeon's eye, stabbed at Dominique, and the jewel sparkled in the gray winter light. "Tell him what you got this afternoon! Tell him about the note from that policeman—that illiterate Kaintuck usurper!—that the police have no further need of your testimony, of anyone's testimony, because they're not going to take the matter further!"

Shocked, January's eyes went to Minou, beautiful in exquisitely cut spinach-green silk with sleeves that stuck out a good twelve inches per side. "Is that true?"

She hesitated for a long minute—probably out of a general unwillingness to agree with anything Euphrasie Dreuze said—then nodded. "Yes. He didn't say in so many words the investigation was being dropped, but I can read between the lines."

"Well, I won't have it!" Euphrasie threw up her arms, as if pleading with heaven, and her bulging eyes fixed on January. "I won't have it! My daughter must be avenged, and if you won't do it, Benjamin January, I will find someone who will!"

"Oh, Ben, don't tell me you're actually *surprised*!"

"Of course I'm surprised!" January dished greens onto Minou's plate, and jambalaya, and handed it to her where she sat at the table, barely conscious of what he did. He wasn't merely surprised but deeply troubled.

Beyond the tall windows of Dominique's exquisite dining room, the small light that got past the wall and rooflines of the houses behind them was fading, though it was barely six. Knowing he'd have to be out at a ball in the Saint Mary faubourg for most of the night, January had slept a few hours after the funeral, but his dreams had been unsettling. When he came down to the kitchen, Dominique was there, an apron over the spinach-green silk, sleeves rolled up, helping Bella and Hannibal wash up tea things. "Mama's over at Phrasie's," she said. "I told Bella I'd get you supper."

"You've been in Paris too long," said Hannibal. He raised his wine glass to Dominique in what was mostly a respectful salute to his hostess but partly a flirtation. She caught his eye and returned him her most melting smile.

"Or not long enough." January returned to the table.

"You really thought the police would investigate the murder of a colored woman if the leading suspects were all white?"

January was silent, feeling the heat of embarrassment rise through him and disgust at himself for the trust he'd felt in the law, in the police, in the Kaintuck officer Shaw. He had, he thought, in fact been in Paris too long. Law-abiding as he was in his soul, it had taken him years to learn to trust authority there.

"What did the note say?" he asked in time. "Because you have to admit, Madame Dreuze's story about Madame Trepagier sending a confederate to plant hoodoo hexes under her rival's mattress isn't something I'd care to take into court."

"Oh, that . . ." His sister made a dismissive gesture. "Everybody in that crowd knew perfectly well that Madame Trepagier tried to swear out a writ late yesterday afternoon to stop the sale of the jewelry and the two slaves, and Madame Dreuze spent the whole morning at Heidekker and Stein's, peddling every fragment, dress, and stick of furniture. Why else do you think Phrasie was carrying on so? She had to cover up. God knows anybody who causes Euphrasie Dreuze inconvenience has got to be the Devil's in-law. Just ask her."

"I had a wife like that once," remarked Hannibal, dreamy reminiscence in his eye. "Maybe more than one. I forget."

Minou rapped him on the arm with her spoon. "Bad man! But no, Ben. It wasn't that."

She rose and crossed to the sideboard where the covered dishes of greens and jambalaya, the rolls, and the wine stood ready, and from a drawer took a half a piece of yellow foolscap, folded small. Hannibal got to his feet and held her chair for her when she returned; she looked as surprised as she would have had her brother performed this gentlemanly office, then smiled at him again, and seated herself in a gentle froufrou of skirts. January had watched his sister at the Blue Ribbon Balls enough to know that, without being unfaithful to Henri Viellard in thought, word, or deed, she always had that effect on men. Certainly, to judge by the warm solicitousness of her eyes, Hannibal was having his customary effect on Minou.

The note was written in the labored hand of one who has acquired the discipline of orthography late and incompletely. At least, thought January dourly, it wasn't tobacco stained.

> *February 16 1833*
> *Mis January:*
>> *Regarding the notes which I askt you to make last Thursday night, many thanks for yor efort and time. It apears now, however, that they will not be necesary, and I would take it as a grate favor if you would put them aside in some safe place where they will not be seen. My deepest apologys for puting you to the trouble of making them.*
>>> *Yr o'bt s'vt, Abishag Shaw*

She was only a plaçée, after all.

January's hand shook with anger as he set the paper down.

"An American," he said softly. "We should have known better than to look for more."

Minou was silent, turning the tall crystal wine glass in her fingers. Henri Viellard was a good provider: The cottage on Rue Burgundy was decorated with expensive simplicity, the table china French, the crystal German. When first he had entered the house last November, January had immediately guessed that the podgy young man had simply given his mistress carte blanche. If tonight's simple meal was anything to go by, her choice of a cook was in keeping with the rest of the establishment—and possibly, though Viellard wouldn't have admitted it, the real attraction of the ménage.

It was not the house of a prostitute, not the house of a woman who sold herself to a man. It was the home of a couple who would have been married had the Black Code not forbidden it, the home of a woman whose man was prevented by law from living with her. The home of that curiously nuanced class of individual, a free plaçée of color. . . .

Whom Americans like Shaw would see only as nigger whores.

With a certain amount of effort he kept his voice even. "Do you have the notes?"

Hannibal was out of his chair and helping her rise before January could make even a belated move in that direction. Thérèse, the servant woman, entered in silence and cleared away plates and serving dishes as Dominique extracted a thick mass of yellow foolscap from yet another drawer in the sideboard, and in equal silence brought coffee things and a little pale brown sugar in a French porcelain bowl.

"So far as I can tell," said Dominique, spreading the papers as the men cleared the cups to one side, "these are the people who were at the ball, and next door in the Théâtre d'Orléans. I checked with all my friends, and all *their* friends, and we figured out even the Americans and decided who had to be at least some of the people in the other ballroom. . . . We know Henri's family had to be there, for instance, because that awful mother of his never lets him go out without taking her and his sisters and Aunt Francine, and we know Pauline Mazanat and the Pontchartrain Trepagiers had to be there because they're the heads of the subscription committee that was running the ball. . . . That kind of thing."

Her long, slim fingers shuffled neatly through the pile of foolscap scribbled with Shaw's uneven lines and the guardsman's pinched hand, sorting them out from the scented buff sheets of her own notepaper.

"The only ones we're not sure of were the men downstairs in the gambling rooms, but of course without tickets, they weren't allowed up the stairs. You can be sure Agnes Pellicot knew *exactly* who was asking her about her daughters. Can you believe that *awful* Henry VIII with his six wives is a man named Hubert Granville who's been talking to Françoise Clisson about her daughter Violette?"

"Were all those six wives his?" asked Hannibal, interested.

"Oh, no." Dominique laughed, and ticked them off on her fingers. "One of them was Bernadette Métoyer, who knows him through her bank—he's the president of the Union Bank and he lent her the money to set up her chocolate business when Athanase de Soto paid her off. Two of them were her sisters who help her in the chocolate shop, one was Marie Toussainte Valcour—Philippe Cournand, her protector, had to attend his grandmother's dinner that night—one was Marie-Eulalie Figes, who is plaçée to Philippe's cousin, and *he* had to dance attendance on Grandma Cournand as well, and one was Marie-Eulalie's younger sister Babette. Marie-Eulalie is trying to come to an understanding for Babette with Jean duBose."

With that kind of intelligence system in operation among the plaçées and their families, January no longer doubted the accuracy or completeness of Dominique's lists. Names were appended in Dominique's small, flowery hand to all the witnesses who had remained to testify, and to all but perhaps twenty of the costumes listed by various persons as "seen." Among those "seen," January was unsettled to note, was "Indian Princess." And she had been seen by at least three people in the upstairs lobby after the music had started playing.

Damn, thought January. The charge that she could have had anything to do with Angelique Crozat's death was ridiculous, but Madame Trepagier had put herself in serious trouble by remaining. Why had she come upstairs after he'd told her to leave? Even without a ticket, a costumed woman could have slipped past the ushers, who were only there to keep out drunks and chance strangers from the gambling rooms. But it was, after all, a Blue Ribbon Ball.

Had she had second thoughts? Something else she had to tell him and was later prevented?

Had she decided to seek out Angelique herself?

In either case, she had lied to him Friday morning when she said she had gone directly back to Les Saules.

I was home by eight-thirty, she had said.

Why the lie?

He scanned the rest of the list.

There were only three other women unaccounted for, "seen" but not identified: "lavender domino," "green-striped odalisque," and "gypsy." "Creole girls spying on their husbands," said Dominique off-handedly, when January asked.

"Silly." She returned his look of surprise with the warm flicker of her smile. "You don't think Creole ladies sometimes try to sneak in and see what their menfolk are up to? We can spot them a mile away. I understand why they want to do that," she added more soberly. "And I . . . I feel sorry for them, even the ones who complain to the police if you go to a restaurant or buy dresses that are too fine. But what good will it do, to see your husband with a woman you already know in your heart exists? It only hurts more. But most of them don't think about that till later."

January remembered himself, standing on the banquette opposite Catherine Clisson's house all those hot nights of his youth and shook his head. It did only hurt more. And he knew that it was a rare man, white or black or colored, who would truly give up a mistress because of the pleading or nagging of a wife. They simply hid them deeper or put them aside for a while only to go back.

He turned the lists over in his fingers, the scribbled and amended and much-crossed chronology of the evening, arranged, he was interested to note, like a dance card, by what songs were being played. Minou's dance card from the evening was included in the bundle—with every dance taken, naturally—and even Shaw's original questions were linked to what music was being played.

Dominique must have suggested it to him. He spelled *waltz,* "*walce.*"

No one had seen Galen Peralta after he'd stormed downstairs following his initial spat with Angelique.

"Was there ever anything between Augustus Mayerling and Angelique?"

Dominique trilled with laughter. "Mayerling? Good heavens, no! He hated Angelique almost from the day they met."

The woman who marries him will have cause to thank the one who wielded that scarf.

"Because of the way she treated young Peralta?"

"If Trepagier and the Peralta boy were both his students," pointed out Hannibal, "it's my guess that's how Angelique met our boy Galen to begin with. Augustus would have had a front-row seat on the whole seduction from the first dropped handkerchief, meanwhile watching her take Arnaud for every cent he had. His . . . antipathy . . . could have been as much disgust as hatred. He's fastidious about things like that."

Hardly a reason for murder, thought January, no matter how fond he was of Galen Peralta. But now that he thought of it, Augustus

Mayerling had been absent from the ballroom for a far longer than would be accounted for by the conference over the duel.

Four dances—slightly under an hour—had intervened between Bouille's challenge and Mayerling's reappearance to ask January to preside as physician over the duel. During those dances—the most popular of the evening—the lobby had been almost deserted. For the same reason, none of Dominique's friends had been willing to absent themselves from the ballroom no matter what portions of their tableau costumes remained unfinished. Galen, storming out of the building, had been smitten with *l'esprit d'escalier* and had gone back to renew his quarrel with Angelique, ascending by the service stair. If Clemence had gone after him down the main stair, she would have missed him. He had presumably departed the same way, and the murderer could have entered quietly from the lobby.

Always assuming, of course, that Galen was not the murderer himself.

"Those names on the last page?" Dominique reached over his shoulder to tap the papers. "Those are the people— Thank you, Thérèse." She smiled at the maid who came in to refill the coffee cups. "Those are the people we know were there that weren't on Lt. Shaw's list, so they must have left either before the murder or just after it, or sneaked out before Shaw could speak to them. Catherine Clisson was one of the ones who sneaked out—or Octave Motet did and insisted she go with him because if anyone recognized her, they'd know he'd been there, too. He's the president of the Banque de Louisiane; he doesn't dare let his name be connected with anything like this. Do you think Galen Peralta was the one who did it? Strangled Angelique, I mean?"

January moved the papers again, studied the lists—who saw whom during the jig and reel, during the Rossini waltz, during the progressive waltz, during the Lancers. Josette Noyelle—Aphrodite in the Greek tableau—had gone into the parlor during the progressive waltz and hadn't seen Angelique then. After the Rossini waltz Dominique had been searching for Angelique, in and out of that room, frequently encountering other friends there as they put up each other's hair, repaired trodden hems, changed or finished costumes for the tableaux.

Only one person—Dominique herself—noted Clemence Drouet's presence at the ball at all. Clemence was that kind of woman. She'd arrived at Angelique's house the following morning in the expectation of seeing her alive, so she must in fact have left the building between her brief encounter with January, just before the quarrel, and the discovery of Angelique's corpse.

And of course, no one had bothered to notify her.

The American Tom Jenkins had clearly been searching as well, if he'd left a laurel leaf in the parlor, but unless he was far cleverer than he looked, he wouldn't have kept searching if he knew she was lying dead at the bottom of an armoire.

"I don't know," he said slowly. "On the face of it, I'd say yes. . . . Except for his age. He's young, and he was crazy possessed by her, even before Trepagier died, I've heard. I'm not sure he'd have had the wits to hide the body and strip her jewelry to make it look like robbery. If he'd killed her, I think he'd have been found by the body."

"You'd be surprised what you do when you have to," pointed out Hannibal, warming his small, rather delicate-looking hands over the coffee cup's aromatic steam. The light had faded from the windows, and Thérèse came in with a taper to light the branches of candles on sideboard, table, and walls. The gold gleam lent color to the fiddler's bloodless features, banishing the dissipated pallor and camouflaging the frayed cuffs and threadbare patches of the black evening coat that hung so slack over his thin shoulders.

"For all he follows Augustus around like a puppy, he wasn't at the duel this morning, and I'm told he didn't attend the Bringiers' ball last night. Not something his father would have let him miss."

"No," said January thoughtfully, leafing through the papers again. "No."

Columbines, Pierrots, Chinese Emperors, Ivanhoes had filled the upstairs lobby and downstairs entry hall; Uncases and Natty Bumpoes (*Bumpi?*, wondered January, recollecting his Latin lessons); Sultans and Greek gods. Men in evening dress and dominoes. Women in unidentifiable garments described by Shaw's laboring clerk as "lace with high collar, violet sash, pearls on sleeves" (except Livia would have pointed out those were not genuine pearls), to which Dominique's more regular hand had appended "lilac princess—Cresside Morisset—w/Denis Saint-Roche (mother/fiancée in Théâtre)."

Out of curiosity, January asked, "Is Peralta Fils engaged to anyone?" *The woman who marries him . . .*

"Rosalie Delaporte," reported Dominique promptly. "The Delaportes are cousins to the Dupages, and there was a big party at Grandpère Dupage's town house on Rue Saint Louis. All of them were there."

Jig/reel—Hubert Granville w/Marie-Eulalie Figes, Yves Valcour w/ Iphègénie Picard, Martin Clos w/Phlosine Seurat . . . Marie-Toussainte Valcour and Bernadette Métoyer saw red/white Ivanhoe by buffet . . . green Elizabethan by doors . . .

He looked again. At least six people had seen "gold Roman" in the ballroom during the Rossini waltz. He'd been William Granger's second for the duel, and thus in Froissart's office at the bottom of the service stair. Xavier Peralta, who'd also been there, hadn't put in a reappearance until almost the end of the progressive waltz, nearly ten minutes later.

He remembered the old man in the night-blue satin, talking long and earnestly with Euphrasie Dreuze, watching the crowds in the lobby, in the ballroom, looking for someone.

He, if not his son, would have had the measure of the cat-faced woman dressed like the Devil's bride. He would have watched that come-hither scene with Jenkins, watched her eyes, her body, as she teased and laughed among the men; watched his son following her, crazy in love. Not being stupid, he would already have asked his friends about her.

A valuable piece of downtown property, a substantial sum monthly, and all the jewels, dresses, horses, and slaves she could coax out of a lovestruck seventeen-year-old boy.

The woman who marries him . . .

A poisonous succubus with a cashbox for a heart.

The meeting in Froissart's office could have continued with Granger and Bouille, of course, after the seconds were dismissed. And Shaw was the only one who would know that.

January folded the papers together, gazing out sightlessly into the early dark. Euphrasie Dreuze's ravings about the dead bat aside, it was quite possible that Lt. Shaw had looked over his notes and come to his own conclusions about just who had the most motive in Angelique Crozat's death: the passionate son, or that powerful, courtly, white-bearded old man.

Maybe he only remembered with the memory of an idealistic young man, but it was his recollection that sixteen years ago, before he left Louisiana, had a white man murdered a free colored woman, the police would have investigated and the murderer been hanged. It had been a French city then, with the French understanding of who, and what, the free colored actually were: a race of not-quite-acknowledged cousins, neither African nor European, but property holders, artisans, citizens.

Shaw had, for a time, appeared to understand. But that was before he'd read these notes.

There was a difference between not quite trusting whites, and this. Being struck in the street had not been as shocking, or as painful, as the realization of what exactly the American regime meant.

" 'Put them aside,' " he quoted dryly, handing the folded sheets back to Dominique, " 'in some safe place where they will not be seen.' It looks like this isn't any of our business anymore."

And so the matter rested, until Euphrasie Dreuze took matters into her own grasping little ring-encrusted hands.

They were all raised to this world, he had said to Madeleine Trepagier three nights ago, with the bands of greasy light falling through the window of Froissart's office onto her masked and painted face. *To do things a certain way. They mostly know each other, and they all know the little tricks—who they can talk to and who not . . .*

January shook his head ironically at the memory of his words as he lounged up Rue DuMaine, with the lazy, almost conversational tapping of African drums growing louder before him beyond the iron palings of the fence around Congo Square.

You don't. Go home, he had said. *Go home right now.*

Even with his papers in his pocket—the pocket of the shabby corduroy roundabout he'd bought for a couple of reales from a back-street slop shop in the Irish Channel—he felt a twinge of uneasiness as he crossed the Rue des Ramparts.

Last night he had said to Dominique, *This isn't any of our business anymore.*

Now who's being a fool?

He slipped his hand in his pocket, fingering the papers with a kind of angry distaste. Before he'd left for Paris, sixteen years ago, the assumption of his status had been unquestioned. He was a free man—black, white, or tea, as Andrew Jackson had said when he'd recruited him to fight the redcoats at Chalmette. He had been shocked when the official at the docks had looked at him oddly, and said, "Returnin' resident, eh? You might want to get yourself papers, boy. They's enough cheats and scum in this city who'd pounce on a likely lookin' boy, and you'd find yourself pickin' cotton in Natchez before you kin say Jack Robinson. Till you do, I'd stay out of barrooms."

He had grown up being called "boy" by white men, even as a grown man. It was something he'd half forgotten, like his wariness of authority. In any case what one accepts as a twenty-four-year-old musician is different from what one expects when one is forty and a member of the Paris College of Surgeons, though he hadn't practiced in ten years. But that at least was something he'd thought about on the boat from Le Havre.

His mother had confirmed that these days a man of color, no matter how well dressed and well spoken, needed to carry proof of his freedom—and a slave of his business—in order to walk the streets alone.

"That is how it has come, p'tit," she said, while in her eyes he saw the reflection of his own blackness—part contempt, but part concern. "It is the Americans, moving in from all sides, with their new houses and their tawdry furniture and their loud women who have no manners. Now more and more they control this town. What do you expect of men who won't even free their own children when they get them on Negro women? They have no understanding of culture, of civilization. To them, we are no better than their slave bastards. If they could, they would lock us all in their barracoons and sell us to make a profit. It is all they think of, the cochons."

She had been, he reflected now, more right than he knew.

She had taken a certain amount of pains, those first few weeks, to introduce him to her friends among the more influential men of color, not only to let them know that he was a music master and in the market for pupils, but to remind them that he was her son, and a free man. For his part he noticed that in the years of his absence, those friends had almost entirely stopped speaking English. It was a way of setting themselves off by language, by style of dress, and mostly by attitude and actions from any association with either the slave blacks or the black American freedmen who worked as laborers in the city.

Another voice came back to him: *He could no more pass himself for a gentleman than our doctor here can pass himself for a white man. . . .*

Or a black one, thought January, shaking his head at himself as he slipped through the gate into the open space of dirt and grass called Congo Square. He wondered whether his blackness, and the memories of a childhood long past, would be sufficient to let him pass for what his mother had been trying for years to get everyone to forget.

The drums beat quicker, two distinct voices, one deep, one high. Somebody laughed; there was a ripple of jokes. The drummers were mocking up a conversation, the deeper drum a man, the higher a woman, and January could almost hear the words. "Come on out behind my cabin, pretty girl?" "Yeah, what's that gonna git me, 'sides sore heels and a round belly?" "Got me some pretty beads here," said the deep drum. "You call them pretty?" laughed the higher drum. "I spit prettier out'n that watermelon I ate last week." You could hear the inflection, the flick of the woman drum's eyelashes and the sway of her hips. More laughter at the deep drum's speculative grumble.

Many plantations—Bellefleur had been one of them—forbade slaves to have drums at all, and when old Joseph had played his reed flutes for dancing after work was done, rhythm was kept on sticks and spoons. There was something about that blood beat speaking across the miles of bayou, swamp, and silent, stifling cane fields in the night that made the owners uneasy. It reminded them of how isolated they were among the Africans they owned.

Those drums had not been making jokes about tussles in the grass behind the cabins.

The memories touched sore places inside him, and he pushed them aside. He didn't belong here. The fact that he looked as if he did troubled him for reasons he couldn't quite define.

January scanned their faces, moving, talking, listening in the just-turned slant of the afternoon light. Distantly, the clock on the cathedral spoke three, answered by the wail of a riverboat's whistle. Up the street, small parties of men and women—white, colored, free blacks, a few devout slaves—would be coming out of afternoon Mass at the Saint-Antoine chapel, holding their prayer books and rosaries tight and crossing Rue des Ramparts so as not to pass the square.

The people here ranged in color as widely as had the attendees at the funeral, though on the whole this crowd was darker. Some of them were almost as smartly dressed. Those would be the skilled slaves, the hairdressers and ironsmiths, the tailors and shoemakers, the carpenters and embroideresses, valets, cooks, and maids. They were outnumbered, however, by those in the coarse grays and browns of laborers and draymen, stablehands and yardmen, laundresses and ironers. The women's tignons were simple muslin or gaudy calico, rather than the silks worn by the women of color in mockery of the Black Code, but like all the colored women in the city they arranged them in fantastic variations of knots, folds, points.

And they all moved differently, spoke to each other differently, from the reserved, careful, soft-spoken members of colored society. The laughter was louder. The men smoked cigars, despite the law that neither black nor colored was permitted to do so in public. Many of the women flirted in a way the carefully reared Catholic young ladies of color never would have dared.

For no reason he remembered a morning, seven or eight weeks earlier, when he'd come to the chapel for early Mass, passing by this square and smelling blood. He had crossed the damp grass and found the beheaded body of a black rooster nailed to one of the oaks, its blood dripping down on the little plate of chickpeas and rice beside the tree's roots, surrounded by a ring of silver half-reale bits. His confessor had told him only a few days ago that he and the other priests would now and then find pieces of pound cake, cigars, or bits of candy at the feet of certain statues in the church.

The drums seemed to have reached an understanding. One could hear it, like the pounding of a lust-quick heart. A banjo joined in, sharp as crickets in summer trees, and a makeshift flute called a night-bird's rill.

"*Calinda, calinda!*" called out someone. "Dance the calinda! *Badoum, badoum!*"

It was nothing like Rossini, nothing like Schubert. Nothing that had to do with Herr Kovald or Paris at all.

Already, men and women had begun to dance.

Leaning against the iron palings of the fence, hands in his pockets and uneasy shame in his heart, January searched the crowd.

The woman he was looking for he hadn't seen in sixteen years.

Dark faces under bright tignons, white smiles gleaming. Shabby skirts swirling, moving, breasts swaying under white blouses, arms weaving. A smell of sweat came off the crowd, and with it the memory of nearly forgotten nights sitting on the step of his mother's cabin, watching the other slaves dance by the smoky blaze of pine knots. Considering how much there had been to do on Bellefleur, the endless weeding and chopping at the heavy cane, repairing barns and outbuildings, cutting cypress, digging mud for levees and causeways, he still wondered how any of them had had the energy to dance, how he himself had managed, even with the wild energy of a child.

More and more were joining in, though, even as they had then. People were shouting, singing, wild and pagan and utterly unlike the music he had been trained to make. Tunes and fragments of tunes unwound like dizzy pinwheels, reeling off into space. A thin girl with a red tignon coiled high like a many-knotted turban danced near him, teasing and inviting, and the brass rattles she wore on her ankles clattered in alien music. He grinned, shook his head. She flashed him a glimpse of calf and petticoat and spun on her way. Across the crowd a face seemed to emerge, half familiar—he realized with a shock it was Romulus Valle, and looked quickly away.

How many others were here? he wondered in momentary panic. Bella—would *Bella* come here on her Sunday afternoons? His mother's cook? He realized he didn't even know if she was still a slave, or had been freed. It had never occurred to him to ask. She was part of his mother's household from time immemorial. . . . In either case she'd never let him hear the end of this if she saw him.

He wondered suddenly if the girl Judith would be here, and what he could possibly say to her about the thing he carried in his pocket.

> *"Her-on mandé,*
> *Her-on mandé,*
> *Ti-gui li papa!"*

Thin, whining, almost hypnotic, the voices rose from deeper in the crowd. More and more were dancing, to the counterpoint rhythm of the drums, the sweet, metallic jangle of ankle clappers. January's mind groped at the meaning of the words, but they were as much African as French—and bad French at that.

> *"Her-on mandé,*
> *Ti-gui li papa!*
> *Her-on mandé,*
> *Her-on mandé,*
> *Do-se dan do-go!"*

Other voices rose up, only slightly more comprehensible:

> *"They seek to frighten me,*
> *Those people must be crazy.*
> *They don't see their misfortune*
> *Or else they must be drunk.*

> *"I, the Voodoo queen,*
> *With my lovely handkerchief*
> *Am not afraid of tomcat shrieks—*
> *I drink serpent venom!"*

Someone shouted, "Marie! Marie!" Turning his head, January saw that a woman had mounted a sort of platform made of packing boxes in the center of the square. She was tall and would have topped many in the crowd even had she not been standing on the makeshift dais—handsome rather than beautiful, with strong cheekbones and very dark eyes. Gold earrings flashed in the torrent of black hair that streamed on her shoulders, and jewels—possibly glass and possibly real—glittered on her white blouse and tempestuous blue skirt. Even without moving her feet she was dancing, body rippling snakelike, eyes closed in a kind of curious ecstasy, though her face was impassive in the long, brazen light.

"I walk on pins,
I walk on needles,
I walk on gilded splinters,
I want to see what they can do . . ."

Other voices were shouting, "Zombi! Papa Limba!" and January's eyes passed quickly across the faces of those who crowded near. The woman had a snake in her arms, the biggest king snake he had ever seen, six feet long and thick as a man's wrist. It coiled around her neck and over her shoulders as she danced, and the droning voices rose against the driving heartbeat of the drums. Through the pickets around the square he could see white faces looking in, women in simple calicoes or the fancier twills and silks, men in the coarse clothing of laborers or the frock coats of artisans or merchants. At the square's four gates, policemen looked on impassively.

How could they? January wondered. How could they simply watch? Did they not feel what these people felt, what he himself felt against his will? The music was electric, drawing the mind and body to it with a force beyond that of childhood memory. It drew at the blood, and even from here, halfway across the square, he could sense the power of the woman with the snake.

He moved nearer. Few of the dancers seemed to notice him, the men dancing first with one woman, then with another, others leaping, shaking, twisting on their own. Looking up at the woman's face, he wondered if she was aware of the crowd around her, or, if not, what it *was* that she saw and heard and felt. The snake moved its head, tongue flicking, and January stepped back. Irrational fear brushed him, that the woman would look down at him with those huge black eyes and say, *You are not one of us. . . . You are here to spy.*

And close by the platform of boxes—marked BRODERICK AND SONS—among the dancers, he saw the woman he was looking for, the woman he had come to this place to find.

She was dancing alone, like the woman on the platform. There were far more women than men around the boxes and many of them moved, eyes shut, in solitary ecstasy. She was thinner than he remembered and her pointy-chinned, flat-boned face was lined. Her clothing, and the orange-and-black tignon that covered her hair, was faded and old. Above the low neck of her calico blouse he could see the points of her collarbone, the beginnings of crepy wrinkles in her neck, and the sight of it went to his heart.

He dared not go up to her, dared not speak. He doubted, in her present state, she would hear him. But the memories were like vinegar, honey, and salt.

"Oh yes, yes, Mamzelle Marie,
She knows well the Grand Zombi . . ."

The woman with the snake stepped down. Eyes open, black as coal, she stretched forth her hands, clasping the hands of the dancers who crowded close. Sometimes she spoke, a low guttural voice January could not hear. Now and then a woman would curtsy to her or a man would kiss her hands. The thin black woman came forward, clasped the voodooienne's hands, and their eyes met, smiling with curious kinship. The two women embraced, and the one they called Marie kissed the other's cheek.

Under the trees someone set up a pot of gumbo, the smell of it thin and smoky in the air. On a packing box a man piled yesterday's bread, and a pralinière stood by with her cart. Men and women gathered around, talking softly and laughing together, then going back into the dancing, as January knew they would be doing all afternoon. But the thin woman turned and walked toward the gate of the square, her patched skirts swishing in the weeds.

She passed between the policemen there, crossed Rue des Ramparts and vanished between the buildings on the corner of Rue Saint Louis. January followed her, angling sideways to pass through the crowd of whites gathered outside the palings. He dodged a carriage and a couple of cabs on the broad street, leaped the gutter, and stepped quickly along the banquette through the shadows that were already growing long.

The attack, when it came, took him completely by surprise. His mind was focused on the woman in the orange-and-black tignon, not only seeking her—pausing at the corner of Rue Burgundy to look for her—but wondering what he would say to her when he came up with her. Wondering if she would recognize him. Or, if she did, whether she would admit to it, and if she admitted to it, whether she would speak to him or simply walk away. He had not been able to locate her before leaving New Orleans, so their last meeting had been an awkward commonplace, with angry words and bitter prophecies of ill on both their parts.

He knew subconsciously that there was someone on the banquette behind him. But only when those footfalls, the rustle of that clothing, came within a foot of him on the uncrowded walk did he turn, startled, and then it was far too late.

They were medium-size men, dark without the lustrous blackness of a pure African. One of them wore a pink-and-black checkered shirt that he remembered seeing in the square. The other man, in coarse red calico and a corduroy jacket similar to January's own, had his arm raised already and the makeshift blackjack he held coming down. January flung up his forearm to block the blow and managed to deflect it a little. It struck his temple with numbing force and stunned him, so that the ensuing struggle was little more than a confusion of punches and knees, of jarring pain in his belly and the hard, crunching smack of his knuckles meeting cheekbone or eye socket. Hands ripped and tore at his shirt and he heard the pocket of his jacket tear. One of them tried to get behind and hold his arms, but January was a very big man and turned, slamming the man in the pink-checkered shirt into the corner of the house nearby.

The next thing he knew he was trying not very successfully to get to his feet with the aid of the same house corner, and two men were propping him, saying "Okay, Sambo, that's enough of that," while his brain slowly identified the thundering in his head as being retreating footsteps pelting away down Rue Burgundy. His skull felt as if it had been cracked, but he did notice that he was not seeing double.

The white men standing over him wore the blue uniforms of the New Orleans City Guard.

"No badge," said one of them. "You got a ticket of leave, Sambo?"

"My name is Benjamin January," he said, straightening up.

He still didn't remember being hit, but his head gave an agonizing throb and the next moment nausea gripped him. The police stepped back, but not very far back, as he reeled to the gutter and fell to his knees, vomiting helplessly into the muddy water.

More footfalls behind him. "Got away," said a voice with a German accent. "What's this one got to say for himself?"

"Mostly 'Here come mah lunch!' "

There was uproarious laughter, and January was hauled to his feet again. He was trembling, humiliated, and cold with shock to the marrow of his bones.

"My name is Benjamin January," he said again, and fumbled in his coat pocket. His hands felt as if they belonged to someone else. "Here are my papers."

"And that's why you was hangin' around the voodoo dance, hah?" said the smallest of the squad. He was a little dark man with the flat, clipped speech of a born Orleanian. He took the papers and shoved them into his uniform pocket, grasped January by the arm. "Let's go, Sambo. I suppose you got no idea who those fellas were you were fightin', hah?"

"I don't," said January, stopping and pulling irritably from the man's grip. His head spun horribly and even that movement brought the taste of nausea back to his throat. Some of the vomit had gotten on his trousers and all he wanted to do was go home and lie down. "One of them was in the square, but . . ."

At the first movement of resistance the three of them closed around him, jerking his arms roughly and causing another queasy surge of weakness. Reflex and anger made him half-turn, but he stopped the movement at once, transformed it into simply bringing his hand to his mouth once more, while he tried to breathe and force back his fury.

His head cleared a little and he realized two of them had their clubs unhooked from their belts, waiting for his next move.

In their faces he saw it wasn't going to do him any good to explain.

"Disturbing the peace, fighting in public and on the Sabbath," said the little officer, slapping January's papers down on the sergeant's desk in the Cabildo's stone-flagged duty room. The corner chamber of the old Spanish city hall faced the river, across the railed green plot of the Place des Armes and the rise of the levee, and the late sunlight visible past the shadows of the arcade had a sickly yellowish cast from the ever-present cloud of steamboat soot.

"No ticket to be out and claiming he's free, but I'd check on these if I were you, sir."

The desk sergeant studied him with chilly eyes, and January could see him evaluating the color of his skin as well as the coarseness of his clothing.

In French, and with his most consciously Parisian attitude of body and voice, January said, "Is it possible to send for my mother, the widow Levesque on Rue Burgundy, Monsieur? She will vouch for me." His head felt like an underdone pudding and his stomach was even worse, and the damp patch of vomit on his torn trouser leg seemed to fill the room with its stink, but he saw the expression in the sergeant's eyes change. "Or if she cannot be found, my sister, Mademoiselle Dominique Janvier, also on Rue Burgundy. Or . . ." He groped for the names of the wealthiest and most influential of his mother's friends. "If they cannot be found, might I send a message to . . . to Batiste Rodriges the sugar broker, or to Doctor Delange? The papers are genuine, I assure you, though the mistake is completely understandable."

The sergeant looked at the description on the papers again, then held them up to the light. There was sullen doubt in his voice. "It says here you're a griffe." He used one of the terms by which the offspring of full blacks and mulattos were described. In January's childhood, the quadroon boys had used it as an insult, though generally not when they were close enough to him to be caught. His mother and his mother's friends had a whole rainbow of terminology to distinguish those with one white great-grandparent from those with two, three, or four. "You look like a full-blood Congo to me."

The papers also said *very dark*. January knew, for he had read them carefully, resentfully, furious at the necessity of having them at all. Behind him, two officers dragged a white man through the station house doors, paunchy, bearded, and reeking of corn liquor and tobacco.

"You stinkin' Frenchified pansy sons a hoors, I shit better men than you ever' time I pull down my pants! I'm Nahum Shagrue, own blood kin to the smallpox and on visitin' terms to every gator on the river! I fucked an' skinned ever' squaw on the Upper Missouri an' killed more men than the cholera! I chew up flatboats and eat grizzly bears and broken glass!"

One of the guardsmen loitering on the benches gestured to the prisoner and said something to another, and January caught Lieutenant Shaw's name. Both men laughed. The sergeant jerked his head toward the massive oak door that led to the Cabildo's inner court. January's papers stayed where they were on his desk.

The central courtyard of the old Spanish city hall ran back almost as far as Exchange Alley, flagged with the heavy granite blocks brought as ballast by oceangoing ships and surrounded on two sides by gal-

leries onto which looked the cells. As the guardsmen led January to
the stairway that ascended to the first of these galleries, they passed a
sturdy, stocklike construction of stained and scarred gray wood, and
January realized with a queasy contraction of his stomach that this was
the city whipping post.

No, he thought, quite calmly, pushing all possibility from his
mind that his own neck might feel that rubbed tightness, his own
arms and ankles be locked into those dirty slots. *No. They don't just
keep people here indefinitely. Someone will send for Livia or Dominique.
In any case nothing will be done without a hearing.*

The knot of ice behind his breastbone did not melt.

The plastered walls of the cell looked like they had been whitewashed sometime around the Declaration of American Independence,
at which time the straw in the mattresses of the cots had probably
been changed, though January wouldn't have staked any large sum on
it. Both cots were already occupied, one by an enormously fat black
man with hands even bigger than January's—although January suspected that spanning an octave and a half on the piano was not what
he did with his—the other by a scar-faced mulatto who sized January
up speculatively with cold gray-green eyes, then turned his face away
with an almost perceptible shrug. Another mulatto, elderly and gray-
haired and incoherent with drink, was fumbling around trying to
reach the bucket in the corner in time to vomit. Three other men, two
black and one white, were seated on the floor. Roaches the length of
January's thumb scampered over the sleeper and in and out of mattresses, bucket, and the cracks in the walls.

"You heave in that bucket, Pop," said the mulatto on the bed, "or
I'll make you lick it up."

The old man collapsed back against the wall and began to cry. "I
di'n' mean it," he said softly. "I di'n' mean nuthin'. I di'n' know them
clothes belonged to nobody, settin' out on the fence that way. I
thought some lady throwed 'em away, I swear—"

"—said I was impudent. What the hell 'impudent' mean?"

"It mean twenty-five lashes, is what it mean—or thirty if you
'drunk an' impudent.'"

No, thought January, putting aside the dread that had begun to grow like a tumor inside him. *Not without seeing a judge. It won't happen.* His palms felt damp, and he wiped them on torn and dirty trousers.

The white man spat. Daubs and squiggles of expectorated tobacco juice covered the wall opposite him and the floor beneath. The sweetish, greasy stench of it rivaled the smell of the bucket.

From beyond the strapwork iron of the door, muffled by the space of the court or the length of the gallery, women's voices rose, shrilly arguing. From further off came a scream from the cells where they kept the insane: "But they did all conspire against me! The king, and President Jackson, they paid off my parents and my schoolmasters and the mayor to ruin me. . . ."

A guard cursed.

The light in the yard faded. Voices could be heard as the work gangs were brought in from cleaning the city's gutters or mending the levees, a soft shush of clothing and the clink of iron chain. The splash of water as someone washed in the basin of the courtyard pump. The cell began to grow dark.

Half an hour later Nahum Shagrue was dragged along the gallery, stumbling, head down, fresh blood trickling from a scalp wound he hadn't had when he'd been brought into the duty room. Mercifully, he was locked in another cell.

About the time music started up in Rue Saint Pierre below the narrow windows in the cell's opposite wall, a youth came along the gallery carrying wooden bowls of beans and rice, gritty and flavorless, and a jug of water. The guards came back with him to collect the bowls afterward. The man who had been 'impudent' smashed a roach with his open hand and cursed drunkenly against someone he called 'that stinkin' Roarke.' The white man continued to chew and spit, wordless as an ox. Outside it began to rain.

The bells on the cathedral struck six, then seven. At eight—full dark—the cannon in Congo Square boomed out, signaling curfew for those few slaves who remained abroad, though the rain, January guessed, would have broken up the dancing long ago.

He wondered about the woman he'd followed from the square and where she lived, and if he'd have to go through this again next Sunday to locate her.

If he wasn't on a boat by that time, he thought bitterly, wedging his broad shoulders against the stained plaster of the wall and drawing up his knees. The man next to him grumbled, "Watch your feet, nigger," and January growled tiredly, "You watch yours." There were advantages to being six feet three and the size of a barn.

On a boat and on his way back to Paris, where he wouldn't have to worry about being triced up in that hellish scaffold in the yard and lashed with a whip because some chaca jack-in-office thought he was darker than he should have been. *Jesus!* he thought, lowering his throbbing head to his wrists. Maybe he couldn't get work as a surgeon in Paris, and maybe the government taxed everything from tooth-brushes to menservants, but at least he wouldn't have to worry about carrying papers around certifying that he wasn't somebody's property trying to commit the crime of stealing himself.

And Ayasha? something whispered in his heart.

Well, not Paris, then. But there were other places in France. Places where every cobblestone and gargoyle and chestnut tree didn't say her name. Or England. The world was filled with cities. . . .

He wondered who were the men who'd attacked him.

And why.

He stifled the rising panic, the fear that nobody would come for him, nobody would come to get him out of this, and thought about those men. One at least had been in the square. Probably both. They'd clearly followed him.

Why?

Coarse clothing, but he thought their shoes looked better than those given to slaves for wintertime wear. In the tangle of the fighting he hadn't had a chance to observe their hands or their clothes, to guess at what they did.

Stay out of barrooms, the official on the docks had said. *They's enough cheats and scum in this city . . . you'd find yourself pickin' cotton in Natchez before you kin say Jack Robinson. . . .*

'Impudent' means twenty-five lashes, is what it means.

NO. It will not happen.

Why hadn't Livia come? Or Minou?

The clock on the cathedral chimed eleven.

The sergeant hadn't sent for them. Was the sergeant being bribed to turn over likely blacks to Carmen and Ricardo or Tallbott, or any of those others who owned the pens and depots and barracoons along Banks' Arcade and Gravier and Baronne streets?

Sitting here in this stinking darkness, it seemed hideously likely.

January closed his eyes, tried to calm the thumping of his heart. Along the gallery, female voices rose again, arguing bitterly, and a man's bellowed, "You hoors shut up, y'hear! Man can't get no sleep!" Other voices joined in, cursing, followed by the sounds of a fight.

I was a fool to return. He wondered why they all didn't leave, all who were able to—all who were still free. *And how long,* he wondered, *would that freedom last, with the arriving Americans, who saw every dark-skinned human being as something to be appropriated and sold?*

It won't happen to me. I'll be let out tomorrow. Holy Mary ever-Virgin, send someone to get me out of here. . . .

Abishag Shaw appeared at the cell door shortly before eight.

January wasn't sure he had slept at all. The night blurred together into a long darkness of intermittent fear; of deliberately cultivated memories of Paris, of Ayasha and of every piece of music he'd ever played; of the prickle of roach feet, the scratching scamper of rats, and unspeakable smells. In the depths of the night he'd fingered his rosary in his pocket, telling over the beads in the darkness, bringing back the words and the incense of the Mass he'd attended that morning before his ill-fated expedition to Congo Square. The familiar promise of the prayers, the touch of the steel crucifix, had comforted him somewhat. At seven, voices in the yard gashed his meditations, a man reading out sentences: "Matthew Priest, for impudence, twenty lashes . . ,"

And the smack of leather opening flesh, punctuated by a man's hoarse screams.

"I am most sorry, Maestro," said Shaw, leading the way swiftly along the gallery and down the wooden steps to the court. As usual he looked like something that had been raised by wolves. As they came to the flagstone court he glanced around him warily, as if expecting an

Indian attack. "I been on another detail these two days, chasin' after complaints about rented-out slaves roomin' away 'stead of stayin' with their masters. 'Course everyone does it—that whole area round about the Swamp's nuthin' but boardinghouses and tenements—but the captain got a flea up his nose about it all of a sudden, and I been talkin' to lodgin' house keepers who look like they'd sell their mothers' coffins out from under 'em. I wouldn't even be back here now, iff'n I hadn't gone by your ma's lookin' for you. . . ."

"Looking for me?" They stopped by the brass pump in the courtyard that allegedly provided for the hygienic impulses of the Cabildo's prisoners. January scooped water onto the stiffened filth on his trouser leg, and sponged at it with a handful of weeds pulled from between the flagstones. His whole body was one vast ache and his head felt as if it was half-filled with dirty water that sloshed agonizingly every time he turned it. Every muscle of his arms and torso seemed to have turned to wood in the night. He'd checked his clothing before leaving the cell but couldn't rid himself of the conviction that it still crawled with roaches.

"Yore ma said she'd got word you was in some kind o' trouble with the law," said the lieutenant, keeping a wary eye on the door of the duty room. "She was some horripilated. . . . No, don't worry 'bout goin' in there, I got 'em." He took January's papers from his coat pocket and held them up, then steered January toward a small postern door that let out onto Rue St. Pierre. "She was some horripilated and said there had to be some kind o' mistake."

"But she wouldn't come down here to see." Bitterly, January took the papers, checked them to make sure they were actually his, then shoved them into his coat.

"Well, she did say she was gonna make sure your sister came down, soon as that man of hers got his breakfast and tied his cravat and got hisself out the door, though God knows how long that'd take him. He looks like he does powerful damage to a breakfast table." Shaw spat into the gutter. "But I said I'd take care of it for her, seein' as how I needed words with you anyway."

January looked away, forcing back a wave of rage worse than anything he had experienced in the darkness of the cell at night.

Of course Minou wouldn't come, as long as that fat flan of a protector of hers needed coddling and kissing. Maybe it was understandable. God forbid she should associate with blacks or with a brother who associated with blacks.

But Livia had no excuse.

After this long, it shouldn't hurt.

Passage to Le Havre was seventy-five dollars. Cheaper, if he'd be willing to forgo the comfort of a cabin and bring his own food. Add in another five dollars or so for a rail ticket to Paris, and fifty to live on there until he could find work. But not in Montmartre. Not anywhere near those quiet northern suburbs. And it would be many years before he trusted himself to return to Notre Dame. Still . . .

The coffee-stand in the market near the river catered to everyone, without distinction: Creole sugar brokers, colored market women, stevedores black and shiny as obsidian, riverboat pilots and exiled Haitian sang mêlé aristocrats; white-bearded sugar planters and their wide-eyed grandsons, gazing at the green-brown river with its forest of masts, hulls, and chimneys belching smoke. Flatboat men every bit as cultured and aromatic as Nahum Shagrue docked rafts of lumber and unloaded bales of furs, hemp, tobacco, and corn; bearded laborers with Shaw's flat Kentucky accents or a Gaelic lilt to their voices sweated side by side with black dockhands unloading cotton and woolen goods, raw cotton, boxes of coffee, liquor, spices from the half dozen steamboats currently in port. Morose and villainous-looking Tockos from the Delta guided pirogues heaped with oysters in to the wharves, calling to one another in their alien tongue.

"Sunday's the worse," Shaw remarked, sipping his coffee standing, as if he had only paused between tables to speak to a friend. January, seated at the same table he'd occupied with Hannibal the morning of the duel with a coffee and a fritter before him, was ironically aware, not for the first time, of the unspoken agreement that appearances had to be kept up.

And indeed, his mother would never let him hear the end of it were she to happen down Rue du Levée and see him eating with so squalid a specimen of the human race as Lieutenant Abishag Shaw.

"And Sunday in Carnival is the worst of the lot," the policeman added. "They was a cockfight round the back of the cemetery, not to speak of the dancin'—not that I saw that, mind. What was you up to there, anyway?" He'd discarded his tobacco, at least. January wondered how he could possibly taste anything. "Seems to me your ma'd like to have wore you out, did she know where you was."

"I noticed she wasn't tripping on her petticoats to get me out of jail."

"Well . . ." Shaw balanced his cup in one big hand and scratched at the stubble on his jaw. "Some folks is like that, not wantin' to admit they got a son ended up in the Calaboose."

"She hasn't wanted to admit she had a son at all," returned January, his voice surprisingly level. "Not a black one, anyway. Nor a black daughter." He sipped his coffee and gazed straight ahead of him, out across the street at the stucco walls of pink and orange and pale blue, the shutters just opening as servants came out onto the galleries to air bedding and shake cleaning rags. He didn't look back at Shaw, but he could almost sense the man's surprise.

"I got th' impression yore ma was right proud of Miss Janvier."

"She is," said January. "Dominique has fair skin and is kept by a white man. It's Olympe Janvier she's not proud of. My full sister. The one I was looking for in Congo Square."

"Ah."

A woman passed, selling callas from a basket on her head, and stopped, smiling, to hand one of those hot fried rice balls to old Romulus Valle, neatly dressed with a rush basket on his arm, out doing the morning shopping as if he'd never spent last night dancing under the spell of Mamzelle Marie.

After a moment Shaw asked, "Find her?"

"I followed her out of the square and down Rue Saint Louis. The men who beat me followed me. I still can't imagine why. Maybe they just thought I looked like I had money on me, or they recognized me as a stranger."

He turned his face away for a moment, not looking at the tall white man who stood over him. The movement pulled at a fold on his trouser leg and he swatted at it, filled again with the morbid conviction that some of the Cabildo's medium-sized fauna were still with him. Then the fact that he was here, beneath the brick arcades of the market, and not still listening to the profanity of his cellmates and the screaming of the insane, brought it home to him, belatedly, that there was something he needed to say.

"Thank you for getting me out of there." He had to force back the childish impulse to mumble the words, force himself to meet the man's eyes. "It was . . . good of you. Sir."

Shaw shook his head, dismissing the thanks, and signaled a pralinière who was making her way between the tables. "I never can get enough of these things," he admitted, selecting a white praline and waving away the offer of change from his half-reale. January bought a brown praline, and the woman gave him a little bunch of the straw-flowers that lined the edge of her basket, for lagniappe.

"Lots of johnnie raws comin' into town all the time," Shaw said, when she had gone. "If it don't bother the folks none if white folks watch 'em dance, what do they care if some out-of-town darky with his big hands in his pockets stares? It ain't like it's a real voodoo dance, not the kind they have out on the lake. You speak to any of the women?"

"I didn't speak to anyone. Maybe I should have."

"Don't see why. You lookin' for Miss Olympe for some reason?"

January hesitated, conscious of the old wariness about showing things to white men, any white men. Then he nodded and felt in his coat pocket not the pocket in which he kept his rosary. The gris-gris was still there, wrapped in his handkerchief. He brought it out carefully and unwrapped it behind his hand, lest the waiters see.

"Madame Dreuze asked me at Angelique's funeral Saturday to prove Madame Trepagier had her servant Judith plant this in Angelique's mattress. A theory," he added dryly, "with which I'm sure you're already familiar."

Shaw rolled his eyes.

"Not that it matters to you anymore," added January, looking down as he made a business folding the handkerchief back around the little scrap of parchment and bones, so that the anger wouldn't show in his eyes. With some effort he kept his voice level. "I don't believe Madame Trepagier had a thing to do with either the charm or Angelique's death, but considering the police have decided to drop the investigation, I thought I'd at least see who did want Angelique dead. Do you know if Madame Trepagier managed to keep Madame Dreuze from selling off the two slaves, by the way? Judith and Kessie? They were both Madame Trepagier's to begin with."

It was something he knew he'd have to find out, and the thought of walking down to the brokers along Baronne Street turned him suddenly cold.

He hoped the sick dread of it didn't show in his face, under Shaw's cool scrutiny, but he was afraid it did.

"Morally they were," said the policeman slowly. "But a woman's property is her husband's to dispose of, pretty much. Neither Arnaud Trepagier nor Angelique Crozat made a will, and he did deed both the cook and the maid to his light o' love. Yes, Madame Trepagier swore out a writ to sue and get 'em back, but both of 'em was sold at the French Exchange yesterday mornin'. Madame Dreuze took maybe half what they was worth, to get 'em turned around quick."

January cursed, in Arabic, very quietly. For a time he watched as a gang of blacks passed by under guard toward the levee, chained neck to neck, men and women alike.

Matthew Priest, for impudence . . . He couldn't get the guard's voice out of his head, or the slap of the leather on skin.

Any man in the city could have his slave whipped in the Calabozo's courtyard by the town hangman for twenty-five cents a stroke.

On the far side of the Place des Armes, he could see the tall wooden platform of the town pillory. A man—colored, but still lighter than him—sat in it, wrists and ankles clamped between the dirty boards, while a gang of river rats spit tobacco and threw horse turds at him, their voices a dim demonic whooping through the noise of the wharves and the hoots of the steamboats. Sixteen years ago, the pillory was still a punishment that could be meted out to whites as well.

A hundred and fifty dollars would get him to Paris. With his current small savings he could probably do it in three months.

That thought helped him. He drew a deep breath and explained,

"Not long before I left for Paris I learned that my sister—Olympe, Minou was only four—had entered the house of a woman called Marie Laveau, a voodooienne, and was learning her trade." He slipped the gris-gris back into his pocket and looked at Shaw again.

"I thought I might still be able to find her at the slave dances, and that she might be able to tell me something about who actually made the charm. A dried bat's a death charm. Someone who wanted to scare her would have put brick dust, or a cross made of salt, on the back step, where she'd be sure to see it. Hiding a conjag like that where she'd sleep next to it every night without knowing it was there—that's the act of someone who really wanted to do her harm."

The lanky Kentuckian slowly licked the remains of the praline from his bony fingers, along with a certain amount of clerical ink, before he replied.

"Someone who sure wanted to do you harm, anyway. Given they was sicced on you by whoever planted that charm. . . . How'd they have known it was you?"

January sniffed. "Everybody in New Orleans heard Madame Dreuze beg me to find her daughter's killer," he said. "And since no one else seems to be taking any further interest in the case . . ." he added pointedly.

"Well, now, that's changed again," said Shaw. "As of this morning. That's why I was over at your ma's."

"So they changed their minds?" said January, anger prickling through him once again. "Decided that a woman doesn't have to be white to merit the protection of the law?"

"Let's just say several folks on the city council have come to see the matter in a different light." Shaw finished his coffee and set the cup on a nearby table, pale eyes thoughtful, watchful, under the overhang of brow. "Captain Tremouille spoke to me this mornin' on the subject, and that's why I's at your ma's—that's why I came hotfoot down to the Calaboose, too, when I heard you was there. Seems they're lookin' for evidence to put the killin' on you."

"Me?" All January could think of was the half-dozen wounded men he'd spoken to after the battle at Chalmette, who said that when first hit by a musket ball, all they felt was a sort of a shock, like being pushed hard. They'd fallen down. Later, the pain came.

"That's right."

Fear. Disbelief, but fear, as if he'd just stepped off a cliff and was only realizing gradually that there wasn't a bottom.

"I didn't even know the woman."

"Well now," said Shaw mildly, "Captain Tremouille asked me to look into that."

"I didn't! Ask anyone! Galen Peralta—"

"Nobody saw Galen Peralta go into that room," said Shaw, "except you, Maestro."

There was no bottom to the cliff. He was plunging through the dark. He'd die when he struck the bottom.

His mother hadn't come to the jail. Nor had his sister.

Only Shaw.

"Captain Tremouille's problem," said Shaw, judiciously turning the fragments of praline over in sticky fingers, "is that he has a colored gal—a plaçée—dead, and the man who looks likeliest to have done it is the son of one of the wealthiest planters in the district. Now, Captain Tremouille believes in justice—he does—but he also believes in keepin' his job, and that might not be so easy once the Peraltas and the Bringiers and the half-dozen other big Creole families that are all kissin' kin to each other start sayin' how let's not make a big hoo-rah and start arrestin' white folks over a colored gal who wasn't any better than she should have been.

"So I got to spend about two days chasin' down slaves sleepin' in attics over on Magazine Street."

"Go on," said January grimly.

"Well," Shaw went on, "yesterday—and maybe only gettin' a thousand dollars for two prime wenches had somethin' to do with it Euphrasie Dreuze figured two could play that friends-an'-family game, and went to see Etienne Crozat, that was her gal's pa. I dunno what she told him, but this mornin' Captain Tremouille called me in first thing and says let's get this murder solved and get it solved quick, and wasn't there any man of her own color who hated her enough to want her dead? He's a powerful man, Crozat. He brokers the crops of half the planters on the river and there's three members of the city council who'll be livin' on beans an' rice if he calls in his paper on them or gives 'em a couple cents less per pound on next year's sugar."

"I didn't know her."

The gray eyes remained steadily on his. "You think that's gonna make any difference?"

He remembered, very suddenly, Shaw handing him his papers in the Cabildo courtyard, taking him out through the postern door. Looking around the courtyard while he, January, washed at the pump, watching like a man in Indian country.

The realization of what Shaw had rescued him from hit him like a wave of ice water.

And the fact that the American had gotten him out of there at all.

"You believe me."

"Well," said Shaw, "I think there's better candidates for the office. At least one who paid them bucks yesterday to rough you up, maybe. Fact remains that gal Clemence Drouet says you was so all-fired eager

to see Miss Crozat, you just about shoved her out of the way goin'
down that hall, and you *was* the last person to see that gal alive."

Voices raised, shouting, at a table nearby: Mayerling and his students. Though it was broad daylight they still wore fancy dress from
some ball the previous night, those who had worn masks having
pushed them up on their foreheads, their hair sticking out all around
the sides. Two had half-risen from their places, dark-haired Creole
youths with anemic mustaches. One of them was the blue-and-yellow
Ivanhoe who'd driven the barouche to the duel.

Mayerling put out one big hand to barely brush the lad's particolored sleeve. "I beg of you, Anatole, mon fils," he said in his husky,
boyish voice, "settle the question of Gaston's manners with words!
Don't deprive me of a pupil. At any rate not until I get my diamond
stickpin paid for."

There was laughter and the boy sat down quickly, laughing unwillingly too. "I'm glad you think I'm capable of it," he said, casting a
withering glare at the haughty young man who had been the object of
his rage.

"If you don't strengthen your redouble the pupil you will deprive
me of is yourself. Unless Gaston goes on neglecting his footwork."

The haughty Gaston bristled, then laughed under his instructor's
raised brow.

"Way those boys carry on you'd think they didn't have the cholera
or the yellow fever waitin' on 'em, to help 'em to an early grave,"
murmured Shaw. "What kind of good's it gonna do their daddies,
spendin' five thousand dollars educatin' 'em and sendin' 'em to Europe and all them places, to have 'em kill each other over the flowers
on some gal's sleeve? *An'* pay that German boy to teach 'em how to do
it."

"I notice Peralta isn't among them," said January. "Was I the last
person to see *him* alive as well?"

Shaw's mouth twitched under a fungus of stubble. "Now, I did
ask after Galen Peralta," he said. His gray eyes remained on the little
cluster at the other table: Mayerling was currently demonstrating Italian defenses with a broomstraw. "His daddy tells me he's gone down
the country, to their place out Bayou Chien Mort. He'll be back

Tuesday next, which Captain Tremouille says is plenty of time to ask him where he went and what he did after his little spat with Miss Crozat."

"Tuesday next?" said January. "He left before *Mardi Gras?*"

"Somethin' of the kind occurred to me." Shaw produced a dirty hank of tobacco from his coat pocket, picked a fragment of lint off it, then glanced at a couple of clerks gossiping in French at the next table over beignets and coffee and put the quid away. "But he was sweet on that gal. Crazy sweet, by all everyone says. May be he just couldn't stay in town."

January looked down at his hands, remembering how the sight of drifted leaves against a curbstone in the rain, the sound of a shutter creaking in the wind, had wrung his heart with pain that he did not think himself capable of bearing. He had packed all Ayasha's dresses, her shoes, her jewelry in her ill-cured leather trunk, and dropped it off the bridge into the Seine, lest even selling the dresses or giving them away to the poor might cause him to encounter some woman wearing one in the market and rip loose all the careful healing of his pain.

"But Bayou Chien Mort? That's forty miles away."

Shaw said nothing. After a moment, January went on, "I came back to this city—where I can't even walk in the streets without a white man's permission to do so—because it was home. Because . . . because there was nowhere else for me to go. But the place out at Bayou Chien Mort is one of Peralta's lesser plantations. It's run by an overseer."

"How you know this?"

"My mother," said January. "My mother knows everything. The place Galen would call home would be Alhambra, on the lake."

"Would it, now?" Shaw didn't sound particularly surprised, or even terribly interested. But January was beginning to realize that for a man who never sounded interested in anything, the lieutenant had taken considerable pains that morning to make sure he, January, was out of the Cabildo's cells before his superiors realized they didn't even need to gather evidence to take him in.

"He may have his reasons," Shaw went on after a moment. "I don't know how well you got on with your daddy, but personally, if

I'd just lost a girl I cared about—and even a kid's stupid puppy love is pretty large to the kid—I'd want to be a lot farther from mine than a couple hours' ride out Bayou Saint John."

And even if he had killed the girl himself, thought January, that might still hold true.

At the same time he recalled the blood under Angelique's nails.

He thought, *She marked him.*

And felt his heart beat quicker.

"And in the meantime," he said slowly, "you're to solve the murder as quick as you can. Before Tuesday next, presumably?"

"I suspect that's the idea. Now, they got no evidence against you 'cept that you was the last person to see Miss Crozat alive. And that you left your job at the piano on purpose right then so's you could see her alone. Half a dozen people saw you go after her."

"I was only away from the ballroom for . . . what? Five minutes?"

"Nobody saw you come out. I asked pretty careful about that."

Even during their conversation in the parlor, thought January, he'd been a suspect.

"Of course nobody saw me come out. Everyone was watching Granger and Bouille make asses of themselves. Hannibal Sefton saw me leave and spoke to me when I returned. He's the fiddler."

"White feller with the cough?"

January nodded. "He lives in the attic over Maggie Dix's place on Perdidio Street. He's the best I've ever heard, here or in Paris or anywhere, but he's a consumptive and lives on opium, so he can't teach or make much of a living."

"He surely was lit up like a High Mass when I talked to him. I'm not sayin' a man can't judge the time of day when he's that jug bit, but they ain't gonna like that in court, if so be it comes to that."

There was a burst of laughter around Mayerling's table, where the sword master had disarmed one of his combative students with a spoon. January remembered that Arnaud Trepagier, too, had been one of Mayerling's pupils.

He turned completely in his chair, fully facing the American for the first time. "I'm glad you're still using that word *if.*"

"I mean to go on usin' it as long as I can," said Shaw gently. "Whole thing smells a little high to me, and higher yet now that somebody's been interferin' with you. Fifteen years ago I'd have said, Don't worry, there's no evidence and you didn't know that woman from Eve's hairdresser. Fifteen years from now I might be sayin', Don't worry, they ain't gonna hang nobody for a colored gal's death, free or not free. Tell you the truth, Maestro, I don't know what to say now."

"Well," said January, "I know what to say." He held out his hand. "Thank you."

Shaw hesitated a moment before taking it, then did so. His hand was large, still callused from plow and ax. "It's my job," he said. "And it'll be my job to arrest you, too, if'n I don't find anybody else. The person who asked you to take a message to Miss Crozat—you want to tell me about them?"

January hesitated, then said, "Not just yet."

Madame Trepagier met him on the gallery, and even at a distance of several yards, as she emerged from the blue shadows of the house, he could see the marks of sleepless tension in her pale face.

"I wanted to thank you for your note," she said, holding out her black-mitted hand for the briefest of contacts permitted by politeness. "It was good of you."

"Not that it did you any good," said January bitterly.

"That had nothing to do with you. And at least I had the . . . the warning of what to expect." Her lips tightened again, pushing down anger that ladylike Creole girls were taught never to express. "Women so frequently turn out like their mothers I don't know why I was even surprised. But that may be unjust."

"If it is," said January, "there's things going on I never heard about."

And some of the tension relaxed from her face in a quick laugh. "And now I suppose I'll have to endure the . . . the humiliation of seeing my jewelry and things my mother wore, and my grandmother, on cheap little chacas and—" She caught herself just fractionally there, and changed the pairing with low-class Creole shopgirls to "American wives." As if through his skin, January knew she had originally started to say, *on cheap little chacas and colored hussies. . . .*

She went on quickly, "And of course Aunt Picard's going to think I sold them myself and offer to buy them back for me."

No, thought January. She wouldn't have told her family about her husband's gifts to his mistress. Her pride was too great.

That pride was now in the quick little shake of her head, as if the matter were more one of annoyance than anything else, and the way she put aside her own concerns in a warm smile. "With what can I help you, Monsieur Janvier? Won't you have a seat?"

She took one of the wickerwork chairs; January took the other. Below them in the kitchen garden, the old slave was back weeding peas, moving more slowly than ever among the pale, velvety green of the leaves.

"Two things," said January. "First, I'd like your permission to tell the police that the message I was asked to deliver to Mademoiselle Crozat came from you."

Wariness sprang into her haunted brown eyes. Wariness and fear. She said nothing, but her *no* was hard and sharp in the way her back tensed, and her hands flinched in her lap.

Slowly, he explained, "I was the last person to see Mademoiselle Crozat alive, Madame. Because I saw her in private, to give her the message from you. Now I've been told that there are some people who are trying to prove that I did the murder."

"Oh, my God. . . ." Her brown eyes were huge, shaken and shocked and—why that expression of being backed into a corner?—of . . . calculation? "I'm so sorry."

"Now, I have no idea what you would have said to her at that meeting, and since Mademoiselle Crozat is dead and the jewelry's gone, you can tell the police anything you want, if they come and speak with you on this. But I need to tell them something."

For a long time she said nothing, her pale mouth perfectly still and her eyes the eyes of a card player swiftly arranging suits to see what can be used and how. Then she looked up at him and said, a little breathlessly, "Yes, yes of course. . . . Thank you for . . . for asking me."

For warning me.

Why fear?

"Will your family be so hard on you, if they learn you tried to see her? I know decent women don't speak to plaçées, but given the circumstances . . ."

She turned her face away quickly, but not so quickly that he didn't see the fury and disgust that flared her nostrils and brought spots of color to her cheekbones as if she'd been struck.

"I'm sorry," he said. "That isn't my business."

She shook her head. "No, it isn't that. It's just that . . . To have the protection of your family there are certain prices you have to pay, if you're a woman. And if you don't pay them . . ."

A hesitation, in which the silence of the undermanned plantation seemed to ring uncomfortably loud. January realized what he had been missing, what he had been listening for, all this time: The voices of children beyond the trees where the cabins would lie, the clink of the plantation forge.

She turned back to him, with the small, simple gesture of the child he had taught. "I wasn't exaggerating when I said I had to get my jewelry back from Angelique Crozat. I *had* to. Two of the fields are on their fourth cropping of sugar. They *must* be replanted, and I have neither money to rent nor to buy the hands we need. Arnaud sold three of our workers in October. To pay for a Christmas ball, he said, but I think some of it went to buy gifts for that woman and her mother, because he suspected—feared—that Mademoiselle Crozat was looking elsewhere. He pledged three more of our hands to cover the costs of renting enough labor to sugar off. I only learned this last Tuesday. I wrote to her—I'd written before—and received no reply."

January remembered the autumn when three of the men on Belle-fleur had died of pneumonia, when the owner hadn't had the money to buy more before sugaring time. The labor had fallen hard on everyone. Though only seven, he'd been sent out to the fields with the men, and he bore far in the back of his dreams the recollection of what it was like to be too exhausted physically to walk back from the fields. One of the men had carried him in. He'd come down sick—very sick—after the sugaring himself.

"There's no way you can get your creditor to defer until after you replant?"

"I'm seeing what I can do about that." Her voice had the unnatural steadiness of one concentrating on balancing an impossibly unwieldy load. "But of course everyone else is planting at this time of year. And to make matters worse the girl Sally, the housemaid, has disappeared. She probably feared I'd send her out to the fields as well, which in fact I might have to do.

"I'm sorry," she added. "This isn't any of your concern. Of course you may tell the police the message came from me, though I . . . Would it be too much to ask if you would not tell them where and when I charged you with that message? Could you for instance tell them that since I . . . since you had been my . . . my teacher, and I knew you would be at the Blue Ribbon Ball . . . ?"

"Of course," said January.

"It isn't as if I was there long or went into the ballroom or saw anyone or spoke to anyone," she went on quickly. "It . . . It was foolish of me to try what I did, and I will always be grateful to you for saving me from . . . from the consequences of that. Thank you. Thank you so much."

She did not meet his eyes. "You said there were two things you wanted to ask?"

"Madame Madeleine?" The door to the house opened, and the old butler, Louis, stood framed in the high opening. Behind him, January could see the central parlor, a medium-size room, beautiful in its simplicity, daffodil-yellow walls and a fireplace mantel of plain bleached pine. The doors onto the front gallery stood open, and a man stood just within them. Though he was attired as a gentleman in a sage-green long-tailed coat and dove-colored trousers, something about him shouted *American*. The square face, with red hair and thick lips framed by a beard the color of rust, was not a Creole face. The eyes—or more properly the way he looked out of those eyes, the set of his head as he sized up the price of the simple curtains and old-fashioned six-octave pianoforte—were not Creole eyes.

Certainly the way he leaned back through the front doors to spit tobacco on the gallery was nothing that any Creole, from the highest aristocrat to the lowest chacalata or catchoupine, would have done.

"Monsieur McGinty's here about the hands."

Madame Trepagier hesitated, torn between anxiety and good manners. January picked up his tall beaver hat from the gallery rail and said, "I'll just walk on over to the kitchen, if it's all right with you, Madame. There is another thing I wanted to ask, if you're still willing to spare me the time."

"Thank you." Had he laid a hand on her arm, he thought, he would have felt her tremble. But when she turned to face the house, to meet the man McGinty's eyes through the doorway, he saw nothing but the same bitter steeliness in her face that she had had the night of the quadroon ball.

"That McGinty might at least have the decency to let her alone about Michie Arnaud's debts till after planting time," grumbled Louis, leading the way down the square-turn steps and across the brick pavement that lay beneath the gallery at the rear of the house. Even in wintertime, the bricks down here were green with moss. It would be the only place bearable for work in the summer heat.

The dining room behind them was shuttered. With the master of the house newly dead and its mistress in the first deeps of mourning, there would be little entertaining.

"Specially now. Seems like troubles don't come one at a time anymore. That Sally gal runnin' off just makes more work for everybody, not that she was any use as a maid to begin with."

January remembered the narrow, sullen-pretty face of the maid who'd passed him three days ago on the gallery, the whip-slim body and the sulky way she walked. A girl full of resentments, he thought, chief of which was probably the unspoken one that she could be sold or rented or given away, as her predecessor had been.

And of course as butler, Louis would have charge of the maids and be responsible for their work.

"She was the one came after Judith, wasn't she?"

"Huh," said the butler. "You coulda had three of that Sally gal and they wouldn't have done the work Judith did, besides always complaining and carrying on, and like as not I'd have to go back and do it myself."

The butler spoke French well, but out of the presence of whites his speech slipped back into the looser grammar and colloquial expressions of the gombo patois. "When she was back doing sewing and laundry, you never heard nuthin' but how the work was too hard and Ursula expected her to do more than her share, but the minute she had to do Judith's work, all we got was how sewing and laundry was what she was really good at, and how could she do this other work? She was a thief, too. She helped herself to handkerchiefs and stockings and earbobs, just as if Madame Madeleine didn't have enough stolen from her by that yeller hussy."

They passed through the brown earth beds and tasseled greenery of the kitchen garden to where the whitewashed brick service buildings stood. Beneath the second-floor gallery the kitchen's shutters were thrown wide, the heat of its open stove warming the cool, mild afternoon air and the smell of red beans cooking sweetly pervasive even against the rich thickness of damp grass. Sheets, petticoats, stockings, tablecloths, and napkins flapped and billowed on clotheslines stretched among the willows that shaded the building's rear, and under the gallery two crones were at work at a table, one of them stuffing a chicken, the other slicing a litter of squash, onions, and green apples.

"Claire, get some tea and crullers for a white gentleman up at the house and some lemonade for Michie Janvier here," said Louis. "You might spare us a cruller or two while you're at it. It's that buckra McGinty again," he added, as the older and more bent of the two women got to her feet and moved into the kitchen with surprising briskness to shift the kettle of hot water more directly onto the big hearth's fire.

"Well, Albert said they didn't find him Saturday when they went into town," remarked the other woman, whose kilted-up skirts were liberally splotched with damp and smelled of soap. "And you know Madame Alicia—that's Madame Madeleine's aunt," she explained in an aside to January, "wouldn't deal with him for her, since he's an American; why Michie Arnaud would deal with an American broker in the first place instead of a good Frenchman is more than I can tell."

"Because they played poker together." Claire came out of the kitchen with a highly decorated papier-mâché tray in her hands. Two cups, saucers, a teapot, a pot of hot water, and a plate of small cakes were arranged with the neatness of flowers on its gleaming dark red surface. "And because he advanced him more money than the Frenchmen would, when he started selling things off to keep that trollop from looking at other men."

There was a brightly colored pottery cup of lemonade on the tea tray, too. This the old cook removed and set on the table and handed the tray to Louis, who carried it back along the brick-paved way toward the rear flight of stairs that led up onto the back gallery of the house.

"Can I help you with any of that?" January nodded toward the pile of vegetables heaped on one end of the table. "There's a word or two I still need to speak with Madame Trepagier after she's done with this Monsieur McGinty, and I hate to sit idle while you ladies work."

His mother would have been shocked and dragged him off to sit at a distance under the trees rather than let him gossip with Negroes, but it crossed January's mind that these two old women might know a good deal more about Angelique's other flirtations than Madame Trepagier would.

The offer to help worked like a charm. Literally like a charm, thought January, sitting down with the blue china bowl of lady peas Claire set in front of him to shell: If he'd gone to a voodooienne for a zinzin to make the cook talk, he couldn't have gotten better results.

"She was flirtin' and carryin' on, and sayin' yes and no and maybe about other men, from the minute she met Michie Arnaud." For hands lumpy and twisted with arthritis, the old cook's fingers seemed to have lost none of their swiftness, mincing, chopping, sweeping aside small neat piles of finely cut peppers and onions as she spoke. "He never knew where she stood with him, so of course no one in his life ever knew where they stood either. That was how she liked it."

"How long ago did he meet Angelique?"

"Five years," said the cook. "He had another gal in town before that, name of Fleur. Pretty gal, real light like Angelique, and a little like her to look at—that height and shapely like her. But when he saw Angelique it was like he was hit by lightning. He followed her for a year, talkin' with her mother and ignorin' Madame Madeleine and Mamzelle Fleur both, and that Angelique would draw him on one day and fight with him the next, swearin' she'd throw herself in the river 'fore she'd let the likes of him touch her . . . and then turn around all sweet and helpless and funny as a kitten, askin' for earbobs or a pin, just to prove he cared. She'd dance with other men at the balls, then lure him on into fights with her about it. He slapped her around, but she knew how to use that, too."

January remembered the mockery in her voice, the way her body had swayed toward young Peralta's even as she'd reviled him. Inviting a blow, which would then turn into a weapon in her hands. Remembered the way her eyes had gazed into his, daring, challenging, as she'd let another man lead her into the waltz.

"And what happened to this Mademoiselle Fleur?" he asked. Claire looked questioningly up at Ursula the laundress, who had come and gone silently during this conversation, carrying away hot water from the boiler in the kitchen and returning to mix up a batch of biscuits.

"She died, along of the fever in 'twenty-eight," said the laundress.

" 'Twenty-eight it was," affirmed the cook. "But even before that happened, Michie Arnaud had put her aside, paid her something and set Angelique up in a house. He bought her a different house, of course, than Mamzelle Fleur. Mamzelle Fleur's mama saw to that. And the new house had to be better, more costive. There are those who said poor Mamzelle Fleur died of shame or grief or whatever Creole ladies die of when they go into a decline, but believe me, Michie Janvier, the fever's always there waitin'."

With an emphatic nod she swept the vegetables she'd chopped into a porcelain dish.

He removed the gris-gris from his pocket, unwrapped it from the handkerchief. "You know anyone who'd have paid to have this put under Angelique's mattress?"

The woman crossed herself and turned back to finish stitching up the chicken's skin. "Anyone on this place would, if they could," she said simply.

"Sally, maybe?" There was something about the timing of her escape that snagged at the back of his mind.

The cook thought about it, then shook her head. "Too lazy," she said. "Too took up with her 'gentleman friend,' with his earbobs and his trinkets and his calico. I ain't surprised she took off, me. We're not so very far from town that she couldn't have just walked in, leastwise to the new American houses on what used to be the Marigny land, and from there she could take that streetcar. Judith, more like. She hated Angelique even before Michie Arnaud gave her to her."

"That Angelique, she had the Devil's temper." Ursula came back drying her hands. "Judith would come back here with her back all in welts and cry with her head in Madame Madeleine's lap, out here in the kitchen where Michie Arnaud couldn't see. He caught 'em once and whipped the both on 'em."

The old woman sat down, glanced across at her still-older friend: wrinkled faces under frayed white tignons. Too old for work in the fields, even in these short-handed times. An inventory would list them as *no value*.

"Thirteen years they was married," said Ursula slowly. "Thirteen years . . . Michie Philippe, he was ten when he died, in the big yellow fever last summer. Little Mamzelle Alexandrine was six. Madame Madeleine, she took on bad after Mamzelle Alexandrine. But after Michie Arnaud took up with Angelique, there wasn't no more children."

"There wasn't no more children for long before that," said Claire, her bright small black eyes cold with anger. "I doctored enough of her bruises, and you, Ursula, you washed enough blood out of her shifts and sheets and petticoats, to know that."

She turned back to January, toothless face like something carved of seamed black oak. "It got worse after he started up with Angelique, and worse after the children died, but you know he always did knock her around after he'd been at the rum. No wonder the poor woman got the look in her eyes of a cat in an alley, 'fraid to so much as take a piece of fish from your hand. No wonder she couldn't come up with so much as a tear after the cholera squished him like a wrung-out rag. No wonder she turned down those cousins of his, Charles-Louis and Edgar and whoever all else, when they asked her to marry them, wanting to keep the land in the family—asked her at the wake after the funeral, if I know Creole families when there's land to be had!"

"It didn't do her any good with the Trepagiers when she turned them down," added Ursula grimly. "Nor will it do her good with them, or with Madame Alicia Picard, if they learn she's tryin' to raise money some other way to keep the place goin', 'stead of marryin' into their families like they think she oughta."

"Raise money how?" asked January curiously. "And I thought Aunt Picard's son was already married."

"Raise money I don't know how," replied the old laundress, rising to head back to the open brick chamber that shared a chimney with the kitchen. "But I can't think of any other reason for her to slip out quiet like she done Thursday night, and take the carriage into town and have Albert let her off in the Place des Armes instead of at her Aunt Picard's. And when she came back, in a hired hack with its lights put out like she didn't want to wake no one up, and came slippin' back into the house through the one door where the shutters hadn't been put up, it was close on to eleven o'clock at night."

"Why did you stay?"

"I . . ." Her hand flinched and she wet her lips quickly with her tongue. In the shadows of the gallery she looked battered and brittle and he regretted asking her, regretted having to ask her.

But if the police were talking about ropes and Benjamin January in the same breath these days, he didn't have much choice.

"What makes you think I . . . ?" She collected herself quickly. "Stayed where?"

"Three people in the police notes mention seeing a Mohican Princess in the Salle d'Orléans, upstairs, late, long after you said you'd gone." No sense getting Claire and Ursula in trouble. In fact two of the people who'd seen her in the upstairs lobby had no idea when they had done so, and the third had mentioned that she'd been present during the first waltz.

"Friday morning you told me you were home by eight-thirty, which would mean you had to have left almost immediately after talking to me. But you mentioned the white dress Angelique was wearing and the necklace of emeralds and pearls. So you stayed long enough to see her."

Her face did not change, but her breath quickened, and long lashes veiled her eyes. She said nothing, and he wondered if silence were the defense she'd tried to use against her husband.

"Was it a man?"

She flinched, the revulsion that crossed her face too sudden and too deep to be anything but genuine. "No." Her voice was small, cold, but perfectly steady. "Not a man."

He felt ashamed.

"You were in the building, then?"

She drew a deep breath, as if collecting herself from the verge of nausea, and raised her eyes to his face again. There was something opaque in them, a guardedness, choosing her words carefully as she had always chosen them. "The reason I stayed had nothing to do with Angelique's death. Nothing to do with her at all."

Every white man of wealth and influence in the city had been there that night. And their wives next door.

But after she'd spoken to him, she'd had reason to hope that Angelique could be met with, pleaded with. . . . Against that hope was the fact that she'd already sent her notes and been snubbed more than once.

Somewhere an ax sounded, distant and clear, men chopping the wood they'd be stowing up all year against grinding time late in fall. The tall chimney of the sugar mill stood high above the willows that surrounded the house, dirty brick and black with soot, like the tower of a dilapidated fortress watching over desolate land. You couldn't get ten dollars an acre for it, his mother had said, and he believed her: run-down, almost worthless, it would take thousands to put it back to what it had been.

Yet she clung to it. It was all she had.

"Yes," the woman went on after a time. "I saw her when she came upstairs, when the men all clustered around her. The way every man always did, I'm told. I can't . . . I can't tell you the humiliation I've suffered, knowing about Arnaud and that woman. Knowing that everyone knew. I was angry enough to tear my grandmother's jewels off her myself and beat her to death with them, but I didn't kill her. I didn't speak to her. To my knowledge I've never spoken to her."

The muscle in her temple jumped, once, with the tightening of her jaw. Standing closer to her, January could see she had a little scar on her lower lip, just above the chin, the kind a woman gets from her own teeth when a man hits her hard.

"I swear I didn't kill her." Madeleine Trepagier raised her eyes to his. "Please don't betray that I was there." January looked aside, unable to meet her gaze. *I doctored enough of her bruises . . . washed enough blood out of her shifts and sheets and petticoats. . . .*

The house, like most Creole houses, was a small one. He wondered if the children, Philippe and Alexandrine, had heard and knew already that they couldn't not have.

She was estranged from both the Trepagiers and her father's family. No outraged sugar planters were going to go to the city council and demand of them that another culprit—preferably one of the victim's own hue or darker—be found.

Or would they? Was that something the city council would demand of themselves, no matter who the white suspect was? The courts were still sufficiently Creole to take the word of a free man of color against a white in a capital case, but it was something he didn't want to try in the absence of hard evidence.

And there was no evidence. No evidence at all. Except that he was the last person to have seen Angelique Crozat alive.

There was a ball that night at Hermann's, a wealthy wine merchant on Rue St. Philippe. He would, January thought, be able to talk with Hannibal there and ask him to make enquiries among the ladies of the Swamp about whether a new black girl was living somewhere in the maze of cribs, attics, back rooms, and sheds where the slaves who "slept out" had their barren homes. The girl Sally might very well have gone to her much-vaunted "gentleman friend," but his rounds as Monsieur Gomez's apprentice, and long experience with the underclass of Paris, had taught January that a woman in such a case—runaway slave and absconding servant alike—frequently ended up as a prostitute no matter what kind of life the man promised her when she left the oppressive protection of a master.

Another of those things, he thought, that most frequently merited a shrug and "Que voulez-vous?"

But when he returned to his mother's house after the Culver girls' piano lesson, he found Dominique in the rear parlor with her, both women stitching industriously on a cascade of apricot silk. "It's for my new dress for the Mardi Gras ball at the Salle d'Orléans." His sister smiled, nodding toward the enormous pile of petticoats that almost hid the room's other chair. "I'll be a shepherdess, and I've talked Henri into going as a sheep."

"That's the most appropriate thing I've heard all day." January poured himself a cup of the coffee that Bella had left on the sideboard.

"Not that he'll be able to spend much time at the Salle," she added blithely. "He'll be at the big masquerade in the Théâtre with that dreadful mother of his and all his sisters. He said he'd slip out and join me for the waltzes."

"I wish *I* could slip out and join you for the waltzes." He turned, and above the yards of ruffles and lace, above his sister's bent head and dainty tignon of pale pink cambric, he tried to meet his mother's eyes.

But Livia didn't so much as look up. She'd been out when he'd returned from the market after his conversation with Shaw—after his visit to the cathedral, to burn a candle and dedicate twenty hard-earned dollars to a Mass of thanks. She had still been gone by the time he'd bathed and changed his clothes for the ride out to Les Saules. He wondered if she had engineered Minou's presence, had maneuvered things so that when he returned—as return he must, around this time of the day, to have a scratch dinner in the kitchen before leaving for the night's work—she would have a third person present, keeping her first conversation with him at the level of unexceptionable common-places.

And when they spoke tomorrow, of course, the easiness of today's conversations would already act as a buffer against his anger.

And what good would it do him anyway? he wondered, suddenly weary with the weariness of last night's long fear and today's exhausting maneuvering in a situation whose rules were one thing for the whites and another for him. If he got angry at her, she would only raise those enormous dark eyes to him, as she was doing now, as if to ask him what he was upset about: Lt. Shaw had gotten him out of the Calabozo, hadn't he? So why should she have come down?

If they'd sent her a message the previous night, she'd deny receiving it. If he quoted Shaw's word for it that she already knew he was a prisoner when Shaw spoke to her, she'd only say, "An American would say anything, p'tit, you know that."

Whatever happened, she, Livia Levesque, that good free colored widow, was not to blame.

So he topped up his coffee, and moved toward the table: *"Don't sit here!"* squealed both women, making a protective grab at the silk.

January pulled a chair far enough from the table so that the fabric would be out of any possible danger from spilled coffee, and said "Mama, have you ever in my life known me to spill *anything*?" It was true that, for all his enormous size, January was a graceful man, something he'd never thought about until Ayasha commented that the sole reason she married him was because he was the only man she'd ever seen she could trust in the same room with white gauze.

"There's always a first time," responded Livia Levesque, with a dryness so like her that in spite of himself January was hard put not to laugh.

"Minou, did you know Arnaud Trepagier's first plaçée? Fleur something-or-other?"

"Médard," replied Livia, without missing a stitch. "Pious mealymouth."

Grief clouded Dominique's eyes, grief and a glint of anger. "Not well," she said. "Poor Fleur."

"Nonsense," said her mother briskly. "She was delighted when Trepagier released her."

"Her mother was delighted," said Minou. "He used to beat Fleur when he was drunk, but she was brokenhearted just the same, that he turned around and took up with another woman that same week. And her mama was fit to kill Angelique. I always thought it served that Trepagier man right, that he had to buy a second house."

"If I know Angelique, it was more expensive than the one Fleur had, too. Houses on the Rue des Ursulines cost about a thousand more than the ones over on Rue des Ramparts. Put one paw on that lace, Madame," she added severely to the obese, butter-colored cat, "and you will spend the rest of the day in the kitchen."

Dominique measured a length of pink silk thread from the reel, snipped it off with gold-handled scissors, neatly threaded her needle again and tied off with a knot no bigger than a grain of salt. "Fleur deeded the house to the Convent of the Ursulines when she entered as a lay sister, and that's where she was living when she died."

"And from what I understand, Euphrasie Dreuze tried to get her hands on that, too," put in Livia. "On the grounds that it was still Trepagier's property, of all things. But what do you expect of a woman who'd use her own daughter to keep her lover interested in her, when the girl was only ten?"

"What?"

"Don't be naïve." She raised her head to blink at him, emotionless as a cat. "Why do you think Etienne Crozat suddenly got so interested in finding Angelique's killer? He was having the both of them. Others, too, the whiter the better and not all of them girls. Whomever Euphrasie could find."

January's stomach turned as he remembered those two quiet-faced young men carrying their sister's coffin—those boys who would have nothing further to do with their mother.

"So she hardly needs *your* services in that direction anymore, p'tit." Livia wrapped two fingers in the gathering threads and pulled the long band of hemmed silk into ruffles with a gesture so heartbreakingly like Ayasha's that January looked aside. Did all women learn the exact motions, the same ways of doing things with needle and cloth, like the positions and movements of ballet? "I hope," she went on crisply, "that we will have no more trouble of that kind. By the way," she added, as January opened his mouth to inform her that yes, they were going to have a good deal more trouble of that kind if they didn't want to see him hanged. "Uncle Bichet's nephew came by to tell you they've had to find another fiddler for tonight. Hannibal's ill."

Minou's dark eyes filled with concern. "Should one of us go down to his rooms? See that he's well?"

"I'll go tomorrow." January got to his feet, glanced at the camelback clock on the sideboard as he put up his coffee cup. The dancing started at eight-thirty at Hermann's, and his bones ached for sleep.

"I've told Bella to get you some supper in the kitchen," said his mother, threading another needle and beginning to whip the ruffles onto the skirt. "Your sister and I will be working for a few hours yet."

Not "I'm sorry you spent last night in the Calabozo," thought January, half-angry, half-wondering as he stepped through the open doors to the courtyard in the back. *Not "I'm sorry I didn't come and get you out."* She didn't even bother to make an excuse: *"I broke my leg. A friend died. I was kidnapped by Berber tribesmen on my way down Rue Saint Pierre."*

Not "Are you in any danger still, p'tit?"

Not "Can I help?"

But he could not remember a time when she would ever have said such a thing.

The company crowded into the great double parlor of the Hermann house on Rue St. Philippe was smaller than that of the Blue Ribbon Ball but considerably more select. Still, January saw many of the costumes he'd been seeing on and off since Twelfth Night, and thanks to Dominique's notes, he could now put names to the blue-and-yellow Ivanhoe, Anatole—attending tonight with the fair Rowena rather than the dark Rebecca—to the Jove with the gold wire beard, to various corsairs, Mohicans, lions, and biblical kings. The Creole aristocracy was out in force, and Uncle Bichet, who knew everyone in the French town by sight and reputation, filled in the gaps left in his knowledge between waltzes, cotillions, and an occasional, obligatory minuet.

Aunt Alicia Picard was the massive-hipped, clinging woman in the somber puce ball gown who never ceased talking—about her rheumatism, her migraines, and her digestion, to judge by her gestures. She had a trick of standing too close to her peevish-faced female companion—her son's wife, according to Uncle Bichet—and picking nervously at her dress, her glove, her arm. January noticed that every time the daughter-in-law escaped to a conversation with someone else,

Aunt Picard would feel faint or find some errand that could be done by no one else.

"I'd rather peddle gumbo in the market than live with Alicia Picard," his mother had said. He began to understand why Madeleine Trepagier would do almost anything rather than be forced by the loss of Les Saules to live in this woman's house.

When Aunt Picard came close to the musicians' bower, January could hear that her conversation centered exclusively on her illnesses and the deaths of various members of her family insofar as they had grieved or inconvenienced her.

Indeed, most of the Creole matrons wore the sober hues suggestive of recent mourning. Madame Trepagier had not been the only one to suffer losses in last summer's scourge. There could not have been a family in town untouched.

"The chances of the cholera returning?" The voice of Dr. Soublet, one of the better-known physicians of the town, carried through a lull in the music. "My dear Madame Picard, due to the expulsion of the febrile gasses by the burning of gunpowder to combat the yellow fever, all the conditions conducive to the Asiatic cholera have been swept from our city, and in fact, there were far fewer cases than have been popularly supposed."

Xavier Peralta, as regal in dark evening dress as he had been in the satins of the ancien régime, frowned. "According to the newspapers, over six thousand died."

"My dear Monsieur Peralta," exclaimed the physician, "please, *please* do not consider a word of what those ignoramuses say in the paper! They persist in the delusion that a disease is a single entity, a sort of evil spirit that seizes on a man and that can be chased away with a single magic spell. Disease is dis-ease—a combination of conditions that must be separately treated: by bleeding, to lower the constitution of the patient, while certain ill humours are driven out with heroic quantities of calomel. What are popularly ascribed as cases of Asiatic cholera may very well have had another source entirely. For instance, the symptoms of what are lumped together as cholera morbus are exactly those of arsenical poisoning."

"I say," laughed one of the Delaporte boys, "does that mean that six thousand wives poisoned their husbands in New Orleans last summer?"

"Slaves poisoned their masters, more like," declared a tall, extremely beautiful Creole lady in dark red. She turned burning black eyes upon Peralta's companion, a tallish trim gentleman in a coat of slightly old-fashioned cut and a stock buckled high about his neck. "You cannot tell me you haven't seen such, Monsieur Tremouille."

The commander of the New Orleans City Guard looked uncomfortable. "On rare occasions, of course, Madame Lalaurie," he said. "But as Dr. Soublet says, a variety of causes can engender the same effect. Frequently if a servant considers himself ill-used—"

"Dieu, servants always consider themselves ill-used," laughed Madame Lalaurie. "If they are but chided for stealing food, they whine and beg and carry on as if it were their right to rob the very people who feed and clothe them and keep a roof above their heads. Without proper discipline, not only would they be wretchedly unhappy, but society itself would crumble, as we saw in France and more recently in Haiti."

"Servants need discipline," agreed a tall man, gorgeously attired as the Jack of Diamonds. "Not only need it, but crave it without knowing it. Even as wives do, on occasion."

"*That* is a matter which can easily be carried to extreme, Monsieur Trepagier." An enormous, ovine-countenanced woman, whom January would have deduced as Henri Viellard's mother even without Uncle Bichet's sotto voce identification, turned to face him, a maneuver reminiscent of the Château of Versailles executing a 180-degree rotation with all its gardens in tow. "And an opinion I would show a certain reticence in expressing, were *I* in quest of a bride."

"Trepagier?" January glanced over at the cellist. "Not the long-lost brother?"

"Lord, no." Uncle Bichet shook his head over his music. "Brother Claud took off right after the wedding with one of Dubonnet Père's housemaids and five hundred dollars' worth of Aunt Paulina Livaudais's jewelry. That's Charles-Louis, from the Jefferson Parish branch of the family. He was there at the Théâtre d'Orléans t'other night, but spent most of his time dallyin' in one of the private boxes with Madame Solange Bouille."

Trepagier's cheeks darkened with anger below the edge of his mask. "Well, begging your pardon, Madame Viellard, but I suspect the women who go on about it are making more of it than it is. Women need to feel a strong hand, same as servants do."

"*I* was never conscious of such a need."

Surveying Madame Viellard, January suppressed the powerful suspicion that the woman had never been married at all and had produced Henri and his five stout, myopic, and nearly identical sisters by spontaneous generation.

"Yet I must agree with Monsieur Trepagier," said Madame Lalaurie in her deep, beautiful voice. "A woman respects strength, needs it for her happiness." Her eye lingered dismissively on Henri Viellard, clothed for the occasion in a highly fashionable coat of pale blue and several acres of pink silk waistcoat embroidered with forget-me-nots. "There is no shame in a young man displaying it. Perhaps your young Galen, Monsieur Peralta, took the matter to an extreme, when not so long ago he took a stick to an Irishwoman who was insolent to him in the street, but ferocity can more easily be tamed than spinelessness stiffened to the proper resolution."

Her husband, pale and small and silent in the shadow of her skirts, folded gloved hands like waxy little flowers and vouchsafed no opinion.

"That incident was long ago," said Peralta quickly. "He was little more than a child then, and believe me, these rages of his have been chastised out of him." His blue eyes remained steady on the woman's face, but January could almost sense the man's awareness of Tremouille—wholly occupied himself with a cup of tafia punch—at his elbow. "These days he would not harm so much as a fly."

"It is his loss," said Madame Lalaurie gravely. "And your error, to rob him of the very quality that will one day make of him a good husbandman for your lands."

"Still," began the pinch-lipped Madame Picard the Younger, "I've heard that young Galen is an absolute fiend in the salon d'épée. He—"

"Lisette!" Aunt Picard materialized at her elbow, fanning herself and rolling her eyes. "Lisette, I'm suddenly feeling quite faint. I'm sure it's la grippe . . . I've felt a desperate unbalance of my vitreous humors all evening. Be a good girl and fetch me a glass of negus. Oh, and Dr. Soublet . . ." She contrived to draw the physician after her as she pursued her hapless daughter-in-law toward the refreshment tables. "Perhaps you could recommend to me . . ."

"Please do not betray me," Madeleine Trepagier had begged, on the gallery of that dilapidated, worthless plantation. To betray her, January understood—as he led the musicians into a light Schubert air and the talk in the room drifted to other matters—would be to cut her off entirely from both the Picards and the Trepagiers. She had rejected their help already, help that would reduce her to the status of a chattel once again, and he guessed it would not take much to widen the rift.

Without the families behind her . . .

What? he asked himself. *They'll hang her instead of me?* He didn't think it likely. And in any case, he knew that whoever it was who'd twisted that scarf or cord or whatever it had been around Angelique Crozat's neck, it hadn't been her.

Near the buffet table a woman was saying, ". . . Well, of course I knew Caroline had actually broken it, but I couldn't say so in front of the servants, you know. I mean, she *is* my niece. So I slapped Rose a couple of licks and told her never to let it happen again."

Cold stirred within him, a dense dread like a lump of stone in his chest.

No matter how many of its younger scions Madeleine Trepagier refused to marry, her family would stand by her if she were accused of a colored woman's murder. And in the absence of hard evidence of any kind, the city would much prefer a culprit without power, a culprit who wasn't white.

January's head ached, fear that it was hard to banish coming back over him in the music's gentle flow. What made it all worse was that he liked Madeleine and respected her: the child he had taught, with her eerie passion for music and her grave acceptance of him as he was; the woman who was fighting to keep her freedom, who trusted him.

He did not really want the decision to come down to a choice between her or him.

He suspected he knew what the choice of those in power would be.

The Peralta town house stood on Rue Chartres, not far from the Place des Armes. A stately building of lettuce-green stucco, it stood three stories high and three bays broad, ironwork galleries decorating the second and third floors and a shop that dealt in fine French furniture occupying the ground floor. At this hour the pink shutters over the shop's French windows had just been opened. A sprightly-looking white woman with her black curls wrapped against the dust swept the banquette outside her doors, while an elderly black man set out planks over the gutter in front of the flagstone carriageway that ran from the street back into the courtyard.

January watched from the corner of Rue St. Philippe until the shopkeeper had gone inside, then walked casually along the banquette, looking about as if he had never seen these pink and yellow buildings, these dark tunnels and the stained-glass brightness of the courts at their ends, until he reached the carriage entrance.

It was not quite eight in the morning. Only servants, or market women in bright head scarfs, were abroad, and few of those. By the smoke-yellowed daylight the street seemed half asleep, shutters closed, gutters floating with sodden Carnival trash.

In his most Parisian French, January said, "Excuse me, good sir. Will this street take me to the market?" He pointed upriver along Rue Chartres.

The slave bowed, frowned, and replied, "I'm not rightly sure, sir." The *sir* was a tribute to the accent: January was not well dressed. "I'm new here in town. Yetta!" He called back over his shoulder. "Yetta, gentleman here wants to know where the market is. You know that?"

A harassed-looking woman appeared, drying her hands on her apron, from the courtyard. "Should be down that ways, I think. . . ." She pointed vaguely in the direction of the river. Her French was the kind called "mo kuri mo vini," heavily mixed with African idiom. "I'm sorry, sir," she added. "We're all of us new here in town, just this week, we're still findin' our way around our ownselves. You from outa town too?" She gave him a sunny gap-toothed smile.

"Paris." January shook his head. "I was born here, but that was some while ago. I haven't been in Louisiana since I was no higher than your knee. I thought I'd remember more, but I confess I feel I've been set down in Moscow."

"Try askin' by the shop," suggested Yetta. "Helga—Mamzelle Richter, what owns the place—she knows this city like a mouse knows the barn. She can tell you the best place to buy what you're after, too."

"Thank you." He smiled and slipped them each a couple of reales, then went into Mademoiselle Richter's shop and asked, just to make sure, commenting that Carnival seemed an odd time to entirely change one's household staff.

"So I thought," said the German girl frankly. She spoke French with an accent indistinguishable from the Creole ladies of Monsieur Hermann's ball last night. "Myself, I think there was a contagion of some sort among the servants. Monsieur Peralta kept the lot of them closed up behind doors for all of one day, until his new lot arrived in two wagons from his plantation on the lake. Then all piled into the wagons, all the old servants—stablemen, cook, laundress, maids, everyone—and left, early on Saturday morning. Did I not live along the street here I would not have seen it at all—I only did because I was coming early to do the accounts. Later in the morning the last few left with a carriage, I think containing Monsieur Galen, for I have not seen him either."

She shrugged. "Me, I lived through the cholera last summer and the yellow fever—and two summers of my husband's sister *predicting* yellow fever that never came. I keep my eye on the newspapers, and listen to what the market women say, and I have heard nothing to frighten me. In any case it's the wrong time of year. So I assume it was something inconvenient, like measles or chicken pox, particularly now at Carnival time. Besides, Monsieur Xavier is still here, coming and going as if there had been no coming and going, if you take my meaning."

Measles or chicken pox? thought January, as he turned his steps along Rue Chartres toward Canal Street and the American faubourg of St. Mary beyond. Or something someone heard or saw, that he or she was not supposed to see?

He remembered again the blood under Angelique's nails.

Tomorrow was Ash Wednesday. Lent or no Lent, there were always small sociabilities on Ash Wednesday from which one could not absent oneself without comment. If he made arrangements this afternoon with Desdunes at the livery, he could leave tonight, after the Mardi Gras ball at the Théâtre d'Orléans was over, riding by moonlight for Bayou Chien Mort.

With luck Xavier Peralta would not leave New Orleans until Thursday.

By then, he thought, he would see what he would see.

The Swamp lay at the upper end of Girod Street, just lakeside of the genteel American houses and wide streets of the faubourg of St. Mary. It was, quite literally, a swamp, for much of the land beyond Canal Street was undrained, and in fact many of the drains from the more respectable purlieus of American business farther down the road, though aimed at the turning basin of the canal not far away, petered out here. The unpaved streets lacked even the brick or packed-earth banquettes of the old city, and the buildings that fronted them—grog shops, gambling dens, brothels, and establishments that seemed to

encompass all three—were crude, unpainted, and squalid beyond description. Most seemed to have been knocked together from lumber
discarded by the sawmills or salvaged from dismantled flatboats. It was
here, among these repellent shacks and transient men, that the yellow
fever struck hardest, here that the cholera had claimed dozens a day.
The air reeked of woodsmoke and sewage.

Mindful of Hannibal's philosophy of proper timing, January had
paused at the market long enough to consume some gingerbread and
coffee, hoping to be ahead of most of the Swamp's usual excitement.
He hadn't reckoned on the stamina of Americans, however, and the
effects, even here in the American sector, of the celebratory spirit of
Mardi Gras. Most of the grog shops were open, barkeeps dispensing
Injun whisky from barrels to long-haired flatboat men across planks
laid on barrels, white men grouped around makeshift tables playing
cards, and small groups of black men visible in alleyways, on their
knees in the mud and weeds, shooting dice. In several cottages the
long jalousies already stood open, revealing seedy rooms barely wider
than the beds they contained, the women sitting on the doorsills with
their petticoats up to their knees, smoking cigars or eating oranges,
calling out to the men as they passed.

"Hey, Sambo," yelled a mulatto woman, "you that big all over?"
She gave him a broken-toothed smile and hiked her skirt up farther.

January grinned and raised his cap to her—he was wearing his
roughest clothes and the sloppy cloth cap of a laborer—and shook his
head. He started to move on but a bearded flatboat man was suddenly
in front of him, piggy eyes glittering with a half-drunken hangover
and tobacco crusted in his beard.

"You leave them hoors alone, boy." He stepped close, crowding
him; January stepped back. As usual, the Kentuckian wasn't by himself. They always seemed to travel in twos and threes, and his friends
emerged from the nearest barroom door, like sullen dogs looking for
something to do.

January was startled into replying, "I was," which was a mistake,
he realized a moment later. It hadn't been accompanied by a grin and
bow.

The man smelled like a privy; the hair of his chest, hanging through his open shirt, was visibly alive with lice. "You was lookin'," he said, stepping forward again. "And you was thinkin'."

About THOSE women? January wanted to say but knew the man —the men, all of them—were actively spoiling for a fight. He managed the bow, but the grin was difficult. "I wasn't thinkin' nuthin', sir, no sir," he said, keeping his eyes down and reflecting that if he ended up in the Calabozo now, he was in serious trouble. There were those in the city guard who might decide his confession would be the shortest way out of everybody's problems, and the thought of what they might do to obtain it turned him cold inside.

He backed from the Americans, stepping with all appearance of an accident into the stream of sewage down the middle of the street. Hating himself, furious, knowing he could pick his assailant up and heave him through the nearest shed wall and not daring to raise his hand, he mocked a little jump of surprise, looked down at his boots, and cried, "Oh, Lordy, now my master gonna wear me out, gettin' my boots all nasty! Oh, Lordy . . ." He pulled a kerchief from his pocket and began to scrub at the filthy slop.

In contempt, the bearded man stepped forward and shoved him, throwing him full-length in the stream. January caught himself on his hands but rolled and sprawled, flinging up his legs to make the fall look worse than it was. He lay where he was, breathing hard, not daring to look up at the laughing circle of men who had gathered, knowing his eyes would betray him. *It's an alternative to being beaten,* he repeated to himself. *It's an alternative to being hanged.*

They moved on after a moment, whooping among themselves and shoving each other: "Lordy, Lordy, mah massa gwine wear me out. . . ."

He heard the whore's voice, "You sure put it to that black buck, handsome," and, a moment later, the ringing sound of a slap and the smack of her body into the doorjamb behind her.

"You keep your bitchy eyes where they belong, nigger."

He got to his feet and moved on, as quietly and inconspicuously as he could. *I will leave this place,* he thought, his hair still prickling with anger that the only choice he had had was to let himself be struck, to degrade himself in order to get away. *The world is wide . . .*

. . . and contains nothing.

He shook away the old despair. *At least most of the world doesn't contain Kentucky swine with their bellies over their belts and no more reading than Livia's cats have. A hundred and fifty dollars.*

Provided, of course, that he survived this at all.

Past another row of cribs—only a few of which were open—he turned right down an alley, glancing behind him to make sure his erstwhile tormentors were not watching. A drunken Choctaw snored under a straggling cypress tree, naked as Adam without even a blanket to cover him. Someone had taken one of his moccasins, but evidently found it wanting—it had large holes in it—and discarded it in the weeds not far away. The other was still on the Indian's foot.

Came into town with his loads of pelts or filé, thought January, *and spent last night drinking up the profits.* He bent, checked the man for signs of exposure, but he was sleeping peacefully. With a shrug, January passed on. In the yard behind the cribs a small group of men were gathered, watching a cockfight. Freed slaves, January guessed, or the men who bought a kind of quasi-freedom from their owners by the day or the week, seeking employment as laborers where they could and preferring whatever sheds and alleyways they could find to sleeping in the cramped slave quarters constantly overlooked by the windows of the whites. A ragged little girl was watching the alleyway—at the first sign of police, the men could disperse leaving nothing but a splattering of chicken blood on the ground.

Whoever had given Shaw the task of running these men down wanted to keep him very busy.

January crossed the yard. The kitchen lay to his right, empty save for a huge mulatto woman nursing a baby while she cooked a panful of grits at the stove. He glanced briefly through the door: the room was alive with roaches and stank of rats, but the woman was crooning a little song about Compair Rabbit, and the child seemed quiet enough.

A rickety stair led up the back of the whorehouse to a ramshackle attic under the roof. January had to bend his tall height to edge through the narrow door, stoop even in the center of the pointed room under the ridgepole. At the far end, under one of the dusty dormers, he could make out books stacked against the wall and a mattress laid on the floor. Mice fled squeaking from the sound of his feet. Down below, he heard the thump and creak of a bed frame striking a flimsy wall and a man's piglike grunts.

"I don't know where they get the energy at this hour of the morning," came Hannibal's voice plaintively from the mattress. "The Glutton—she's the second from the far end—has been at it since eight o'clock. Even at five cents a turn she has to be making a fortune. Nine of them so far. I've been married to women who didn't perform that much in a year."

January knelt beside the mattress. In the dusty light the fiddler looked awful, his face ghastly white and sunken in the dark frame of his long hair. Blood spotted the sheet over him and blotched the rags thrown down near a water pitcher not far away, and the threadbare nightshirt he wore was damp with sweat. His pulse was steady, however, and his nails, when pinched, returned to color quickly, and when January put his ear to his friend's chest he heard none of the telltale rattle of pneumonia.

"I'm sorry I missed the Hermanns' ball," said Hannibal, when January sat up again. "Did you get someone to replace me?"

"Bichet's nephew Johnnie."

"Then I completely abase myself. That's the best you could do? The boy couldn't keep time with a clock in his hand to help him. I'll be there tonight, I promise."

January looked gravely down at him, the bled-out pallor and shaky hands. "You sure?"

" *'How has he the leisure to be sick, in such a justling time?'* I'll be there. I need the money."

More thumping and rattling below. A man cried out, as if startled or hurt. Hannibal shut his eyes.

"Besides, this place was bad enough last night. Tonight's Mardi Gras, and I'd much rather be at the Théâtre d'Orléans snabbling oysters than here listening to the bedstead symphony and the fights in the barroom. The Butcher came up and sat with me a little last night—she's the one who brought me the water—but they'll all be busy tonight, so I'd just as soon brush up my good coat and make my appearance in society. Which reminds me, I don't know what French privies are like, but in this country we go into them from the top, not the bottom."

January looked down at his coat and laughed bitterly. "Evidently not in Kentucky," he said, and Hannibal looked quickly away.

"Ah. I should have . . . Well."

"My mama'd tell me that's what you get when you go past Canal Street and mix with the Americans. She—"

The outside door opened. The big woman entered, having replaced the baby with a bowl of grits and gravy in one enormous hand, two cups of coffee on saucers balanced easily in the other. In spite of her size and girth—coupling with her would be like mounting a plow horse, thought January admiringly—she was beautiful, if one had not been raised to believe white skin and delicate features constituted all of beauty.

"I saw you was up here, Ben," she said, kneeling beside him and handing him the cup. It wasn't clean, but he'd drunk from far worse, and the coffee was strong enough to kill cholera, yellow fever, or such of this woman's customers as survived the woman herself. "How you feelin', Hannibal?"

"Ready to imitate the action of the tigers." He sat up a little, poked at the contents of the dish, and ate a few mouthfuls without much enthusiasm. The woman reached into her dress pocket and produced a small bottle. "I found this in Nancy's room. There ain't much left, but if you water it some it may last you."

Hannibal held the bottle to the light, and January smelled the swoony alcohol bitterness of laudanum. The fiddler's mouth quirked—evidently Nancy had consumed most of the contents—but he said, "Thank you, Mary. At least I've been into every pawnshop in town enough that most of the pawnbrokers won't take my violin anymore," he added philosophically. "So the girls have quit hocking it. And of course the books are perfectly safe."

"I went down by Tia Hojie and got you this," Mary went on. She produced a small bag of red flannel from the same pocket, put it around Hannibal's neck on a long, dirty ribbon. "Don't you open it," she added, as he made a move to do so. "It's healin' juju—a black cat bone and mouse heads and I don't know what all else. You just wear it and it'll help you. I got a green candle to burn here, too."

"Thank you," said Hannibal, reaching out to take the woman's hands. "That's good of you, truly. What'll Big Mag say about having a candle up here? She took away the lamp I had to read by," he added to January. "When it gets dark, all I can do is lie here and listen to the fights downstairs."

"I'll put it in a glass jar," promised Mary. "Besides, Big Mag gonna be busy tonight; she won't know nuthin'. I'll put the mark on your shoes and burn this here candle while you're gone, and you feel better in the mornin'."

Hannibal coughed, fighting the spasm, then managed a smile. "I'll feel better knowing I can pay Mag her rent money," he said. "Thank you."

The woman collected the blood-crusted rags, checked to see there was water in the pitcher, and departed. Hannibal sank back on the mattress with the barely touched bowl of grits next to his hand and fell almost immediately to sleep. January shook his head, covered the bowl with the saucer, and descended the stairs. On a sudden thought he crossed the kitchen yard, to where Fat Mary was fussing around the kitchen once more. As he had suspected, there was a residue of brick dust on the kitchen steps, and a little smear of ochre on the doorsill.

"Maybe you can help me," he said, and she turned, the baby on one hip again and a square black bottle of gin in her hand.

"Maybe I can," she smiled.

"I hear there's a new girl around this part of town; skinny Congo girl name of Sally. Runaway from one of the plantations. You know where she'd be, how I can talk to her?"

"Sally." The woman frowned, searching her mind. She spoke English with a rough eastern accent, Virginia or the Carolinas, slow and drawling after the flat, clippy vowels of New Orleans speech. "Name don't sound familiar, and I know most of the girls on the game roundabouts here."

"She may not be on the game yet," said January. "She ran off with a little bit of money. She's got a new calico dress, new earbobs, maybe. She ran off with a man."

"She runned off with a man, she end up on the game fast enough." She refreshed herself with a swig of gin, and rocked her child gently, swaying on big, bare, pink-soled feet. "But I ain't seen any of the men round about here—not the ones with money to go buyin' calico and earbobs for a woman—with a new gal. I'll ask around some, though."

"Thank you, Mary." He slipped an American fifty-cent piece onto the table where she could pick it up after he left. He saw her note it with her eye, but she made no comment. He wasn't exactly sure what he thought Sally could tell him, but he was beginning to be very curious about exactly what Madeleine Trepagier had done Thursday night and in what state her clothing had been when she returned home.

Sally would know. And, if Sally were sufficiently resentful of her mistress to run away, Sally could probably be induced to talk. It would at least give him somewhere else to look, some other avenue to point out to Shaw.

"One other question? I'm trying to find a voodooienne name of Olympia. I don't know what her second name is these days, but she's about so tall, skinny, real dark, like me. She's under Marie Laveau."

"Everbody under Mamzelle Marie these days," said Fat Mary, without animosity. "She make damn sure no other queen operatin' on her own in this town. Olympia?" She frowned. "That'd be Olympia Corbier, over Customhouse Street—Olympia Snakebones, she called. She got big power, they say, but she crazy." She shrugged. " 'Course, they all a little crazy. Even the nice ones, like Tia Hojie."

"Where on Customhouse Street?"

" 'Tween Bourbon and Burgundy. She got a little cottage there. Her man Corbier's an upholsterer, but he don't got much to say for himself."

"If I was married to a voodooienne," said January, "I wouldn't have much to say for myself, either."

He turned away from the kitchen door. From the barroom at the far end of the line of cribs a sudden commotion of shouting broke out, whoops and screams and curses. Someone yelled "Look out! He's got a knife!" Through the window that looked into the yard a man's body came flying, bringing with it a tangle of cheap curtains, glass, and fragments of sash. The man sprawled, gasping, in the some three inches of unspeakable water that puddled most of the yard, as another man came crashing through the remains of the window and half a dozen others—all white, all bearded, all wearing the filthy linsey-woolsey shirts and coarse woolen suspendered pants of flatboat men—came boiling out through the rear door. The audience from the cock-fight in the corner of the yard gravitated at once to the far more inviting spectacle and the man in the mud was yelling "Christ, he's killed me! Christ, I'm bleeding!"

The smell of blood was rank, sweet, hot in the bright air. January strode across the yard, forced his way to the front of the crowd in time to see the man on the ground sit up, face chalky under a graying bush of tobacco-stained beard. His thigh had been opened for almost a hand's breadth, brilliant arterial blood spouting in huge gouts. The man fell back, groaning, back arching.

Without thinking January said, "Bandanna," and Mary, who'd come running out of the kitchen beside him, pulled off her tignon and handed it to him. He knelt beside the boatman, twisted the blue-and-yellow kerchief high around the man's thigh, almost into the groin, and reached back, saying, "Stick—something . . ."

Somebody handed him the ramrod from a pistol. He twisted it into the tourniquet, screwing it tight, his hands working automatically, remembering a dozen or a hundred similar emergencies in the night clinic at the Hôtel Dieu. "Bandanna," he repeated, reaching out again, and a neckerchief was put into his hands. It smelled to heaven, was black with greasy sweat, and crept with lice, but there was no time to be choosy. He folded it into a pad, pressed it hard on the wound, the additional pressure closing it.

The patient groaned, reached out, and whispered, "Whisky. For the love of God, whisky."

January took the bottle somebody handed down and poured it on the makeshift dressing. The man screamed at the sting of it, grabbed the bottle from his hand, and yelled, "Git this nigger away from me! Nahum! Git him away, I say! Who the hell let him touch old Gator Jim? I killed niggers his size 'fore I was old enough to spit straight!"

"He shouldn't have whisky," said January, as someone else held out another bottle. "He needs to have that cut cleaned and stitched, cauterized if possible."

"The hell you say!" yelled the patient, trying to sit up.

"T'bacca juice'll clean it just as well," added another one of the boatmen, and that seemed to act as a license—every one of the men had a remedy. Gator Jim swigged deeply of the whisky and when January tried to stop him two men pulled him back, thrust him away into the muddy yard.

"You can't—" began January, as the boatmen carried their friend back into the saloon. One stepped clear and stood in his path.

For some reason he recognized the man called Nahum Shagrue, whom he'd last seen at the Calabozo.

"Saloon's for white men, boy." Shagrue's voice was very quiet, but his eyes were the eyes of a wild pig: intelligent, ugly, and deadly dangerous, calculating where and how to attack. He had a pistol and two knives in his belt, another knife protruding from the top of one boot, and the end of his nose was a flattened mass of scar tissue, as if someone had bitten off the tip of it long ago. The cut he'd got on his forehead from the city guard was a crusted mess over one spiky brow, and tobacco juice made brown stains as if roaches had been squashed in his blond beard. He spit now, copious and accurate, on January's foot.

"He needs to have that wound cleaned if he isn't going to get blood poisoning," said January. "And he needs to have it stitched, and the tourniquet loosened every five minutes if—"

"What, you think you're some kinda doctor, boy?"

January had enough sense not to reply.

"We kin take care of our own 'thout no uppity nigger tellin' us what to do," said Shagrue. "Now you git, 'fore you're the one needs cleanin' an' stitchin'.'"

From within the saloon, January could hear the harsh upriver voices. "Holy Christ, get him some whisky." "I hear cowshit on a wound'll draw the poison right out." "Lady over on Jackson Street got a cow. . . ." "The hell with them fancy French doctors, get me old Injun Sam. . . . Sober him up first. . . ."

January knew the man would die.

He turned, and his eyes met those of the boatman before him; pale like broken glass, cold and intolerant and abysmally ignorant.

And proud of it.

He turned away.

Olympe Corbier opened the door of her small, ochre-stuccoed cottage on Rue Douane and stood looking across at her brother for some moments, her thin face blank beneath the orange-and-black tignon. Behind her the room was filled with light and thick with the smells of incense and drying herbs. A cheap French chromo of the Virgin was tacked to the wall under a wreath of sassafras; on a narrow table of plank and twig before it stood a green candle on one side, a red one on the other, amid a gay tangle of beads. That was all January could see past her shoulder. Somewhere in the house a child was singing.

She said, "Ben."

It was the woman who had been at Congo Square.

"Olympe."

"Marie said you was back." She stepped aside to let him in. When he mounted the tall brick steps he gained over her in height. Tall for a woman, she was nowhere near his own inches. She was dressed much as she had been Sunday, in a bright-colored skirt badly frayed and the white blouse and jacket of a poor artisan's wife. The fine wrinkles that stitched her eyelids and were beginning to make their appearance around her lips detracted nothing from the vivid life of her face.

"Marie?"

"The Queen. Laveau. But it was all over anyway, that Widow Levesque's big son was back from France and playin' piano like Angel Gabriel. Nana Bichie told me in the market, where I buy my herbs. That you had a lady in France, but she died, and so you returned."

Her French had deteriorated. Even before he had left, it had begun to coarsen, the *j*s shifting into *z*s and the *a*s to *o*s, the endings and articles of words fading away. Like his, her voice was deep and made music of the sounds. In another room of the cottage—or perhaps in the yard behind—a young girl's voice sounded, and the singing child stilled for a moment. Her eyes changed momentarily as she kept track of what was going on, as mothers do—or as other children's mothers always had. Just a touch, then her attention returned to him.

"You never came."

"I didn't know you'd want me to," he said. "We'd fought. . . ." He hesitated, feeling awkward and stupid but knowing that their quarrel sixteen years ago was something that still needed getting past. "And I felt bad that I hadn't come back, hadn't made the time to look for you, before I left for France. I was stupid then—and I guess I didn't quite have the nerve now. I don't know how long it would have taken me to get the nerve, if I didn't need your advice."

"About Angelique Crozat?"

He looked nonplussed. Her dark face split into a white grin and the tension of her body relaxed. She shook her head, "Brother, for a griffe you sure white inside. You don't think everybody In town don't know about that silly cow Phrasie Dreuze hangin' herself all over you like Spanish moss at the funeral and layin' it on you to 'avenge her daughter's murder'? It true like she sayin' that somebody witched her pillow?"

"Put this in her mattress." He produced the handkerchief from his coat pocket—his slightly-better corduroy coatee, not the rough serge roundabout he'd worn to the Swamp. Bella had shaken her head over the damp and stinking bundle he'd brought down to her upon his return to the house that morning: "Fox go callin' on a pig, gonna get shit on his fur," she'd said.

Olympe led the way to a very old, very scarred settee set beneath the lake-side window, nudged aside an enormous gray cat, and sat beside him, turning the gris-gris carefully in the light. She kept the handkerchief between the dried bat and her palm, touched the dead thing only with her nail, but her face had the businesslike intentness of a physician's during the examination of a stool or a sputum. The cat sniffed at January's knee, then tucked its feet and stared slit-eyed into sleepy distance once more.

"John Bayou made this," Olympe said at last. "It's the kind hangs in the swamp near the lake where he goes, and you can still smell the turpentine on it." She held it out for him to sniff. "He favors snuff and turpentine. Dr. Yah-Yah woulda made a wax ball with chicken feathers, 'stead of huntin' down a bat. It's bad gris-gris, death written all over it." Her dark eyes flickered to him. "You been carryin' this in your pocket?"

He nodded.

"You lucky you get off with just a couple beatin's." January's hand went to the swollen lips of the cut cheek he'd taken Sunday afternoon. The gris-gris had, of course, been in his pocket at the time. Also today in the Swamp.

"What?" she said, seeing his face. "You thought it would only work against the one whose name was spoke at its making?" Her face softened a little, and the old, ready contempt she'd flayed him with at their last meeting was tempered now by years of bearing children and dealing with the helplessness of other people's pain. "Or they teach you in France it was all nigger hoodoo?" Once she would have thrown the words at him like a challenger's gauntlet. Now she smiled, exasperated but kind.

"Where would I find this John Bayou?"

"I wouldn't advise it," said Olympe. "He mean, Doctor John." Her coffee-dark eyes narrowed, like the cat's. "And what was Angelique Crozat to you?"

"A woman they're saying I killed."

"Who's saying?"

"The police. Not saying it right out yet, but they're thinking it louder and louder." And he told her what had happened that night,

leaving out only who it was who had given him the message to take to
Angelique—"someone who couldn't be at that ball"—and what Shaw
had told him later.

"Phrasie Dreuze," said Olympe, as if she'd bitten on a lemon, and
her eyes had the look of an angry cat's again. "Yes, her man made it
worth her while to keep her mouth shut about him and her daughter.
Mamzelle Marie had her cut of that, for showin' Phrasie how to pass
off Angelique as a virgin to Trepagier when the time come. But some
people knew. Anybody who knew Angelique as a child didn't have far
to go to guess. No wonder she didn't have much use for men."

She shook her head. "Phrasie know you were the last person to see
her girl alive?"

"I think so. She was there when Clemence Drouet told Shaw
about it, but I don't think she's smart enough to put two and two
together. Even if she was, I don't think she'd care."

"No. So long as she's got her revenge." She turned her head, to
regard the withered bat on the windowsill. "I'll need a dollar, two
dollars, to find out from Doctor John."

He took them from his wallet, heavy silver cartwheels, and she
placed them on the sill on either side of the bat. The cat jumped up
and sniffed the money, but didn't go near the gris-gris. January told
himself it was because the thing smelled of snuff and turpentine.

"Anybody ever ask you to witch Angelique?"

Olympe hesitated, but her eyes moved.

"Who?"

She pushed the silver dollars to and fro with a fingertip. "When
you talked about goin' to France, brother, you talked about becomin'
a doctor. A real doctor, a go-to-school doctor. You do that?"

January nodded.

"You take that oath they make doctors take, about not runnin'
your mouth about your patients who come to you with secrets? Secrets
that are the seeds of their illness?"

He looked away, unable to meet her eyes. Then he sighed. "Looks
like it's my day to be double stupid. Now you got me talkin' gombo,"
he added, realizing he had slipped, not only into the softer inflections
of the Africanized speech, but into its abbreviated forms as well.

"You always did set store on bein' a Frenchman," smiled Olympe. "You as bad as Mama, and that sister of ours with her fat custard moneybag, pretendin' I'm no kin of theirs because I'm my father's child." Her mouth quirked, and for a moment the old anger glinted in her eyes.

"I'm sorry." His hand moved toward the money. She regarded him in surprise.

"You change your mind 'bout Doctor John?"

"I thought you just told me you wouldn't tell."

"I won't tell on the person who paid *me*," she said, as if explaining something to one of her younger children. "Might be some completely different soul went to John Bayou, and that's none of my lookout. I should know in two, three days."

"I'll be back by then." He thought he said the words casually, but there was more than just interest in the way she turned her head. "I'm leaving town for a few days. Riding out tonight, as soon as the dancing's through."

He felt his heart trip quicker as he spoke the words aloud. It was something he didn't want to think about. Since he had returned to Louisiana, he had not been out of New Orleans, had barely left the French town, and then only for certain specific destinations: the Culvers' house, the houses of other private pupils.

In the old French town, the traditions of a free colored caste protected him. His French speech identified him with it, at least to those who knew, and his friends and family guarded him, because should ill befall his mother's son, ill would threaten them all.

Whatever family he might possess in the rest of the state, wherever and whoever they were, they were still picking cotton and cutting cane, without legal names or legal rights. In effect, everything beyond Canal Street was the Swamp.

"Can't that policeman go?" she asked. "Or won't he?"

"I don't know," said January softly. "I think they're keeping him busy, keeping him quiet. And I think . . ." He hesitated, not exactly sure what to say because he wasn't exactly sure what it was he was going to Chien Mort to seek.

"I think he really wants to find out the truth," he went on slowly.

"But he's an American, and he's a white man. If in his heart he really doesn't want the killer to be Galen Peralta, he'll be . . . too willing to look the other way if Peralta Père says, 'Look over there.' And you know for a fact he's not going to get a thing out of those slaves."

Olympe nodded.

January swallowed hard, thinking about the world outside the bounds of the city he knew. "I think it's gotta be me."

Through the open doors to the rear parlor he could see a girl of twelve or so, skinny like Olympe but with the red-mahogany cast of the free colored, with a two-year-old boy on her knee, telling him a long tale about Compair Lapin and Michie Dindon while she shelled peas at the table.

He thought, *They can walk twelve blocks downstream or six blocks toward the river and they'll be safe . . . my nephew, my niece.* But he knew that wasn't even true anymore.

"I'll be back," he said. His voice was hoarse.

"Wait." Olympe rose, crossed to the big étagère in the corner. Like the settle—and all the furniture in the room—it was very plain, with a patina of great age, the red cypress gleaming like satin. Its shelves were lined with borders of fancifully cut paper, and held red clay pots and tin canisters that had once contained coffee, sugar, or cocoa, labels garish in several tongues. She took a blue bead from one canister and a couple of tiny bones from another, tied the bones in a piece of red flannel and laced everything together onto a leather thong, muttering to herself and occasionally clapping her hands or snapping her fingers while she worked. Then she put the entire thong into her mouth, crossed herself three times, and knelt before the chromo of the Virgin, her head bowed in prayer.

January recognized some of the ritual, from his childhood at Bellefleur. The priest who'd catechized him later had taught him to trust in the Virgin and take comfort in the mysteries of the rosary. It had been years since he'd even thought of such spells.

"Here." She held out the thong to him. "Tie this round your ankle when you go. Papa Legba and Virgin Mary, they look out for you and bring you back here safe and free. It's not safe out there," she went on, seeing him smile as he put the thong into his pocket. "You had that gris-gris on you for near a week, and there's evil in it, the kind of evil that comes from petty anger and grows big, like a rat stuffin' itself on worms in the dark. Wear it. It's not safe beyond the river. Not for the likes of us. Maybe not ever again."

The sun was leaning over the wide crescent of the river as January walked back along Rue Burgundy toward his mother's house. In the tall town houses and the low-built cottages both, and in every court-yard and turning, he could sense the movement and excitement of preparations for the final night of festivities, the suppressed flurry of fantastic clothing and the freedom of masks.

He'd already made arrangements with Desdunes's Livery for the best horse obtainable. Food, and a little spare clothing, and bait for the horse lay packed in the saddlebag under the bed in his room. *It's not safe beyond the river.*

The land that he'd been born in, the land that was his home, was enemy land. American land. The land of men like Nahum Shagrue.

His heart beat hard as he walked along the bricks of the ban-quette. If he could get evidence, find a reason, learn something to tell Shaw about what was out at Bayou Chien Mort, he thought the man would go. And despite all the Americans could do, the testimony of a free man of color was still good in the courts of New Orleans.

But it had to be a free man's testimony, not that of subpoenaed slaves.

A couple of Creole blades came down the banquette toward him, gesturing excitedly, recounting a duel or a card game, and January stepped down, springing over the noisome gutter and into the mud of the street to let them pass. Neither so much as glanced from their absorption.

As he crossed back on some householder's plank to the pavement, January cursed Euphrasie Dreuze in his heart. At his mother's house he edged down the narrow passage to the yard and thence climbed to his own room above the kitchen. At the small cypress desk he wrote a quick letter to Abishag Shaw—keeping the wording as simple as possi-ble just to be on the safe side—then took his papers from his pocket and copied them exactly in his best notarial script. He started to fold the copy, then flattened it out again, and for good measure made a second copy on paper he'd bought last week to keep track of his students' payments. The inaccuracy of the official signature didn't trouble him much, given what he knew about the educational level prevalent in rural Louisiana. He placed the original in the envelope with the letter to Shaw, and closed it with a wafer of pink wax. One copy he folded and put in the desk, another in his pocket.

As a lifeline it wasn't much, but it was all he had.

It was half a block from his mother's house to Minou's. The two houses were nearly identical, replicas of all the small cottages along that portion of Rue Burgundy. He edged down the narrow way between Minou's cottage and the next and into the yard, where his sister's cook was peeling apples for a tart at the table set up outside the kitchen door. The afternoon was a cool one, the heat that poured from the big brick kitchen welcome. Inside, January could see Thérèse ironing petticoats at a larger table near the stove.

"She inside," said the cook, looking up at him with an encouraging smile, which also told him that Henri Viellard was not on the premises. It would not have done, of course, for his sister's protector to be reminded that Dominique had a brother at all, much less one so dark. She had been her usual sweet, charming self when she'd told him to check whether Henri was present before approaching her door, but after the morning's events, and after Sunday night in the Calabozo, he felt a surge of sympathy for Olympe's rebellion.

"But I warn you, she in God's own dither 'bout that ball."

In a dither over the ball, was she? thought January, standing in the long French doors that let into the double parlor, watching his sister arranging the curls on an enormous white wig of the sort popular fifty years before.

And how much of a dither would she be in if someone told her that she could be murdered with impunity by a white man? Or was that something she already knew and accepted, the way she accepted that she could not be in public with her hair uncovered or own a carriage?

"Ben." She turned in her chair and smiled. "Would you like tea? I'll have Thérèse—"

He shook his head, and stepped across to kiss her cheek. "I can't stay," he said. "I'm playing tonight, and it seems like all morning I've been up to this and that, and I need to go to church yet before the ball."

"Church?"

"I'm leaving right after the dancing ends," said January quietly. "Riding down to Bayou Chien Mort to have a talk with the Peralta house servants—and to have a look at Michie Galen if I can manage it. The girl you mentioned him being affianced to—is he in love with her?"

"Rosalie Delaporte?" Dominique wrinkled her nose. "If you're planning to deliver a letter, you'd have better luck saying it's from that fencing master of his. That must be who he's missing most."

January shook his head. "His father approves of the fencing master."

"His father approves of Rosalie Delaporte. Skimmed milk, if you ask me." She removed a nosegay from too close attentions by the cat. "You might tell him you have a note from Angelique's mother. But his father approved of that, too."

"Did he?" January settled onto the other chair, straddling it backward. The table was a litter of plumes, lace, and silk flowers, hurtfully reminiscent of Ayasha. The apricot silk gown lay spread over the divan in the front parlor, gleaming softly in the light of the French doors. "I wonder. And what he approved of when Angelique was alive, and what he'll countenance now, are two different things. Do you have anything of Angelique's? Something that could pass as a souvenir, something she wanted him to have?"

"With her mother selling up everything that would bring in a picayune? Here." Dominique got to her feet and rustled over to the sideboard, returning with a pair of fragile white kid gloves. "She and I wore the same sizes, down to shoes and gloves—I know, because she borrowed a pair of my shoes once when a rainstorm caught her and never returned them, the bitch. These should pass for hers."

"Thank you." He slipped them into his pocket. "What do I owe you for them?"

"Goose." She waved the offer away. "It'll give Henri something to get me on my next birthday. Why is it men never know what to buy a woman? He has me do the shopping when he needs to buy gifts for his mother and sisters. Not that he ever tells them that, of course."

"You sure he isn't having some other lady buy the presents he gives you?" suggested January mischievously.

Dominique drew herself up. "Benjamin," she said, with great dignity, "*no* woman, even one who wished me ill, would have suggested that he buy me the collected works of Jean-Jacques Rousseau."

"I abase myself," apologized January humbly. "One more thing." He took from his breast pocket the envelope and handed it to her. "I should be back Sunday. I'll come for this then. If I'm not—if I don't—take this to Lieutenant Shaw at the Calabozo immediately."

And if worse came to worst, he added mentally, *hope to hell somebody—your Henri, or Livia, or somebody—would be able to come up with the $1,500 it would take to buy me out of slavery.*

If they could find me.

As he had predicted, the crowd at the public masquerade held in the Théâtre d'Orléans was far larger than that at the quadroon ball going on next door, and far less well behaved.

The temporary floor had been laid as usual above the seats in the Théâtre's pit, stretching from the lip of the stage to the doors. Bunting fluttered from every pillar and curtain swag, and long tables of refreshments had been set out under the eye of waiters to which—both John Davis, the owner of both buildings, and the master of ceremonies had informed the musicians in no uncertain terms—only the attending guests would have access. In the vast route of people bustling and jostling around the edges of the room or performing energetic quadrilles in the center, January recognized again all the now-familiar costumes: Richelieu, the dreadful blue-and-yellow Ivanhoe, Henry VIII—sans wives—the laurel-crowned Roman. The Roman was accompanied by a flaxen, flat-bosomed, and rather extensively covered Cleopatra, and some of the other American planters and businessmen

by their wives, but they were far fewer, and the Creole belles evident
were of the class referred to by the upper-class Creoles as chacas:
shopgirls, artisans, grisettes.

The young Creole gentlemen were there in force, however, flirting
with the chaca girls as they'd never have flirted with the gently bred
ladies of their own station. Augustus Mayerling, who for all his exper-
tise with a saber seemed indeed to be a surprisingly peaceable soul,
had to step in two or three times to throw water on incipient blazes.
Other fencing masters were not so conscientious. There were noticeably more women than men present, at least in part because the
Creole gentlemen had a habit of disappearing down the discreetly
curtained passageway to the Salle d'Orléans next door, where, January
knew, the quadroon ball was in full swing. Occasionally, if there was a
lull in the general noise level, he could catch a drift of its music.

Philippe Decoudreau was on the cornet again. January winced.

He didn't hear them often, and less so as the evening progressed.
In addition to the din of the crowd, the hollow thudding of feet on
the suspended plank floor and the noise of the orchestra—augmented
for the evening by a guitar, two flutes, and a badly played clari-
nette—the clamor in the streets was clearly audible. The heavy curtains of olive-green velvet were hooped back and the windows open.
Maskers, Kaintucks, whores, sailors, and citizens out for a spree
thronged and paraded through the streets from gambling hall to caba-
ret to eating house, calling to one another, singing, blowing flour in
one anothers' faces, ringing cowbells, and clashing cymbals. There was
a feverish quality to the humid air. Fights and scuffles broke out
between the dances, sometimes lasting all the way out of the hall to
the checkroom where pistols, swords, and sword-canes had been de-
posited.

"Do you see Peralta?" asked January worriedly at one point, dab-
bing the sweat from his face and scanning the crowd. The press of
people raised the temperature of the room to an ovenlike stifle, a
circumstance that didn't seem to affect the dancers in the slightest
degree. Almost no breeze stirred from the long windows and the air
was heavy with the smells of perfume, pomade, and uncleaned costumes.

Hannibal, white with fatigue and face running with sweat, swept the room with his gaze, then shook his head. "Doesn't mean he isn't here," he pointed out. His hoarse, boyish voice was barely a thread. "He might be in the lobby—I went out there a few minutes ago, it's like a coaching inn at Christmas. Or he might be next door."

Or in Davis's gambling rooms up the street, thought January. *Or at some elegant private ball. Or riding back to Bayou Chien Mort tonight, to make sure no one comes asking awkward questions about his son.*

In the cathedral, where he'd gone to make his Lenten confession early and pray desperately for the success of his journey, January had been tormented by the conviction that Peralta would walk in and see him, recognize him, somehow know what his plans were. It irritated him that he should feel like a criminal in his search for the justice that the law should be giving him gratis. Confession and contrition and the ritual of the Mass had calmed his fears for a time, but as the evening progressed and Peralta did not make an appearance, like scurrying rats the fears returned.

The band occupied a dais set on the stage, and with the temporary floor slightly below even that level, January had a good view of the dancers. Dr. Soublet was there, arguing violently with another physician who seemed to think six pints of blood an excessive amount to abstract from a patient in a week.

Though the buffet tables were situated on the opposite side of the room from the windows, Henri Viellard—duly garbed as a sheep—seemed to have chosen gourmandise over fresh air; he patted his forehead repeatedly with a succession of fine linen handkerchiefs but refused to abandon proximity to the oysters, tartlets, meringues, and roulades. In his fluffy costume he bore a more than passing resemblance to a bespectacled meringue himself, with an apricot silk bow about his neck. His sisters, January noticed, were likewise clothed as fanciful animals: a swan, a rabbit, a cat, a mouse (that was the little one who looked like she'd escaped from the convent to attend), and something which after long study he and Hannibal agreed probably had to be a fish.

"Which I suppose makes Madame Viellard a farmer's wife," concluded January doubtfully.

"Or Mrs. Noah," pointed out Hannibal. "All she needs is a little boat under her arm."

He glimpsed both William Granger and Jean Bouille, moving with calculated exactness to remain as far as possible from one another while still occupying the same large room. As Uncle Bichet had remarked, Bouille's wife did seem to disappear up to the screened private theater boxes every time Bouille vanished down the passageway to the Salle next door. When the dance concluded and Granger and Bouille led their respective partners toward the buffet in courses that threatened to intersect, the master of ceremonies scurried to intercept Bouille before another disaster could occur.

While Monsieur Davis's eye was elsewhere, January rose from the piano and moved discreetly along the wall to the buffet. He didn't like the white look around Hannibal's mouth, or the way he had of leaning inconspicuously against the piano as he played. He looked bled out, the flesh around his eyes deeply marked with pain, and the watered laudanum, January suspected, was not doing him very much good. As he drew close to the buffet Mayerling caught his eye, signaled him to stay where he was, and wandered over himself to collect a glass of champagne and one of the strong molasses tafia, then strolled back up to the stage as January returned to his place at the piano.

"I wanted to thank you again for standing physician the other day," said the fencing master. "You behold your competition."

Soublet and his adversary had reached the shouting stage and were brandishing their canes: It was obviously only a matter of time until they named their friends.

"Maybe not being able to practice in this city is what the preachers call a blessing in disguise," said January.

"And a fairly thin disguise at that. You know Granger is now claiming that he deloped—fired into the air—and Bouille is hinting to everyone he thinks will listen that his opponent flinched aside at the last moment—in other words, dodged out of cowardice, surely one of the most foolish things to do under the circumstances since most pistols will throw one direction or the other, especially at fifty feet."

He nodded toward Bouille, deep in conversation with Monsieur

Davis, who was steering him in the direction of a group of Creole businessmen and their wives. "So now we can only hope to keep them apart for the evening. After tomorrow, of course, they will both be sober more of the time."

"Thompsonian dog!" screamed Dr. Soublet, his opponent evidently favoring the do-it-oneself herbalist school of that well-known Yankee doctor.

"Murderer!" shrieked the Thompsonian dog, and the two men fell upon each other in a welter of kicking, flailing canes, and profanity.

"Birds in their little nests agree," sighed Hannibal, draining the tafia,

> *"And 'tis a shameful sight*
> *When children of one family*
> *Fall out, and chide, and fight."*

Monsieur Davis and half a dozen others hustled the combatants from the room.

Mayerling remained where he was, shaking his head in a kind of amazement. Hannibal picked up his violin again, playing to cover the chatter of the crowd; the music was frail as honey candy, but with an edge to it like glass.

"I never saw the point of dueling, myself." January turned back to the keyboard. His hands followed the trail the violin set, a kind of automatic embellishment that could be done without thinking. "It might be different were I allowed to give challenges, or accept them, but I don't think so."

"Of course not," said the Prussian in surprise. "You have your music. You are an intelligent man, and an educated one. You are seldom bored. It is all from boredom, you know," he went on, looking out into the room again. "It is like the Kaintucks in the Swamp or the Irish on Tchoupitoulas Street. They have nothing to do, so they get into fights or look for reasons to get into fights. They are not so very different from the Creoles."

He shook his head wonderingly.

". . . It's not like she's got room to be so damn choosy," said a man's voice, beside one of the boxes on the stage. "If Arnaud sinned he must have had his reasons. No man whose wife is making him happy goes straying like that."

There was a murmur of agreement. January turned his head sharply, saw that it was the Jack of Diamonds, Charles-Louis Trepagier, and another man, shorter than he but with the same sturdy, powerful build. The shorter man wore the gaudy costume of what Lord Byron probably had conceived a Turkish pasha to look like, ballooning pistachio-colored trousers, a short vest of orange and green, an orange-and-green turban with a purple glass jewel on it the size of an American dollar. An orange mask hid his face, orange slippers his feet, a long purple silk sash that had clearly started its life as a lady's scarf wrapped two or three times around his waist.

"It isn't like she hasn't had offers," added another of the Trepagier clan resentfully. "Good ones, too—I don't mean trash like McGinty. She thinks she's too good . . ."

"Too good! That's a laugh!" The stranger threw back his head with a bitter bark. He leaned closer, lowering his voice but not nearly enough. "If the woman's turned you down it's because she's got a lover hidden somewhere. Has had, since she shut Arnaud out of her bed. I've even heard she's put on a mask and come dancing."

"At public balls?"

"Public balls, certainly," said the pasha. He nodded back over his shoulder toward the discreet doorway of the passage to the Salle. "And other places, maybe not so public."

"Sir . . ."

January hadn't even seen Mayerling move. The young fencing master slipped through the crowd like a bronze fish, a dangerous glitter of blue-and-black jewels like dragon scales, his big, pale hands resting folded on the gems of his belt buckle. Behind the modeled leather of his mask, his hazel eyes were suddenly deadly chill.

"I assume," said Mayerling, "that you are speaking third-hand gossip about someone whom none of you knows. Certainly no gentleman would bandy any woman's name so in a public place."

The Trepagier boys regarded him in alarmed silence. In his five years in New Orleans the Prussian had only fought three duels, but in each he had killed with such scientifically vicious dispatch, and such utter lack of mercy, as to discourage any further challenges. The wolf-pale eyes traveled from their clothing to their faces, clearly recognizing, clearly identifying.

"This is fortunate, since I only duel with gentlemen," Mayerling went on quietly. He turned to regard the pasha in green. "Should I happen to find," he said, as if he could see the face behind the garish satin of the mask, "that a woman's name is being spoken by those whose blood would not dishonor my sword, then of course, as a gentleman, I should have no choice but to avenge that lady's honor and put a halt to that gossip in whatever way seemed best to me."

The yellow gaze swept them like a backhand cut. There was no cruelty in it, only a chill and terrifying strength. January could almost see the line of blood it left.

"I trust that I make myself clear?"

The pasha opened his mouth to speak. The Jack of Diamonds reached out, put a hand on his pink silk arm. To Mayerling, he said, "It was, of course, a woman of the lower classes of whom we spoke, a chaca shopkeeper who betrayed her husband, nothing more."

"Even so," said Mayerling softly. "Such talk disturbs me. Perhaps you should study to ape gentlemen a little more closely—whoever you are."

None of them replied. Mayerling waited for a moment, giving them time to declare themselves gentlemen and offended, then turned his back and vanished into the crowd.

January leaned over, and touched Uncle Bichet on the shoulder. "Who was that?" he asked, the old man looked at him in some surprise.

"Just a couple of the Trepagier boys."

"No—with them."

The cellist turned his head to look, but the pasha was even then vanishing through the curtained doorway that led to the Salle d'Orléans, deep in conversation with the purple pirate.

The Trepagier brothers—there were at least four of them, two of whom were married and none of whom were boys at all—were bullying and insulting a much younger man who had dared flirt with a flustered and feathered damsel garbed as a gypsy, evidently secure in the knowledge that he would not dare challenge them, and they were correct.

Uncle Bichet shook his head, and glanced at the program card. "Those lazy folks been standing long enough," he said, and January turned, unwillingly, back to his music.

Sally, he thought. Whoever the green pasha was, he had to have spoken with the runaway servant girl Sally. Or he recognized Madame Trepagier at the ball Thursday night, either by her movement, stance, and voice—as he himself had done—or because she'd worn that silly Indian costume somewhere before.

And if that were the case, thought January with sudden bitterness, *for a man attending a quadroon ball he had a lot of nerve criticizing a woman he recognized there.*

The dancing lasted until nearly dawn. Technically Lent began at midnight, but there was no diminution of champagne, tafia, gumbo or pâté, though having made his confession that afternoon January abstained all evening even when the opportunity presented itself. Eventually Xavier Peralta made his appearance, clothed in the red robe and scepter of a king with his cousin the chief of police still at his side. The waltzes and quadrilles grew wilder as the more respectable ladies took their departure, the fights and jostling more frequent. Everyone seemed determined to extract the final drops of pleasure from the Carnival season, to dance the soles off their shoes, to dally on the balconies above the torchlit river of noise surging along Rue Orléans.

Also, as the night wore on, more and more of the wealthier men disappeared for longer and longer periods of time. The Creole belles, though perhaps not of the highest society, stood abandoned along the wall, whispering among themselves and pretending not to care. Most of them, January suspected, would stop at home only long enough to wash off their rouge before attending early services in the cathedral. The American women whose husbands were still in attendance whispered about the half dozen or so whose men had "stepped out for a bit of air." Most of them appeared and disappeared a number of times, but the Roman soldier stayed gone. The deserted Cleopatra involved herself in an animated discussion with several other ladies but kept an eye on the door, and when the errant Roman at last returned, there was promise of bitter acrimony in her greeting.

They bring it on themselves, January thought, but he knew it wasn't that easy. Like everything else about New Orleans, it was a bittersweet tangle, and you could not run from it without leaving pieces of your torn-out heart behind.

No wonder everyone tried to dance and be gay, he thought, as he walked toward the livery stable in the tepid mists of predawn. Costumed maskers still reeled along the banquettes of Rue Orléans, and from every tavern music could be heard, brassy street bands and thumping drums. Under the flicker of the street lamps whooping Kaintucks pursued masked and laughing prostitutes. The air, thick with the smell of the river, was also weighed with wine and whisky and tobacco and cheap perfume.

He collected his rented horse from a sleepy stablehand and rode down to the levee, where the flatboat captain he'd contracted yesterday waited for him in the white ocean of mist that rose from the river. The river itself was very still, the levees on either side rising like ridges of mountains from the thinning vapors. Behind them in the last starlight the town dozed, exhausted at last.

There was only so much—deception financial and romantic, the monstrosity of slavery, and the waiting horrors of yellow fever—that could be masked behind the bright scrim of music, the taste of coffee and gumbo, the shimmer of the moonlight.

Mardi Gras was done. The greedy consumption of the last good food, the draining of the last of the wine, a final, wild coupling in the darkness before the penitential death of Lent.

He watched the dark shore of the west bank approaching with terror in his heart.

S I X T E E N

Morning found him eight miles from the city, riding west along the levee with the rank trees and undergrowth of the batture at the foot of the slope on his left, the dark brown earth of fields on his right. In places they were rank with winter weeds, but as the sun first gilded, then cleared the writhing stringers of the Gulf clouds, groups of slaves could be seen threading their way along the paths, hoes on their shoulders, bare feet swirling the ground mists. Once a white man called to him in slurry New Orleans French and asked to see his papers, but when January produced them—and a receipt from Desdunes's Livery, to prove he hadn't stolen the horse—the patroller seemed to lose interest and barely gave them a glance.

The man had to tuck his whip under his arm to take the papers. Down in the field below, the workers sang as they hoed, a steady-paced song in almost incomprehensible gombo, clearing the land for the new crop of cane.

January remembered that song from the plantation on which he had been born.

Since he had been back, he had been afraid to leave New Orleans, fearing for his liberty—fearing, too, the sight of the changes that had taken place as Americans took control of the land and that the whites would see him as a slave and perhaps make him one again. The smell of the earth and the sweat of the workers; the beat of the morning sun on the backs of his hands and the twitterings of birds in the oaks that surrounded the fields; the occasional drift, like pockets of lingering mist, of the field songs brought back to him his own days of slavery, of childhood, of innocence, a terrible mingling of sweetness and pain.

For thirty years, like Livia, he had pretended it wasn't he who'd been a slave. Now it came to him, as it hadn't in years, that he never knew what had become of his father.

Or of that child, he thought—that little boy running through the cane fields before first light or lying on the batture picking voice from voice in the chorus of the frogs when the sun went down.

For a time it seemed to him that he still didn't know.

He stopped frequently to rest the horse, knowing that there was no chance of trading for a fresh one between the city and Bayou Chien Mort. He cut overland to avoid the wide loop of the river past McDonoughville, passed through swampy woods of cypress and hickory that hummed and creaked with insect life in the dense sun of the forenoon. The land here was soggy and crossed with marshes and bayous like green-brown glass under hushed but wakeful trees. Some time after noon he bought a bowl of gumbo and half a pone of corn bread for a picayune from a trapper whose cabin lay in a clearing among the marshes. The house was barely a shack and only with difficulty distinguishable from the byre that sheltered the single cow and the litter of pigs, but he knew, by the man's eyes, that had he asked to come in he would have been denied. They were Spanish, like the *isleños* in the Terre des Boeufs to the south, and barely understood his French. From around a corner of the house half a dozen filthy, skinny children watched him, but no one said a word.

Bayou Chien Mort itself lay some twenty-five miles southeast of New Orleans, in Plaquemines Parish, country that was still largely French where it was anything at all. In a way that made him feel more comfortable, for the small farmers and trappers of the backwoods here were less likely to kidnap a black man and sell him as a slave. The enterprise would have required far too much energy. He'd seen them in the market in New Orleans, simply clothed in homespun cotton striped red and blue, abysmally poor and surrounded by swarms of children who all seemed to bear names like Nono and Vévé and Bibi, cheerfully selling powdered filé and alligator hides and going away again without bothering, like the Americans did, to sample the delights of the big city. Even more than the Creoles, who despised them, these primitive trappers belonged to a world of their own, cut off from the rest of the world until even their language was almost obscure.

Nevertheless he felt safer among them than he would have in the more American north or west, though no black man traveling alone was truly safe. Even when he picked up the course of the river again he kept his distance from it, holding to a muddy trace through the silent stillness of the forest that lay behind the plantations. The river was far too heavily traveled for comfort, and the keelboat men—Nahum Shagrue and his spiritual kin—were only a step above river pirates themselves and sometimes not even that.

He had hoped to stop and sleep at the heat of noon, but the execrable nature of the forest road slowed his progress, and as the sun's slant grew steeper he dared not halt for more than the hour or so needed from time to time to rest his horse. Once or twice he dozed after foddering the animal on the oats he'd brought—save for four hours after Hermann's ball he had not done more than nap in almost two days—but every time the wind brought him the hoot of a steamboat on the river he'd jerk awake in a sweat, fearing Xavier Peralta had canceled all the family breakfasts and Ash Wednesday dinners to hasten to his exiled son.

An hour or two before sunset he reached Chien Mort. He came at it from behind, seeing light where the trees thinned, and then beyond that the slightly mounded rows of a cleared field, short trenches cut along the centers of the rows to receive the half-fermented stalks of last year's cane.

They were well ahead on their work, he thought. According to his mother, Peralta usually remained at his chief residence—Alhambra—on Lake Pontchartrain. He must have an efficient overseer here.

Keeping to the woods, he rode along the edges of the cleared land to within sight of the house, identifying various outbuildings, landmarks, fields, and trying to memorize them as he had once memorized landmarks as a child. If anything went wrong he might need to orient himself in a hurry, and in the dark. There were fields of second-crop cane, just beginning to sprout bristles of dark, striped stalks—Batavia cane, which hadn't even been introduced in the country when he was a child—and fields whose turned earth told him by its pattern that it would soon be planted in corn.

Past those lay the levee, with its thick line of sycamores. A little band of woodland hid the home place from him, but he could see the brick dome and tower of the refinery, and beyond it, barely glimpsed past an orchard, the whitewashed wooden cabins of the slaves. The house itself and the overseer's cottage, the dovecotes and smokehouses and stables, all lay hidden among the darkness of gray-bearded oaks.

He clucked softly to the horse and moved along.

Between the cane fields and the corn lay a ridge of land, thick with nettles and peppergrass. Two or three sycamores stood on it, left, January guessed, to provide shade to the workers when they stopped for nooning.

He reined around, picking his way along the edge of the cleared ground until he'd worked back to the trace once more. A few miles earlier he had seen another path leading back into the woods and smelled smoke among the trees where the land grew boggy. Patient retracing led him to the place again, and though it was farther from the Peralta fields than he liked, he didn't know the area and this was his best hope. The path was a seldom-used one and led into swamp and hackberry thickets along Bayou Chien Mort itself, but as the afternoon was dimming he found what he sought: a small house constructed of mud, moss, and cypress planks, its gallery overlooking the still water of a narrow bayou, its yard swarming with black-eyed, unkempt, barefoot children, descendants of Canadian French exiled here almost a hundred years earlier.

"Papa, he up the bayou, him," explained the oldest girl to January's question. The smoke he'd smelled an hour ago had been from her cook fire, the kitchen being also the main room of the little house, rich with the smells of onion, pepper, and crawfish. "But Val, he take a message to Peralta, if you want."

Val—fetched from the shed where he was scraping muskrat hides—proved to be fourteen, with black hair and the strange pale gray-green eyes the Acadians sometimes had. All the children grouped around the kitchen table while January wrote his message, marveling either at the fact that a black man could write or at the miracle of literacy itself; then they sat on the gallery with him while he ate some of the jambalaya the girl had been cooking ("It ain't sat long enough to be real good," the girl said.), and he left them marveling over the coins he gave them as he went on his way.

They reminded him of Ayasha's description of the Moroccan peasants who lived on the edge of the desert: *They know their prayers,* she had said, *and how to tell genuine coin from the most convincing counterfeit. And that is all.*

He smiled. He wondered what she would have made of all this: the Spanish woodcutters, the Italian ice-cream vendors in the market, the strange, tiny colony of Tockos in the deep Delta who fished for oysters and sang Greek songs and occasionally drowned themselves when the moon was full, the Germans and the degraded remnants of the Choctaw and Natchez nations. There was supposed to be a colony of Chinese somewhere on the Algiers bank of the river.

And Africans, of course.

In the shifty dimness of twilight he sought out a place to hide the horse. He hadn't dared ask the children about such a thing directly, having represented himself as a man in too much of a hurry, and going in the wrong direction, to stop at the plantation himself. But he'd gathered that "Ti Margaux, up the bayou," had recently died, and there was no one occupying his house or barns. In the jungly stillness of the swamps it was anybody's guess which way "up the bayou" was—bayous flowed sometimes one way, sometimes another, and frequently lay eerily still under the dense green canopy of cypress and moss—but after considerable searching and backtracking January located the place, raised on stilts and built, like most of these small houses, of mud and cypress planks.

Already neighbors and family had carried away everything of any conceivable value, including about half the planks of its gallery roof. The barn had been likewise stripped, but its doors remained, at least.

In gathering darkness January found a holey and broken bucket whose chinks, once stopped with moss, didn't leak too badly while he carried up water for the horse. He rubbed the animal down, gave it fodder, and latched the door behind him, praying that no neighbors would be by to glean behind the earlier reapers. He didn't think so. The place looked comprehensively sacked.

Bedroll on his shoulder and Minou's kid gloves in his pocket, he set off once more for Chien Mort.

"Hey, who dat, settin' out in the dark?"

His mother—or any of his schoolmasters—would have flayed him alive. He'd said to Olympe she'd got him talking as he used to when he was a child, and it was startling how easily his tongue burred *j*s into *z*s, how the ends of words trailed away into nothing and all the cases slurred into that single all-purpose *l*.

The old black, sitting on the doorstep of his cabin and playing a sort of reed panpipe, looked up and grinned toothlessly by the light of the few pine-knot torches still burning. "Who dat, sneakin' out of the fields like a whipsnake lookin' for rats?"

He had followed the music in from the fields, guided through the darkening cane rows toward the whitewashed line of cabins behind the big house: panpipes, a banjo, the rattle of bones. Lively music, dancing music, weird and pagan in the darkness: the bamboula, the counjaille, the pilé chactas. It was a music that brought back to him again that hurt of nostalgia and grief, memories of sitting on the plank step of a slave cabin as the old man was sitting—as three or four children were still sitting a few cabins down the way—watching the fire-gilded faces of men and women swaying in the darkness, dancing loose the ache of work in their muscles, dancing to find the only freedom their hearts could have.

The dancing was over now, but only just. A man on the step of the next cabin was still tinkering songs on his banjo, quiet songs now, a fragment of a jig Hannibal sometimes fiddled, the trace of an opera air. Young women were playing eyes with young men. Only a few crickets could be heard this early in the year. The frogs were croaking below the levee beyond the big house. He recalled the names he'd given their voices as a child: Monsieur Gik, Monsieur Big Dark, little Mamzelle Didi. It was cool enough that the fire someone had built in the widening of the street felt good.

"Just a handful of leaves, blowin' over the ground," smiled January, as the old man moved aside to let him sit. "And damn glad to hear a little music."

"You headin' for the woods?" asked the man with the banjo, a euphemistic way of asking if he were a runaway.

"Well, let's just say I'm headin' away from town." January gave him a wink. "I'm on my way down to Grand Isle, see my woman and my children. Figured what with balls and parties and everybody in town runnin' around in masks and too drunk to tell who's who even without, nobody's gonna even know I'm gone till I'm back."

"I hear you there," said a stout, sweet-faced young woman whose calico dress and bright-colored head scarf identified her immediately as one of Peralta's hastily transplanted town house servants.

"You been up to New Orleans?" asked January, with innocent surprise.

And got the whole story.

In pieces, and with digressions concerning the conduct of neighboring servants and the husbands, wives, boyfriends, and girlfriends of the town house staff, it was this: Galen Peralta had met the mistress of Arnaud Trepagier, his fellow pupil at the swordsmanship academy of Augustus Mayerling, and had fallen desperately in love. The boy's father had taken him to Blue Ribbon Balls in an attempt to interest him in some other young sang mêlé, but it was of no use.

"And she wasn't pushin' him away much, neither," added the woman, who turned out to be Honey, the Peralta household cook.

"Pushin' with one hand and makin' bedroom eyes while she did it," added another woman, the wrinkles of advancing age beginning to line her strong-chinned face. "Just as well Arnaud Trepagier came down with the cholera like he did, or there woulda been trouble." She spoke with malicious satisfaction in her voice and spite in her eyes, for which January couldn't blame her. After living in New Orleans for most, if not all, of her adult life, exile to a backwater plantation at a moment's notice had to be galling, disorienting, and terrifying.

Angelique went into mourning.

("Some mourning," sniffed the elderly maid. "I seen more modest dresses paradin' up and down Gallatin Street." "Well, she did wear black," amended the kinder Honey. "I seen her in the market.")

Michie Galen sent her notes. Michie Xavier said it wasn't proper. Michie Galen didn't care. He was seventeen and in love.

("Lord, a man doesn't need to be seventeen to make a damn fool of himself over a girl," grinned a woman on another doorstep, a wrapped bundle of baby sleeping at her bare breast and a four-year-old boy, sleeping also, cradled against her other side. Her field-hand husband, sitting beside her, gave her a hard nudge with his elbow and a smile with his eyes. Everybody except January had obviously heard this story already, but it was new enough to still have bright edges of interest in the telling.)

Michie Galen begged his father to speak to Madame Dreuze. They went to the Mardi Gras quadroon ball. "First thing anybody hear about it, Michie Xavier come in when it's near light, which is late for him. He ain't one to stay out howlin' at the mornin' star. He ask, has Michie Galen come in? We say no, and just then there's knockin' at the gate, and Charles, he go open it, Michie Xavier right on his heels and most of the rest of us followin' after. And in the light of the street lamps we see Michie Galen, drunk as a wheelbarrow and hangin' on the side of the gate, with his mask hanging off, and his face all scratched up, scratched deep an' bleedin'."

January was silent, but he felt exactly as he had when, as a child, he'd gone hunting with a sling and stones and seen a squirrel drop off a branch under a clean and perfect hit.

Angelique's face returned to him—the enigmatic cat face, surrounded by lace and jewels—and that scornful, razor-edged voice saying *How dare you lay a hand on me?* Saying it for the second time, with the tones exact as music well rehearsed.

The fire fell in upon itself with a silky rustle. The field hands gathered close, to hear the end of the tale. Someone glanced nervously along the street, in the direction of the overseer's cottage, but from the dark windows came no sound.

"Michie Xavier and Michie Galen just stand there for a minute, starin' at each other," the cook went on. "Then Michie Xavier turn to us and say, real quiet, 'Shut the gate now, Charles. And don't you open it tomorrow mornin'. Honey, we got enough food in the kitchen for meals for a day without goin' out to the market?' Ain't nobody said what happened, but I figure it, Michie Galen got drunk and in a to-do with some low-down woman, and his pa didn't want word of it gettin' out to Rosalie Delaporte that he's engaged to."

"To Thierry Delaporte, you mean," put in a small, dignified, middle-aged man whose rough clothing and coarse moccasins were alike new and unsettled on his thin frame. There were bandages on two of his fingers. Charles, the Peralta butler, January guessed. Put to some lesser task for the nonce, since Galen Peralta, staying at the big house here alone, would scarcely need the formality of more than a cook and a maid to keep the place clean. "Rosalie Delaporte's pa," he added, to January, by way of explanation. "He has a big plantation out in Saint Charles Parish, and they been talkin' of marryin' his girl for years."

"It'll be years, if Michie Galen takes up with that Angelique gal," retorted the maid. "I hear she pure poison."

"Come mornin'," Honey went on, after a brief digression on the family ties between the Peraltas, the Delaportes, the Tremouilles, and the Bringiers, "Michie Xavier sends Momo over there"—she pointed to a young man who was quite clearly making himself at home with the local girls—"up to Alhambra by the lake with a message, askin' for Tia Zozo the cook there and people to be butler and maid and coachman and all, to take our places so we could come down here for a couple weeks, so there'd be no blabbin'."

"Couple weeks, you think?" said the maid bitterly. "Whether word gets out now or later, it'll still make trouble for him and that Delaporte girl his pa's so set on him marryin'. You dreamin', girl. We gonna be here a long time."

There was smoldering rage in her eyes.

January thought about the miles of swamp and bayou and road

he'd ridden over, the utter isolation of this place. This woman—all of the house servants—had been taken from their friends, from husbands or lovers, from the place they knew, literally at a day's notice and for what appeared to them to be sheer caprice. He saw the grief come into Honey's eyes, and the fat woman looked away.

"Michie Xavier wouldn't do that to us, Anne," said Charles gently. "I know him. I worked in his house forty years. He said to me, as we were gettin' in the wagon, that we'd all be back soon."

"Ha! So where is he?"

"On his way, most like. He had to stay around for Ash Wednesday, to go to church at the cathedral, and have fish supper at the Bringiers'. Now he'll be on his way, to see Michie Galen, if nuthin' else."

"Besides," pointed out January, remembering his own childhood terror of leaving Bellefleur Plantation for the city, "who's he got cookin' for him and brushin' his clothes? If you all are here clearin' cane fields, what are those folk from Alhambra up there doin' in place of you? He'll get sick of wrinkly shirts and dust bunnies under his desk in no time."

The maid Anne did not look convinced, but Honey smiled gratefully. The talk ran on a little longer, about the death of Xavier's first wife in childbed with the boy Galen, and his second in the yellow fever four years ago. There were evidently three little girls as well. Every detail of the family's life and movements were aired—January had almost forgotten how much house servants knew about their masters' business. He'd been too young to care much during his own days in the quarters, though it was one of the maids who'd kept him posted on the progress of his mother's sale. Later, Livia had tried to keep him separate from the slave children in the French town, though with poor success. He remembered, too, Olympe's stories about how the voodoo doctors and voodoo queens gathered information from subtle, far-flung networks of informers, learning everything about who went where and for what purposes about people who were totally unaware of how closely they were observed.

At length the old man with the panpipe said, "Little Dog-Star risin'. Ol' Uhrquahr look out his window and still see fire here, he be out. Uhrquahr the overseer," he explained to January. "I'd tell you spread your blanket here in one of the cabins, but Uhrquahr, he mean. Better not chance it."

"Thank you kindly," said January. "Fire and a chance to talk was what I needed, and to set a spell. I'll be movin' on before it gets light."

It had been a long time, he thought, striding quietly through the starlit fields toward the cornfield and its sycamores, since he'd sat listening to that kind of talk, the lazy back-and-forth of the field hands and yard servants as they wound down for sleep. It was not that he missed that life, though he knew whites who would claim he did, in his heart of hearts. The anxiety, dread, and helplessness that were the underpinning of those days were too strong, even yet, in his memory. The whites were fools who said that slaves enjoyed their slavery, much less that they "liked a strong hand." Like most people they got along as best they could, taking happiness where and how they found it, in the knowledge that even that could be taken away at some white man's whim.

What he had missed, without being aware of it, was the beauty that had slipped in between the bars of that childhood cage: the soft chill of the spring evening, the smell of the newly turned earth. The rattle of the bamboula in the darkness and the friendliness of those companions in misfortune.

That he had never had his mother's love, he had known at the time. But he had had his father's, and every woman on Bellefleur had been his aunt. He had not realized how deeply he had missed that feeling. Having been raised in so close-knit a community—first on Bellefleur and later in the French town—it was no wonder he yearned for it all the years he had been in Paris.

No wonder, he thought, that when he had been wounded unto death in his heart, it was to that community he returned. *It's here that I belong,* he thought, without even a sensation of surprise. *Not Europe. Not Paris. Not Africa. Here among these no-longer-Africans, not-really-French.*

And Nahum Shagrue?

It was a riddle he couldn't answer.

Behind him he heard far-off voices, raised in one last song, like the voices of ghosts in the dark.

"Misery led this black to the woods,
Tell my master I died in the woods."

The gibbous moon stood high above the trees. As he lay in his blanket under the sycamores, telling over his rosary and watching the drift of clouds come and go by the wan light of muzzy stars, Paris seemed infinities distant. In Paris, he wondered if Ayasha had ever felt that way about Algiers.

SEVENTEEN

From the sycamores, he could see Galen Peralta coming across the cane fields in the clear gray-pink of first light.

The rise of the unplowed ground, slight though it was, gave him a clear view in all directions, thankfully unimpeded by the cane that by autumn would be tall enough to conceal an army. Smoke drifted from the kitchen buildings between the big house and the overseer's cottage, though the morning was warming and there was none from cottage, cabins, or house. Far on the river, the whistle of a steamboat floated in the thick stillness of morning. Conceivably Peralta Père could have left the city as late as midnight last night, in which case he would be arriving any minute.

January tried his best to recall if he'd heard a boat last night. He didn't think so, but so taken up had he been with what the servants had to tell, he had forgotten to listen. The currents below the city were swift, and a downriver boat wouldn't need to make speed by sticking to the tortuous channels near the shore. The moon was waxing. He'd heard there were pilots who'd travel on moonless nights. He supposed that in sufficiently desperate circumstances he'd even pay to ride with one.

Narrowing his eyes, he squinted into the dove-colored light. At least he hoped that was Galen.

The boy came nearer. On foot, of course, to avoid questions about taking a horse out so early. The reedy, rather delicate frame was the one he recognized from the Salle d'Orléans, worlds different from the stocky, straight-backed form of Peralta Père. Under a wide-brimmed hat, the face was shadowed, but the man did not move with the confident stride of an overseer.

January tried to calm the pounding of his heart. The steamboat wouldn't come in for some time yet. He had time to get out, to get clear.

He didn't have to say much to this boy, but he had to see him face-to-face, to verify—and to be able to testify—about what he had been told.

After a week, the scratches were still livid, though fading. In another week they'd be gone. The marks were clearly the rakes of a woman's nails, cheekbone to chin, both sides; scabbed in places, and in others clear pink lines across the delicate, pale brown skin that still retained the porcelain quality of a child's. Galen squinted up at him from under the brim of his wide hat, the first time January had seen him up close.

Large, clear blue eyes, and an almost invisible blond mustache clinging ridiculously to the short upper lip. Fair hair bleached fairer by the sun at its tips. Blue smudges marked his eyes, and strain and grief and sleepless nights had put lines around his mouth.

January had worked the night shift at the Hôtel Dieu too long to think it impossible, or even unlikely, that a man who would strangle a woman he loved in a fit of rage would afterward lie awake weeping for her at night. He had seen men howling with tears and attempting to cut their own wrists over the bodies of wives or lovers they had themselves disemboweled with broken bottles. And for all that she had the skin of a white woman, Angelique was colored, lesser in the eyes of the law and perhaps in her lover's eyes as well.

Perhaps that was what hurt him so much.

"Yuh-yuh-you have s-something for me?"

"Yes, sir." January removed his soft cap and deliberately made his accent as backstreet as possible. "M'am Dreuze sent this." He produced the clean bandanna from his jacket pocket, in which were wrapped Dominique's gloves.

The boy unwrapped them, stood looking down at them, and January could see the muscles of his jaw harden with the effort to command himself.

Unlike Charles-Louis Trepagier, this was not a young man who accepted violence casually, not even the violence of his own nature. January wondered what Xavier Peralta had said to his son that first dawn, after the servants were dismissed.

"D-did she . . ." He swallowed, and tried again. "D-did she s-send anything else?"

"No, sir."

The boy looked up again, fighting hard not to shed tears in the presence of a stranger and a black man at that. "I s-see." The downy brows pulled together for a moment, puzzling. At his height, January knew he was difficult to mistake, and he'd been one of the few in the building that night who wasn't masked.

They'd passed within twelve inches of each other in the doorway of the retiring room.

All of Galen's mind, all his heart, had been centered on that white, glittering Fata Morgana laughing at him in the candle-light . . . but it was just possible that he remembered.

Panic went through him like a douse of ice water and he slumped his shoulders a little and scratched his chin. He'd found it was true also that many whites looked less closely at blacks or colored whom they did not know. "But she say, deliver 'em into your own hand, not to nobody else, so that's what I do." Anything not to sound like someone who would be in the ballroom that night. "You got a message for me to take back to her?"

He could have cut out his tongue a moment later. If Galen said, *Yes, wait here for two hours while I go back to the house and write one,* the odds of Xavier Peralta returning in the meantime would be hideously multiplied. And of course a white would think nothing of telling him to wait half the morning. It would in any case cost him precious time to backtrack to where he'd hidden the horse.

The thought that it might have been stolen flashed across his mind and turned him sick. On foot he'd have no chance at all in this country.

A steamboat could cover the thirty miles from the city in five or six hours, depending on how many stops it had to make and what cargo had to be unloaded at any one of them. If Peralta had left at midnight . . .

"N-no," said Galen. "N-no, it's all right." He looked very young. He wrapped the gloves in the bandanna again, and slipped it into the pocket of his coarse tweed jacket. From his trouser pocket he took a Mexican silver dollar, which he put in January's hand. "Thank y-you. If you'd c-care to come back to the house they'll give you s-something in the kitchen."

"If it's all right with you, sir, I'll be gettin' on." He touched his cap brim politely. "M'am Dreuze, she gave me that 'cos she knew I was headin' down to Grand Isle to see my wife, but it's best I be on my road. Thank you kindly, though."

The excuse sounded hideously lame—what traveler would pass up the chance for free food and a chance to gossip at the plantation kitchen?—but Galen was clearly too shaken to notice any discrepancy. He turned back toward the house without a word, the last of the ground mist dissolving around his feet, his hand moving a little in his pocket, caressing the gloves.

Minou's gloves.

January felt a little ashamed of himself.

He strangled that woman whose body you found, he told himself. *And he's trying to shift the blame onto you. Passing off a souvenir d'amour that actually belonged to your sister is the least of what he deserves.*

It was difficult to say, however, what it was that Galen Peralta did deserve.

Justice, he thought. *Only justice. But we all of us deserve that.*

The slaves were emerging from the street between the cabins, singing softly in the dawn, as January picked his way along the packed trail between the fields, headed for the woods like a fox for its earth.

It was years since January had traveled in rough country. Even as a child, he'd never formally learned woodcraft, only such that every country-raised slave knew: three sticks in a triangle, pointing back the way you came, blazes on tree trunks, watch your feet and legs, and be careful around anything a snake could bask on or hide under. The day was warm with the new warmth of the Louisiana spring, a damp, debilitating heat unlike the hottest days he had known in Paris. Among the oak and sweet gum woods the air felt dense, breathless, and its weight seemed to increase as he went. He tried to keep the brighter daylight beyond the thinning trees to his left, skirting the cane fields without losing sight of them, for he knew how easy it would be to lose his bearings completely in those endless woods.

Distantly, like the sound of wind around the eaves at night, the singing from the fields still came to him.

> *Little ones without father,*
> *Little ones without mother,*
> *What do you do to earn money?*
> *The river we cross for wild berries to search,*
> *We follow the bayous a-fishing for perch,*
> *And that's how we earn money.*

Mechanically his trained mind analyzed the eerie, descending scale, the loose embellishments of the rhythm, and the meandering syncopation of implied drums, but the song whispered to something deeper in his heart. Like the calinda, it had nothing to do with Schubert and Rossini, but its power called his name nonetheless.

A warbler sang in a thicket of hackberry. Farther off, a buzzard cried.

Then stillness.

Silence.

January halted, listening, wondering if the winds had shifted over. Far off he heard the alto hoot of a steamboat.

The cane fields lay between him and the river. The singing had ceased.

Something tightened, a knot behind his sternum, and he quickened his pace, trying not to run, for running would leave more sign and put him in danger of tripping, a serious matter in the leaves and fallen branches underfoot. If he ran, he would very likely lose his way.

In his mind he could see a horseman—two horsemen, perhaps— riding out from the big house, waving for the overseer *(Uhrquahr, he mean . . .),* the workers silent as they watched. . . .

Or maybe it was just that someone was getting a talking-to. That would be enough to stop the singing, for as long as it lasted. He strained his ears, but the singing did not resume.

He moved on, quicker now, trying to remember the landmarks. They'd looked different in last night's gathering darkness from the way they had in the afternoon, and far different now, coming back the other way. He found one of his own trail markers near a red oak veiled in Spanish moss like a mourning widow, and had no recollection whatsoever of the place. He knocked the sticks flying as he moved on. How soon would it be, he wondered, before they organized to follow?

At Bellefleur when he was six one of the field hands had run away. He remembered how the overseer had called for men to hunt, and the men had gathered. There had been more white men in the posse from neighboring plantations, since Bellefleur, close to New Orleans, had not been nearly as isolated as Chien Mort, but it was planting time and few could be spared. Most of the hunting had been done—and done willingly—by the runaway's fellow slaves.

He'd as much as told them he was a runaway. And he was no kin nor friend of theirs. For a break from the monotony of clearing the fields, of course they'd follow.

Rain started, thin and steady. It would cover his scent if they were using dogs but made tracks likelier in soft ground, and it further obscured the landmarks. A respectable music master in Paris, he'd worn boots for sixteen years, and Livia had seen to it in the years before that that he'd gone shod like a respectable colored, not barefoot like a black. Though his boots would leave a sharper track he didn't dare take them off and try to flee barefoot.

Around him the woods grew thicker and the ground boggy, cypresses rising ghostly among the oaks. It was farther than he had thought to the small tributary bayou he'd followed to old Ti Margaux's shack. His clothes grew leaden on his back and dragged at his limbs. His mind, always too active, conjured the picture of that exhausted, hag-ridden young man coming back to the whitewashed plantation house to meet his father standing on the threshold, newly returned from the steamboat landing.

Who brought you those gloves?

A b-big n-nigger from town.

And you let him see you? You let anyone from town see your face?

He thought about the girl Sally, simply walking away from Les Saules. As the cook Claire had remarked, it was only an hour to the American streetcar line. Out here he'd have a long way to run before he came to safety.

He came through trees and found himself facing water he'd never seen before, jewel green with duckweed and scaled over with the expanding rings of water drops in the rain. Cypress like old gray gods in rags crowded along its edge, pale against the bright green of the pines behind them. In the water itself their knobby knees rose up like wading children sent ahead to scout the shallows. A turtle blinked at him from a log.

Thank God the alligators are still sleeping this time of year, he thought, turning back on his own tracks, casting around for the blaze he'd left—he thought he'd left—hereabouts. The water in front of him might be the bayou along which Ti Margaux had his broken-down house, or might be a tributary of it, or might lead somewhere else altogether. The rain came harder, rustling in the leaves of the live oaks, the needles of the pines. By the water the air was cool, but in the trees again, even the rain didn't seem to affect the damp heat, only keep him from hearing the sounds of pursuit. He stumbled in a tangle of wild azalea, and very suddenly, found himself face-to-face with a young black man in the coarse trousers of a field hand, a club in his hand.

"Here he is!" shouted the man. "Here he—"

January covered the distance between them in two long strides, wrested the club from the hunter—who was too surprised at being attacked, instead of fled, to use it—and cracked him a hard blow across the side of the head. The young man went sprawling, stunned, and January sprinted in the direction he thought he'd been going immediately before the encounter. The rain pelted harder around him, blurring the green-on-green-on-green of water and vegetation into a confusing monochrome.

He turned toward the thicker growth along the water, but voices were calling out from the high ground, so he knew he couldn't go to earth. Instead he veered for the high ground himself, where the water ash and cypress and palmetto gave place to loblolly pine that killed most undergrowth with its needles. His long legs pumped, his body settling into its stride. He was tall, but he hadn't run in years, and his boots were heavy on his feet. Too many years, he thought, as his breath burned suddenly in his lungs. Those boys back there would be young, and fit.

He skidded, wove, plunged back toward the water again. Something gray caught his eye, and he saw that it was the old house of the deceased Ti Margaux, impossibly on the other side of the water. He had no idea how he'd gotten himself turned around, but the place was unmistakable. For a moment he considered lying low and letting them run past, but they'd see the house as well, know he'd head there. The snakes would be sleeping in winter, like the gators—*Please God, let the snakes be still sleeping!* Then he pulled off his coat and plunged into the bayou.

It wasn't wide—twelve or fifteen feet—nor particularly deep. He only had to strike out and swim for a stroke or two, holding the coat and his papers aloft, then his boots were slushing thickly in unspeakable mud and a tangle of alligator weed that dragged at him like steel nets. Underwater leaves slit at his thighs and sides as he dragged himself ashore, stumbled up the slope, dragged open the door of the old barn and caught up the bridle, remembering to work evenly and without haste as he coaxed the bit into the horse's mouth, buckled chin strap and band. He flung himself, dripping, onto the horse's back without benefit of saddle and kicked the animal forward out the barn door at a gallop.

Outside there was only a tangle of cypress and red oak, buckler fern and butterweed and creeper slowing the horse's stride. January ducked, keeping his head down under the low-hanging branches, wet moss trailing over his back as he tried to find the narrow trace that had led him here.

Then men were on him, springing out of the jungles of verdure, black, half-naked, armed with clubs and yelling with the hunt. January drove his heels into his mount's sides but hands were already dragging at the bridle, at his legs, pulling the panicking horse down and dragging him off. He swung with his club and felt it connect, but blows rained on his shoulders, stunning him. He felt his own makeshift weapon ripped from his hands, then he was pinned, still struggling, to the ground.

A white man's voice said, "Let him up."

They did, still holding his arms, crowding close around him, the rain not quite washing the rank smell of his own sweat or theirs or the swamp from him.

Three white men stood on the slightly higher ground before him. Evidently none had tried to ride through the swamp, following, like the blacks, on foot. One was a square-built, fair-haired man of thirty or so with bristling mustaches and whiskers, a blacksnake whip hanging coiled at his belt—Uhrquahr the overseer. The second, still in the tweed coat and hunting breeches he'd worn to walk to the cornfield that morning, the rain dripping from the broad brim of his palmetto hat, was Galen Peralta.

The third, white hair bare to the rain and eyes cold and hard as blue glass, was Xavier Peralta.

Peralta turned to one of the field hands holding January's arms. "Is this the man who came to the cabins last night and asked about Michie Galen?"

"Yes sir, it is."

He turned back at January. He, too, looked exhausted, as if the nights that had passed in obligatory family revelry had been harrowed by sleeplessness. It wasn't yet noon, which meant he'd taken the earliest boat he could that morning.

"You told my son that you'd been sent by Madame Dreuze with a keepsake—a gesture I find not in the slightest like the woman, for all her protests of sentimentality—and you told my servants that you were a runaway bound for Grand Isle. I think that you were lying both times. Tell the truth to me now. Who are you?"

"My name is Benjamin January," said January. "I'm a free man of color." He reached into his pocket—the field hands never releasing their hold on his arms—and produced the papers.

Uhrquahr took them and tore them up without looking at them. "You a slave now," he said, and smiled.

"Bring him," said Peralta and turned away.

The sugar mill was one of the few buildings on the Peralta place constructed of brick. There was a chamber to one side where the wood was stored against the voracious fires of the winter harvests, but with winter barely over the wood room was nearly empty, the brick floor swept clean. The backbreaking work of filling it would be a constant through the coming year, like hoeing up the fast-sprouting weeds before they smothered the cane or keeping the ditches clear.

On the opposite side of the mill, past the silent dark shapes of the rollers and the long line of the empty boiling vats, cones of sugar cured in another chamber on their wooden racks, leaching out the last of the molasses under stretched squares of gauze to keep the roaches away. The thick, raw-sweet smell of it filled the gloom.

"Spancel him to the upright." Peralta's voice echoed coldly in the high rafters, beneath the thrumming of the rain. His horse, and Uhrquahr's, had been waiting at the edge of the trees, the ankle chains in their saddlebags. "Just by the ankle will do," he added, as the overseer made a move to shove January back against one of the squared cypress pillars that supported the dome of the mill chamber itself. "I'll call you if there's trouble."

They had to pull off January's boots to lock the chain. It chafed the flesh of his foot and drove deep into the skin the blue bead of Olympe's charm.

From beneath his coattails Peralta took two pistols, one of which he handed to Uhrquahr. For all his soaked clothing, dripping into a puddle around his feet, the old planter radiated a kind of quiet anger, a deadliness more to be feared than the overseer's blind, raw exercise of power.

"Mr. Uhrquahr, will you stand outside the door of the wood room? Should I raise a cry you are to come in, but not before. I doubt this will take long. Have Hephastion send the men back into the fields as soon as the rain clears."

The overseer touched the brim of his soaked slouch hat and departed, the sound of the rain momentarily louder as he opened the door from the wood room outside. As he stepped out into the light Uhrquahr glanced sullenly over his shoulder, disappointed and angry.

January leaned his back against the pillar, his hands at his sides, watching Peralta in silence. The old man stood at a distance, the white hair making wet strings on his collar, his blue eyes cold as glass. There was something in the way he stood that told January he was waiting for him to speak, to hear what the first rush of words would be, explanations and excuses, perhaps pleas. So he kept his silence, as if both men were abiding until the turn of some unknown tide. The sound of the rain was very loud.

It was Peralta who finally broke the silence. "I did not know the police hired free blacks as agents."

January almost protested that he was sang mêlé, not black, then realized how ridiculous that would sound. Maybe Olympe was right about him being whiter than their mother inside.

"The police didn't send me," he said, and shook his head a little as a thread of water trickled from his close-cropped hair down into his eye. His voice was soft in the near dark. "Didn't you ask Monsieur Tremouille not to send anyone? Not to investigate at all? I'm the man they'll hang in the place of your son."

Peralta looked away. In the shadows it was impossible to see his expression, or whether his fair, pinkish skin colored up, but the tension that hardened his shoulders and back was unmistakable, his silence like the scrape of a cotton-press wheel screwed too tight.

Shoot me and walk out, thought January, too angry at this man now to care what he did. He'd seen a lot of death, and at this range, a bullet was going to be less painful and quicker than the rope and the drop. *Shoot me and walk out or say something.* He would not volunteer another word.

"You were . . . one of the musicians. The pianist."

"That's right," said January. "And your son can tell you that I was in the room talking to Mademoiselle Crozat when he came in, and that when I walked out she was still alive."

There was no sound but Peralta's breathing and January's own.

"He's the only witness to that fact," January went on. "But you probably already know that."

"No." The old man moved his shoulders, shifted his weight from one hip to the other, breaking the hard watchfulness. "No, I didn't. I did not discuss the matter at any great length with the police. My son . . ." He fell silent a very long time. "My son said nothing about you."

"And did your friend Captain Tremouille tell you that I was the only witness to the fact that your son came into the room when he did? After everyone saw him storm off down the stairs following his quarrel with Angelique?" January kept his eyes on the white man's left shoulder, knowing the rage in them showed even so but almost too angry to care.

"I don't have to listen to this." Peralta turned away.

"No, you don't," said January. "Because you've got a gun and I'm chained up. You don't have to listen to anything."

It stopped him. January guessed Peralta wouldn't have stopped if he'd said, *Because you're white and I'm black.* Might very well have struck him, in fact. In a sense, it amounted to the same thing, though of course a white man wouldn't see it that way. But as he'd known in the ballroom on the night of Bouille's challenge to William Granger, Peralta considered himself a gentleman, a man of old-fashioned honor. He was a man who prided himself on knowing the rules, on not being like the Americans.

"I told my friends where I was coming," said January. He made a subconscious move to fold his arms, and stopped himself from taking a stance too threatening, too challenging, too "uppity." His very size, he knew, was threat enough, and he was treading an extremely narrow road here. "If I'm not back, they'll take what I've written to the police. Not that it'll do me a flyspeck of good if you've decided a rich man can kill a poor one who's in his way, but I respect the truth and want it told."

Peralta turned slowly back. The implication of a lie touched him to the quick. He opened his mouth, within the rain-beaded circle of white mustache, but couldn't refute the words. Still, as a man of honor, a Creole gentleman of the old traditions, he couldn't let the words go unanswered. And gentlemen told the truth.

"He's my son," he said at last. "And I'm not going to kill you."

The cold clutch of panic tightened around January's heart, knowing what that probably meant. But he said steadily, "My friends will still come looking."

Who? he thought bitterly. *Livia? Dominique?*

"Unless you plan to sell me out of the state."

"No," said Peralta simply. He drew a deep breath, and met January's gaze again. "I know it's . . . hard. But I don't see what else I can do. Uhrquahr!"

The door opened fast. Uhrquahr came in with his gun trained; January reckoned Peralta was lucky his man hadn't stepped in shooting and killed them both before his eyes adjusted to the shadows.

"Put him in the jail," said Peralta quietly. "We'll be keeping him here for a few days."

Mambo Susu, the oldest woman on Bellefleur when January was growing up, had always said that it was bad luck to build a house out of brick and stone, things that had no spirit. It had made sense at the time, since all the slave cabins were made of wood and the inhabitants of the big house seemed to be as crazy and alien as living in a house without spirit would make them.

Later, watching the hard rains and hurricane winds from the windows of his mother's house on Rue Burgundy, January had remembered those dripping nights and the steady, hacking coughs most of the hands developed in time and revised his opinion.

In any case the slave jail on Chien Mort was built out of brick.

The bars of the single high window were wood rather than expensive iron, but the knowledge did January little good, as he was shackled to the rear wall with a short chain around his right wrist. It could have been worse, he reflected. Chronic runaways were frequently chained lying on their backs, butt to the wall with their feet manacled to rings set in about four feet off the floor. The floor was brick. The whole room smelled of mildew and very old piss.

Examining the bolts that held the chain to the wall, January reflected on the difference in sound between Bayou Chien Mort and Les Saules. Bayou Chien Mort, small and somnolent and out-of-the-way as it was, at least sounded alive: The voices of small children rang shrilly from the direction of the cabins, and from far off came the faint, steady suggestion of the chop of mattocks and hoes, of voices singing.

> *"They chased, they hunted him with dogs,*
> *They fired a rifle at him.*
> *They dragged him from the cypress swamp,*
> *His arms they tied behind his back,*
> *They tied his hands in front of him . . ."*

It was a forbidden song, a secret song, about the rebel slave leader Saint-Malo. Uhrquahr must not be near. January shivered and scratched with a fingernail at the mortar around the screws.

As he'd suspected, it wasn't mortar proper but hardened clay, poorly adapted for its job. He gathered the chain in his hand, wrapped the slack around his arm above the elbow, and twisted his whole body, watching for the telltale give in the bolts.

A little, he thought. *A little.*

He canvassed his pockets.

They'd taken his knife and spoon, the only metal he'd had on him, all his money, and his silver watch. The only thing they'd left him was his rosary.

Blessed Mary ever-Virgin, he prayed, *give me an idea. Show me some way.* He folded the beads back up again, put them away. He moved his feet, still bare since they hadn't given him back his boots, and his anklebone brushed the blue bead on its thong, a rosary to the old gods.

Papa Legba who guards all the doors, he thought, *I could do with some help from you, too.*

He took the rosary beads out of his pocket again, and turned them over in his hand. The beads winked at him, bright blue, like the bead on his ankle. Cheap glass.

With a cheap steel crucifix.

Blessed Mary ever-Virgin, he prayed, *forgive me for this, but I've got to get out of here.*

He began to scrape, cautiously, at the mortar around the bolts with the inch or so of steel at the bottom of the cross.

He heard the bolt lock on the door rattle and had a moment of horrified panic when he realized there was a little heap of powdered clay and broken fragments of mortar on the floor under the bolt. Falling to his knees, he swept it with his hands along the join of wall and floor and just barely stood up again in time to shield the ragged gouge in the clay with his body. His right hand he shoved in his pocket, rosary and all; six hours of steady work had left palm and fingers a raw mass of blisters and blood.

The sun had gone over to the other side of the building. The room was in shadow, until the light fell in like a fog of glare from the open door.

It took him a moment to realize who was standing there.

It was Galen Peralta.

"Puh-puh-Papa . . ." he began, and stopped. "P-Papa s-s-says you're the one who's taken the b-blame for . . . for what happened."

January said nothing.

"And thuh-that y-you c-came here tuh-tuh . . ." He could barely get the words out, his face contorted with frustration, with the fire of his inarticulate temper. "To see my face. To tuh-tell the police. That's why you came."

"You expect me to just sit there and let them hang me in your place?"

"But I duh-duh-duh . . ." He stepped through the door, shaking his head with desperation, fists clenching as if he would strike himself or anything near him in his need. "I duh-didn't do it!" He dragged in his breath hard, forcing a kind of steadiness. "I really, really d-didn't hurt her! I was d-drunk . . . I got duh-drunker . . . B-but I remember enough of the night to know I d-didn't hurt her! I wanted—I wanted—she laughed at m-me and I wuh-wanted to kill her, w-wanted to break her neck . . ."

"Perhaps your young Galen," Mme. Lalaurie had said, *"took the matter to an extreme, when not so long ago he took a stick to an Irish-woman who was insolent to him. . . ."* But unlike the Trepagier boys, it was Galen's cross rather than his crown.

"I left," he whispered. "I had t-to leave. Even Puh-Papa doesn't believe me."

He sounded desolate. In other circumstances, watching his struggle even to make himself understood on the simplest possible level, January knew he'd have felt pity for him. But at the moment he had little to spare.

"Whether I believe you or not isn't going to matter one bit when I'm chopping cotton in Georgia."

"N-no," said Galen quickly. "P-Papa's not going to do that! He's a hard m-man—st-st-stern . . ." He flinched a little at some thought. "Buh-but he'd n-never . . . He'd never be unjust like that. You're a free man."

January glanced around him at the jail's brick walls and said nothing.

"He's just g-going to keep you here until . . . until the m-marks on my f-face heal up. He said it's . . . it's hard to kn-know the right thing to do. Buh-but he's going to give you some m-money and see

that you get on a ship, to Europe or England or M-Mexico or wherever you want, just so long as it's not N-New Orleans."

*Exactly as he'd shipped all the house servants out to the farthest of his
plantations, regardless of their families, relationships, lives.*

"Just so long as I never see my home or my friends or my family
again," said January softly. "For something you know—and your
father knows—I didn't do."

A little defiantly, Galen said, "It's buh-buh-better than hanging!
He's doing the best he c-can for you, when Uhrquahr . . ." He
hesitated.

"When Uhrquahr wants to sell me," finished January for him. He
deliberately made his shoulders relax and slump a little, and bowed his
head, mostly so Galen wouldn't see his eyes. "I understand. Thank
you . . . and thank him." *You vain little cowardly popinjay.* It was
cleaner than his humiliation in the Swamp, though it came to exactly
the same thing.

But it relaxed the boy and brought him a step back into the room.

"It isn't as if . . . as if . . . It isn't as if I'd d-done it," argued
Galen. He rubbed at the lines of scab on his face. "B-but no one will
b-believe me. If my own father doesn't buh-believe . . ."

"She scratched you in the room there?"

Galen nodded, wretched. A lock of fair hair fell down over his
forehead. "She said to m-me . . . She said . . ."

*She said the things women with a cruel streak generally say to the men
who love them.*

"I cuh-cuh- . . . I c-can't say this."

The boy was consumed with guilt. January made his voice gentle,
as if he were back in the night clinic of the Hôtel Dieu.

"Were you lovers?"

He nodded again. "It was as if she w-wanted me t-to st-st-strike
her, w-wanted me to . . . to be violent. To hurt her." The words
jammed in his throat, and he forced them out, thin and panting, like
watered blood. "She . . . She used to d-do that. I tuh-try to k-keep
my temper, I've tuh-talked to Père Eugenius ab-bout it, again and
again. I've p-prayed about it, t-talked to Augustus—to M-Maître

M-Mayerling . . . Then she'd b-bait me and t-taunt me into hurt-
ing her, and hold it over me."

He shook his head, a desperate spasm of a gesture. "It was—It was
as if she w-wanted to get me to m-make love to her thuh-there in the
room," he whispered. "God knows I w-wanted to. Suh-suh-seeing her
d-dance that w-way. . . . I d-don't know if it was fighting or love-
making or what, that we did, b-but I pushed her away from me and I
left. I felt sick. I went b-back down the service stairs, the way I'd come
up. I was afraid I'd meet m-my father downstairs. I went . . . I
d-don't know where I went. The Verandah Hotel, I think, and the
Saint Louis Exchange. I just went in whatever d-doors I saw and got
liquor. It wasn't until I was cuh-cuh-coming back to the ballroom that
I met some men, and they said there'd been a muh-murder. The
d-dusky damsel in the c-cat mask, they said. I ran back and the police
were there. . . ."

He turned away and covered his face. "The first thing I thuh-
thought was that I shouldn't have left her. If I'd stayed w-with her she
w-wouldn't have been alone. She w-wouldn't have been k-k-killed. It
was only later when I got home that Puh-Puh-Puh- . . . that Papa
looked at me that way."

His arms wrapped around him, hugging himself with wretched-
ness, and January struggled to put his own anger at them aside—anger
at the boy who would let an innocent man take his punishment, a
man who would let an innocent take the punishment of a boy whom
he truly believed to be guilty.

Behind his flank he flexed his gouged and bleeding hand.

Stay silent. Stay silent and learn.

But maybe, he thought, part of his own anger was only envy. He
didn't like to think so, but he suspected that if it had been Minou
who'd been jailed, their mother would have been at the Cabildo that
night raising seven kinds of Cain until her child was freed. Even if she
thought Minou had killed a man.

"I never thuh-thuh-thought it was p-possible to love someone like
that," the boy went on, his voice a hoarse whisper now, speaking
almost to himself. He might have taken the silence for sympathy, or
he might have gone beyond awareness of January's existence, only

needing to confess to someone who was not his father, someone of whom he wasn't afraid.

"I never thuh-thought I c-could love someone that . . . that wild. She was n-nothing like I'd ever thought about, or d-dreamed about, but I c-couldn't get her out of my mind. It was like one of those c-crazy, dirty d-dreams one gets. I n-never thought I'd violate another man's wuh-woman, or go through all those st-stupid little subterfuges, meeting her at night after he'd left, s-sending her secret letters, everything they do in n-novels. I didn't know what to do. And now at n-night all I c-c-can think about is her voice, and the times she'd be like a child who needed me. It was m-my fault," he added softly. He was shivering now, hands clutched together, pressed to his lips. "M-my fault she was alone when . . . when he came into the room."

"And you have no idea who he might have been?" asked January in the voice of his own confessor.

The boy raised his head, stared at him blankly, as if such a thought had never crossed his mind. As if Angelique's death had been like one of Byron's poems, some catastrophe engineered by malevolent gods to harm the bereaved, not attached to other matters in the victim's life.

As if, January realized, in Galen Peralta's mind, Angelique had no other life than as the center of *his* consciousness.

"Do you know who might have hated her?" he asked. "Who might have wished her dead?"

Of course you don't, he thought, as the boy simply gazed with those tear-filled blue eyes. *You never spoke to her about a single one of her other concerns, did you?*

"I . . . n-no," he stammered. "Who w-would have w-wanted to harm her?"

The blind naïveté—the complete ignorance—of the remark made him want to hoot with laughter, but that, he knew, would be his death.

"An ex-lover?" January suggested gently. "A rival? Someone she had wronged? If she had a crazy temper, she'd have taken it out on someone other than you."

The boy shook his head and looked away, face darkening in the gloom as he realized, perhaps for the first time, that he had not known very well the woman he had professed to so madly love.

"Was there someone you saw on the stairway?" asked January. "Someone you passed in the courtyard on the way out?"

"I d-don't . . . I d-don't remember anything. Look, my p-papa says we should let this all blow over. . . ."

"But then the man who did this will get away." January made his voice low, both grave and sympathetic, as if he were speaking to one of his students or to some poor soul at the night clinic. "Listen, Michie Peralta." He carefully used the idiom of the slaves, like a dog lowering itself down before another dog so as not to get killed. "I'm grateful to your father for sending me away rather than doing some worse thing, because I know it's in his power to do so." *The arrogant bastard.* "But one day I want to clear my own name, and to do that I have to find who really did it. If you can tell me everything you remember about that night, I can write to my family from France or Mexico or wherever I end up, and they can talk to the police, investigate this thing. Clear *your* name as well, not just with the police but with your father."

The boy licked his lips with a pale, hesitant tongue, but his watery eyes brightened a little. "I . . . I underst-stand. But I d-don't . . . I really d-don't remember."

Just as his love for Angelique had been a matter of concern to him alone, thought January, so in his mind he saw only himself at their parting and not anyone around him.

"How did you leave the building?" asked January in a coaxing voice, trying to ignore the agonizing pain in his hand. "Down the service stairs?"

Galen nodded. "I d-didn't . . . Everybody was in the upstairs lobby. But I heard . . . voices . . . in the office when I came out the b-bottom, so I w-went through the lobby and out into the c-court that way."

His father's voice, thought January. *In Froissart's office, talking to Granger and Bouille.*

"Did you see anyone in the lobby? Anyone you know? Or would know again?"

"I d-don't . . . I d-don't know." Galen shrugged helplessly and looked around, casting about for a reason to leave. "They were all w-wearing masks."

"What kind of masks? Anything really pretty? Really vulgar? Really ugly?" If the killer had ascended the service stair sometime during the progressive waltz, he—or just possibly she—would have almost certainly passed this distraught boy in the lobby or the court-yard.

"There was that vulgar p-purple p-pirate," said Galen promptly, his brow unfurrowing with relief at being able to recall something or someone. "M-Mayerling was d-down there, I . . . I hurried p-past because I didn't want him to see me. I didn't—I c-couldn't—do with speaking to anyone. There was a w-woman dressed like an Indian in b-b-buckskin. . . ."

He frowned again, struggling with the mental effort as much as with his stutter. A very perfect young Creole gentleman, thought January dourly: competent with a sword or a horse and slowly being inculcated to the endless, careful work of running a sugar plantation, but utterly without imagination. Or perhaps with just enough imagi-nation to sense that he was being pressed and molded against his will, the will he was not allowed to have, into something he was not. Enough fire in him to rebel against his father's demands by seeking out a creature of fire like Angelique Crozat.

"There was a k-kind of Turk in an orange t-turban," he went on after a moment. "He was in the c-courtyard. I remember thinking his t-turban looked like a p-pumpkin under the lanterns in the trees. And as I c-came down the steps I s-saw Angelique's little f-f-friend, C-Clemence. She was st-standing in the courtyard, looking for s-someone. But I c-couldn't stand to talk."

His face contracted again with sudden pain, and he turned away. "Duh-duh-don't . . . Don't let my father know I s-said all this," he whispered. "I have to g-go. I have to be out at the w-woodlot now. I just wuh-wuh-wanted you to know I d-didn't . . . I d-didn't kill her. Do you believe me?"

"I believe you," said January. *You cowardly little wretch.* And, hearing the anger in his own voice, the threat of sarcasm fighting to rise to the surface, he added humbly, "Thank your father for me. And thank you."

"It's all I can d-do," said the boy softly. "I hope . . . I hope your friends c-can find who really d-did it. I hope what I've t-told you is some help. Because I c-can't even c-confess this, you know? I cuh-cuh-can't . . . I cuh-can't c-confess that I left her alone."

You're condemning me to exile from everyone I know, thought January, as the door closed behind Galen, the labored squeak of the bolt echoed again. *From the only home I have. And you expect me to pity you because you can't confess?*

Have your own nightmares, boy. I'll shed a tear for you on my way back to New Orleans on foot.

He turned back, gritting his teeth hard as the steel arms of Christ's cross pressed, then grated, in the raw meat of his palm, and began to gouge at the clay once more.

> *"Boss-man say, Gonna sell that big black boy,*
> *Boss-man say, Gonna sell that big black boy.*
> *Tell the Big Boss he run off in the night,*
> *But take him out, take him on up to Natchez town . . ."*

January swung around, heart pounding hard at the sound of the thin, wailing song beneath the jailhouse window. A woman singing, he thought, standing in the near-complete early darkness of the evening, her voice almost hidden by the singing of the hands as they came past on the pathway to the cabins.

Singing to him. There was no other reason for her to be there, close enough to the jail for him to touch, had he not been chained.

> *"Mama, take this food, hide it in the black oak tree,*
> *Mama, take this food, hide it in the black oak tree,*
> *Where the bayou bends,*
> *My food, my boots, they wait for me . . ."*

Something dark flashed between the bars of the windows; a moment later he heard the soft strike of metal on the packed dirt of the floor.

Uhrquahr, thought January, in a sudden flash of cold rage. So Uhrquahr had his own plans to benefit from the windfall his employer had too much honor to pick up.

The anger helped him. Exhausted, the agony in his hand sapping the rest of his strength, without that fury he wasn't sure he'd have been able to tear free the loosened chain from the wall.

The thought of Uhrquahr did it, though. He wrapped the chain twice around his arm and wrenched, half-blind with anger, and the staple popped free with a force that sent him staggering into the opposite wall. He stumbled, fell, gasping and in a pain he had never experienced in his life, aching in every muscle.

And knowing that he wasn't done yet, for he had to cut through the wooden bars.

He couldn't even stand up to cross the cell to the window. On hands and knees, in the pitch dark, he crawled, back muscles crying out with agony as he swept the invisible dirt before him with his left hand. His right was a useless root of pain. He literally had no idea how he'd manage to cut the bars.

He knew he'd have to manage. There was food and his boots waiting for him in the black oak where the bayou curved—a short distance from the path that led back to Ti Margaux's house, for he'd noticed the tree there. God knew how he'd get the spancel off his wrist or where he could get sufficient alcohol to keep his hand from mortifying—at a pinch, a willow-bark poultice would probably suffice, if he had time to make one. But once he ran, he'd better not get caught again.

His fingers touched metal, lumpy and heavy. It was the head of a mattock, razor-sharp on its edge and capable of chopping through the toughest roots.

Blessed Mary ever-Virgin, he thought, reaching down to touch the rosary in his trouser pocket, with its battered and twisted steel cross, *I owe you as many Masses as you want to name.*

And I owe you too, Papa Legba—the opener of doors.

A waxing moon had risen midway through the afternoon, and pale silver flickered on the waters through a gauze of mist when January finally reached the black oak where the bayou curved. Heart pounding with fear of snakes, wildcats, and nests of sleeping hornets, he groped in the crotch of the brooding dark shape, wreathed with fog and Spanish moss, and almost at once his fingers touched cloth. It was a slave's blanket, not his own, wrapped around a good store of ash pone and dried apples, a holed and ragged linsey-woolsey shirt, a corked gourd, which even from the outside smelled of raw cheap rum, and his boots.

Thanking God with every breath he drew, January pulled on the boots first. His feet were bleeding from a dozen scratches and so swollen he could barely get the boots on, but even at this early season, he knew there was danger from snakes. His own shirt he'd torn to make a bandage to keep the dirt out of his raw and throbbing hand, and to tie up the chain to his right arm. He shed the remains and replaced them with the linsey-woolsey garment, which if old and ragged was at least whole.

He tore another strip from the old shirt, squatting in a broad fletch of moonlight on the edge of the field, and gritted his teeth as he pulled the crusted, sticky wrapping from his hand. The new strip he soaked in rum and wrapped tight, put another on top of it, the pain of the alcohol going right up his arm and into his belly and groin as if he'd been stabbed.

The river, he thought. *They'll search the west bank first.*

As the thought went through his head his heart sank. He was a strong man, and after Galen Peralta had left him, one of the children had brought him pone and pulse and greens on a cheap clay plate, probably what they all lived on in the quarters. But he'd been living soft. He could feel the exertions of yesterday in the muscles of his thighs and back and legs; his bones telling him in no uncertain terms that he was forty. Even with the logs and planks and uprooted trees that drifted down and caught in the snags of the river bars to float his weight, he wasn't sure he'd be able to swim the river at this point. The current was like a millrace below the city, powerful and treacherous.

But he didn't really have a choice. He knew that.

The stream was high, but by the weeds and mud on the banks the peak of the rise was past. There was no guarantee that another rise wouldn't come down while he was halfway across, and if that happened he could be carried halfway to the ocean and perhaps drowned. As he picked his way among the moonlit tangle of weed and scrub on the levee, one or perhaps two plantations up from Chien Mort, he understood why slaves became superstitious, praying to whatever saint or loa they thought might be listening and collecting cornmeal, salt, mouse bones and chicken feathers in the desperate hope that they might somehow avert catastrophes over which they had no control.

It was the alternative to a bleakness of despair he hadn't known since his childhood.

And in his childhood, he recalled—waist-deep in water, his boots hung around his neck as he struggled to clear a floating tree trunk from half-unseen obstructions, the chain weighing heavier and heavier on his right arm—he had been as avid a student of the rituals of luck and aversion as any on Bellefleur. If he'd thought it would do him any good in reaching the east bank in safety he wasn't sure he wouldn't have taken the time to snap his fingers, hop on one foot, and spit.

Thin mist veiled the water in patches, but he could discern the dark line of trees that was the far bank. Above him the sky was clear, and the moon far enough to the west that the stars over the east bank were bright. From the tail of the Dipper he sited a line down the sky to two brilliant stars, identifying their positions and hoping he could do so again when in midriver and fighting the current's drag.

He tied his food, clothing, blanket, and boots to the tree trunk he'd freed, took two deep swigs of the rum, which was worse than anything he'd ever tasted in his life, laid his chained arm over the trunk to carry the weight of his body, and set out swimming.

I didn't kill her, Galen Peralta had said.

And January believed him.

He didn't want to, because the alternative it left would be even harder to prove . . . and hurt him with the anger of betrayal.

The Indian Princess at the foot of the stairs. The flash of buckskin, half-glimpsed through the crowd around the ballroom doors. *I must see her . . . I MUST.*

He'd offered to take the message. Had she assented only to be rid of him, to make him think that she'd left? The desperation in her eyes came back to him, when she'd spoken of her grandmother's jewels, cold desperation and anger. The way she'd set her shoulders, going in to talk to the broker who held her husband's debts. *That trash McGinty,* her husband's relatives had said . . . A man who undoubtedly was using the debts to urge marriage on a widow. For an upriver American on the make, even a run-down plantation was better than nothing.

She was a woman, he thought, backed into a corner, and the way out of that corner was money enough to hang on to her property. Money that could have come through those jewels that had been her grandmother's, and then hers. Jewels she would still regard as hers by right, and the woman who took them a whore and a thief.

Mist moved between him and the bank. He kicked hard at the moving water beneath and around him, stroked hard with his left arm, and kept his eye on the clearer of the two guiding stars. The sheer size of the river, like a monstrous serpent, was terrifying, the power of it pulling at his body, as if he were no more than a flea on a dog. The willow trunk he held on to, bigger than his own waist, was a matchstick on the flood, and he wondered what he'd do if a riverboat, or a flatboat, came down at him from the north, without lights, emerging from the fog.

There was nothing he could do about that, he thought. *Just keep swimming.*

The problem was, in spite of all of the information he had he knew she hadn't done the murder.

He could probably have made a case against her—possibly one that would even stick, given that her family had half disowned her and her husband's relatives wanted clear title to Arnaud Trepagier's land and she was refusing to marry any of them.

But it might not save him, even at that.

And he knew she hadn't done it.

In all the trash on the parlor floor, there hadn't been a single black cock feather.

Yet she was lying and had been lying from the start. She knew something. Had she seen something, staying on as she did? Spoken to someone?

Sally. Hannibal could find out from the girls in the Swamp, if he asked enough of them. Possibly even Shaw would be able to track her down, once January had told him.

Told him what? he thought bitterly. *That a white Creole lady might know something, when Angelique's father can see a perfectly good man of color to convict of the crime to satisfy Euphrasie's vengeance on the world?*

He supposed the gentlemanly thing to do was to keep silent about whatever his suspicions were, to help Madeleine Trepagier cover whatever her guilty secret was. But he knew he'd have to find it and twist her with it; he'd have to threaten to tell to force her to give him whatever answers she could.

He felt like a swine, a swine running squealing from the hammer and the rope.

He kicked hard against the drag of the water around him, struggling with waning human might against the King of Rivers. Weariness already burned in his muscles, weighted his bones.

He could flee he supposed. Ironic, that Xavier Peralta had offered him exactly what he'd been planning to save his money for. Père Eugenius always did say, *Be careful what you pray for.*

Not that Uhrquahr would let the chance of $1,500 clear profit slip out of his hands so easily.

He was a surgeon, and there were surgical hospitals in London, Vienna, Rome . . .

Cities where he knew no one, where there was no one. He wasn't sure exactly when his feeling had changed, or how. Perhaps it was Catherine Clisson's smile of welcome, an old friend glad to see him, or the voices of the workers singing in the fields. He understood that he had been lonely in Paris, until he'd met Ayasha. He had been a stranger on the face of the earth, in every place but New Orleans, where his family was and his home.

In New Orleans he was a man of color, an uneasy sojourner in a world increasingly American, hostile, and white. But he was what he was. At twenty-four he'd been strong enough, whole enough, to seek a new life. At forty, he didn't know.

He'd spoken to Angelique in order to help Mme. Trepagier, Madeleine, his student of other years, trying to play the part of the honorable man. Trying to reestablish his links with that old life. And this was his reward.

The water rolled against him, a wave like a solid wall, his leaden limbs fighting, driving him across the currents toward the shore. His two cold stars watched him, disinterested, as the moon dipped away toward the tangled west.

There was nothing of this in Bach, he thought, his mind striving to throw off the creeping weight of exhaustion, the growing insistence that even on the breast of the river, what was best for him now was sleep. Skirls of music flitted through his mind, Herr Kovald's light touch on the piano keys, Mozart, Haydn, the Water Music . . .

Swimming against the river's might, struggling with exhaustion and the heavy smells of the mud and the night—fleeing injustice and servitude toward a town where those things passed under other names—the only songs that came to his mind were those of his childhood, the dark wailing music of the African lands. Those spoke in his muscles and his bones, as he pulled against the current and kept his eye on his guardian stars.

He reached the far bank aching but knew he dared not stop. Plantations stretched in an almost uniform forty arpents inland—two or three miles—before petering out in a wilderness of bayou, cypress swamp, and pine wood. He climbed the levee on his hands and knees, like an animal, and lay on the top, panting, staring at the dark water, all sparkling with the silver of the sinking moon. It was early spring, the world very silent but for the lap of the river below. Inland all creation breathed one damp cold breath of turned earth, where a new crop of sugar was being prepared for, trenches chopped like bridal beds in the long dirt hills. He knew it wouldn't be many hours before the slaves would be out again.

He ate some bread, which was wet in his pack, and drank as much of the rum as he dared spare, knowing he'd need it for his hand, and got to his feet again. His legs felt like rubber.

Daddy, wherever you are, he thought, for no particular reason, *your son's thinking of you.*

He traveled like this for two days, and a little more.

He struck the chain off his arm as soon as he was far enough from habitation that the hard clang of the mattock head on the shackle wouldn't be heard—or he hoped it wouldn't be heard—and carried the iron half of Friday before he decided the drain on his strength wasn't worth the possibility that he might need it. He buried it under a hollow log.

He kept close enough to the rear of the plantations to follow the line they made, the line of the river that would lead him eventually back to town, but it terrified him. He guessed Peralta would be offering a large reward for his capture—*Big black buck,* it would say. *Runaway.* And there were always patrols. In older times there'd always been coming and going between the plantations and little colonies of runaways—marrons—in the woods, but heavier settlement and the death of the rebel leader Saint-Malo had put a stop to that. Sometimes he heard riders in the woods and hid himself in the thickets of hackberry and elder, wondering if he'd been sufficiently careful about keeping to hard ground, wondering if he'd left some sign. He was surprised how much of his childhood woodcraft came back to him, but he knew himself incapable of navigating, once he got out of sight of the thinning in the trees that marked the fields to his left.

In the afternoons the singing of the work-gangs in the fields came to him, and as it had on the breast of the river the music took him by the bones. Lying in the thickets with the gnats dense around his head, drawn by the scent of the rum on his hand as he bandaged it, and of his sweat, he listened to those voices and thought, *This is the music of my home.*

> *"Ana-qué, an'o'bia,*
> *Bia'tail-la, Qué-re-qué,*
> *Nal-le oua, Au-Mondé,*
> *Au-tap-o-té, Au-tap-o-té,*
> *Au-qué-ré-qué, Bo."*

African words, not even understandable by those who sang them anymore, but the rhythm of them warmed his tired blood. He wondered if Madeleine Trepagier's girl Sally had felt anything like this, running from her mistress—running to New Orleans.

Probably not, he thought. She'd fled with a man and had had his promises to reassure her: his gifts and his sex to keep her from thinking too much about whether he'd keep his word, from wondering why a white man would suddenly get so enamored of a slave.

If she hadn't been in the Swamp three days ago, he thought—with the tired anger that seemed to have become a part of his flesh—she would be soon.

On the Saturday he met Lucius Lacrîme.

He heard the *tut* of hooves, the rustle and creak of saddle leather, at some distance, but the woods were thin. He turned and headed inland, not fast but as fast as he dared, seeking any kind of cover that he could.

Thin with pines on the weak soil, the woods here seemed as bare of cover as the ballroom of the Salle d'Orléans.

The hooves were near and he knew they'd see him for sure if he kept moving. He crouched behind the roots of the biggest tree he could find, wadding his big body down flat and small to the earth and tucking the dwindling bundle of blanket and food between belly and knees. He'd feel a fool if they saw him, hiding like a child behind a tree.

As if, he thought, feeling a fool was the worst thing that would happen then.

". . . Wench over to the Boyle place." American voices, quiet. "Cooks a treat, but ugly as a pig."

"Put a bag over her head, then. Christ, what you want for a— You there! You, nigger!"

Every muscle galvanized as if touched with a scientist's electrical spark, but he forced stillness. *A trick, a trap . . .*

Then another voice said in bad English skewed by worse French, "You talkin' to me, Michie?"

"Yeah, I'm talkin' to you. You see any other niggers hereabouts? Lemme see your pass."

"That ain't him, Theo, that's just old Lucius Lacrîme. Got a place hereabouts." The hooves were still. January heard the chink of bridle hardware as one of the horses tossed its head. "You seen a big black buck, Looch? Headin' toward the city, maybe?"

"Not headin' toward the city, no, sir." Lucius Lacrîme had an old man's voice, thin and slow and almost sing-song, a broken glass scritching on a rock. "Big man? My nephew he say there somebody holed up someplace along Bayou Désolé. Big man by his track, and black my nephew say, but wearin' boots like a white man. That be him?"

The woods were so still January could hear the far-off boom of the steamboats on the river, four miles away, and the ringing of an ax. Bridle hardware jingled again, this time sharply, and a horse blew.

"That'll be him," said the man who was fastidious about the appearance of cooks. "You know Bayou Désolé, Furman?"

"I know where it lies. Bad country, peters out in a swamp. Just the place a runaway'd hole up, I guess."

The hooves retreated. The voices faded into the mottled buffs and blacks of the early spring woods. January didn't raise his head, knowing in his bones that Lucius Lacrîme still stood where he'd been.

In time the old voice said in English, "You can come out, son. They gone." There was a stillness, January not moving. Then, in French, "You're safe, my son. I won't harm you." He barely heard a rustle, until the old man got almost on top of his hiding place. Then he stood up.

"Thank you, grandfather." He nodded to the flattened weeds behind the cypress knees. "There's not much cover here."

"They're searching, all around the woods." Dark eyes like clear coffee considered him from within an eon of wrinkles, like the eyes of a tortoise on a log. He was a middle-size man who looked as if he'd been knotted out of grass a thousand years ago, dry and frail and clean. Tribal scars like Uncle Bichet's made shiny bumps in the ashy stubble of his beard.

"They say they look for a runaway field hand, but no field hand wears boots or needs them." He held out an arthritic claw and took January's left hand, turned and touched the powerful fingers, the raw welt that the rope had left when they'd bound him. "What they think you pick for them, flowers?"

January closed his hand. "No dealer in Natchez is gonna ask about why a field hand's got no calluses, if the price is cheap. Thank you for sending them on." He reached down for his bundle, but the old man caught his right hand with its crusted wad of wrappings, and turned it over in his bony fingers.

"And what's this, p'tit? Do they know you hurt? They'll spot you by it."

January shook his head. "I don't think they know."

The old man brought the bandage up to his nose and sniffed, then pushed at the edges, where the shackle had chafed raw the skin of his wrist. He nodded a few times, and said, "You a lucky child, p'tit. Old Limba, he look out for you. But headin' on back to town, that the first place they look. Stay in the bayous, down the southwest across the river, or back in the swamps. You can trap, fish, hunt. . . . They never find you." His grin was bright, like sun flecking off dark water. "They never found me."

"They'll never look." January settled his weight against the tug of Lacrîme's hand. "Not so long as I'm out of their way. Not so long as I don't come back to the city. So long as I don't come forward as a free man, claiming what's mine, they don't care if I'm dead or a slave or on a ship heading back to Europe. Just so long as I don't bother them. And I'm not going to give them that."

It was the first time he'd said it; the first time he'd expressed to himself exactly what it was that had carried him against the current of the river, that had kept him moving through the long exhaustion of the previous days and nights.

The songs in the field. The blue bead on his ankle. The twisted steel cross in his pocket. They were verses in a bigger song, and suddenly he was aware of what the song was about. And it wasn't just about his family, his friends, and his own sore heart.

Lacrîme peered up at him with those tortoise eyes. "They who, p'tit?"

An old man who figured an innocent black man's life was worth less to him than the life of the son whom he believed to be a murderer. The boy who hadn't the guts to go against his father's will.

The woman he'd taught to play Beethoven, all those years ago.

And whoever it was that she would lead him to.

"White men," he said. "I'm going on to town. Is there a path you can point me out to get there?"

Lacrime took him by way of the swamp tracks, the game trails, the twisty ways through the marsh country that lay back of the river, toward the tangled shores of Lake Pontchartrain. They were old tracks, from the days when networks of marron settlements had laced the boscages. The old man looked fragile, crabbed up with arthritis and age, but like a cypress root he was tough as iron. He scrambled with bobcat agility through thickets, bogs, and low-lying mud that sucked and dragged at January's boots and seemed to pull the strength out of him.

"T'cha, you get soft in this country," the old man chided, when January stopped to lean against a tree to rest. "Soft and tame. The boss men all ask for a man bred in this country, a criolo, instead of one who came across the sea. They all uppity, they say, princes and kings and warriors. When we fought the Dahomies, we'd run this much and more, through the bottomlands by the river, and woe on any man who let the enemy hear him. He'd be lucky if he lived to be brought to the beach and the white man's ships."

"Were you?" asked January. They stood knee-deep in water, skimmed over in an emerald velvet whisper of duckweed, the woods around them gray-silent, hung with silver moss, dark leaves, and stillness. More rain had fallen earlier and the world smelled of it, and of woodsmoke from some distant squatter's shack. Maybe bandits, and maybe others like Lacrîme.

"Ah." The old man spat and turned to lead him once again along the silent traces in the woods. "They took our village, filthy Dahomies. We twelve, we young men, came back from hunting to find it all gone. Big stuff, the stuff of great tales. We followed them through the jungle, along the rivers, through the heat and the black night. And they left what traces they could, our parents, our sisters, our little brothers, and the girls we were courting. It would have been a great tale if we'd taken them back. A great song, sung all down the years."

He shook his head, with a wry mouth that such innocence could have been. "Maybe we sang a verse or two of it to each other, just to try it out, to hear how it would be.

"But there was no tale. Not even with my own village was I put in a ship, but with a bunch of people—Hausa from up by the great lake, Fulbe and Ibos—whose language I didn't even know. Young men are stupid."

He glanced back over his shoulder at January, laboring behind him.

"Nobody will give you justice, p'tit, no matter how much truth you shove down their throats. I'd been better to go north with my friends and look for another tribe of the Ewe, who at least knew the names of my gods."

"Did you ever find them again?" asked January. "Your own people, your family—those who spoke your tongue, who knew the names of your gods?"

The Ewe shook his head. "Never."

January followed in silence, as twilight settled deep over the green-gray land, then night.

They traveled on through night, sleeping only little. The food was gone and the rum January had been putting on his hand to keep infection at bay. He checked the wound whenever they stopped, which wasn't often, until daylight failed; the mess of the raw flesh was ugly, but looked clean, as far as he could tell, and he felt no fever. He was weary, however, weary beyond anything he'd ever known, even working in the fields—even the weariness after fighting, hiding in trees and blasting away with a rifle at the advancing red-coated troops with the expectation of losing his own life any minute, hadn't been like this. He guessed this was one effect of the wound, but the knowledge didn't help him much. He wanted only to sleep.

"Not safe to sleep, Compair Rabbit," the old man said, shaking January out of his doze where they'd stopped to rest by the foot of a tree. "Bouki the hyena, he's out riding the tracks. Used to be there was farms in the boscage, villages like in Africa. We'd live like we did, and they couldn't find us. When they came, we'd just melt away in the woods. Now Bouki and his hyenas, they ride the trails, hire Americans from up the river. Compair Rabbit better not sleep now when Bouki's out hunting."

They found a pirogue on the tangled banks of the long bayou that stretched from the lake in toward the town and hugged the bottomless shadows of its banks where the moonlight didn't touch. In time they followed in the waters of the canal toward the grubby scatter of wooden cottages, mud and stucco houses that made up the Faubourg Tremé, the newer French suburb. Though it was long after curfew, Orion and his hunting dogs sinking west toward their home beyond the trackless deserts of Mexico, January was conscious of lamps burning, ochre slits behind louvered shutters, threads of amber outlining shut doors. All around him, as Lucius Lacrîme drew the small boat close to a floating wooden stage and led the way up and into the rough gaggle of unpaved and unguttered streets that smelled of out-

houses, January sensed a kind of movement in the dark, a certain life
flitting in the dense black of the alleyways. Once he heard, dim as a
drift of smoke, a woman singing something that had naught to do
with Mozart or Rossini, with polkas or ballads or the loves and griefs
of whites.

Lacrîme led him around the back of a whitewashed cottage whose
stucco was chipped and falling and badly in need of repair. Tobacco
smoke rode over the stink of the privies in the dark of the yard. There
was a gleam of gold, like Polyphemus's brooding eye, halfway up the
outside stair to the attic.

"Hey, Compair Jon," breathed Lacrîme—though January had no
idea how he could have seen or recognized anyone in the density of
the shadows.

"Hey, Compair Lacrîme," replied a soft voice from above. The
smell of smoke increased as the man took his cigar from his mouth
and blew a cloud.

"There room up there for my friend to sleep?"

"Being he got no objection to featherbeds and lullabies, and beautiful girls bringing him cocoa in bed when he wakes."

"You got any objection to that, Compair Rabbit?"

January looked up at the glowing coal. "You just tell them girls
that cocoa better not have skin on it, and make sure those lullabies are
by Schubert and not Rossini—leastwise not anything Rossini's written
lately."

He heard the soft snort of laughter. "Mozart right by you?"

He made a deprecating gesture, like a housekeeper haggling in the
market. "If that's all you got, I guess I'll put up with it." He felt he
could have been happy on bare boards, which he suspected would be
the case, just so long as he could lie down and sleep.

"They'll be looking for you in town, you know," said Lucius
Lacrîme's soft, scratchy voice at his elbow. He'd told the old man a
little of what had happened in Chien Mort—that he was a free man
who'd lost the proofs of his freedom, and what had passed between
him and Galen Peralta. "Even those that don't know what went on
know runaways mostly head for town nowadays."

"People know me here," said January.

"And people know old man Peralta. And if you think you got a chance against him in court of law, you're a fool."

January knew he was right. The thought of going into a courtroom, of trying to persuade a jury that he was innocent on his cloudy assertions that a white woman was involved in some kind of scandal— a jury of white men, possibly Americans—frightened him badly, worse than he had been afraid chained to the pillar in the sugar house. It was like holding a line in combat: stand and fire, knowing that if you ran you were a dead man, but facing some other man's loaded gun.

If he didn't run now, he thought, he might not be able to later.

But the line hadn't broken, he thought. They'd kept firing, and the British had eventually fallen back.

That the Americans hadn't even thanked him for his trouble was beside the point.

"I have to stay," he said. He didn't know what else he could say, besides that.

In the darkness it was impossible to see, but there was a rustle of fabric, a glint of eyes, as the old man shook his head. "That's how I ended up taking a ride in a great big ship, p'tit," said Lucius Lacrîme sadly and clapped him softly on the back. "And nobody'll sing that song about your courage."

The thought of starting again elsewhere, of giving up what little he had left without a fight, dragged at him, like the time as a child he'd caught a fishhook in his flesh. The thought of letting Peralta, Tremouille, and Etienne Crozat win. He was at Chalmette again, loading his musket and watching red blurs take shape in the rank brume of powder smoke and fog.

"I still have to stay."

"You lay still, then, until you know what the hyenas are doing, Compair Rabbit. And when you break cover, you watch your back."

January didn't hear him go.

TWENTY

The attic over the store was one of those places Abishag Shaw had been told to shut down, a sleeping place for slaves who preferred to rent their own bodies from their owners for cash money, and find their own food and housing and employment, rather than exist in the enclosed compounds behind the white folks' houses. In a room twenty feet by thirty—blocked off by a wood-and-plaster wall from the attic storeroom of the shop below—ten men slept, as January had guessed, on the bare floor, rolled in blankets with their heads on their spare jackets or shirts. The place stank of unwashed clothes, unbathed flesh, of mice and roaches and of the smoke leaking through the brick of the two chimneys that rose up along the dividing wall. January had to feel his way gingerly down the center of the room so as not to trip over anyone, as he sought the place he'd seen in the little dim moonlight let in when he'd opened the door.

There was a dormer on the other side of the slanted roof—which, like Hannibal's attic in the Swamp, rose to a point a foot and a half short of his own height—and after a few minutes his eyes adjusted to the still denser dark, so that he could guess at the shapes that lay all around him, breathing deeply, heavily, in the vermin-infested dark.

Still, it was less crowded than the jail cell, quieter and far cleaner. By the last threads of blue moonlight he could see the man nearest him, and beyond him the little bundle of clothing, tin cup and plate, and the tin identification medal that showed him to be a slave working rather than a runaway when he walked about the streets.

He was sleeping under a roof he'd chosen for himself.

January closed his eyes.

His hand slid into his pocket, fingering the battered rosary as he told off prayers of thanks.

The illusion of freedom was tiny, he thought—maybe as tiny as his own illusion of justice—but they made do with it. It was better, to them, than the marginally more comfortable accommodations under a master's roof. Better than leaving everything he owned, everything he had worked for, everything he had left in the world, for the convenience of whoever had put that scarf around Angelique Crozat's ivory silk throat.

Save for a few hours snatched along the way, he had been without sleep for two nights and most of a third. Sleeping, he dreamed of the soft wailing voices of the workers in the fields, under the glassy weight of the new sun.

> *"They say go north, find us new kin,*
> *They say go north, find us new kin,*
> *We try save our folks,*
> *We never come back again."*

But the dream's light changed, from the early spring sun, harsh on the cane fields, to moonlight heavy as quicksilver, a black ocean strewn with phosphor galaxies, the black shape of a ship riding silent in the dark.

Dark blots on the ivory silk beach, like messy scabs; a tangle of walls and pens, shacks and fences; charred flesh and the smell of human waste and branding fires; the muted whisper of weeping. The glint of eyes that showed twelve young men, watching from the clotted shadows of the mangrove swamp.

"Without my folks, is no land home,
He say without my folks, no land be home,
I'll die on that beach,
Before I live my life alone."

"I walk on needles, I walk on pins," sang a voice back, whirling through dark and time like the smell of a burning house. "I know well the Grand Zombi . . ."

The throb of drums swept aside the beat of the surf on the shore. Voices cried, *"Calinda!* Dance the *calinda! Badoum, badoum!"*

Rain smell, and the throbbing in his hand as if it had been pounded with a hammer. It was only marginally more painful than the rest of his body: legs, arms, back. Downstairs, two people argued in gombo French over the price of a half-pound of sugar.

Leaky gray light showed him the slant of the roof, the bundles of blankets, tin cups, spare shirts that were shoved into corners and around the walls. When he sat up mice went scurrying, but the roaches were less concerned. Possibly, thought January wryly, because some of them were almost as big.

No one was in sight. The dancing in Congo Square generally didn't start until well after noon. The door onto the stairway stood open, the noise coming through it clearly. He limped over, stooping under the rafters and stepping through, stood on the little porch just outside, looking across the muddy yards, the wet, dark slate tiling of slanted roofs, and the cypress and palmetto that marked an area only recently and incompletely claimed from woods and swamps.

A rabble of plane trees and the white spire of the Church of St. Antoine showed him where the square lay. He was, he guessed, within a mile of his mother's house.

And that was exactly where the police would look for him, if they were looking.

Bouki the hyena, he's out riding the tracks, whispered a rusty voice in his mind. *When you break cover, you watch your back.*

Painfully—feet aching, legs aching—he descended the wooden stairs to the yard.

"It's two bits to sleep the night." A man came out of the store that occupied half the downstairs of the building. His face was the color of well-worn saddle leather, and about as expressive. He stood with folded arms in the muddy way that led back from the yard to the street.

The voice wasn't the same as the one Lacrîme had spoken to last night. At a guess, the owner of the store collected money from the men who slept in his attic, but asked no questions about who came and went. The man with the cigar had been one of the other slaves.

"I have no money," said January. "I can get some. I'll bring it, later in the day."

"You'll bring it and six white horses too, huh?"

"I'll bring it." January's head ached, though not nearly as bad as his body or his hand. Fatigue and hunger made him feel scraped-out, as if the marrow had been sold out of his bones. He felt he should argue with this man, or produce some telling reason why he should be trusted, but he couldn't think of any at the moment. He'd have to pay Desdunes for his horse, too.

Even anger had gone to ash. He could have struck him, he supposed—from a great distance—but that would mean someone would call the police.

"I hold on to your boots," said the storekeeper. "When you come back with my two bits, you get your boots back."

So it was that January was barefoot, ragged, his hand wrapped in dirty bandages, and his whole body sweating like a nervous horse with fear that someone would stop him, ask his business, or worse yet recognize him, when he slipped down the narrow walkway and into his sister Dominique's yard. Becky, standing under the kitchen gallery ironing the intricate cut-lace puffs of a dress sleeve, looked up and called, "What is it? What do you want?" in a hard, cross voice, then looked again and set the iron down quickly.

"Michie Benjamin!" She ran toward him, stopped, staring, as he held up his hand. "What in the name of heaven?"

"Is my sister here?" And, as she started for the rear door of the house, "Don't speak of me if there's anyone here but her."

Becky went inside. January waited under the gallery, hesitant even to go into the kitchen with his scratched feet and muddy clothes. All he could think was, *Mama will never let me hear the end of this.*

He wondered what his mother would do, if Xavier Peralta had already used his influence to send the police for his, January's, arrest.

He wasn't entirely sure he wanted to know.

Minou appeared in the dark of the house, stepped outside, like a blossom of Queen Anne's lace in lavender-striped muslin sprigged with violets. Another figure flashed in the darkness, emerged into the light. Olympe, her blue skirt and rusty persimmon-red blouse and tignon giving her the look of a market woman against the dull gray of the afternoon light.

"Dear God!" cried Minou, but for a moment there was only worried watchfulness, swift calculation in Olympe's dark eyes. Then, "What happened? That policeman was here this morning, to talk to you, he said."

A riverboat would have brought Peralta back to town in eight hours, maybe nine, thought January. Enough passed on the lower river that he could have signaled one within a few hours of the disappearance being discovered.

"I gave him your letter, Ben. Becky, heat some water now, immediately. You said if you hadn't returned by Sunday, and he said he'd been to Mama's house already. Ben, you didn't—?"

He shook his head. "Can you send someone to the grocery on the upstream lakeside corner of Rue Conti, a couple of blocks above the turning basin? Give the owner two reales and get my boots back. And send Thérèse over to Mama's house and get me some clothes."

"I'll send one of my boys," said Olympe, in her Hecate voice of silver-veined iron. "We don't know what the police know, or what they think, but that policeman who came, he's no fool." As she spoke she slipped past the cook and into the kitchen, coming out with a blue-and-white German-made dish of jambalaya and a pone of bread. "You got your papers?"

Again he shook his head. "They're in the desk in my room. Top left drawer." He resolved, as soon as he had the time, to forge five or six more copies. "What did Shaw say?"

"That he wanted to talk to you." Dominique seated herself on another of the bent-willow kitchen chairs, while January gouged into the jambalaya like a gravedigger in a fever summer, alternating the rice and shrimp with gulps of coffee only partly warmed. "I asked him if you were in any trouble. He said you could be, and would be if he couldn't find you. Ben, what happened?"

"Peralta's overseer tore up my papers," said January. "Galen Peralta didn't kill Angelique, but his father thinks he did. He said he'd hold me there until the boy's face healed up—Angelique scratched him pretty badly and a jury might take that amiss—then put me on a boat for Europe or New York or wherever I wanted to go. Some of the slaves told me that night the overseer was planning to take me and sell me himself and claim I'd escaped. They slipped me a mattock head to hack through the window bars."

"Oh, Ben." Her voice was barely a whisper, her hand to her mouth. *Fear for me?* wondered January. Well, yes—Dominique was a warm-hearted girl, with a ready sympathy, and cared for him with the unthinking happy love she'd shown when she was four and he her great, tall brother twenty years her senior. But was part of the shock he read in her eyes a realization of how little her own freedom meant?

Or didn't she understand that yet?

"What . . . What do they want you for? You have papers. I mean, you are free, and here in town people know you."

"Peralta may tell the police some story that makes it seem I did the murder, rather than his son." Thin rain had started to fall again, as it had fallen all day, pattering the muddy ground beyond the gallery where they sat. Becky moved silently in the kitchen behind them, grinding fresh coffee and feeding the fire under the big iron boiler.

"He's the guards' captain's cousin, and the guards are under pressure from Etienne Crozat to find someone, anyone, to punish for the crime. I think I can find who really did it, but I'll need proof. And that proof had better be strong enough to stand up against the fact that the killer was almost certainly white, and I'm black."

By the time January had finished bathing and had shaved five days' bristle of graying beard from his face, Olympe had returned with his boots and a bundle of clothes from their mother's house. Both sisters were waiting for him in Dominique's parlor when he crossed the yard through the thin, driving needles of rain; he wondered why he'd never realized how much alike they looked.

Probably because he'd never seen them together as adults. It occurred to him to wonder what Olympe was doing here at all.

"I need to find a runaway, a girl name of Sally," said January, as he came into the rear parlor where both women sat. "So high, thin, as black as me. Full-blood Congo, they say. She ran off from Les Saules Plantation a week ago Friday, probably with a man." At the moment, he reflected, finding her might be safer than another trip out to Les Saules, at least while the sun was up.

"I think she knows something, and I'm pretty sure she talked to someone about something." He'd examined his hand in the kitchen and had found it still clean. The bandages Becky had pinned over the dressings and salves he'd put on it gleamed starkly white against the dark of his flesh.

"I'll ask around," said Olympe. "She could be anywhere, if she ran off with a man. White man?"

"I don't know. I think so, since he was able to give her expensive gifts."

"A two-dollar dress length still cheaper than buying a girl at the Exchange," remarked Olympe cynically. "I found who paid Doctor John for your hoodoo."

A carriage passed in the street, the wheels squishing thickly in the mire. Dominique turned her head quickly, toward the two tall French doors that opened onto Rue Burgundy—standing open, for the day, though rainy, was warm. Olympe's bronze lips twisted. "Don't worry. We'll be out of here when he comes."

Dominique sniffed. "That isn't going to be until ten at least. I swear, on Sunday afternoons you could wipe out the entire French population of the city with five cannonballs if you knew where to aim them."

"Maybe that's why the Americans don't have aunts and in-laws and cousins-thrice-removed to Sunday dinner," remarked Olympe, lazily stroking the fat white cat. "Like rabbits in a field, they don't all graze in a herd."

"Darling, you know it's for reasons of domestic economy." Minou flashed back at her the identical smile. "The LeBretons must spend a hundred dollars on those Sunday dinners, once you pack in all the Lafrenières, Borés, Macartys, Chauvins, Viellards, Boisclaires, Boisblancs, and Lebedoyere connections, even if they don't have dancing afterward—which they will, Lent or no Lent. No American would stand for it, isn't that so, Ben? That awful Culver woman had the nerve to haggle with Ben over teaching her repulsive little girls to play piano!"

January smiled in spite of himself. "They aren't repulsive," he said. It was like looking back on something that had happened years ago. "And I think one reason the Americans don't have everyone in the world for Sunday dinner is because most of them are new to this city. They come in from New York or Philadelphia or Virginia; they bring their wives and children, but they haven't had time to get grandmamas and sisters' husbands and the brother's wife's widowed aunt and her four children yet. Give them time."

Dominique made a little noise of disbelief in her throat, and crossed to the secrétaire. "From everything I hear, they're going to *take* that time whether anyone *gives* it to them or not. Could the person who bought the gris-gris have been at the ball?"

"*Could* have?" said Olympe. "She *was* there, chérie, and right in Angelique's pocket the whole time."

January's eyes met hers, and he knew with a sinking sense of shock of whom she spoke. *"Clemence Drouet?"* And then, "That's ridiculous. She worshiped Angelique."

The eyes of both sisters rested on him, older and younger, with the same exasperated patience, the same slight wonderment at his blindness. It was Dominique who spoke.

"Oh, Ben, you don't think the plain girls, the fat girls, the ones who fetch and carry and follow around after the pretty ones, don't know *exactly* how they get talked about behind their backs?" There was pity and a little grief in her voice. "You think Clemence couldn't have hated Angelique at the same time she loved her?"

"Doctor John, he say he made Clemence a couple fine gris-gris," said Olympe. "The one you gave me and another that may still be under the back step, and it can stay there, for all of me, if Phrasie Dreuze is going to live in that house. Mamzelle Marie tell me," she added, as Dominique went to pull a bundle of yellow notepaper from the drawer of the secrétaire, "the men who beat you up was Clemence's brother Marquis and his friend, tryin' to get that gris-gris back before you could find out who laid it and tell on her."

January remembered how the men's hands had torn at his coat. For money, he'd thought at the time. Remembered too the young woman's round, tear-streaked face in the shadows of Angelique's house, the look of terror in her eyes as Euphrasie Dreuze had wailed of murder. *She's been underfoot all morning,* his mother had said.

"Mostly they do stop at gris-gris, you know," added Olympe quietly, leaning back on the divan like a slim black serpent and stroking the cat's white feet. "Women who have hate in them. They'll put a pasteboard coffin on somebody's back step, or a cross of salt, as a way of doing murder and not doing murder. Some of them, it makes them stop and think."

"I know last fall that American Jenkins came over and talked to Clemence, at just about every Blue Ribbon Ball," said Dominique. She lowered the papers, her dark eyes sad. "But of course Angelique never could stand to see men paying attention to anyone but her. Still, I'd never have thought Clemence would harm a hair of Angelique's head."

"Nor would she," said January softly. "If she went to Doctor John for a gris-gris, she could have gone for something else. Poison, to slip in her glass—and she'd have had every opportunity in the world. Even an emetic on the night of the ball, if she wasn't up to doing murder. Strangling her with a scarf at a public ball . . ." He shook his head.

"Chéri, *I* was ready to strangle her with a scarf at that ball," retorted Dominique, returning to shuffling her papers. "And *I* hadn't just seen her walk off with the first man who'd paid me any attention in my life. There," she said, poking her finger down. "I thought I saw her go running downstairs just after Galen did. She could have come back up the service stairs."

"What *is* that?" January craned his head to see what was written. "I thought Shaw came and got his notes when they opened the case again."

"Silly." She crossed to him, handed them over—neat, small, perfect French handwriting on creamy gilt-edged notepaper. "I copied them. If there's going to be a nine days wonder in this town, of course I'm going to make sure I'm the one who has all the facts."

Minou had rearranged the notes in chronological order. At quarter of nine, Clemence Drouet was listed as "downstairs—court? lobby?" Also listed in the court at the time was the orange-and-green Turk, and Indian with a question mark, which could have been anyone.

Shortly thereafter, Xavier Peralta had been seen going into Froissart's office with the dueling party—Granger, Mayerling, the purple pirate, Bouille, Jenkins—but when one Doucette Labayadere (costumed as a mulberry tree—*a mulberry tree?*) saw them emerge, the party had consisted solely of Froissart, Granger, and Bouille. The others, presumably, had left at some earlier time.

No one had seen Galen Peralta in the downstairs lobby after the progressive waltz, but at least one other person had seen Augustus Mayerling.

He sat for a time, turning the notes over and over in his hand.

Mayerling was an outsider. A white man, true, but a man raised outside of slave-holding society. A man who would pick a surgeon on the grounds of experience rather than color.

If nothing else, it was worth asking what he knew.

"May I take these?"

"You may not!" retorted his sister indignantly. Then, relenting, "I'll make you out a copy; you can get it tomorrow."

"You're a peach." He kissed her hand, then looked out the open French doors, where the light was fading to final, rainy dusk. "Something tells me we may need an extra copy where we can get at it."

"I have the original notes, too," she said. "I mean the ones the officer made that night. Monsieur Shaw left them here when he had his fair copy and I just put them in a drawer. Will you be speaking to Monsieur Shaw?"

January set down the notes. "I don't know," he said. "If I can do it without being arrested on the spot, yes. You say you gave him my letter. Did he read it?"

She nodded.

"Did he say anything?"

"Nothing. Just put it in his pocket. But he can read," she added quickly. "I saw him read these notes when he took them."

Olympe sniffed, sounding extremely like their mother. "There's miracles every day. Will you need a place to stay, brother? This Shaw will know Mama's house—this house, too," she added, and January noted, a little cynically, that for one tiny unguarded second Dominique looked relieved. "If worse comes to worst there are other places you can stay as well, until we can get you out of town."

"Good," said January bitterly. "So I can be a fugitive, because witnesses don't want to testify anything that'll make a jury think a white killed that woman."

"Better than bein' a corpse for the same reason." She shifted the cat off her lap and fetched an oiled-silk umbrella from behind the door. "I'll find somebody who can get a letter to this Shaw, set up a meetin'." She went to the French doors, looked out at the street, where the oil lamps suspended high on the walls cast flashing coins of light in the dark water of the gutters. "Darn few on the streets now, so you should be safe enough."

January put on the jacket she'd brought him, kissed Minou, and stepped down from the French doors, helping his sister—who needed it no more than a gazelle—down to the brick banquette, and from there across the plank to the street. Only a few spits of rain flecked them now, but the darkening sky was heavily pregnant with more.

"I'll still want to find this Sally girl and speak to Clemence Drouet if I can."

"You really think that poor spaniel of a girl was clever enough to know if she killed Angelique in public that way, people'd go lookin' in all directions but at her?" Olympe shook her head. "Unless she was clever all these years—deep clever—I'd say if she killed her friend in anger over her walkin' off with Jenkins, she'd just have sat down beside the body and howled."

"Maybe," agreed January, knowing Olympe was probably right.

"I've told you what I know about it," his sister went on, "and so I'll ask you this, Ben: Be careful what you do with that knowledge. I think Clemence went off cryin' into the night, same as that boy Galen did. But Clemence is a colored gal, where Galen's white. And she did pay for that gris-gris. If the law's out lookin' for someone to hang, like you say, all you'll have to do is speak her name and she'll be a dead woman, for no more crime than hating a woman she wasn't strong enough to leave."

January was silent, knowing again that Olympe spoke true and wondering wearily how he had happened to have the responsibility not only for Madeleine Trepagier's freedom yoked to his shoulders, but for the life of a girl he'd barely met. For some reason he remembered that Apollo was not only the god of music and of healing but of justice as well.

Monsieur Gomez had taught him, *Make your diagnosis first, then decide on treatment when you know the facts.*

Augustus first, he thought. *Then we'll see what else we need to know.*

"I didn't know you knew Minou," he remarked, as they drew near the corner of the Rue Douane.

"Not well. I've kept track of her, of course, but Thursday was the first time I ever went through her door." The dark eyebrows pulled down, troubled by some unaccustomed thoughts. "I didn't think I'd like her, to tell the truth, though she was sweet as a little girl. I was surprised."

"Why Thursday?"

"I went looking for you when I learned who paid for that gris-gris, and told off them boys to give you a poundin'." She frowned again. Her front teeth were just prominent enough to give her face a sharpness, a feral quality, like her watchful dark eyes. He wondered if she knew Lucius Lacrîme. "And then, I was worried about you. The hairball I keep told me you were in trouble, or hurt." She glanced down at his bandaged hand.

January cast back in his mind and told himself that it was coincidence that his capture by Peralta, the interview in the sugar mill, and the long torture of escape had taken place on Thursday.

"I was there today because she asked me to come back, asked my help," Olympe went on. "She's with child, you know."

Something that wasn't quite anger—but was close to it—wrenched him hard. But he only said, "I didn't think Henri had enough red blood in him to make a child."

Olympia Snakebones glanced sidelong up at him, under the umbrella's shadow. "He's good to her," she said. "And he'll be good to the child. They mostly are, as long as those children do what they're told to do, be what they're told to be, and don't go askin' too many questions about why things are the way they are."

January was silent a moment, stopping at the corner of Rue Bienville, a few blocks above the tall house where Augustus Mayerling had his rooms. Then he sighed. "Nobody's got a monopoly on that, sister. Not the whites, not the blacks, not the sang mêlé."

Her smile under the shadow of the umbrella was bright and wry. Then she turned away, crossing a plank to the street and holding her blue skirts high out of the mud as she splashed across, to return to her home, her husband, and her daughters and sons.

Augustus Mayerling occupied two rooms on the top floor, high above a courtyard full of banana plants and plane trees and a shop that dealt in coffees and teas. The rain had eased again to thin flutters, glistening in daffodil patches beneath the streetlights. As he climbed the wooden steps from gallery to gallery, January was surrounded by the rising smells of foliage and cooking from the courtyard beneath him. The high walls of the house muffled the noises of the street, the distant hoot of the steamboat whistles, and the cries of a few final oyster vendors giving up for the day.

While he and Olympe had been walking down Rue Burgundy

they'd heard the cannon by the Cabildo, closing down curfew for the night. The rain had damped the dancing in Congo Square some hours before. If he were stopped by the guards he'd have to present his papers, to prove himself free. The thought made him uneasy. The city seemed very silent without the jostling voices of maskers in the streets, the thump and wail of brass bands in the taverns, the riot of parades.

And indeed, thought January wryly, within a week the Creoles would be hiring him to play at discreet little balls again no matter what the church said about surrendering one's pleasures to God in that time of penitence—provided of course he wasn't in jail or on a boat. Life went on, and one could not content oneself with backgammon and gossip forever.

Certainly no gambling hall in the city had closed down. But that, as any Creole would say with that expressive Creole shrug, was but the custom of the country.

The topmost gallery was dark, illuminated only by the thin cracks of light from the French doors of Mayerling's rooms.

January had just reached the top of the stairs when the doors were opened. Mayerling looked right and left, warily, the gold light glinting on close-cropped flaxen hair and a white shirt open at the throat. Clearly not seeing that anyone else stood there in the dark, he beckoned back in the room behind him.

A woman stepped out, clothed in widow's black.

January felt his heart freeze inside him. The light strength of her movement, the way her shoulders squared when she turned, was—as it had been not many nights ago—unmistakable.

"The back stairs are safer," said Mayerling's husky, boyish voice. "The slaves won't be back for a little time yet." Reaching back into the apartment, the Prussian brought out a cloak, which he settled around his shoulders. Putting a hand to the woman's back, he made to guide her into the dark curve of the building where the back stairs ran down to the gallery above the kitchen.

The woman stopped, turned, put back her veils, and raised her face to his. Dim as it was, the honey warmth of the candles within fell on her, showing January clearly the strong oval lines of the chin, the enormous, mahogany red eyes of Madeleine Trepagier.

TWENTY ONE

Madeleine Trepagier and Augustus Mayerling.

I was a fool not to guess.

Concealed behind the corner of a carriageway halfway down the street, January watched the sword master help his mistress into a hired fiacre. The banquette was otherwise empty; Sunday, Lent, and Creole dinner parties completing what the rain had begun.

It wasn't only Trepagier's mistress who'd met Peralta through Mayerling's school. Mayerling himself had met his pupil's beautiful wife.

Whoever he marries will have cause to thank the person who wielded that scarf.

I should have no choice but to avenge that lady's honor. . . . Why hadn't he seen it then, less than two minutes after Mayerling had attributed all dueling to boredom, ignorance, and vice?

Perhaps because of the disgusted horror in Madeleine's eyes when she'd said, *Not a man* . . .

The cab moved away from the banquette. Fair head bowed in the rain, Mayerling turned and vanished into the pitch-dark carriageway from which he and Madame Trepagier had come.

She'll change from the fiacre to her own carriage somewhere, thought January. *Probably the Place des Armes.*

He stepped out of hiding and moved through the rainy, lamp-blotched darkness after the fiacre, the mud and water washing over the street's uneven paving-blocks slowing its progress and making it easy for him to keep it in sight.

Augustus was a foreigner. White, but a Prussian. A jury might just rule on the evidence and not the color of the defendant's skin.

But everything in him was saying, *No, no* as he followed the dark bulk of the carriage through the streets toward the cathedral.

Not a man, Madeleine had said, with a loathing in her eyes that had told its own tale of Arnaud Trepagier as surely as had the old cook and laundress of Les Saules. Working at the Hôtel Dieu, January had met women who had been raped and abused, had seen what it did to them ever after. That any man would have been gentle enough, caring enough, to lead her out of that prison of terror and rage was a miracle and a gift.

Looking back at that Thursday night at the Salle d'Orléans, January could see everything with blinding clarity.

Everything except what he should do.

In a novel the answer would be obvious. *"Missy, ain't been no joy in this old world for me since my woman done died."* Followed by a quaintly ill-spelt confession and the rope—or maybe a ticket to France if the novelist was in a good humor.

But New Orleans was his home. And Uhrquahr and Peralta weren't the only enemies advancing through the mist.

By the rustling darkness of the cathedral garden, literally a stone's throw from the Orleans ballroom, the fiacre came to a halt. It was raining more heavily now, but Madame Trepagier, her face hidden by the long veils of a widow, stepped down and paid the driver, then turned and hurried into the alley that ran between the church and the Cabildo, a black form swiftly swallowed by the dark.

Dominique ran that way, the night of the murder, thought January, following her into the dark. But during the bright Carnival season there had been lamps in every one of the shop fronts along the alley that were now closed up and dark, revelers staggering back and forth in a steady stream between Rue Royale and the Place des Armes. With the cathedral clock striking eight, and the leaden ceiling of cloud mixing with the eternal pall of steamboat smoke, the alley was pitch-black, with only a window or two throwing gold sprinkles on the falling rain.

Creole Sunday in New Orleans, thought January. *Of course Madeleine Trepagier would have dinner with Aunt Picard, with all the Trepagier cousins in attendance, pressing their suits. Why not? Why not? A woman can't run a plantation alone.* It would be the easiest thing in the world to claim a headache and retreat to the arms of the one man whose touch she could endure without nausea. Her own coachman would have instructions ahead of time to pick her up in the Place des Armes. There was no one at Les Saules now to mark the time she returned, except her servants.

A chill went through him as he thought, *And one of them's gone.* For the first time he wondered what exactly it was that Sally might have seen, and whether she had left Les Saules at all.

That far from other houses, as Madame Trepagier herself had pointed out, a woman was at the mercy of her husband, but so a slave girl would be at the mercy of a mistress who had something to hide.

He saw her shape, reflected ahead of him against the few lamps burning in the Place des Armes, and quickened his step. Then there was a blurred scuffle of movement, and her scream echoed in the brick strait of the alley like the sudden sound of ripping cloth.

There was a scuffle, a splash, a glimpse of struggling forms in the dark, and a man's curse in river-rat English. Madeleine screamed again and there was another splash, but by this time January was on top of them, grabbing handfuls of coarse, greasy cloth that stank of tobacco and vomit and pissed-out beer. He shoved someone or something up against the brick of the alley wall and smashed with all his force where a face should be, grating his knuckles on hair. A voice from the square shouted "Madame Madeleine! Madame Madeleine!" and there was gasping, screaming, cursing and the slosh and stench of gutter water.

The man January had struck came back at him like a bobcat, but January was a good five inches taller and far heavier and lifted him bodily, slamming him to the pavement like a sack of corn. He kicked

him, very hard, then turned to seize the second man, who was wading
knee-deep in the heaving stream of the gutter, knife flashing in his
hand, above the billow of black petticoats and floating veils beneath
him. He stomped his foot down, pinning Madame Trepagier under
the water, then cursed in surprise and fell on top of her. January was
on them by then, dragging him up by a wad of dripping, verminous
hair.

The knife slashed and gleamed. January twisted sideways, losing
his grip, and then the man was pelting away along the building fronts
of Rue Chartres, as a slender old man with a coachman's whip came
running up unsteadily, gasping for breath, his face ashy.

Madame Trepagier was trying to rise, her dragging skirts and veils
a soaked confusion about her, trembling so badly she could barely
stand. She shrank from January's steadying hand with a cry, then
looked up at his face. For an instant he thought she would break
down, cling to him weeping, but she turned away, hugging herself
desperately in her soaked winding-sheets of veils. "I'm all right." Her
voice was tense as harp wire, but low and steady. "I'm all right."

"Madame Madeleine, Madame Madeleine!" The old coachman
looked as if he needed to be propped up himself. "You all right? You
hurt?" In the shadows of the alley mouth only his eyes and teeth and
silver coat buttons caught the reflection of the lights along the
Cabildo's colonnade. Like a drenched crow in mourning weeds, wet
veils plastered over her cheeks, Madame Trepagier was little more than
a sooty cloud. "Come on, Madame Madeleine. I'll take you back to
your Aunt Picard's, get those wet clothes off you—"

"No," she said quickly. "Not my aunt's."

Not, thought January, if she'd left there three hours ago with a
manufactured headache.

He put a steadying hand under her elbow. She stiffened, but did
not pull away.

"Come," he said. "I'll get you to my sister's."

"It . . . was foolish of me. Walking down that alleyway, I mean."
Madeleine Trepagier made a small movement with her hand toward

her unraveled torrent of dark hair, and Dominique said, "Sh-sh-sh," and moved the trembling fingers away. Her own hands worked competently with the soft pig-bristle brush, stroking out the long, damp swatches, less now to untangle them than to let them dry and to calm the woman who sat in the chair before her, laced into a borrowed corset and a borrowed dress and with a cup of herb tisane steaming before her. The honey-gold moire of the gown, with its ribbons of caramel and pink, set off Madeleine's warm complexion as beautifully as it did Dominique's. January wondered how long it would be before the woman abandoned her mourning and returned to wearing colors like this again.

"I never thought ruffians would be lurking that close to the police station," continued Madeleine, folding her hands obediently in her lap. "I was just walking back from my Aunt Picard's over on Rue Toulouse."

Dominique's dress was cut lower than a widow's high-made collar, and the small gold cross Madeleine wore around her throat was just visible in the pit between her collarbones. January saw again the way her head had fallen back to receive the sword master's mouth on hers, the desperate strength with which they had held each other in the thin spit of the rain.

Augustus and Madeleine. A glimpse of deerskin, as golden as the dress she wore now, in the doorway as he began the first waltz. Looking for him? And the Prussian in his black-and-green Elizabethan doublet, crossing the downstairs lobby as Galen Peralta descended after his fight with Angelique.

Questions crowded his mind, a jam of logs at high water behind his teeth, and the first of them, the largest of them, was always, *What do I do?*

He was glad of Dominique's prattle, of her presence in the room. It gave him time to think.

"Cathedral Alley isn't so very far from the levee," he pointed out in time. "Or from Gallatin Street. We had Kaintucks all over town during Mardi Gras."

Dominique sniffed. "And I'm sure the significance of Ash Wednesday completely escaped them. One would think after a week they would get the hint." If she felt any uncertainty at all about the presence of a white lady in her parlor, she certainly didn't show it. "You poor darling, thank God Ben was there. What were you doing down on Rue Royale, anyway, Ben? I thought you were going to Olympe's."

"I thought I saw someone who could give me an explanation about the night of the murder," said January, and his glance crossed Madeleine's. Her eyes, downcast with confusion at finding herself in the house of a plaçée, went wide with shock and dread.

"Now, don't talk about murders," said Dominique severely, and patted Madeleine's shoulders. She hesitated for a long moment, then picked her words carefully. "My brother is helping the police investigating Angelique Crozat's murder—for all they're doing," she added tartly. "Personally, I'm *astonished* the one who was strangled wasn't that awful harpy of a mother. I was *speechless* when I heard how she'd sold off all your jewelry and dresses . . . and do you know, Ben, she's been flouncing around town for days in a mourning veil down to her feet, and the most dreadful cheap crêpe dress. It streaked black all over Mama's straw-colored divan cushions. Excuse me, dears, I'll just go to the kitchen and see if your coachman is all right."

Not even random violence that could have ended in murder, thought January wryly, *could shake Dominique's sense of caste.* Watching his sister through the arch into the rear parlor, and thence through the French door at the back and into the rainy yard, he knew that the coachman would be shown all consideration, given a cup of coffee and some of Becky's wonderful crêpes, in the kitchen. The rain had let up almost completely, and through the open French doors to the street a few droplets still caught the lamplight as they fell. The streaming brightness flashed on the millrace of the gutter, and on the slow, lazy drips from the abat-vent overhead. A fiacre passed, the driver cursing audibly at the Trepagier carriage that stood, horse blanketed, before the cottage. A few streets away a man's voice bellowed, "Now, don't you push me, hear! I am the child of calamity and the second cousin to the yellow fever! I eats Injuns for breakfast. . . ."

Madeleine shuddered profoundly and lowered her forehead to her hand. Very softly, she said, "Don't ask me about it tonight, Monsieur

Janvier, please. Thank you—thank you so much—for helping me, for being there." Her shoulders twitched a little, as if still feeling the grasp of heavy hands, and she brought up a long breath. "I know why you were there. You followed me from . . . from Rue Bienville, didn't you? I thought I saw you as the fiacre pulled away."

"Yes," said January softly. She raised her face, her eyes meeting his, steadily, willing him to believe.

"He is innocent. I swear to you he had nothing to do with the murder. I—" She took a deep breath. "I strangled Angelique. Please, please, I beg you . . ."

"You didn't," said January quietly, "and I know you didn't, Madame. That outfit of yours was leaking black cock feathers all over the building and you were never near that parlor. And you had nothing on you that could have been used for a garrote. Did you stay to see him?"

"No! He had nothing to do with it, I swear to you."

"Were you with him?"

She hesitated, searching in her mind for what the best answer would be, then cried "No!" a few instants late. "I saw him—that is, I saw him across the lobby. . . . I saw him the whole time. But we weren't . . . we didn't . . ."

She was floundering, and January turned away. The woman sprang to her feet, caught his arm, her face blazing like gold in the soft flicker of the lamp. "Please! Please don't go to the police! Please don't mention his name! Come . . ." She hesitated, stammering, scouting, staring up into his face, trying to read his eyes. "Come to Les Saules tomorrow. I'll talk about anything you want me to then. But not tonight."

"So you can get a note to him?" asked January.

Her eyes flinched, then returned to his. "No, of course not. It's just that—"

She got no further. Hannibal Sefton, threadbare coat and long hair damp with the rain, singing a von Weber aria and more than slightly drunk, sprang lightly through the French door from the banquette outside directly behind Madeleine's back, caught her around the waist, and gave her a resounding kiss on the neck.

Madeleine screamed, pure terror in her voice. She wrenched herself free with a violence that knocked away the chair by which she stood and ripped her assailant's face with the clawed fingers of both hands. Hannibal recoiled with a gasp of shock, almost falling back through the doorway. January caught at the terrified woman but she tore herself from him and staggered a step or two into the middle of the room, sobbing and shaking. The next instant Dominique came flying through the dining room door and caught her in her arms.

"It's all right! It's all right! Darling, it's all right, he's a friend of mine—a very impudent friend."

Hannibal stood, violin case forgotten on the floor beside him, clinging to the doorjamb with one hand while the other felt his bleeding face. His eyes were those of a dog who has come up expecting a pat and received instead a forceful kick in the teeth. "I'm sorry," he said. "Madame, I'm so sorry, I didn't—" He looked pleadingly from Dominique to January, aghast and helpless. "I thought it was Minou. I swear I thought it was Minou."

"Oh, and that's how you treat me, is it?" retorted Minou, furious at the result rather than the deed, but furious nonetheless. Held tight in her arms, Madeleine was still racked with long waves of shaking, head bowed over, as if she were about to be sick. If she was faking, thought January, he had never seen it so well done.

And somehow, he did not think her horror at a man's touch was a fake.

"It's all right." He put a hand on Hannibal's shoulder. "I'll explain outside. Minou, would you go out to Les Saules with Madame Trepagier? I don't think she should be alone."

"Oh, of course! I've already told Thérèse to tell Henri—*if* that slug ever puts in an appearance—that I've been called away by an emergency, and to give him tisane and flan and everything he might need. Now you get out of here, you bad man." But she touched Hannibal's forearm to reassure him, as January herded him out the long doors and onto the banquette once more.

Glancing back, January saw his sister help Madame Trepagier into a chair, still trembling violently; heard Madame Trepagier whisper "Thank you. . . . Thank you."

"Augustus Mayerling, hm?" said Hannibal, when January had finished his narration. Even along a relative backstreet like Rue Burgundy, oil lamps still burned on their curved brackets from the stucco walls of the houses, their light gleaming in the gutters and the wet pavements beyond. Beneath the outthrust galleries of the town houses and shops and the abat-vents of the line of cottages, they were almost completely protected from the increasing rain.

In every house, past the iron-lace balconies and behind spidery lattices of wooden louvers, warm light shone, working a kind of magic in the night. Somewhere someone was playing a banjo—strictly against the rules of Lent—elsewhere voices sounded from the two sides of a corner grog-shop, shutters opened all the length of the room onto the street, where free blacks and river-trash played cards, cursed, laughed.

"I hate to think it was him," January finished after a time, "because I like the boy. But of everyone in the Orléans ballroom that night, it sounds to me like Mayerling had the best reason for wanting Angelique dead. And Madame Trepagier knows it. And much as I like him, and much as I don't blame him for doing it, it's him or me . . . and I want to look around his rooms for that necklace."

"And if you don't find it, then what?" asked Hannibal. His voice was a faint, raw rasp, and he coughed as they crossed the planks at the corner of Rue Conti. "It could have been anyone in the ballroom, you know."

"Then why protect him? Why beg me not to so much as speak his name to the police? Why risk her own neck, if all that would happen to him was a night or two in jail until he was cleared? Other women have lovers. It isn't spoken of, but everyone in town knows who they are. It isn't as if she were deceiving a husband, and the plantation is hers to dispose of as she will, no matter what her family says. She doesn't have to say they were together in the ballroom. She can say they met elsewhere, if she's going to lie about it. But she doesn't. Why would she deny his involvement in anything so completely, if what he did doesn't bear scrutiny?"

"It's not what he did," said Hannibal quietly. "It's what he is."

January looked at him blankly. For a moment he thought, *With that complexion he can't POSSIBLY be an octoroon trying to pass.*

Hannibal hesitated a moment, then said, "Augustus Mayerling is a woman."

"What?" It stopped January dead on the banquette.

"Augustus Mayerling is a woman. I don't know what his—her—real name is." Hannibal started walking again, with that kind of loose-jointed scarecrow grace, his dark eyes turned inward on the recollection.

"But it isn't that unusual, you know. There was that woman who served for years as a man in the Russian cavalry recently. Women fought at Trafalgar and Waterloo disguised as men. I've talked to men who knew them. I found out about Augustus—well, I guessed—almost by accident. About two years ago he picked me up outside a saloon in Gallatin Street where I'd been playing for dimes. Of course they robbed me the minute I was out the door, and he took me back to his place, since I was almost unconscious. I was feverish all night, and he cared for me, and I—it was probably the fever—I could tell the difference. I kissed his hand—her hand—we just looked at each other for a minute. I knew."

Of all people, thought January, *Hannibal would know.*

The fiddler shrugged. "Later we talked about it. I think he was glad to have someone else who knew. I've covered for him now and then, though he seems to have worked out long ago all the little dodges, all the ways of getting around questions, things like keeping shaving tackle in his rooms and staying out of certain situations. But, that wouldn't be possible, for even a day or two, in jail. God knows he's far from the first person to manage it. You're the only one I've told. Don't . . ."

"No. Of course not." January walked along, feeling a little stunned.

Fighting is either for joy, or for death. . . .

He could still see the Prussian's cold yellow eyes as he said that, bright as they spoke about the passion of his art. And he'd seen Mayerling fight, in the long upper room that was his salle des armes on Exchange Alley: whalebone and steel and terrifyingly fast. He'd heard about the men he had killed.

Suddenly he remembered Madeleine Trepagier as a child, attacking the Beethoven sonatas like a sculptor carving great chunks of marble in quest of the statues hidden within, drunk with the greedy strength of one lusting to unite with the heart of an art.

Hers was music, like his own. Her lover's was steel.

But the passion was the same. Of course they would find it in each other.

"I understand," he said softly. "In a way it could be no one else."

"No," said Hannibal. His dark eyes clouded. "Too many women who have been . . . injured like that . . . don't find anyone."

But that was not what January had meant.

They walked in silence, January remembering the occasional couple in Paris—usually prostitutes who came from five or ten or twenty men a day back to the arms of their lady friends. But there had been one pair of middle-aged and smilingly contented daughters of returned aristo émigrés who ran a hat shop in the Bois de Boulogne and made fortunes off their bits of flowers and lace.

But none of that, he thought, meant that Augustus Mayerling hadn't been the one to wind that scarf around Angelique's neck.

"I still want to have a look around his rooms," said January after a time. "In any case he'll want to hear what happened tonight."

He cannot pass himself off as a gentleman, Jean Bouille had said of the American Granger, little realizing that the spidery-thin sword master who had taught him was doing exactly that.

Only the mask he wore was his cropped fair hair, thought January, *and the scars on his face.* But a mask it was, as surely as the elaborate thing of jewels and fur that had hidden Angelique's face on the night of her death. The man's coat and trousers were a costume as surely as that stolen white silk dress had been, more subtle because they used the minds of those who saw as a disguise.

I wear trousers, therefore you see a man.

Your skin is black, therefore I see a slave. Except, of course, that Augustus was one of the few people in this country who saw a musician, and a man. Beside him, Hannibal said again, "Will she forgive me? Will Minou make her understand? I thought it was Minou. She was wearing Minou's dress—I thought it was Minou. I'm so sorry."

January started to say, "It's all right, she was just scared—" and then stopped, and it seemed to him that the blood in his veins turned colder than the rain.

"Oh, Jesus," he whispered.

Hannibal halted too, looking up at him, baffled. "What—"

"She was wearing Madeleine's jewels," said January softly.

"Who was? Minou . . ."

"She was wearing Madeleine's jewels, and whoever killed her thought she was Madeleine." January still stood in the middle of the banquette, staring into space, shaken to his bones but knowing, as surely as he knew his name, that he was right.

"They killed the wrong woman."

"Who did? Why would anyone . . . ?"

"The plantation," said January. He made a move back toward Rue Burgundy, then halted, knowing the carriage had moved away from the banquette moments after he and Hannibal had left the house. "Les Saules. It butts up against the Gentilly place—wasn't one of the proposed streetcar routes Granger and Bouille were fighting over out past Bayou Gentilly? If the route goes out there the land will be worth a fortune. If she sells it all to that McGinty fellow for debts . . ."

"McGinty?" said Hannibal, startled. "McGinty was one of Granger's seconds. The pirate with the red Vandyke, holding the horses."

The two men stared at each other for a moment, pieces falling into place: McGinty's coppery whiskers clashing with the purple satin of his pirate mask, the faubourgs of New Orleans spreading in an Americanized welter of wooden gingerbread and money, Livia's dry voice reading aloud William Granger's slanderous accusations of Jean Bouille in the newspaper, the efforts to discredit Madeleine before Aunt Picard could marry her off.

"Come on!" January turned and strode down Rue Bienville, Hannibal hurrying, gasping, in his wake.

"How did they know she'd be at the ball?"

"Sally. The girl who ran off. The one who had a 'high-toned' boyfriend—a white boyfriend. You or Fat Mary ever find out anything of where she went?"

The fiddler shook his head. "Not a word of her."

"Ten to one the man she ran off with was McGinty or someone connected with him. He'd been around the plantation on business."

"And tonight . . ."

"It's got to be someone connected with the Trepagier family. Someone who stands to inherit—and my guess is it's Arnaud's brother. Claud, the one who's been in Texas." He strode along the banquette, heedless of the rain. "Anyone connected with the family would know she'd be at her Aunt Picard's tonight. Anyone could have arranged an ambush."

"Then if the attack this evening wasn't chance . . ."

"They'll have followed her out of town to try again."

TWENTY TWO

Hannibal's breathing had hoarsened to a dragging gasp by the time they reached the gallery outside Mayerling's rooms. The rain was heavy now, streaming down from a tar-black sky and glittering in the lamps hung under the galleries. In the amber glow of the candles that the Prussian brought to the open door, January could see no difference, no clue to confirm what he now knew. The epicene ivory beakiness was the same. His only thought was, *Even without the scars, that's one homely woman.*

"Madame Trepagier is in trouble," said January, as the Prussian stepped out onto the gallery, clothed in vest and shirtsleeves, the short-cropped blond bristle of hair still damp from its earlier wetting in the rain. "Where do you keep your chaise?"

"Rue Douane. Where is she?" He reached back through the door and fetched his coat from its peg. "And how do you—?"

"Bring your guns."

Mayerling stopped, his eyes going to January's, then past him to Hannibal, leaning on the upright of the gallery stair and holding his ribs to still his coughing.

"What's happened? Come in." He strode away into the apartment, where another branch of candles burned on a table before an open book. The place was small and almost bare, but in one corner of the room stood a double escapement seven-octave Broadwood piano, and music was heaped on its lid and the table at its side.

The Prussian flipped open an armoire, pulled a drawer, drew forth the boxed set of Manton pistols with which Granger and Bouille had missed each other, and a bag of shot. From the wall beside the armoire he took down a Kentucky long rifle and an English shotgun.

During this activity January explained, "Someone attacked Madame Trepagier after she left here." Mayerling turned his head sharply, but January went on, "She was assaulted in Orléans Alley by the cathedral. I stopped them, sent her off home, but now I think they'll try again. Her brother-in-law's behind it, he's got to be."

"Claud?" Mayerling handed January the shotgun—thereby, January reflected wryly, breaking Louisiana state law—slung the powder box under his arm, and shrugged his coat on top of it, to keep it out of the rain. The last time he had had a gun in his hands, thought January, had been at the Battle of Chalmette. "I'd heard he was back in town, staying with the Trepagier cousins."

"When?" asked January, startled.

"I don't know." Their feet clattered on the wood of the stairways, down one gallery, two. "Mardi Gras itself, I think, or the day before. At least that's when he sent a message to Madeleine asking to see her."

"Did she?"

"No." His voice was dry and very cold. "I think she knew he was going to propose to her."

"Try to murder her, more like. She's lucky she didn't go. You know what he looks like?"

"No. Which is as well," he added softly, "from what she has told me of the man. But why would he have men attack her? Why would he—"

"To inherit Les Saules," said January as they reached the street.

The sword master checked his stride for a moment to regard him in surprise. "The plantation? But without slaves it's worthless. The land's run-down, there are too few slaves to work what they have, they need to replant every one of the fields . . ."

"The land will be worth a hundred dollars an acre if they put the streetcar line out from Gentilly, instead of from LaFayette like Granger's company proposed."

"Granger." Mayerling's light, husky voice was soft. "The duel was over Bouille's decision, of course. Since it went against Granger the line will of course be from Gentilly. And Granger's friend McGinty would have known that. He's been pressing Madeleine to sell to him for months now."

"And at a guess," said Hannibal, reaching out one hand to prop himself just slightly on the iron post of the gallery, "Claud Trepagier is the fellow in the green Turk costume who was talking to McGinty in the Salle d'Orléans a few minutes before Angelique came in."

"*Äffenschwänz*," said Mayerling coldly. "The horse is at the livery just down the way. It will take me minutes . . ."

"Pick me up on Rue Douane below Rampart. Hannibal, you sound like you'd better stay here."

The fiddler coughed, and shook his head violently. "You'll need a loader."

There was no time to argue, so January simply handed the shotgun to Hannibal and took off up Bienville at a lope. A few minutes brought him to Olympe's cottage, where a boy of eleven or so opened the French door into the front bedroom, instead of to the parlor where he had been before.

"Mama, she with a lady, sir," said the boy politely, in slurry Creole French. "You come in, though, it pourin' out." He stepped aside. Through an open door into the other bedroom January could see three more children, like little stair steps, sitting cross-legged on a big bed with a large, broad-shouldered, very kindly-looking mulatto man who was reading to them from a book.

The man got up at once and came in, holding out his hand. "You must be Ben. I'm Paul Corbier."

Once upon a time January could have pictured Olympe marrying no one less impressive than the Devil himself. Looking at his brother-in-law's face he understood at least some of his sister's mellower mood. "I need to speak to Olympe, now, quickly. I think our sister's in trouble . . . Dominique. I need somebody to find Lieutenant

Shaw of the police—or any of the police—and send them out to the Gentilly Road, out to the Trepagier plantation at Les Saules, quickly. There's an ambush been laid, murder going to be done."

"They'll want to know how you know this," said Corbier.

January shook his head. "It's not something I can prove. Lieutenant Shaw will know, it's part of the Crozat murder case. Tell him I think Madeleine Trepagier is going to be ambushed there and we may need help. I'm going out there now."

Harness jingled and tires squelched in the mud, and turning, January saw over his shoulder the chaise that had carried them out to the Allard plantation for the duel. Dark-slicked with water, the horse shook its head against the rain. By the oil lamp in the bracket above the door, and the lesser gleam of the carriage lamps, Mayerling's scarred face was a pale blur in the dark of the leather hood.

"Dominique's with Madame Trepagier. Get Olympe to go, or send one of the children, but hurry!"

January sprang down the high brick step, across the banquette, vaulting the gutter and scrambling into the chaise, crowding its two occupants. His last glimpse of the light showed Paul Corbier turning to give some urgent instruction to the oldest boy as he shut the louvered door.

Mayerling lashed the reins. The wheels jarred and lurched in ruts and mud and jolted as they passed over the gutters, sprays of water leaping around them with the black glitter of liquid coal.

"Hannibal tells me your sister Dominique is with her."

"I had to take her somewhere. Minou knows enough not to speak of it later."

"Trepagier will have hired his men in the Swamp," said Hannibal, clinging to the two long guns and swaying with the violence of their speed. "For a dollar Nahum Shagrue's boys would sack the orphanage if they thought they could get away with it. *The mutable, rank-scented many* . . . Keelboat pirates . . . killers."

"I've met Monsieur Shagrue." January remembered those pig-cunning eyes, and the stink of sewage dripping off his coat.

"The green Turk was with Charles-Louis Trepagier at the Théâtre on Mardi Gras night," said Mayerling in time. "I remember his words concerning Madeleine." The thin nostrils flared with silent anger. "I'm sorry now I didn't settle the matter there and then, in the courtyard. Capon. I suppose by then he had decided that he would rather kill than wed her."

"McGinty would have told him a proposal wasn't any use," said January. "He'd already tried it, as soon as Arnaud was dead—which means he knew there was a chance of the streetcar line going through even then. That must have been when he sent for Claud, and when he started romancing Sally, to keep an eye on Madame Trepagier's movements. Of course as a broker who'd handled Arnaud's affairs he'd have met her. It must have been Sally who told him Madame Trepagier was going to the quadroon ball to talk to Angelique."

"Told him she was going," said Hannibal, "but not what she would wear."

"And Claud hadn't seen Madeleine since her wedding to his brother, thirteen years ago. He couldn't have, if he'd embezzled money and stolen a slave. So when he saw a woman of her height and her build, wearing her jewels. . . ."

"It refreshes me to know," said Mayerling, never taking his eyes from the road, "that upon occasion, some people do get what they deserve. By the way," he added, "thank you for telling her to get out of there. I had no idea of her intention until I saw her, looking in at the ballroom door."

"She was with you until ten, wasn't she?" January kept his voice steady with an effort, for Mayerling drove like the Wild Hunt, and once beyond the lamps of the Faubourg Marigny the road beneath the overhanging oaks was pitch-dark. An occasional glimmer of soft gaslight through colored curtains flickered through the trees like a fashionable ghost to show where houses stood, but even those grew more sparse as the road got worse.

"Yes," said the sword master. "I glimpsed her outside the ballroom and slipped away from that silliness in Froissart's office as quickly as I could. I suppose I should have simply put her in a fiacre at once and sent her home, but instead we went through the passageway to the Théâtre and found our way up to one of the private boxes. We have, you understand, little chance to be together. Foolish, I admit, and dangerous. I beg you make allowances for a man in love."

January glanced sharply sidelong at him, suddenly conscious of the thinness of those shoulder bones pressed so tightly into his arm. Mayerling met his gaze with frosty challenge, then returned his attention to the road as the chaise crashed through a minor lake across their way, water spraying around them in muddy wings.

"It is a long time," said the Prussian quietly, "since I have thought of myself as anything else. I suppose in France you ceased after a time to think of every white man as someone to beware of. To look down when one spoke to you?"

"In France I didn't have to lie every day about what I am."

"Every day I tell the truth about what I am," replied Mayerling calmly. "I merely leave out the one fact—the one facet of my entirety—which would, in everyone's eyes, obliterate all the rest. Two facets, now. I used to lie awake nights, worrying about what would happen if I fell in love."

The thin face split into a sudden grin, like an impish boy's, save for the saber scars. "I never thought it would be a woman I fell in love with, you see. Not until I met her. And then it was like coming out of a dark room into sunlight."

He shrugged. "But, I have the advantage of being physically mannish enough to—as the octoroons say—pass, something I have done since the age of seventeen. *Pass for a gentleman,* I believe Monsieur Bouille put it. . . . There!"

Through the metallic glint of carriage lamps on rain the slow-moving brougham appeared, a dark loom in the road ahead. Mayerling slashed with the reins again, and the horse leaped forward heavily, the chaise rocking like a drunken thing in the flooded ruts. Beyond the narrow zone of the lamps' illumination, nothing could be seen, the evergreen roof of live oak shutting out the black sky above, the Spanish moss dripping in wet curtains of cobweb around about. The coachman, rigid with disapproval of Madame Madeleine's choice of companions, half-turned on his box, trying to maneuver the carriage out of the narrow way to let the swifter vehicle pass. Mayerling pulled his horse to a walk, leaned from the chaise to cry, "Albert! It's me, Mayerling!"

"Monsieur Mayerling, sir!" The coachman saluted with his whip. "What you doin' out on a night like this? And that horse of yours look in a regular lather."

The door of the carriage opened abruptly, Madeleine's face framed suddenly in its darkness, and she had to stop herself visibly from speaking her lover's Christian name in front of her servant. "What is it?" Her voice sounded perfectly composed, but her face was haggard with exhaustion and strain.

January shook himself forcibly free of the sensation of foolishness that overwhelmed him at the sight of the carriage, unmolested, unambushed, untouched. There was danger—if not tonight, then tomorrow, or the next time she went out.

Augustus bowed, sweeping off his hat in the rain. "A complete false alarm, I hope. I'll explain when we reach the house, but Monsieur Janvier has a theory—and I think he's right—about the Crozat woman's murder. And if he's right, the attack on you this evening was no accident, and you may need escort back to Les Saules."

"Ben?" came Dominique's voice from the carriage. "Ben, what theory? And what does it have to do with Madeleine? She wasn't even there that night, in spite of what that horrid Charles-Louis Trepagier has been saying all over town."

"I'll explain at the house," called January from the chaise. He tossed the long rifle, which Augustus caught with an expert hand. "Put out the carriage lamps. Can you see well enough without them to walk at the horse's head?"

"I think so. It's not far from here."

"Put out the carriage lamps?" protested Albert. "Now why on earth . . ."

"Just stay on the box, if you would," ordered Augustus, flipping open the glass to blow out the candles within. "And keep silence. There may be men waiting along the road. They'll hear us coming, even over the rain, but at least we can keep from making targets of ourselves. Here." He walked around to the door again, and passed one of the pistols through it.

"I didn't know you could shoot a pistol." January heard Minou's voice, a sweet thread, as the black ghost that was all he could see of Mayerling drifted back to the coach horse's head, took the bridle, and began to walk forward, boots crunching on the crushed shells of the roadbed.

"My uncle Gustave taught me. He said . . ." Her voice lowered, drowned in the clatter of rain on the chaise roof, and January settled into the slow, cautious business of following the carriage in almost total darkness among the trees. Evidently any constraint Madame Trepagier felt about being in a carriage with a courtesan had been dealt with between the two women already.

Knowing the rain would hide any sound of ambush, he strained all his senses, trying to listen to the forest of oak and sycamore on either side, trying to hear something besides the patter of falling water and the soggy crunch of the wheels in oak leaves, shells, and mud. In time the darkness before them seemed to grow lighter, and the rain fell more heavily on his face. They came out from the trees, turned the corner, with the water of Bayou Gentilly on their left, and to their right, a dim white shape showed behind the oak trunks, like a smudge of chalk on black velvet.

Lights burned in the upstairs parlor of Les Saules, a welcoming glow of saffron through the murk. A lamp had been kindled likewise in the stairway that led from the paved loggia beneath the rear gallery. Augustus, visibly relieved, walked around from the horse's head to the carriage door, while Albert, on the box, raised his voice. "You, Louis! Get your lazy bones out here with an umbrella for Madame Madeleine!"

There was no light in the kitchen.

January was already standing to shout a warning when he saw the second giveaway—the muddy tracks caked thick on the flagstones of the lower gallery, the stairs leading up. He shouted, *"No!* They're in the house!" and Mayerling froze, his hand on the carriage door, startled face a blur in the shadows as he turned toward the chaise where January was already gathering the reins. "Drive for it, Albert, they're—"

From the upper gallery of the house a rifle cracked. Mayerling flung himself down as the ball hit the side of the coach with a leathery thump; a second shot boomed hollowly, and the carriage horse reared, screaming, then fell in the traces. January grabbed the shotgun and sprang out on the far side of the chaise, dodged and sprinted toward the house, and reached it in time to catch the first of the rivermen as he bounded like a tiger down the stair with a knife in his hand.

January fired into his chest with the shotgun from a distance of four feet or so. The man went slamming back against the steps, blood spouting from his chest, mouth, and nose; someone on the stair above said "Fuck me!" and there was a clomping of unwilling feet, then the flat, splintering shot of another rifle as Mayerling fired into the lighted openwork of the stair.

A dozen things seemed to happen then, Mayerling's horse rearing, then foundering in the shafts, which January had expected, amid the flat snaps of more rifles. Mayerling, Albert, and the two women raced in erratic zigzags across the two or three yards of open lawn to the shelter of the house gallery; a hoarse, boyish voice gasped, "Give it," in January's ear and Hannibal pulled the shotgun from his hand to load. January wondered obliquely where Hannibal had learned that in a close-quarters fight the loader had better identify himself before touching a man who was likely to turn around and knock him flying in mistake for another assailant.

Sobbing, Madeleine clawed open her black mourning reticule and pulled out keys, opened the shutters of the dining room door. Footsteps thundered and bumbled on the gallery overhead but Mayerling fired his pistol at the man who tried to come down to fetch the casualty lying in the stairwell, and the muddy boots retreated upward again. The wounded man screamed, "Get me out'n here! Get me out'n here!" The smell of blood was like burned metal. It dripped in sheets down his shirt, down his chest.

At the same moment January heard a groan behind him, and by the banked ember glow of the dining room fireplace within saw Dominique supporting the coachman Albert, his blood mixing with rainwater to dye the whole side of her pale dress. The elderly servant was gasping, his hand clutching at his side, eyes tight shut with agony and face already ashen with shock.

"Ben, what on earth—?" sobbed Minou.

"Not now. Can you load?" He ducked through the door, stripped away the old man's coat as he spoke. Madeleine jerked the doors shut behind them, barred them as January ripped the white shirt, wadded it into a pressure bandage—he looked swiftly around for something to tie it with and without a word Augustus pulled Dominique's tignon from her head, releasing a torrent of black curls around her shoulders. The bullet had gone clean through, shattering the lowest rib. Albert cried out with pain at the pressure but seemed to have no trouble breathing.

"No! I—"

"Don't they teach you girls anything besides Italian and cross-stitch?" demanded Hannibal, pulling her away to where Madeleine stood in the shelter of the study door and the light fell through from the lantern in the stairwell outside. "Ball—just enough powder to cover the ball—first the powder, then the ball—wad—in she goes—ram, and I mean *hard*—pinch in the pan." He handed the pistol to Madeleine, took Augustus's rifle, repeated the procedure, his teeth clenched against a sudden spasm of coughing. "There. Now you know something Henri doesn't know."

"*You* shut up about Henri." It was her flirt voice. She was over the first shock.

"With me." Madeleine strode across the darkness of the dining room, pausing only long enough to shove the table out of the way, then opened the French doors that looked toward the bayou and parted the heavy shutters a crack. She said, *"Bleu,"* a ladylike little oath, and fired the pistol. A man's voice bellowed, "Shit-eatin' nigger!" and there was the sound of something falling, and the confusion of footsteps on the front gallery as well. Dominique rammed home the next charge before the smoke had completely cleared and returned the pistol to her, and Madeleine called across to Augustus, "Thank God you brought the good pistols, dear."

"I think that's the one that throws to the right."

"My leg's broke! Shit-fuck, my leg's broke!" howled a voice outside.

January tied the final knot in the pressure dressing, strode across the dining room to the door of the small study beyond.

There was one window, set high in the wall and shuttered fast. He listened a moment to the ceiling above his head, then ducked through the door again. "Madame! Is there a gallery on that side of the house?" He tried to remember, but he'd only ridden up to it from the back.

"No."

"Out this way, fast. With any luck they won't see us."

"There's an oak a hundred yards straight out," said Madeleine. She snapped off a final shot, slammed the shutter, and bolted it again. "I know the fields in that direction. They don't."

"Night fights for he who knows the land." Mayerling was bending already, lifting the coachman as gently as he could to lean on his shoulder. "Can you make it, Albert? Hannibal?"

The fiddler nodded, though his face was scarcely less taut than the slave's and he leaned on the dining table.

"Fast, then, before they realize we're making an escape."

The room was pitch-dark and nearly empty save for the table at which Mme. Trepagier did her accounts. Dominique and January lifted it to move it under the window, lest the scrape of its legs on the tile floor alert anyone above; January sprang up, flipped the latch, and squeezed through. As he dropped the five feet to the grass beneath he heard a man shout, "There's one of 'em!" and a shot splintered stucco from the wall near his head, from the corner of the front gallery.

He looked fast—two flatboat men were standing at the end of the front gallery, looking around the corner of the house, one reloading already and the second bringing his rifle to bear. It could only have been chance that they'd been standing where they could see the window. With only the shotgun in his hand there was no way he could return fire. All this he saw and thought in a split second; then he heard Mayerling yell, "Run!" and the flat hard roar of a Baker rifle, and what might have been a cry of pain.

He heard the crunch of feet in the grass as a man dropped off the gallery and saw the glint of a knife; heard, also, Madeleine Trepagier sob out Mayerling's name, as he turned and plunged away alone into the darkness of the night.

TWENTY·THREE

Another rifle cracked out, the thud of the ball striking not far to January's left as he raced into the darkness. Feet trip-hammered the ground behind. It wouldn't take Napoleon to figure out that if Madeleine had an armed escort, reinforcements weren't far behind. The attackers couldn't afford to let anyone get away. January shucked his coat as he ran, ripped free his shirt, legs pumping, dodging and weaving but running with all the speed in his long legs. The lights from the house barely touched the trunks of the willows around the main buildings, glimmered on the trailing leaves and the beards of moss on the oaks.

Beyond them it was lightless, Erebus under a sky of pitch.

January leaped six or seven feet sideways and fell to his face on the earth.

The soft crunch-crunch-crunch of pursuing feet stopped.

Loading? Aiming? Taking his time to site on a sitting target?

Or baffled by the sudden silence, the utter dark into which his skin blended like glass into water, one with the damp velvet obscurity of the night.

Lying on the ground, just beyond the line of weeds where the dug fields began, January could see his pursuer as a blocky shape against what dim illumination filtered through the trees. The shape moved a little. Turning its head? Waiting for eyesight to adjust?

January lay still.

The man would have stalked Indians in the Missouri woods and been stalked by them. He would have the patience of the hunter.

And for a long while, in fact, he stood exactly as he was, only turning his head the slightest bit—January guessed rather than clearly saw the movement—as he listened. Now and then a gunshot cracked out from the direction of the house. Sometimes he could hear a man swear.

Then, very cautiously, the pursuer began to move. By the way he moved—slowly, cautiously, but straight ahead—January knew that he was himself invisible against the dark earth. And just as slowly, timing his movements with those of his hunter, he crawled.

The ground sloped down, wet and thick smelling. He was between the bare humped earth of the cane rows, the hunter moving to his right. He heard the wet suck of mud on the man's boots, saw dimly, dimly, the black shape of him move. He'd seek higher ground and be looking in the direction of his feet.

January struck.

He was within a few feet of the Kaintuck, though the smell of the rain-wet earth drowned all the feral sweat-and-tobacco stench of him. It was easy to reach out and grab the man's legs, jerk them back, drop the man down with a cry into the soft earth. January was ready. The Kaintuck was not. The man flailed with his knife as January rammed his knee below the breastbone, grabbed verminous handfuls of hair and beard, and slammed the head around and sideways. There was a quick crack like an oak stick breaking underfoot, and the smell of voided waste.

"Lordy, Lordy," murmured January under his breath. "My massa gwine wear me out for sure."

He supposed he'd have to confess this next Friday—not, of course, in any church in the old town, nor would he mention the color of the man he had killed—but he had to admit that he felt not the smallest twinge of remorse.

He knew enough to stay low as he searched the body, appropriating knife, powder horn, and long rifle. He checked the load with the ramrod, felt the rod's end jar on patch and ball.

He'd expected it, but had to be sure.

More shots, echoing in the night. January turned back, saw figures moving among the trees, around the house. He thought, *They'll have locked up the slaves somewhere,* only to realize in the next instant they'd have chained them as well. Probably in the sugar mill, the only brick building large enough to hold even so small a contingent as Les Saules's. He wondered if Claud Trepagier and McGinty would sell them later or blame the whole business on a slave uprising.

Not if the bodies were shot, he thought.

And then, *But to cover that, all they'd have to do is . . .* The smell of woodsmoke reached him, sluggish on the warm spring night.

All they'd have to do is fire the house.

Flames were licking up over the gallery already, bright on the wooden railings and the heavy strapwork shutters. Wood from the kitchen and the smokehouse had been piled against all the shutters on the bayou side of the house, the flame leaping from it huge and orange and new, the smoke white and fresh, billowing into the black of the sky. Against the brightness of the fire January could see the shapes of men, outlined in red, coarse shirts of plaid or trade goods or rough linsey-woolsey, homespun pants slick with grease, the glitter of cold animal eyes. They stood in a rough semicircle, facing inward toward the house, their guns pointed at the door.

If he stepped from the shelter of the willows, January thought quite calmly, the firelight would show him up, but a Kentucky long rifle would take the distance easily.

There were six men on this side. The rest would be around the front. They all had their backs to him, but nevertheless he recognized the Irishman McGinty's copper-colored hair. The beard had seemed darker in the shadows of the house, the day January had seen him. Recognized also the way he stood, legs apart, hands thrust in the pockets of his sage-green long-tailed coat. The man beside him, dark-haired and medium-size with a look of a panther to his big body, wore a long-tailed coat also, natty but threadbare, and the fire glistened off the pomade in his hair.

He was the same build as the Turk in green, and like the Turk wore a gold signet on one hand that caught the light of the fire.

It was to him one of the rivermen spoke. "C'n we have the woman 'fore we kills her?"

"No," said the dark-haired man, and held up his rifle to firing position, looking down the barrel at the door. His voice was the voice of the orange-and-green Turk. "I want to be sure this time."

By the glaring leap of the fire January recognized Nahum Shagrue.

"Damn better be sure this time," growled McGinty. "Damn up-pity bitch, I damn near swallowed my tongue when I come out here next mornin' and saw her."

"I told you I hadn't seen her in years."

"What you bet the woman comes out first?" said someone else softly.

"Which woman? White dress or gold?"

"White."

"Nah. Gonna be the blond jasper with the scar. Twenty-five cents on it."

"You got it."

"There—the door moved."

Still completely unseen, January checked the site, made completely sure of his aim—for he knew he would only have the one shot—and with quiet deliberation, squeezed the trigger and blew off the back of Claud Trepagier's head.

Even as the Creole's body pitched forward January caught up his shotgun, ducked behind the nearest oak and yelled at the top of his voice, "Fire at will, men!"

At the same moment a shot cracked out from the house and Shagrue flung back his head with a gasp, clutching and grabbing a hole the size of a teacup at the base of his neck. Someone fired in January's direction but McGinty was already running for the trees.

The rivermen knew the folly of standing between an enemy and flame. Their chief gone, they fled, melting into the darkness on the heels of their employer without waiting to see who or how many their assailants were. Without a chance of getting paid it no longer mattered.

Emerging from the smoke-filled lower story of the house, Madeleine and Augustus got off a couple of pistol shots, but—aside from Augustus's first target on Shagrue—hit nothing.

Four of the rivermen were picked up later by Lt. Shaw's guardsmen on the road. McGinty was arrested the following afternoon on the levee, trying to get steamboat passage to St. Louis. He was subsequently hanged.

Lt. Shaw came walking out of the darkness as January was checking old Albert's wound, the coachman laid out on the damp grass of the garden border on a quilt fetched from the kitchen. Madeleine, who went to the kitchen to bring whatever bandages she could find, found Claire the cook and Ursula the laundress tied to their bedsteads, bleeding and bruised. Claire returned with her, bearing medicines and a pitcher of tafia. She bound the ripped graze in Augustus's arm with perfunctory speed, and when Shaw appeared was dividing her solicitude between Dominique—who she assumed to be on the threshold of miscarriage in spite of Minou's assertions to the contrary—and Hannibal, stretched on another quilt and coughing bits of blood as well as smoke.

The house blazed like a massive torch, flames rising thirty feet from its roof. By that livid glare Madeleine, in her honey-colored gown, looked like a gold idol burning in sunset. She brought the rifle up at the muted squeak of the policeman's boots on the grass, and Augustus, scarred face smudged with soot and hair a spiky tangle, called out, *"Qui vive?"* and slipped into the deeper shadows of the willows, just in case.

"Lieutenant Abishag Shaw," called out that high, nasal Kaintuck voice. "You folks all right?"

"We have two men wounded and one ill." January rose and went forward to meet him. From the kitchen quarters Madeleine had also brought him a shirt, rather short in the sleeves over his powerful arms.

"Can your men help us carry them to the overseer's house? There's nothing that can be done for the house here," he added.

Shaw considered the conflagration thoughtfully, cracked his knuckles, and said, "I have to 'low you're right on that. And those fellas?"

He nodded toward the two bodies that still lay between the house and the trees, the blood smell almost drowned by the gritty stink of smoke.

"One of them is my brother-in-law, Claud Trepagier," said Madeleine, with soft dignity. "The man who was behind this—ambuscade. The man who murdered Angelique Crozat in mistake for me." Her dark eyes were very calm, looking up at the tall policeman with a kind of defiance. "The other man is one of those he hired, first to ambush me, then to come here ahead of me in the hopes of catching me alone. They locked my servants in the mill house. We . . ." She passed her hand quickly across her brow, and that steely strength wavered. "They're probably chained. The keys . . ."

"They'll be on Claud's body," said January. Together, he and Shaw walked to the sprawled mess that had been Claud Trepagier.

"Nahum Shagrue," remarked Shaw and spat into the glittering grass. "As I do live and breathe. I wondered where he came by that money he was gamblin' yesterday. Mighty pretty shootin'," he added. "What was it, a long rifle?"

January hesitated, then said, "It looks that way." He bent to empty the man's pockets. There was a black iron key there on a ring—simple, a pattern he recognized of old. Looking at it in his bandaged palm brought back the wave of anger he had felt in Peralta's sugar house, the rage that had carried him across the river, that had burned in him when he'd come, barefoot and in rags, to his sister's yard.

He closed his eyes and turned away, unable, for the moment, to keep his eyes either on the key or on the white man kneeling on the other side of the American's body.

He wanted to throw the thing away, drop it in the bayou, after freeing the prisoners in the sugar mill, but he knew the feeling was ridiculous.

They'd only forge more.

Shaw took it from his hand. "I'll tell off Boechter to go let 'em out."

January nodded. For a time he couldn't speak; didn't know what he could say. Only that he did not want to go near the mill house, see those black faces packed in the darkness, hear the chink and rattle of chains.

In silence he walked back toward the group by the willows, Shaw pacing quietly at his side.

Before they reached them—Madeleine speaking softly to her coachman as two of the constables lifted the old man between them—Shaw extended a bony hand to touch January's sleeve. He stopped, and they looked back at the bodies on the grass.

"Nice shooting, in this light from over in the trees." Shaw considered January for a moment, the ragged osnaburg shirt hanging open over his chest and his trousers, boots, flesh smudged thick with the damp earth of the fields and the wet grass and leaves from beneath the trees around the house. "My men tell me they found another of these fellers with his neck broke six or ten rods yonder from the house. You happen to see how either of them events happened? As a free man of color, of course your testimony'll be wanted before the coroner's court."

"Oh, eh bien!" said Dominique hotly. "And what if my brother had killed them? Those American salauds try to murder us, and because Benjamin has black skin he would not be allowed to—"

"He's allowed to *testify*," Shaw cut her off, and fixed her with his mild gray eye. The constables moved away, bearing Albert toward the overseer's empty cottage. "Courts do frown on it, Miss Janvier, should a colored man kill a white."

"Bah! And I suppose defending oneself and one's loved ones becomes more acceptable the lighter a man's skin is?"

The deep-set gaze moved back to January again. "Well," said Shaw gently, "I guess in some parts it do."

"I shot him," said Augustus, Hannibal, and Madeleine, almost in chorus. Then they looked at each other in some embarrassment, while Shaw contemplated their almost completely unmuddied boots and seemed to consider at length the fact that Hannibal at this point was not even capable of sitting up.

"I shot Trepagier," said Augustus again. "Or maybe it was one of his own men. I forget." His white shirt hung open at the throat and soot and blood striped his gaudy waistcoat, the yellow firelight in his eyes gave him the feral look of something out of a play by Euripides.

"One of his own men, looks like," remarked Shaw, and scratched his jaw. "Seein' as how he were shot from behind. Ain't likely we'd catch 'em all. And that feller in the field, looks like he just fell and broke his neck. You better get them boots of your'n clean, Maestro," he added to January. "Seems to me like . . ."

A small man in the blue uniform of the city guards appeared from the shadows of the trees. "Carriage comin', sir. We cotched two, the boys is out lookin' still."

From the rough shell drive came the crunching rattle of wheels, and a very stylish landau appeared from the darkness, the flames of the burning house burnishing the sleek sides of its team to coppery red. The coachman drew rein at the sight of the fire. The door flew open and an enormously fat, fair, bespectacled man scrambled down, his round moon face stricken with horror at the sight.

"Henri!" Dominique sprang to her feet from Hannibal's side, flew toward him with arms outstretched. Her hair lay around her shoulders like Egyptian darkness, blood and powder smoke matted the fragile muslin of her dress, and her face was scratched and bruised.

The fat man cried, "Minou!" in a desperate voice, and they fell into one another's arms, her slender hands not quite meeting around his broad back while his chubby, white, unworked sausage fingers clutched in handfuls at the sable hair. "Oh, Henri," she whispered, and fainted in his arms.

Madeleine, pistol still in hand, put her fists on her hips and glanced up at January. "Well, I've seen *that* better done."

Augustus nudged her with his elbow. "Don't spoil it for him."

Lt. Shaw came back to them, watching over his shoulder as Henri tenderly bore his beloved in a welter of muddy and grass-stained white petticoats to the carriage. "It does appear," he said, "that you're right,

Madame Trepagier, about that bein' your brother-in-law. I will say Monsieur Tremouille, not to speak of Monsieur Crozat, is gonna be glad to have the whole thing solved so convenient. But I'm purely sorry about your house."

"It doesn't matter," said Madeleine quietly. "I was never happy there, and I would have sold it within a few weeks in any case."

TWENTY · FOUR

At the end of March, Madeleine Trepagier sold the plantation of Les Saules to an American developer for $103,000 and four parcels of the subdivided land, to be disposed of later at her discretion. The first house of the new subdivision—a very large and very Grecian mansion for a Philadelphia banker and his family—began construction before Ascension Day. The main street, paralleling the route of the Gentilly and Pontchartrain Streetcar Lines, was called Madeleine Street. Jean Bouille also included in the development plans side streets called Alexandrine and Philippe, after the two children who had died. There was no Arnaud Street.

The Trepagier family—both its Pontchartrain and New Orleans branches—was outraged. Livia, getting her information through the Rampart Street or octoroon side of the clan, said it was because they were getting none of the resulting money, an opinion with which January could find no fault, though Charles-Louis Trepagier fulminated to Aunt Alicia Picard in terms of letting family land be lived upon by sales américaines. Madeleine sold a number of the field hands to neighbors and members of the family, but kept about twelve, whose services she hired out to the lumber mills upriver at a handsome profit. Louis, Claire, Albert, and Ursula she retained for her own household, purchasing a tall town house of shrimp-colored stucco on Rue Conti and investing the remainder in warehouse property at the foot of Rue LaFayette. One of the first things she did, while still living with her Aunt Picard, was to contact Maspero's Exchange and learn the name of the Cane River cotton planter who had purchased Judith and buy her back. It was, of course, never mentioned by anyone that she had been in Dominique Janvier's house, nor Dominique in hers. When the two women passed on the street, they did not speak.

"Funny," said Shaw, leaning against the brick pillar of the market arcade, next to the table where he'd located January with his coffee and beignet. "She wins her own freedom from that family of her'n, and the kindest, the most humane thing she can think to do is go to all that trouble to find that gal Judith and buy her back as a slave." He shook his head.

"She's a Creole lady." There was ironic bitterness in January's voice. "It's the custom of the country. Expecting her to see any connection is like thinking my mother's going to stop acting like my mother. Or that you're going to sit down at this table with me. Sir."

A slow smile spread across the Kaintuck's unshaven face, the gray eyes twinkling with amusement. "I suppose you're right about that." He stepped away from the brick arcade for a moment and spat in the general direction of the gutter. January hoped for the sake of peace in the town that the man's aim was better with firearms.

"We found the boardin' house on the Esplanade where Claud Trepagier stayed for the week before he showed up at the Trepagier town house claimin' to have just stepped off a steamboat. Everythin' was there: that necklace and letters from McGinty dating back about three weeks after Arnaud's death."

"I suppose it took about three weeks for McGinty to realize that he couldn't pressure or badger Madame Trepagier into marrying him."

"That'd be my guess, though of course McGinty wouldn't say so. He did say there was some hurry-up about it, on account of them cousins of her'n offerin' marriage theirselves. The woman who runs the boardin' house says she remembers Claud goin' out that Thursday night in that green Turk costume, and she remembers McGinty comin' by to see him a couple times. The girl who works in the kitchen found this, stuffed in the garbage-bin one day that week. She don't recollect what day."

From his pocket he produced a long scarf or sash of orange-and-green silk, tasseled at the ends and dabbed and blotted with blood.

"The sash he was wearing at the Mardi Gras ball itself was purple," said January slowly. "I remember thinking it didn't match. It was a later replacement—probably part of McGinty's pirate costume."

"It don't prove anythin', of course—that blood coulda come from a dog or a chicken or wherever—but it gave Mister Crozat somethin' to show that mother of the murdered girl—and Lord, didn't she carry on! Not that I blame her. It was her only daughter, her flesh and blood."

January turned his coffee cup in his hands, remembering the way Angelique's brothers had turned their faces from their mother at the funeral. Remembering what Hannibal had said, and his mother.

Shaw went on after a thoughtful moment, "But she carried on a damn sight worse when Captain Tremouille broke the news to her that necklace was goin' back to Madame Trepagier, because it hadn't even been rightfully Trepagier's to give away in the first place. Now *that* was grief."

A woman with a basket on her head walked by along the Rue du Levée, singing about gingerbread. January could see she wore a thong about her ankle, with a blue bead and a couple of brass bells. Under boot and sock he still wore the one Olympe had made him. Whether it had gotten him safe out of Bayou Chien Mort he wasn't sure, but he certainly hadn't been beaten up since.

"I don't know why I didn't see it earlier," he said slowly, as the Kentuckian folded the sash and restored it to the seemingly depthless pocket of his frayed green coat. "I knew it was Madame Trepagier's dress Angelique was wearing—she'd told me so—and my sister mentioned that she and Angelique also wore the same size dresses. Both women were dark-haired. Both had the same coloring."

"Well," said Shaw, "leavin' out the poor taste of the thing, it ain't that uncommon. You see lots of men who'll marry a woman looks just like their dead wives, or the men who'll always ask for a blonde or a tall girl or whatever in a parlor house. Trepagier prob'ly never gave it a thought, that barrin' the faces, his mistress looked pretty much exactly like his wife."

"Only one was colored," said January. "And if her mother hadn't resorted to blackmail, her death might never have been looked into at all." He glanced sidelong up at the tall man standing beside the table. "Did you ever find anything of the girl Sally?"

"On the subject of colored girls whose deaths don't get looked into, you mean?"

"Yes," said January. "That's what I mean."

The policeman rubbed his unshaven chin and cracked his knuckles with a noise audible several feet away. "I got a couple of the men the city hires to clean the gutters—not bein' able to spare any constables, you understand—and dragged around the bayous some. We found a woman's body about the right height in Bayou Gentilly two days ago, that looked like it'd been there since right around Mardi Gras, but what with the water and the crawfish there wasn't much face left on her. And I did check with Maspero's and over by Carmen and Ricardo and the other big dealers, and nobody answerin' McGinty's description had sold a black girl that age." He stepped away from the vicinity of the tables and spat into the gutter again. "I got word out to the dealers upriver, but myself, I think that was her. Mrs. Trepagier's cook Claire said as how Sally's fella was redheaded, but of course we can't use her testimony in a court of law."

January said ironically, "Of course not."

The cathedral bell called out across the Place des Armes; Rue du Levée was filling up. The last mists of the morning were burning off and the day was already turning hot. Most of the planters had left the city right after Easter, which had fallen early that year. Already the dark striped cane was head high in the fields, and Bella had put up the mosquito bars in Livia's house and the garçonnière.

A gray-suited form jostling along the banquette paused for a fraction of a second, and looking up, January met the blue eyes of Xavier Peralta. The planter paused for a moment, midstride, then turned his face away and kept walking.

" 'Why, thank you, I'm just fine too,' " murmured Shaw. " 'What? No, it weren't no trouble to clear your son of murder, long as I was clearin' my ownself anyway, glad to do it, sir.' "

January covered his mouth with his hand, but could not smother his laughter. He finally managed to say, " 'Sugar mill? What sugar mill?' " He didn't know why he laughed. It was that, he supposed, or hate the man—and all planters—and all whites—forever.

But his laughter was bitter. Maybe he would hate them anyway. He didn't know.

"Well, if you ever decide you do want to go back to Europe and be a doctor," said Shaw at length, "I suppose you could go to him and ask for passage. I don't think he'd thank you for it, though."

At the foot of the Place des Armes along the levee, queer in the livid, soot-dyed glare of the sun, boats were loading with cotton, wines, pineapples, silk, coffles of slaves, and Russian cigarettes. Bound upriver, or out for New York or Philadelphia, for Le Havre or Liverpool. The *Boreas*, the *Aspasia*, the *Essex*, and the *Walter Scott*. Bound for anywhere but New Orleans.

January thought about it as he walked home.

Two evenings later there was a knock at the door of Livia Levesque's cottage on Rue Burgundy, at the time when the oil lamps above the street were being lit.

Spring heat had settled on the city, and the air was thick with smudges of tobacco and lemon grass, burned to keep the mosquitoes at bay. Livia had spoken over dinner of renting lodgings out on the lake, as the Culvers were already doing and the parents of several others among January's pupils. The French doors were open to the street and to the yard behind the house, so that the rooms all breathed with the smell of that afternoon's light rain and the whiff of crawfish gumbo and red beans.

January's shrunken class had taken their leave. In the weeks between Mardi Gras and Easter he'd acquired several new students, who would, he knew, be back in the fall, and one of them at least—a tiny boy named Narcisse Brêzé—showed promise of real genius. After the students departed January remained in the parlor, playing the pieces that pleased him, Bach and Haydn and von Weber, letting the music roll from the instrument as dusk gathered in the little cottage and slowly, unwillingly, the day's heat withdrew. In time Hannibal appeared, waxen and shabby as usual—without saying a word about it, Livia had begun including him at her dinner table now that entertainments in the town were growing thin. He unpacked his violin and slipped into accompaniment, the fiddle like a golden fish in the dark strong waters of the piano's greater voice: jigs and reels and sentimental ballads, and snatches of melody from the Montmartre cafés that had been popular in Paris two years ago. Dominique came in, and then Livia, simply sitting and listening as the evening deepened and the crickets began to cry.

Livia had just risen to kindle the lamp when the knock came. A hooded woman on the doorstep said, "I heard the piano and knew you had to be home." The gold light flared and broadened. It was Madeleine Trepagier, discreetly veiled and dressed in a gown of dull-rose dimity beneath her cloak, with Augustus—slim and dapper and inconspicuously dressed, at least inconspicuously for Augustus—at her side.

For the first time since he had left for Paris sixteen years ago, January saw her face in repose, without fear or wariness in the clear brown eyes.

"I came to thank you," she said, "for all the help that you gave me, and for all that you did."

January shook his head. "I'd like to say it was my pleasure to aid you," he said, "but it wasn't. And I was doing it to save my own neck."

Madeleine smiled. "Maybe," she said. "But it was my doing that you were put in that position in the first place. And I have your honor to thank that my name never came into it with the police. Your honor, and your belief in me. Thank you."

She hesitated, looking down at her hands, still standing on the banquette outside the door. Then she raised her eyes to his again. "And I wanted to let you know," she said, "that Augustus and I are going to be married. By Protestant ceremony," she added, holding his eyes as his mouth fell open in protest, "up the river in Natchez. But the announcement will appear in the newspapers this week."

Although he was almost completely certain that no such ceremony would actually take place—Sapphic love being one thing but deliberate profanation of a sacrament quite another—January was still shocked speechless. He looked from her to Augustus, but before he could gather his thoughts Hannibal said, from the parlor behind him, "Good. I'm glad. And since my colleague is too overcome with delight for you both to speak, I hereby volunteer the pair of us to play at your homecoming reception."

"But . . ." Upon later reflection January wasn't sure what it was about the idea that took him aback—perhaps only the way he had been raised. But Dominique sprang to her feet and rustled in a silvery froufrou of petticoats to his side, to grasp both Madeleine's hands and —after a quick glance up and down the street to make sure they were unobserved—bend from the doorway to kiss her cheeks.

"Darling," she said, and straightened up. "Now Ben," she added firmly, "don't get all Creole and high horse. Madame Trepagier married once to please her family, and look what came of it. Even if he's a fencing teacher and hasn't a sou, I think she's entitled to be with the one she loves."

January looked at them in the gold square of the lamplight, the beaky-nosed, scar-faced sword master and the brown-eyed girl whose teacher he had been. Augustus raised one straight, pale brow.

"If we do not marry, people will begin to talk."

"Ben's just being stuffy," snapped Livia from behind him. "Of course a widow can marry whom she pleases. Really, Ben, I'm surprised at you."

January sighed and bowed his head, fighting a rueful grin. "Yes," he said. "Yes, Madame—you are entitled to be with whom you love. And I will be most honored to play at your reception." He hesitated, looking down into her face. More softly, he said, "It might be, you know, that you'd be happier in Paris than here."

"It might," said Madame Trepagier, more softly still. "And one day it may come to that. But with all its faults—with my family and the Americans coming in and . . . and all else—New Orleans is my home."

She lowered the veil to cover her face once more. Their dark forms moved off down the banquette. In the Place des Armes a cannon fired, signaling the curfew for all slaves to be indoors—all men of color, if they had not good proof of their business abroad. The hoot of a steamboat whistle answered it, bound upstream to the American towns that swarmed with the riffraff of Kaintucks and rivermen, or downstream to the coastwise trade with the slave states to the east. In either direction, and not very far off, lay the lands where it mattered even less than here that a man was legally free, if he showed the smallest trace of African descent; where a man could lose all his rights and his liberty—and that of his children—in the time it took a white man to tear up a piece of paper.

January turned back to the lighted parlor. Livia had gone into the rear of the house. Dominique had resumed her seat and picked up her sewing again, an intricately smocked and embroidered christening gown for the child that now made a soft round of her belly under her loose-fitting short gown. Her face was beautiful in the glow of the lamps; she was one of those women whose beauty increased with pregnancy.

Having in the past several weeks made better acquaintance with his Corbier nieces and nephews, January found himself looking forward to having another.

And that, he thought, was home.

Not Africa, nor Paris, but here, this place where he'd grown up. Sitting at the piano again he let his hands wander, sketching a tune he'd heard in the fields of Bayou Chien Mort, an echo of older tunes, and Hannibal's violin trailed and threaded around it like a skein of gold.

Dominique looked up, smiled, and said, "That's pretty, Ben. What is it?"

He only shook his head. In his mother's household, he thought, it wouldn't be considered at all respectable.

Then from the other room he heard Livia's deep smoky voice

half-hum, half-whisper half-remembered words she had put behind her and tried to eradicate from the lives of her daughters and her son.

"An-a-qué, an'o'bia,
Bia'tail-la, Qué-re-qué,
Nal-le oua, Au-Mondé,
Au-tap-o-té, Aupe-to-té,
Au-qué-ré-qué, Bo.

"Misery led this black to the woods,
Tell my master I died in the woods."

But if he spoke to her, he thought, she would deny it, of course.

A native of southern California, Barbara Hambly attended the University of California and spent a year at the University of Bordeaux, France, obtaining a master's degree in medieval history in 1975. She has worked as both a teacher and as a technical editor, and holds a black belt in Shotokan karate. *A Free Man of Color* is the first of a series of novels about Benjamin January and New Orleans in the 1830s. The second novel, *Fever Season,* will appear in 1998.

Ms. Hambly lives half-time in New Orleans and half-time in Los Angeles with two Pekinese, a cat, and another writer.